THE FUSION CAGE

Dean Crawford

ISBN: 1514381168
ISBN-13: 978-1514381168

Also by Dean Crawford:

The Warner & Lopez Series
The Nemesis Origin
The Fusion Cage

The Ethan Warner Series
Covenant
Immortal
Apocalypse
The Chimera Secret
The Eternity Project

Atlantia Series
Survivor
Retaliator
Aggressor
Endeavour
Defiance

Independent novels
Eden
Holo Sapiens
Soul Seekers
Stone Cold

Want to receive notification of new releases? Just sign up to Dean
Crawford's newsletter via: www.deancrawfordbooks.com

Dean Crawford

I

Amber Ryan knew that there was something wrong the moment she reached the edge of the forest. She crouched down amid the sun dappled trees, the dark green and black disruptive pattern material of her camouflage smock blending in perfectly with the light from the setting sun shimmering through the long grass.

The town below her was nestled deep within the confluence of three valleys and intersected by the silvery line of Hope Creek that wound its way down from the highlands of the Logan Creek Conservation Area. The high hills created a natural, shadowy haven surrounded by deep forests of pine and aspen within which the tiny town of Clearwater had lain since the gold rush of two centuries before. A population of just three hundred fifteen. One road in, one road out. The next town was more than ten miles away.

Amber, her eyes shielded from the sun's glare by her sunglasses, slowly lay down in the long grass. She shifted her position to avoid crushing the bodies of two grouse hitched to her belt as she slipped the rifle she carried off her shoulder and removed the protective plastic shields on the telescopic sights.

Clearwater's deep location within the surrounding mountains meant that it saw sunlight only in the very height of summer and by sundown was always deep in shadow. Amber had normally navigated her way home via the town's twinkling street lights, an obvious and clearly visible marker in the wilderness as soon as one crested the ridge high above the settlement. But this time, things were different.

The street lights were all out and there were blockades on both of the town's exit routes. From her vantage point high in the hills Amber could not make out any details until she pulled the rifle into her shoulder and aimed it down at the blockade on the west entrance to the town, not so much a proper road as a logging track winding in from the deep forests.

Amber's heart skipped a beat. Two vehicles, both of them painted a drab green, were parked nose to nose across the road, and in front of them were a series of boards painted with vivid yellow and black hazard chevrons. Behind the boards stood four soldiers, all cradling what looked like assault rifles.

Amber swept the rifle to the east and immediately tracked the position of a second barricade on the far side of the town, likewise manned by armed soldiers. Amber scanned the vehicles but saw no markings to identify which army unit they were assigned to, and the soldiers' uniforms betrayed no patches or insignia that she could recognize from so far away. Concerned but not alarmed, it took a while for Amber to realize what it was that was truly bugging her, an out–of–place sensation that she could not shake off.

As her sights swept slowly across the town she realized that the main street was devoid of either pedestrians or vehicles. Clearwater was a redneck haven, always filled with trucks and four by fours plastered with mud, burly loggers making their way either to or from *Old Rigger's*, a crumbling joint that served the town's only alcohol. An equally shabby Colonial style hotel on the opposite side of the town provided a place for them to live during the season, after which Clearwater's population halved as the loggers left.

But now there was not a single car in the town, and through her sights Amber could see that the businesses were closed and some of the windows of the houses were already boarded up. She slowly lowered the rifle and stared in amazement at the sight of her town completely abandoned. She'd left Clearwater four days before for a weekend camping trip in the wilderness, a country girl at heart who longed to escape the stifling routine of college. Amber's father had stayed behind, the man who had taught her to love and live in the countryside too old now to venture far out across the rugged wilderness. Besides, he had been busy in his workshop, his head down on yet another crazy idea he'd had, something he'd wanted to build for …

Amber saw movement, men emerging from a building near the west edge of the town where most of the residential homes were located up on the foothills, elevated away from the creek that in the winter could swell to twice its normal depth and width as rainfall on the mountains swept down into the myriad gullies and creeks that slashed across the forested valleys.

Amber set her rifle down and pulled a small set of folding binoculars from her smock as she saw eight soldiers carrying something on their shoulders, some kind of pallet. Atop the pallet was something concealed beneath a camouflaged tarpaulin that rippled in the evening breeze gusting through the valley, and she saw the tarpaulin edges flapping as more soldiers hurried into view and began trying to tie it down more securely.

As one soldier yanked down on one corner of the tarpaulin so the opposite edge was hauled upward, and in an instant a fierce flare of blue–white light burst from beneath the cover like a supernova, as though a new born star had blossomed into life. Amber saw the brilliant light fill her vision and she almost screamed as she jerked her eyes away from the optics and threw her hands instinctively over them.

The darkness behind her hands was scorched by the afterglow of the infernal brightness and Amber realized that she was weeping, that she may have permanently damaged her eyes. The vicious light had seemed so intense that it had imprinted upon her eyes a bizarre negative image of the town below, cast in shades of gray and black, the brilliant orb blazing at its centre. Amber tried to open her eyes and whimpered as she saw her vision marred, clear around the edges but filled with blackness at its centre. She turned her head to one side, wiped the tears from her face as she tried to get a last glance at the mysterious object being hauled onto a small truck that had appeared on main street. Through the periphery of her blurred vision she watched as the object was properly secured and concealed, and moments later the barricades were removed and the object was driven out of Clearwater.

Amber reached out with one hand for her rifle and by touch alone she slung the weapon on her shoulder, remaining prone amid the tall grass for fear of being spotted by the troops still in the town. Her vision sparkled and pulsed with kaleidoscopic colors orbiting the blackness, and she stifled her sobs as she withdrew back into the cover of the trees and lay down on the cool grass with her eyes closed. She reached down to her side for a canteen of water, and after drinking from it she poured the cold water across her face in the hope that the damage to her eyes might somehow be mitigated.

She tried to relax as she set up a small camp, more by touch than by sight, relying on her experience and skills to build a simple makeshift shelter on which she laid down, and the soft caress of the warm evening breeze and the whispering of the wind through the trees lulled her into a doze.

Amber did not know how long she was out for, but when she was awoken by the cold air she opened her eyes and for a moment panicked as she saw nothing but absolute blackness.

Amber sucked in a deep breath of air and rolled onto her back, and there above her appeared a sky filled with a panorama of glittering stars. Her gaze swept the dense star fields and she almost wept again as she realized that her blindness had been temporary, the brutal glare of whatever she had seen now nothing but a memory. Amber rolled onto her side once more and looked down into the valley and saw nothing but an absolute and impenetrable blackness, the mountains around her dark against the pale glow of a new dawn, the sky to the east tinged with its light.

She got to her feet and once again used her binoculars to scan the town, but under the faint starlight the only thing of which she could be sure was that the barricades were gone from the tracks and that the power was still off.

Amber strode out of the treeline and descended the hillside toward Clearwater, passing through thick forest glades and hearing the first waters whispering through the creek as she approached the town. She slowed as she joined the logging trail that crossed the base of the foothills before her, cautious of her approach to a town that she had called home for all of her seventeen years. In the dim light she could make out the narrow bridge that crossed the creek onto Main Street and she hesitated for a moment before she crouched down, enshrouded in inky blackness.

Amber pulled a flashlight from her smock pocket but refrained from switching it on, cautious of revealing her presence. She searched the darkness for some sight or sound of humanity but found nothing. Instead, she waited in the cold as the light to the east grew stronger and cast its glow down the valley toward Clearwater and finally brought enough illumination to the town for her to see her way.

Amber crept forward across the bridge toward Main Street, and as she reached it so she slowed as her jaw hung open and her grip on the flashlight failed. The flashlight dropped onto the wooden bridge with a crack that sounded deafeningly loud in the absolute silence around her.

The old barber's shop opposite her still stood alongside the former mine shop that was now a tannery, horses still a popular mode of transport on the more rugged local trails. Both properties were silent and dark, as was the rest of the town, but what stunned her was that they both also appeared to have been untouched for perhaps decades. The paint on the walls was peeling, exposing old woodwork beneath, and the windows were caked in filth. Amber paced forward onto Main Street and stared in disbelief as she realized that debris was strewn across the street, old newspapers and pieces of junk scattered as though nobody had cleaned the streets for weeks or even months.

Amber turned left, heading instinctively for home. Her footfalls sounded unusually loud in the absolute silence as she walked past the small chapel, the white clapperboard building decayed and the roof collapsed. She quickened her pace, hurrying past vacant lots and houses stained by decades of disrepair, and then she began running up the old road that led to her home.

Amber was out of breath by the time she reached it, and she stared in silence as the rising sun cast shafts of golden light through the faint mist hanging in the air. The glow bathed her home in its warm light, the house that she had grown up in, the one that she had left just days previously. The dawn light passed through the skeletal remains of the property, piercing old roof timbers and broken down walls as Amber's legs gave way beneath her and she sank to her knees on the stony track.

Like the rest of the entire town, her home looked as though nobody had lived in it for half a century.

***

Dean Crawford

II

Defense Intelligence Agency,

Joint Base Anacostia, Washington DC

'Any news on where the fire is?'

The driver of the unmarked sedan glanced in his rear–view mirror at Douglas Jarvis and gave a brief shake of his head, his face cast into sharp relief by the brilliant light of the sun rising above the city. The vehicle was moving between lanes of light morning traffic on the 295 just east of the base, heading for the off ramp that would take them into one of the United States' most secretive locations just inside the District of Columbia: Anacostia–Bolling Air Force Base and the home of the Defense Intelligence Agency's DIAC Building.

Jarvis had not really expected the driver to have any real knowledge of what was awaiting him inside the building, although on occasion in the past his former boss at the DIAC, General Mitchell, had forwarded files out to him to peruse on the way in and bring him up to speed. These days, however, security was more paramount than ever – what happened inside the DIAC, stayed inside.

Jarvis had been summoned by the Director of National Intelligence, Lieutenant General J. F. Nellis, a former United States Air Force officer who had recently been appointed DNI by the current president. Jarvis, a former career Marine Corps officer and later an intelligence analyst with the DIA, had been selected by Nellis to run a small, almost invisible investigative unit designed to root out corruption within the intelligence community while remaining beyond the prying eyes of senior figures on Capitol Hill. Jarvis had been chosen due to his prior success in operating a similar unit within the DIA that had conducted five investigations into what were rather discreetly termed as "anomalous phenomena" and attracted the attention of both the FBI and the CIA before being shut down. Jarvis had spent some twenty years working for the DIA and been involved in some of the highest–level classified operations ever conducted by elements of the US Covert Operations Service. Most of them he would never be able to talk about with another human being, even those with whom he had served. Jarvis knew the rules and had obeyed them with patriotic fervour his entire career.

What bothered Jarvis was that since the formation of the new unit most of his meetings with Nellis had occurred at the DNI's own office in Tyson's Corner, Virginia, and not here in the district and within a stone's throw of both Capitol Hill and the White House.

The driver eased the vehicle toward the heavily guarded entrance to the DIAC, modern silvery buildings that glowed a burnished gold in the sunrise, and passed through numerous checkpoints and bomb–sweeps before being allowed to continue on toward a parking lot shielded from scrutiny beneath one of the array of buildings before him. Whatever the reason for Jarvis being brought here, Nellis was still keeping his presence under wraps, the buildings were ringed with vast open–air lots that could have been used, but all of which would allow Jarvis's arrival to be observed.

The car came to a halt near one wall of the lot, which was virtually empty at this early hour, and the driver indicated an elevator door close by.

'Access code number seven–zero–four, select level five, room two–zero–one.'

The driver spoke the words mechanically, having clearly memorized them, and looked at Jarvis to ensure that he had understood. As soon as Jarvis had climbed out and closed his door the car slid away again toward the exit. Jarvis accessed the elevator and stepped inside, selected level five, and took a deep breath.

Room *201* was a non–descript briefing room on the fifth floor, and the only one that Jarvis encountered on his journey that was open. Furthermore, it had not escaped his attention that the floor in the immediate area was entirely empty: for whatever reason, Nellis had seen fit to ensure that no DIA staff would witness whatever was about to take place in the room.

Jarvis approached the open door cautiously and knocked once.

'Enter.'

Jarvis felt a brief moment of relief as he recognized Nellis's voice and entered the room, the DNI standing from behind a bare desk and extending a hand.

'My apologies for the unusual choice of location,' Nellis explained. 'I have a briefing with both the president and the Director CIA in an hour in DC.'

'No problem,' Jarvis replied as he closed the office door and took a seat opposite Nellis. 'What's the story?'

Nellis was just one year into the role of DNI and he had already aged visibly, swamped by the sheer volume of information he was required to process as a matter of daily routine. Nellis sat back down and retrieved from a briefcase by his side a slim file that he slid across the table to Jarvis.

'Classified Cosmic, naturally, and cannot leave the room,' Nellis said. 'We need to be quick and develop a strategy rapidly before we both leave the building separately. I have a car waiting and my staff think I'm up here revising the presidential briefing, not talking to you.'

'Understood,' Jarvis nodded as he opened the file and began scanning the contents as fast as he could.

Speed–reading was an advantageous skill to any intelligence agent, the very nature of the business governed by how much information an individual could absorb, process, analyse and utilize in as short a time as possible. Jarvis's eyes swept across the pages and words leaped out at him as others poured into his sub–conscious.

Disappearances. Nigeria. Specific excess heat anomaly. Siberia mass murder. Viktor Schauberger, Austria, implosion research. Zero point. Neutron pulse detection. More words flashed by his eyes as his brain soaked in the information on the pages before he reached a final line.

Clearwater, Missouri.

'What happened at Clearwater?' Jarvis asked.

'Four days ago, a B–2 Spirit Stealth bomber of the 509th Bomber Wing operating out of Whiteman Air Force Base, Missouri, landed after a routine training mission and downloaded data from its reconnaissance computers to servers at the DIA for analysis. Most of what was there held little interest other than to confirm that the aircraft's sensors were working correctly, however just before sunset as the aircraft was turning for home it detected an anomalous energy burst from the mountains down in the south east.'

Jarvis raised an eyebrow. 'And that's the big deal?'

'The big deal,' Nellis replied, 'is that the energy burst registered on the aircraft's systems as being equivalent to around fourteen thousand pounds of TNT.'

Jarvis, a former Marine, did not need an explanation of how much devastation would be caused by the detonation of such an enormous volume of high explosives. An airburst of fourteen thousand pounds would create a truly immense blast that would shatter windows for miles around. A below–terrain blast would cause shockwaves sufficient to level major structures and would be detected by the USA's Advanced National Seismic System and the Seismological Service.

'I saw nothing on the news, and there's no way anybody could conceal a detonation that large.'

'That's because there was no detonation,' Nellis explained.

'What about laser pulses or other directed energy weapons?' Jarvis suggested. 'Could the B–2 have simply been in direct line–of–sight to a smaller energy beam that made it look much larger?'

Nellis grinned. 'A great idea, but we already checked it out. There's nothing out there that could have emitted such a pulse and besides, we have a secondary detection that confirms the magnitude and location of that made by the B–2.'

Nellis handed Jarvis a photograph that had not been in the file, and this one was clearly taken from orbit. Jarvis instantly recognized the data stream across the bottom of image identifying a NAVSTAR satellite, normally used for GPS navigation systems. A little–known secondary role of this satellite array was its ability to detect both surface and nuclear detonations via the disturbances they caused to the Earth's ionosphere, which in turn created minute alterations in the signals relayed to and from the orbiting satellites. Part of the USA's Integrated Operational Nuclear Detection System, the photo in Jarvis's hand was backed up by a visual image captured by an orbiting KH–12 *Keyhole* spy satellite.

In the center of Missouri's mountain territory, where deeply forested hills surrounded a network of creeks and rivers, a bright blue–white flare of light was clearly visible that matched the NAVSTAR's time anomaly data.

'Something went bang,' Jarvis said finally. 'Do we have any imagery post–blast?'

'Yes we do,' Nellis said as he handed Jarvis a final image. 'We sent a B–2 over the sight the following day to take a single optical shot, and that's where things got really interesting.'

Jarvis looked at the second image and frowned. This one, in full color and high resolution, showed the town of Clearwater in the aftermath of the intense blast. What bothered Jarvis about the image was that the town was entirely intact. He looked up at Nellis.

'Has anybody spoken to the inhabitants of the town?'

'We sent two agents down there yesterday to ask a few questions,' Nellis replied. 'When they got there they said that the entire town was deserted, that it looked like nobody had lived there for fifty or more years.'

Jarvis stared down at the photo in his hand and he saw flash through his mind the brief description of Clearwater in the original file that Nellis had handed him.

'The US Population Census recorded Clearwater as having a seasonal maximum population average of three hundred or so residents,' he said. 'That census is only a few years old.'

'Agreed,' Nellis said, 'and yet apparently within forty eight hours of this blast being recorded the entire population of Clearwater vanished and the town now looks like it was abandoned half a century ago. I checked the current Census records, and they've been altered: Clearwater is listed as abandoned. That would be odd enough, were it not for the fact that this isn't the first time something like this has happened.'

'Amelu Alam, Nigeria,' Jarvis recalled from the file as he set it down before him on the table. 'An entire village of nearly two hundred people vanished overnight, after witnesses in a nearby village reported seeing bright lights so powerful they couldn't look directly at them.'

'And Royenka, Siberia,' Nellis added. 'Eighty nine people disappeared after what was presumed to be an explosion of some kind. By the time emergency services were alerted and able to access the remote town, there was nobody there any longer. None of them were ever seen again.'

Jarvis sat back in his seat and thought for a moment. 'Your two agents weren't able to make anything of this, so why call me in?'

'This is what your people specialize in, Doug,' Nellis explained, 'and there's something going on here that I'm not being informed about. You and I both know that when it comes to matters of the highest security, both the DIA and my own office are being kept out of the loop.'

'Majestic Twelve,' Jarvis said. 'You think that they're somehow behind this?'

'People don't just disappear in their hundreds without a reason,' Nellis said. 'In Nigeria it could be put down to the actions of rebel factions slaughtering innocent villagers and in Siberia anything goes, even severe weather. But what interests me is that in all of these cases there has been an absolute and complete media blackout. Again, I could perhaps understand it in Saharan Africa or high in the Siberian wastelands, but here in the United States?'

Jarvis nodded his agreement.

'These people must have had families outside of the town, friends, acquaintances – there must be a trail, but I don't sense any reason to suspect a connection to Majestic Twelve.'

'Look more closely at the first image, Doug, just outside the town.'

Jarvis peered closely at the photograph and after a moment he saw it. Barricades on the roads, what might have been jeeps alongside them.

'Ours?' he asked.

'No deployment of military personnel to that location is recorded by any unit at the time that image was taken, meaning they're under the Black Budget or paramilitary. And that's not all.'

Nellis folded his hands beneath his chin as he spoke.

'After my meeting with the president, he and his entourage are departing for Holland, as are the leaders of dozens of countries and a fair proportion of the CEO's of the largest corporations in the USA and overseas.'

Jarvis raised an eyebrow. 'I wasn't aware of any major governmental gatherings scheduled for this month?'

'That's also because of a similar rigidly–enforced media blackout that occurs once every single year,' Nellis explained. 'The president and the rest are all attending an annual conference known as the Bilderberg Meeting.'

'Bilderberg,' Jarvis echoed. 'You think that MJ–12 are involved with it?'

'I've come to believe that Bilderberg is to some degree the vessel through which Majestic Twelve coordinate their activities.'

Jarvis was aware that few people knew of the existence, let alone the relevance, of the Bilderberg Group. Members of the Bilderberg, together with their sister organisations – the Trilateral Commission and the Council on Foreign Relations, were charged with the post–war take over of the democratic process. The measures implemented by the group provided general control of the world economy through indirect political means.

Bilderberg was originally conceived by Joseph H. Retinger and Prince Bernhard of the Netherlands. Prince Bernhard, at the time, was an important figure in the oil industry and held a major position in Royal Dutch Petroleum, also trading as Shell Oil, as well as Societe Generale de Belgique, an influential global corporation.

In 1952 Retinger approached Bernhard with a proposal for a covert conference to involve NATO leaders in general discussion on international affairs. The meeting would allow each participant to speak his mind freely because no media representative would be permitted inside; nor would there be any news bulletin about the meeting or the topics discussed. If any leaks occurred, the journalists responsible would be "discouraged" from reporting it.

In 1952 Bernhard approached the Truman Administration and briefed them about the proposed conference. However it was not until the Eisenhower Administration when the first American counterpart group was formed. From the outset the American group was influenced by the Rockefeller family, the owners of Standard Oil. From then on, the Bilderberg meetings reflected the concerns of the oil industry in its meetings.

Bilderberg took its name from the Bilderberg Hotel in Oosterbeek, Holland, where the first meeting took place in May, 1954. The concept of Bilderberg was not new, although none attracted and provoked global myths in the way that Bilderberg did. Groups such as Bohemian Grove, established in 1872 by San Franciscans, played a significant role in shaping post–war politics in the US. The Ditchley Park Foundation was established in 1953 in Britain with a similar aim.

Around a hundred and fifteen individuals attended each conference, each chosen based on their knowledge, standing and experience – just like the members of the rumoured Majestic Twelve, a cabal of shadowy, powerful figures whom Nellis was trying to expose.

'What does Bilderberg have to do with Clearwater, Missouri?' Jarvis asked.

'The president's briefing of this morning,' Nellis replied. 'It includes reference to major projects ongoing in the area, requested directly by the president himself. If what I'm sensing here is true, whatever happened in Clearwater is of interest to those attending this years' Bilderberg Conference in Holland, and I want to know why. I need you to send your best two agents into Missouri and find out what the hell is behind those disappearances, and you need to be extra careful with this one Doug.'

'How so?'

'Three hundred people cannot just disappear in the United States without the involvement of at least one major government agency. Even if Majestic Twelve does have the influence to initiate such an event, they won't have access to the kind of manpower required to complete the task.'

Jarvis nodded cautiously.

'CIA, or maybe FBI,' he replied.

'They'll be watching you,' Nellis agreed as he stood up. 'Watch your backs.'

***

III

River Forest, Chicago,

Illinois

'I'm just saying that it doesn't have the same kind of *ring* to it, you know?'

'No I don't know, and besides it's not up to you any more is it?'

Ethan Warner folded his arms and shrugged as he looked up at the new sign his partner, Nicola Lopez, had installed above the door to their office. Lopez was beaming as she surveyed her work, her dark and exotic eyes sparkling with delight as she set an electric drill down on the sidewalk and pulled a band out of her pony tail to release a fall of dense black hair that reached half way down her back.

The original faded paint of *Warner & Lopez Inc* had been replaced with a brand new *Lopez & Warner Inc* in polished aluminium plate that shone in the dawn sunlight as Ethan surveyed it. The change of name had been Lopez's idea – her insistence, when they had agreed to reform their partnership. After Ethan's prolonged absence from the business, during which Lopez had struggled on alone, he had found it difficult to justify denying her the indulgence.

'We're going to have to buy new paperwork, business cards and register the new business name change with the IRS,' Ethan pointed out.

'Already done,' Lopez replied, still admiring her handiwork.

'You're enjoying this.'

'Yes I am,' she said. 'Things get done when I'm in charge.'

'Speaking of which, what's next on the list of jobs? Do we have much work coming in to this brave new empire of yours?'

Lopez's studied delight deflated somewhat and her shoulders slumped as she led him into the office.

Ethan Warner pulled off his leather jacket and tossed it onto a couch beside the door. The small office contained little more than two desks, some filing cabinets, a security safe, a cooler and a small television. Posters on the walls portrayed numerous bail–jumpers in the Chicago area, right out as far as the border with Michigan. Bail bondsmen wasn't a glamorous part of their work, and nor was being hired as private detectives, but it paid the bills.

'Seventeen cases as of this morning,' Lopez informed him as she surveyed their current case–load. 'All bail jumpers, none of them high value and all likely in the Chicago metropolitan area or within easy reach of it.'

Ethan nodded as he gave the walls a cursory glance. 'Not quite what was here before I left. Have you cleaned up Chicago's streets single handed?'

'It's tough trying to do a two–person job on your own, case you hadn't noticed,' Lopez shot back with a dirty look. 'Our reputation for speed and success took a hit for the year you were hiding out in the middle of nowhere, and the competition picked up the slack.'

Ethan raised his hands, not wanting to provoke Lopez into an argument.

'I know,' he said. 'Let's just get onto the best–paying case we've got and go from there, okay? Any word from the DIA?'

In recent years Ethan and Lopez had been fortunate enough, or unfortunate enough depending on how he looked at it, to have been contracted by the Defense Intelligence Agency to investigate cases the rest of the intelligence community had rejected as unworkable. The connection to a high level agency like the DIA had come from a former colleague of Ethan's named Douglas Jarvis. The old man had once been captain of a United States Rifle Platoon and Ethan's senior officer from his time with the Corps in Iraq and Afghanistan. Their friendship, cemented during Operation Iraqi Freedom and later, when Ethan had resigned his commission and been embedded with Jarvis's men as a journalist, had continued into their unusual and discreet accord with the DIA where Jarvis continued to serve his country.

'Nothing,' Lopez admitted. 'They've been quiet since Argentina.'

Ethan thought back briefly to their last investigation that had reached its conclusion high in the mountains of South America, when they had first encountered armed forces deployed by an unknown but extremely well equipped organisation that seemed to operate entirely outside the US Government. The discovery that he and Lopez had sought to protect, the remains of an alien species excavated from ancient Incan tombs high in the Andes, had been confiscated by the mysterious group in return for them escaping with their lives.

'I suspect the DIA has their work cut out for them right now,' Ethan surmised as he flopped down into a chair. 'Whoever went up against us represents a huge threat if they can operate with impunity from the government. Jarvis won't want to face them in open battle again without further investigating just who the hell they are.'

Lopez winced as she leafed through a case file. 'Jarvis doesn't face anybody in open battle, Ethan. He just sends us in to do the shooting for him.'

'He's in his sixties, Nicola,' Ethan pointed out. 'Hardly an age for crashing through doors.'

Lopez shrugged, munching on a donut as she read from the file of an alleged *Mickey Cobras* killer by the deceptively impressive name of John Valiant, who had skipped bail out of Cook County a month earlier. Like most members of the *Cobras* gang, Valiant was an African American operating out of the Fuller Park area of the city, the gang's collective operations involving drug trafficking, extortion, robbery and murder. Arrested for the homicide of an enforcer from the rival group *Gangster Disciples* during a drugs dispute that turned into a gunfight on the corner of West 35th Street, Valiant had been sprung on bail and vanished.

'He could be anywhere,' Ethan pointed out as he observed the file. 'The Cobras have enough cash behind them to tuck him away anywhere around the country.'

Although smaller in number than most of their rival gangs, the Cobras were successful enough to command the title of *super–gang* according to the US Attorney.

'You said to start with the highest value target,' Lopez pointed out.

'Highest profit is what I meant,' Ethan replied. 'There's not much point in us tracking Valiant down if it takes us two months to do so.'

Lopez dropped the file as if it had vanished from existence as she looked across her desk at him.

'Then you should say what you mean,' she informed him. 'This is why I'm in charge now.'

Lopez popped the last morsel of donut into her mouth and smiled as she ate.

'Okay then, go for your life,' Ethan suggested. 'What's our next target?'

Lopez was about to reply when a new voice interjected.

'Missouri.'

Ethan turned in his seat to see Doug Jarvis standing in the office doorway, his hands in the pockets of his neatly pressed pants as he leaned against the jam.

Lopez almost coughed out her donut as she shot to her feet.

'Change of leadership,' she said hotly. 'You're dealing with me, now.'

Jarvis raised an eyebrow at Lopez as he glanced questioningly at Ethan.

'She's the boss,' Ethan explained with an airy wave in Lopez's direction. 'Humor her, for both our sakes.'

'It's not about humor,' Lopez insisted. 'This business gets things done when I'm at the helm, and I'll decide what cases we'll be taking on.'

Lopez stepped out from behind her desk and perched on the edge of it as she folded her arms and raised an enquiring eyebrow at Jarvis. 'And how can we help you?'

Jarvis, his elderly features sparkling with bemusement, moved across to a spare seat and sighed as he sat down.

'The DIA has detected an anomaly out in forest country in south Missouri, and wants us to check it out.'

'You mean,' Lopez corrected him, 'you want *us* to check it out for *you.*'

Jarvis glanced at Ethan again. 'How long's this been going on?'

'It feels like years already.'

'Hey, grandpa!' Lopez snapped as she clicked her fingers in Jarvis's face. 'I'm standing right here, so state your case or take a walk.'

Jarvis was unable to prevent his mirth from spilling over and he laughed. 'Ownership of business deeds doesn't a drill sergeant make, Nicola. Take it easy.'

Lopez smiled without warmth. 'I'll take it easy when I'm happy that any work we take on for you benefits the people concerned, and not just you or the government.'

Jarvis inclined his head in agreement as he replied.

'Five days ago, three hundred people vanished without a trace from a town called Clearwater. The town now looks as though nobody has set foot in it for fifty years. I want the both of you to go down there and find out what the hell happened.'

Lopez's studied indignance vanished almost immediately as she digested what Jarvis had said.

'How is that possible? Did some sort of time warp just whisk them away or something?'

'Intelligence resources detected a powerful energy emission in the area and a very bright light, but other than that we have absolutely nothing to go on.'

'Why us and not DIA agents or paramilitary troops?'

'DIA boots have already been on the ground at Clearwater, two agents sent down to take a look at the scene. They didn't find anything significant but my boss doesn't want to expose our awareness that anything untoward has occurred there, in case … '

'Majestic Twelve,' Ethan finished the sentence for Jarvis. 'You guys think they're involved.'

'Nellis can't be sure but similar events in other countries mean that this could be an MJ–12 job, and he doesn't want to let them know that we're onto them. He wants you two to go and take a look and figure this thing out.' Jarvis glanced at Lopez. 'That's if you're not too busy, of course.'

Lopez studied her fingertips for a moment.

'We may have the time to take a quick look,' she replied. 'How come the media's not all over this story already? They'd have a field day.'

'Nobody knows, as far as we can make out,' Jarvis replied. 'There are ghost towns all over Missouri state and many others, a legacy of the gold rush and mining towns long abandoned. It seems like a cover up, but what we don't understand is why they've decided to shut this town down, what they've done with the residents, and how come it is that if they're still alive they're not talking to anybody about what happened to them.'

Ethan looked across at Lopez, who in turn stood up and offered Jarvis a mild grin.

'We'll take the case,' she said. 'How are we getting down there?'

'That, I'm afraid, is up to you,' Jarvis replied. 'Unless the case develops enough for Nellis to prioritize it, the days of military jet flights on commandeered aircraft are long over, although you can still bill the office for gas use – after all, you've only got to travel one state over. Have a nice day.'

***

Dean Crawford

IV

Piedmont, Missouri

'It's at times like this I actually miss that battered old Catalina airplane your friend owns.'

The sky above them was a crisp, clear blue, the horizon bright with the glow of a new dawn as Ethan drove south through the small town of Piedmont, the streetlights still glowing and most cars still parked in their drives awaiting the dawn commuter rush.

'Arnie?' Ethan asked, and chuckled despite his weariness from the long drive down from Illinois. 'The last thing he said to us after Argentina was that if he ever saw us again he'd shoot us, and if he missed, he'd shoot himself.'

Lopez was sitting in the passenger seat with her boots up on the dashboard, shades pulled down over her eyes and her arms folded across her chest. She had slept like that for the last few hours, after taking the first stint as driver out of Chicago. Ethan, significantly taller than his partner, had spent an uncomfortable few hours curled up on the back seat before taking over somewhere outside of Springfield, Illinois.

'I kind of liked him,' Lopez replied, 'mostly because he didn't like you.'

'Charmed, I'm sure,' Ethan shrugged as he drove slowly through the town while consulting a local map for the correct logging trail off the main road that led to Clearwater. 'But he would have been useful here. Most of these trails are the only access points to the deep forests, and he could have landed us on one of the lakes instead.'

The logging trail was just south of Piedmont, a dusty track that switched back off the main road and plunged deep into the shadowy forests. Ethan had wanted to reach the site on or around sunrise, both to avoid the traffic around major towns and also to limit the possibility of ambush out in the wilderness. Neither he nor Lopez had any doubts about the determination or ruthlessness of the assets assigned to Majestic Twelve after their experiences in Peru and Argentina.

The logging track wound for miles through dense forest, the tops of the trees rising high above the vehicle as it crunched along the gravel track. At times it simply wasn't possible to see more than a few feet around the car, rare openings in the forest through which Ethan could see the occasional, unnaturally dead straight path of fire breaks between the trees.

It took almost an hour to traverse the wild terrain before they finally reached a deep valley. Below them was the glassy surface of a slow–moving river winding between the soaring hills.

'There's a bridge ahead,' Lopez said as she pointed out the windscreen.

Ethan looked ahead and saw a white painted bridge, constructed from wood and with the paint peeling as though it had been left untended for many years. It crossed from the wooded hillside on the opposite side of the river, and as the car turned the corner on the track he could see the road straightening as it led into Clearwater.

Ethan reached down instinctively beneath his left arm and felt the reassuring cold metal of his pistol. One of the few advantages of them once again working for the Defense Intelligence Agency was a licence to carry weapons as part of official government business. Although they were not allowed to officially associate themselves with the agency itself, presenting the permits to any law enforcement officer would result in a computer search clearing them with a "right to carry". Satisfied that his weapon was close by and ready, Ethan continued to drive toward the small town. The car crept to a halt on the dusty gravel just as the sun was rising behind them in the east, casting a warm golden glow across distant clapperboard houses, church, and rows of old shops that stretched away down Main Street and turned right into the woods.

Ethan pulled into a lay–by in the forest and killed the engine as he glanced at Lopez.

'This is it,' he said simply as he opened his door. 'Let's see what we can find.'

'The town's that way,' she replied, pointing ahead.

'Indeed, and we don't know what's waiting for us in there, so we'll take a hike and watch for a while from an elevated position. Infantry tactics, one–oh–one.'

Lopez got out of the car. 'I think you've already forgotten who's in charge here.'

'It's not about authority, it's about common sense. Unless you're going to just head in there on your own?'

Lopez snorted something in response but followed Ethan out of the car and up a nearby hillside, deep forest concealing their path as they climbed up and around to a position that overlooked the town. Ethan located a suitable spot and they settled down to watch.

'Is this really necessary?'

Lopez's voice was a whisper as she lay in the deep, damp grass overlooking the small town. Below them stretched the silvery thread of the river that wound its way between the deep valleys and beneath the rickety old bridge that crossed the river into the small town.

Ethan lay beside Lopez, a pair of binoculars in his hands as he surveyed the town. The sun was not yet fully up, the horizon glowing and tendrils of mist draped like fallen angel's wings across the forests around them.

'We don't know what we'll find down there,' Ethan said in a soft whisper as he swept the town once more with the binoculars. 'I'm not about to walk into another trap like we did in Argentina.'

'That was different. We already had people after us at that point, but nobody knows we're here.'

'As far as we know,' Ethan cautioned as he watched the town.

Clearwater was barely a spot on a map, an old mining town that had been left behind by the rest of the world fifty years before. Logging and forestry work kept the town's three hundred inhabitants in work, if three hundred people could be called a town at all. The fact that the state had not seen fit to pave the road that led into the town from the highway several miles away across the wilderness revealed how little the town had to offer the outside world.

Small town America was often seen as the quaint, grassroots heart of America, but the small towns were the first to go during economic crises. In his time Ethan had often driven long range across America, and more than once passed through the boarded–up remains of what had once been a thriving community, or witnessed the remains of modern houses and apartment complexes sitting alone far out in the wilderness, the funds for construction having dried up long ago. Both types of ghost town seemed like memorials to the past, the American dream gone bad.

'My ass is wet.'

Ethan rolled his eyes as he looked across at Lopez. 'It's not like this is your first rodeo in the woods, Nicola.'

'I certainly hope it's my last,' she shot back. 'We came to check the town out up close, not sit on a hillside in the damp heather. Are we going down there or not because I'm not sitting up here for another hour waiting to freeze to death?!'

Ethan sighed and took one last look through the binoculars. 'Fine, let's go.'

The air this far out in the wilderness was scented with the odours of pine and cedar and possessed of a freshness Ethan rarely experienced in Chicago. It was also entirely silent, no sound of birdsong and only the whisper of the river passing by in glassy silence beneath the nearby bridge to accompany them as Ethan led the way into the town.

'Looks like nobody's been here for quite a while,' Lopez observed as she looked at the various shops lining the right–hand side of Main Street.

Most of the windows were opaque with grime, once bright colors now faded and the wood peeled with age. Several of the roofs of the buildings had collapsed, many of their windows broken. Main Street ahead of them was littered with debris, and Ethan could already see that the church that dominated the town had probably not heard a service in decades.

'Clearwater is not really mentioned any more on the census,' Ethan said as he recalled the contents of the file that Doug Jarvis had handed to them. 'According to official documents nobody has lived here for about forty years. Clearwater is one of countless ghost towns across the USA.'

'It's off the grid enough that nobody would notice if the place had vanished entirely,' Lopez agreed. 'Always makes me wonder who lived here and what happened to them?'

'Especially now,' Ethan said as he turned towards some of the shops lining the parade nearby.

A series of wooden steps lead up onto the parade, a simple fence across the front cut from trees many decades before and likely used to tie up horses in the days before vehicles. Ethan put a foot out and tested the first step, cautious of such old timbers collapsing beneath his weight, but he found it solid and firm beneath his touch. He climbed up onto the parade and looked into the windows of an old supply store, wiping the grime from the glass and peering inside. The interior was almost completely empty, stripped of any wares the owner of the shop might once have sold.

Ethan frowned thoughtfully, then stepped back from the window and looked at the line of shops. All of the properties were built in a similar style, well over a century old and with roofs that were tiled with different materials over the decades. The parade on which he stood was dusty, the paint long since scoured from the wood by years of rain and burning sunshine.

'You sure Jarvis is right about this place?' Lopez asked. 'It sure looks like nobody's been here for a long time.'

Ethan's eyes drifted across the street alongside them, his gaze falling on other properties further up Main Street that were likewise dilapidated in their appearance. Something was missing, something important that he could not put his finger on.

'I don't know,' he murmured thoughtfully.

Ethan crouched down and stared at the wooden planks of the parade beneath his feet. The paint had peeled, but the planks themselves were still dead straight, not warped by the sunlight and the constantly alternating bitter cold of winter and heat of summer. He would have expected many of the planks to have bowed under the change in temperatures over the years, and then those bows to have filled with standing water during the rainy season, rotting the wood.

Suddenly he realised what was missing. 'Scat,' he said.

'What?'

Ethan surveyed the parade and then the fronts of the houses, the shops and even the bridge itself.

'There's no animal scat,' he repeated as he stood up and looked around. 'Rats, foxes, birds, all sorts of vermin should have been all over this place for years but I'm seeing nothing, barely any bird droppings even.'

Lopez looked around, clearly beginning to realise what Ethan was getting out, and as he looked further so he saw more things that did not make sense.

'The bridge is still intact and looks solid,' Lopez observed, 'even though the paint has peeled off it still looks like it could hold us.'

Ethan nodded, glancing up at the parade of shops. 'Some of the shops windows have been broken, and the interiors look like they're filled with dirt and debris, but there are no plants growing inside them. One of the first things that happens with old towns like this is that nature takes over, tree roots grow up through foundations and such like. These properties are just clapperboard constructions, the kind of thing that plants would have no problem pushing through in a matter of months let alone years.'

Lopez turned and looked at a nearby property and then the lawn in front of it.

'Grass isn't overgrown,' she pointed out. 'That must have been cut a few days ago, a few weeks at the very most, because we're already in summer. It should be up to our knees by now.'

Ethan nodded as he stepped down off the parade and began walking down Main Street with Lopez alongside him. He began searching in earnest as they walked, seeking further evidence that what they were witnessing was not an aged ghost town at all.

On the edge of one lawn, itself covered with a layer of short grass that must have been cut recently, he saw a series of tyre treads where somebody had backed out of the drive and just clipped the edge of their lawn. Ethan hurried over and examined the track.

'Wide tread, deep too,' he said as he glanced up at the house, 'left by a modern vehicle, not something from the 1950s.'

Ethan set off up the drive toward the front door of the house, which was hanging open from a timber frame covered in curls of peeled paint. Ethan reached up to brush some of the paint off, which fluttered to the ground like brightly colored leaves. Ethan touched the timbers themselves, the bare wood smooth and hard to the touch.

'The wood hasn't rotted here either,' Ethan said.

Beside him, Lopez reached beneath her jacket and produced a pistol that seemed too large for her hands.

'I don't like this,' she murmured softly as she peered into the darkness and the gloom of the house.

Ethan eased inside with Lopez covering him. Although he felt certain the town was indeed deserted, he now had serious question marks in his mind about how it had come to be so. Ethan crept forward, glancing to his right into a living room devoid of furniture, the paint on the walls faded with age, the floorboards uncarpeted.

They moved on slowly into a large kitchen that faced out across broad open lawns, the grass short and glistening as the sunlight struck early morning dew.

'Look at this,' Lopez said from one side.

Ethan walked across to where she was crouching down on the floor beside a grubby square mark on the tiles where a chiller had once stood. She pointed down to the skirting boards that lined the wall where it met the tiles, and there among the grime were a few morsels of food that must have spilled from the chiller when it was moved.

'Peas, if I'm not mistaken,' Lopez said. 'And they haven't rotted, yet.'

'Three hundred people skip town, taking all their possessions with them, and within days the town looks as though it hasn't been occupied for decades. It must have taken a lot of work to make this town look the way it does.'

'My guess is that the townsfolk were in on it,' Lopez replied. 'They made the town look this way on purpose, but what on earth could cause three hundred people to just leave their homes behind and take everything with them and disappear into history?'

Ethan shook his head slowly as he led the way back out of the house and into the glowing golden sunshine outside.

'Every one of them must have made use of paint stripper to age their properties, and I suppose it's possible they could have loaded vacuum cleaners with dust and set them on reverse to spray all this muck over everything. Mixed with a mild adhesive it would have stuck quite easily to the windows and surfaces, ageing them overnight.'

'It doesn't make any sense,' Lopez said. 'What about the collapsed roofs?'

Ethan glanced up at one of the skeletal remains of a colonial style house's roof. 'It doesn't take much to saw out some wood and let the weight of tiles and rafters do the rest. It's an extra touch and it's quite nice but I suspect if we went up there we'd find that the beams are cleanly cut, and not rotted away and...'

Ethan broke off as he saw movement up on the hillside over the river. He froze for a moment as he sought the source of the movement and saw a shape hiding in the grass, just below the treeline above an open, grassy clearing on the slopes. Almost at the same moment he saw it struggle, the grass waving around it, a frantic movement and then something burst from the forest behind it.

The figure moved with immense speed and grace, leaping like a gazelle across the slope as it charged in on its captured prey, and Ethan saw the flash of a blade in the sunlight as the figure plunged down on what must have been a rabbit or similar prey captured in a trap in the grass. Moments later the blade flashed down and the creature stopped struggling.

Ethan and Lopez stood in silence for a long moment before Lopez finally looked at him.

'Did I just see that?'

Ethan nodded. 'You take the right flank, I'll take the left.'

***

Dean Crawford

V

They moved out together, spreading apart as they eased down the hillside, moving from cover to cover. Ethan kept his eyes fixed upon the figure crouched over the prey at the base of the hill. He could not tell whether it was a man or a woman, the shape completely broken up by dense foliage that had been used as camouflage, woven into their clothing to break up their outline in the manner of a ghillie suit and avoid detection by whatever it was they were hunting. The fact that they were hunting at all suggested that whatever had happened to Clearwater, it had occurred long enough ago that there were no longer any food resources within the town. If the person at the base of the hill was a survivor, Ethan knew instinctively that it was essential they were captured and questioned.

He glanced out to his right and saw Lopez moving with silky grace between the tall grasses, staying low and moving almost out of sight as Ethan crept into a glade of trees. A narrow path between the trees led to the base of the hill and the increased cover allowed him to move more quickly, but it also concealed from view his target.

Ethan reached the base of the hill and crouched low, not really seeking to see the target but listening instead. On the faint whisper of a breeze he could hear the sound of a blade cutting skin as the survivor prepared the animal they had caught for cooking later on. He distinctly heard the faint tearing of flesh as he crept slowly forwards through the glade. The sounds stopped as he reached the edge of the tree line, with the open grasses ahead glowing in the sunrise before him.

Ethan squinted and raised one hand to shield his eyes from the brilliant flare of the sunlight as he tried to see where the hunter was crouched.

'Don't move.'

Ethan remained silent and still, although he cursed himself as from his right he heard faint footsteps. He swivelled his gaze to see a tall figure completely enshrouded in a make–shift ghillie suit, a powerful–looking rifle in their grasp and a steely gaze directed at him.

'I'm not here to hurt you.' Ethan said.

'Is that why you're carrying?' the figure asked, a female voice.

'It's licensed,' Ethan explained. 'I'm here to find out what happened to the town of Clearwater.'

The figure stood in silence, legs splayed and the rifle pointed unwaveringly between Ethan's eyes.

'What would you know about it?'

'I know that recently this was a thriving little town,' Ethan shrugged, holding his arms out to either side to show her that he was not about to draw his weapon. 'Somebody's made this place look like it's fifty years old, and I want to know why.'

'What's it to you?'

Ethan managed a faint smile. 'I was about to ask you the same question.'

'Yeah? Well, I'm the one holding a rifle.'

The voice that replied didn't belong to the hunter.

'And I'm the one holding a pistol.'

Lopez eased out of the treeline from behind the hunter, a service pistol aimed at the back of their target's head. Ethan smiled broadly as he got to his feet and saw the hunter rolled her eyes as she lowered the rifle.

Ethan took a pace toward her and yanked the rifle from her grasp. She put her hands in the air but stared into the distance rather than meeting Ethan's gaze. Ethan check the rifle over, made it safe, and then looked into the hunter's eyes and forced her to meet his.

'If we were here to hurt you, I'd probably shoot you right now.'

Ethan turned the rifle over and pressed it back into her grasp. The woman stared at him with a slightly surprised gaze as she took hold of the rifle once more, and Ethan gestured for Lopez to lower her pistol.

'Should have known you wouldn't be out here alone,' the woman said as she glanced over her shoulder and saw Lopez standing behind her.

'Yes you should,' Ethan agreed. 'But you caught me out. Who are you?'

The woman reached up and pulled the hood of the ghillie suit off to reveal a surprisingly young face and long black hair tied tightly behind her head. A stud sparkled in her nose, and her eye liner was a little too heavy, a look that Ethan recalled as being referred to as *emo*. Her thick black hair, pale skin and permanently disgruntled expression made her a virtual poster–girl for teenage adolescence.

'My name is Amber,' she replied.

'Does Amber have a second name?' Lopez asked.

'Not for now.'

Considering that her entire town appeared to have vanished, Ethan had some sympathy for her desire to remain anonymous until she had figured out who was confronting her.

'We need to talk,' Ethan said. 'Do you have any idea what happened here?'

Amber sighed and then gestured for them to follow as she struck out of the glade across the hillside.

'I was on a camping trip, part of my college break,' she explained as they walked. 'I came back through here four days ago, heading home ready to go back to college the following day. When I got here it was almost sunset, and the town was barricaded from both sides by troops and vehicles. They took something out of here, and when I got a glimpse of it on the back of a truck it was so bright that it blinded me.'

Ethan looked at Lopez, who shot him serious glance.

'Jarvis mentioned something about an energy burst that got picked up by one of the local airbases.'

'This energy or light that you saw,' Ethan asked. 'Do you have any idea what it was?'

Amber shook her head. 'No. By the time I recovered my sight it was the following morning. The trucks were gone and the town looked like it does now. I don't know what the hell happened and I felt like I was losing my mind, like I'd gone back in some bizarre time warp and been left here all alone. It was only when I saw airliners cruising through the sky that I knew something else must have happened.'

'You've been staying out here all alone?' Lopez asked. 'You didn't think to go for help?'

'From here?' Amber challenged. 'Military troops made my entire town's inhabitants disappear, and then went out of their way to make this town look like it's been abandoned for half a century. I don't know what happened to any of the people that lived here, but I have a suspicion it's not good. I wasn't about to reveal that I was still alive.'

'They probably already know,' Ethan said. 'Whoever did this will have had a census of the town's inhabitants, the entire population. They will know that you're missing.'

'Which is why I kept my head down and stayed out of sight,' Amber agreed. 'I was hoping that perhaps the townsfolk would come back eventually, that this was all some sort of mistake or that maybe Hollywood had hired the entire town to shoot some movie or something. Wishful thinking, I guess.'

Ethan was already thinking himself, although none of his thoughts were wishful at all. Military troops were involved in whatever had happened here and the town's inhabitants were gone. Yet they had not sought to hunt for the missing Amber, and that suggested to him that they did not have the resources to conduct such an overt operation out here, despite the undoubted sensitivity of whatever it was they were trying to cover up.

'Small unit, covert operations,' he said as he looked at Lopez.

'Paramilitary unit,' Lopez replied in agreement. 'I don't suppose they'll have wanted to attract attention to this operation using helicopters or heavy lift aircraft of any kind. This would have been a very quiet operation to get everybody out, make the town look old and then just disappear.'

Amber nodded her agreement.

'I was never camped more than ten miles from the town, and I never heard any unusual aircraft in the area or anything that suggested there were major forces deployed. From what I did see I think there were no more than about fifty soldiers in all.'

Amber crouched down in the grass and lifted a dead rabbit, its skin already removed and its guts a slimy mess on a rock nearby. Lopez winced faintly as she watched Amber hook the carcass onto her belt.

'You're not going to be able to stay out here forever!' Ethan pointed out to Amber. 'Sooner or later we have to figure out what happened here.'

Amber turned to him and raised one delicate eyebrow.

'How did you know about what happened here?' she demanded. 'Why has none of the emergency services or even the media come down here to report on this?'

'We work for the Defense Intelligence Agency,' Ethan explained. 'It's our job to figure out things like this. If you live here, then why don't you take us to your home and maybe we can start trying to understand what's going on?'

Amber's face fell. 'My home is gone.'

Lopez stepped forward. 'Did you have family there?'

Amber nodded. 'My folks, they're gone too.'

'Towns don't disappear without a reason, nor do family,' Ethan said. 'And this is not the first time it's happened.'

'What do you mean?' Amber asked.

'The DIA has evidence of towns disappearing in remote parts of the world such as Africa and Siberia, and it's happening more frequently than you might imagine,' Lopez explained. 'This is the first time it's happened on US soil as far as we are aware. If you want to find out what happened to your parents, then we're going to need an idea of why it was that this town would be made to disappear instead of any other in the United States. Was there anything at all unusual going on in Clearwater before the population disappeared?'

Amber sighed softly and nodded.

'Four weeks ago, the entire town was cut off from the National Grid.'

Ethan raised an eyebrow. 'I'm surprised it was connected in the first place, it's so remote.'

'A lot of the properties used oil burners,' Amber agreed, 'but we also had mains electricity.'

'So what, the population left after the power was shut off?' Lopez suggested.

Amber shook her head.

'No, the town was disconnected from the National Grid but the power wasn't shut off. That's what I'm assuming is behind this. Clearwater was generating its own power and no longer needed to be a part of the National Grid at all. None of us were using oil or gas or coal anymore.'

'I don't see a wind tower,' Ethan said as he looked around.

'That's because there wasn't one,' Amber insisted. 'That's kind of the point. We didn't need any energy at all because we were getting it all for free.'

***

VI

'Say that again?'

Amber sat down on the lawn of what had once been her home, the rifle resting against her shoulder and pointed at the sky as she spoke.

'My father was an inventor who worked for the government for almost thirty years,' she explained. 'He worked on numerous projects involving nuclear fusion at the National Ignition Facility in California. I don't fully understand exactly what it was that he did except that it involved novel ways of producing energy.'

Ethan nodded as he recognized the name of the famous facility in Chicago.

'They're the guys that are trying to produce nuclear fusion on earth right?'

Amber nodded. 'My father explained it in the sense that they were trying to create a small sun on earth. They have these chambers that are able to contain immense pressures and temperatures just like those found in the sun. If they are able to do so, then the energy produced is far more than the actual energy required to start the process in the first place: dad calls it the "ultimate free lunch", getting more out than you put in.'

'I didn't think that was possible,' Lopez asked, 'something to do with the law of conservation of energy?'

Amber looked at Lopez with renewed respect.

'Dad mentioned that from time to time, that it's impossible to get more energy out of something than you put in. However, nuclear fusion is the same way that a nuclear bomb works except of course that in a bomb the energy is not contained but allowed to radiate outwards as a blast. He said once that this process is the conversion of matter into pure energy, E equals MC squared and all that techy stuff. That's why nuclear bombs are so powerful, they convert everything back into raw energy.'

Ethan recalled from a previous investigation for the DIA of just how much power nuclear fusion was able to create. A scientist who had worked at similar laboratories once explained to him that if he was to take the button from his shirt and convert it into pure energy, it would explode with enough force to level an entire city block. Even the largest nuclear fusion bombs that had ever been detonated contained only a fist–

sized chunk of matter, usually plutonium, and yet they were capable of levelling cities and laying waste to entire regions.

'So what happened? Did this ignition facility finally manage what your father was working on?'

'Not in his time working there,' Amber said. 'My father was at the forefront of the pioneering technology being developed to create true nuclear fusion on earth as a power source, but the new scientists coming through from the universities were overtaking him in the understanding of what was happening. My father thought it wiser to relinquish his position to allow them to continue the work while he pursued other avenues.'

'Other avenues?' Ethan echoed.

'My father had become disillusioned with the idea of creating nuclear fusion on earth, chiefly because he thought it was an expensive and inefficient way of generating such vast amounts of energy.'

'Inefficient?' Lopez asked. 'I don't know much about nuclear fusion, but I did understand it to be very powerful and without any exhaust gases that pollute the atmosphere.'

'That's very true,' Amber agreed. 'And despite what the green movement says, nuclear fusion is in fact very safe. It's the opposite of nuclear fission, which is the process of splitting an atom. In that process, if the cooling of the reactor is not maintained then the process can run away with itself. That's what happened at Chernobyl in 1986. Nuclear fusion, however, is very safe because it's the process of forcing the atoms together under high pressure. If the process should fail for some reason, perhaps the reactor chamber being breached, the first thing that happens is that pressure is lost and the process immediately ceases.'

'So what was the problem then?' Ethan asked.

'My father was of the opinion that it was possible to produce nuclear fusion without requiring the intense pressures and temperatures of a nuclear fusion reactor. He had done sufficient research, or so he kept saying to anyone who would listen, that he believed it possible to build a reactor that was not the size of a small town but that you could fit in a boiler room at home.'

Ethan glanced at Lopez. 'Something like that would be worth silencing an entire town for.'

'If it existed,' Lopez pointed out. 'Did your father managed to build something like that?'

'I don't know,' Amber admitted. 'After he retired from the National Ignition Facility, dad spent countless months in his workshop labouring on something. He wouldn't tell me what it was about and was really shady about revealing to anyone what he was doing in there. I didn't really understand why until now.'

'Understand what? And was it your father's invention that was powering the town after it separated from the National Grid?'

Amber rubbed her temples with one hand as she replied.

'According to dad, many people in the past have claimed to have invented devices that produce energy for free. Most of them are charlatans, snake oil salesman who have ripped off people for thousands or even hundreds of thousands of dollars and then disappeared. However, he said that a few people have created devices that have then suddenly disappeared, all trace of their existence vanishing and in one case their house actually being reduced to nothing but foundations literally overnight. News reports would then appear on the Internet claiming them to have been charlatans that had fled the country with others people's money, or likewise slanderous comments made denigrating their reputation.'

'Sounds like conspiracy theories to me,' Lopez pointed out. 'Any time somebody claims to have invented something spectacular and is then challenged to produce evidence to support their claims, they mysteriously find themselves unable to do so or simply disappear.'

'My dad is not one of those people!' Amber shot back. 'He had a different plan in mind.'

'Such as?' Ethan asked.

'My father was going to give the device away to the world for free.'

Ethan and Lopez remain silent for a long moment as they considered the implications of this. It was without doubt that anybody who could develop such a remarkable device, one that could power the world for free, would become incredibly wealthy in an instant. Like, Rockefeller or Gates or Branson wealthy. Literally every home and every vehicle in the world would want one of the devices, would relish being able to sever ties with power companies that made such gargantuan profits from the populations of so many countries. To give something so valuable away for free seemed literally insane.

'Nobody ever does that,' Lopez said. 'Everybody sells out.'

Amber smiled up at Lopez as she replied. 'So you'd imagine, but in fact the world is changing much faster than I think a lot of governments and corporations would like. Freeware and shareware is becoming the new norm, with people developing programs and software for computers and not selling them but simply sharing them for free across the Internet with peers.'

'Software is a bit different from a world–changing energy source,' Ethan pointed out.

'Is it?' Amber challenged. 'Where do you think the World Wide Web came from?'

'The United States military,' Lopez replied. 'They were using it as a communication device and the technology trickled down to the civilian realm.'

'Wrong,' Amber replied. 'The World Wide Web was invented by Sir Tim Berners–Lee, a British scientist who developed it to communicate with other scientists quickly and then realised the potential of what he had created and resisted all offers from major American corporations keen to profit from the technology. It was he, one man alone, who gave us the World Wide Web and thus the Internet for free. He surrendered the chance of becoming a multi–billionaire in favour of returning something to the world that would benefit the public in more ways than even he himself could have imagined at the time.'

Ethan crouched down alongside Amber in fascination.

'Your father was going to develop a device that would power the world for free and then he was going to give it all away. What's his name?'

Amber smiled again.

'Stanley Meyer,' she replied, and then her features saddened once more. 'And my mother is Mary. She's also missing.'

'You're Amber Meyer?' Lopez asked.

'Amber Ryan,' she replied. 'I was adopted. Stanley and Mary couldn't have children, so they adopted me at the age of two. Mary was an electrochemist and they met as undergraduates at university. I think that because they couldn't have children they made their careers their priority, and then later in life decided to adopt me.'

'Philanthropists,' Ethan guessed. 'They were giving things back all the time.'

'They consider acts of such altruism as the future of our species,' Amber said. 'Dad said that corporate capitalism, a price and a profit for any service, had become so grotesquely mutated that it no longer served a purpose for those who needed it the most. He didn't want his legacy to be a billionaire's fortune – he wanted it to be a legacy that would last for all time.'

Ethan shook his head in wonder. 'That's pretty amazing.'

'I considered him an idiot for even suggesting it,' Amber retorted with a shrug. 'He could have become a billionaire overnight. He deserved the success. I'd have taken the money and then handed the device to somebody else, let them duck the bullets, but dad isn't like that.'

'Fossil fuel companies would become worthless,' Lopez pointed out.

'Not to mention the collapse of oil–bearing nation's economies,' Ethan added.

'That's what he was afraid of,' Amber said. 'I think that he felt that governments and major corporations would seek to silence him if they had discovered what he was working on. It's why he came back here from Chicago, back to our hometown. It's quite remote and I think he preferred basing himself here far from the prying eyes of Washington.'

Ethan sat back on his haunches thoughtfully as he considered what Amber had told him.

'So let's say Stanley was successful, and that bright object you saw being taken away by troops was what he created. He must then logically have revealed the device to the townsfolk and helped them disconnect from the National Grid.'

Amber nodded. 'That's what I figured. He had to prove that the device works, because they wouldn't believe him otherwise. So he disconnects the town from the National Grid and wires it up to whatever he created. It looks like doing that was enough to alert the government to what he was up to.'

Lopez joined them as she spoke. 'The government sends somebody down to take a look at things, realise what's happening here and decide to shut it all down before word gets out.'

'They make Clearwater look like a ghost town that's not been lived in for many years,' Ethan went on. 'But then what's happened to the townspeople? Surely they haven't decided to murder three hundred people to cover this up?'

Lopez shook her head as she looked around them.

'I don't doubt that the government would want to keep this under wraps, but I also doubt they would murder so many people in order to do so. Washington has been behind quite a few alternative energy programs for some years now and everyone knows about climate change.'

'Then they must have bought them out,' Ethan said in amazement. 'Every last one of them.'

'No way,' Amber said. 'My father would never have agreed to silence over this, not for any money.'

'Then your father is in a great deal of trouble,' Ethan said, 'because whoever is behind this would likely go to any lengths to ensure his silence. The question is, who?'

Amber looked up at the surrounding hills.

'There is a major company that was involved in a legal dispute with the town's council over mining rights out in the mountains near here. It's something to do with the new mining process which literally slices the tops off of mountains in order to gain access to coal inside. Apparently the process has poisoned the fresh water supplies to many towns, and our councillors were fighting the company for the right to maintain the pristine wilderness around here.'

'If that company found out about your father's device,' Lopez said, 'then they would have had a very clear motive for ensuring nothing ever got out of Clearwater.'

Ethan rubbed his chin thoughtfully. 'Who was winning the legal battle?'

'The corporation, predictably,' Amber replied. 'They had access to legal eagles far more powerful than anybody in Clearwater or even St Louis. There was no way we were going to win that case ... '

'Unless your father revealed his device to the world,' Lopez finished the sentence for her.

Amber reached into her clothes and produced a cell phone. 'I could call my mother, she could explain everything to you better than I could but I haven't been able to reach her and ... '

Amber went to activate the phone and Ethan lunged forward and caught her hand. 'No!'

'Why not?' Amber gasped, shocked.

'She's not answering because she can't or doesn't want to be found, and I suspect if you use that cell phone the people who shut down Clearwater will come for you too.' Ethan released his grip on Amber, cautious of frightening her. 'What's the name of this company?'

'Seavers Incorporated,' Amber spat as though removing something unpleasant from her mouth.

***

VII

Northern Kentucky International Airport,

Hebron, Kentucky

Huck Seavers was not normally a nervous man, but he could feel tension in his body and a prickly heat irritating the back of his neck as he sat in the Gulfstream jet's luxurious interior and awaited his guest. The temptation to hide his rugged, wide–jawed features beneath the brim of his Fedora was almost overwhelming.

'Are you all right sir?'

The stewardess on the flight was leaning over him, concern writ large over her perfect features.

'Never better!' Huck boomed, one thick hand slapping down on his jeans with a sharp crack. 'How are you, honey?'

Huck's broad, white smile and sparkling eyes glittered at the stewardess, who smiled as she stood up once more.

'Fine, thank you, sir.'

The stewardess moved off, and Huck retreated once more into his sombre mood.

He did not know the man he was waiting for, not who he worked for and indeed not even what he wanted. The only thing he did know was the man's name, Aaron Mitchell, and that his influence and power had been instrumental in allowing Seavers to further develop his plans to begin mining the mountains of Missouri for coal. Seavers Incorporated was one of the largest mountaintop mining companies in the United States with a portfolio of over $5 billion worth of operations across the Appalachian mountains in the eastern United States.

Mountaintop removal mining, also known as mountaintop mining, was a form of surface mining that involved digging the summit ridge of a mountain. Coal seams were extracted by removing some four hundred feet of overburden to expose underlying coal seams. The excess rock and soil was then dumped into nearby valleys in what were called "holler fills". The process was less expensive to execute and required fewer employees than conventional mining, and had begun in Appalachia in the 1970s as an extension of strip mining techniques. The process had spread across Kentucky, West Virginia, Virginia, and Tennessee as conventional seams had been exhausted, and Huck's father had been there to take advantage of the new process.

The late, great Jeb Seavers had started the company in the early 70s, a period during which America had witnessed great financial and economic upheaval, fuel shortages and oil crises in the Middle East. Sensing an opportunity in the new and novel form of mining, Huck's father had developed an empire that was continuing to this day to provide fossil fuel power for the United States. Over the decades since, and with Huck's assistance, Seavers Incorporated had acquired allies both in Congress and the White House across multiple presidencies, valuable assets in the constant fight against environmentalists who seemed determined to remove all forms of power production from the United States in favour of returning humanity to living in mud huts and burning scrap wood for heat.

Seavers sighed softly as he looked out of the window of his jet and watched a regional aircraft take off, bound to destinations unknown. Big coal, as it was known, was a dirty business in almost every way and Huck was more than aware that many of the mountaintop mining companies had sought every means possible to ignore environmental and human rights issues in the pursuit of profit from their work. Seavers disliked the name itself – *big coal*, which made him sound like some corporate monster hell–bent on the destruction of nature. In truth, Seavers could not be further from such a caricature.

On the fold–down table before him was a picture of his wife and three children, in front of their beachfront property in Malibu, California. The bright blue sky, burning sunshine and luxurious villa were a sharp contrast to the drizzle and gray skies of Kentucky. Seavers could hear the rain drumming on the windows of the jet as he waited, and he reminded himself of why he was doing what he was doing. There were those who depended upon him, and the world was not a place that favored the weak or, sadly, the altruistic.

Seaver's assistant, Allison, moved to the door of the jet and heaved the locking mechanism open. The door swung down and a series of steps unfolded automatically under hydraulic pressure to allow a man in a dark suit to stride up into the aircraft. He wore a long black coat, presumably to defend against the gusting rain outside, but nonetheless it made him look somewhat sepulchral. A black suit with a white shirt and black tie, his obsidian skin dark and his hair salt–and–pepper gray, his bulk large and intimidating even from this distance. Seavers could not imagine a more perfect image for the kind of man he was being forced to deal with.

Aaron Mitchell strode to the seat opposite Huck and sat down, his hair and face beaded with drops of rain to which he seemed oblivious. Dark eyes and a humourless expression stared back at Seavers as though from another world.

'It is done.'

Seavers felt some of the tension slip away from his body and he could not help the sigh of relief that escaped from his lips as he nodded.

'They all folded?'

'All but one.'

Seavers felt his blood run cold again. He stared at Aaron for a long moment waiting to hear what had happened to the individual who had apparently decided to turn down the offer of a lifetime.

Aaron spoke quietly, but his voice nonetheless seemed to reverberate through Huck's chest.

'Stanley Meyer fled the town of Clearwater approximately two hours before we arrived. We have not been able to locate either he or his wife and daughter.'

Despite his consternation Seavers felt a ripple of relief once more flash through his system. He knew what the men he was doing business with were capable of, and had half expected a report that Meyer had been severed into multiple pieces and posted to the four corners of the country.

'And what of his fusion cage?'

Aaron inclined his head. 'It is now in safe hands.'

Seavers leaned forward on the table, his hands clapsed before him.

'Stanley Meyer can reproduce that device almost anywhere he chooses,' he insisted. 'He can move from town to town and will be extremely difficult to trace. We both know that he is aware of who we are, of what we're trying to do.'

'Measures have been put in place,' Aaron replied. 'Disinformation has been spread. Meyer will not be able to get funding for his device no matter where he goes, and if he ever does surface will likely be arrested for fraud.'

Seavers rubbed his temples and shook his head. Despite the importance to him of maintaining his company's work and future, he was aware that what he was doing to Meyer was every bit as distressing to the old man as it would be were somebody to undermine Seavers' own company, just as environmentalists often did with smear campaigns and lies.

'Meyer will not stop,' Seavers said. 'How much money was he offered?'

Aaron Mitchell stared back at Seavers. 'Enough. He refused.'

Seavers looked at Mitchell and began to wonder whether he would have been better served travelling to visit Meyer himself, although he knew Stanley would likely have shot him on sight if Huck had stepped across his porch. Seavers was the opposite of what Meyer strove to be, the corporate monster that everybody love to hate, the powerful one, the successful one, the one for whom no fortune was large enough. Seavers bitterly regretted breaking contact with Meyer, with whom in the past he had often discussed the promising future of nuclear fusion and Seaver's interest in investing in any new breakthrough technologies that might have emerged from the National Ignition Facility in California. But Huck could not have predicted just how far the old man would have come, just how much he would have achieved using nothing more than the tools available to him in the back of a goddamn garden shed.

Seavers leaned back in his seat in exasperation. 'You told me that your people had power to find anybody, anywhere, at any time. You said you'd be able to deal with this, quietly.'

Mitchell's expression did not change, as though he were a waxwork, his mouth the only moving part and his voice a monotone rumble that seemed strangely soothing and threatening at the same time.

'Ours is a small unit and we do not have the resources to pursue an individual across the country. It would appear that Meyer and his family are smart enough to understand how to stay off the grid. Without a paper or digital trail we are as powerless as anybody to find them.'

'And what if they go public?!'

Seavers slammed a clenched fist down on the table between them, surprising himself at his anger in front of the formidable man sitting before him. Mitchell did not blink at the sharp crack nor appear even mildly concerned at Seaver's fury.

'It will take Meyer time to construct another device, and in order to prove its worth it would have to go public in one way, shape or form in order to once again attract attention. As soon as he does, we will be upon him.'

'And if that's too late?'

'That's your problem,' Mitchell said finally.

'It's *my* problem?' Seavers uttered. 'The last time we spoke you suggested to me that covering this up would not be an issue.'

Finally, Mitchell moved. He leaned forward and folded his massive hands before him as he spoke in a voice so deep it sounded as though he were underwater.

'The issue has been covered up,' he growled. 'Three hundred people have been silenced at great expense to the people I work for, your mining claims will face no further opposition and you have required our assistance to make it all happen. There are limits to what we can do, and thresholds to the risks we are prepared to take on behalf of others.'

Seavers clenched his fists and replied through gritted teeth, unable to understand why Mitchell was failing to grasp the problems that he was facing.

'If Meyer's device ever reaches the light of day my company will become worthless overnight. The cost of paying redundancies, dismantling equipment and environmental rehabilitation programs in the areas we have already begun excavating will leave the business completely crippled.'

If Mitchell was capable of showing any sign of emotion, Seavers could not see it.

'Your business practices are your concern,' Mitchell replied. 'My superiors have far wider global affairs to concern themselves with. Their part in this bargain is complete, and anything else that stands in your way will have to be dealt with by your own people.'

Mitchell stood up and turned to walk toward the aircraft exit. Seavers fumed in silence for a moment before he called out.

'Wait!'

Mitchell stopped walking but did not turn back to look at Seavers. Huck stood up from his chair and closed his eyes as he spoke, feeling every bit the man who was walking blindly off the edge of a cliff with the certainty of doom before him and yet unable to stop his legs from moving.

'What would it cost to ensure the complete removal of any risk to my company's future?'

Aaron Mitchell turned on the spot, his hands in his pockets.

'That would require your complete control of Meyer's device, would it not?' Mitchell said.

Seavers felt a sudden pulse of excitement as he considered this new and novel approach to his problem. An alliance instead of enmity with

Meyer. Seavers cursed himself for not thinking of it before, and then he saw the look on Mitchell's face.

'This is what you wanted,' he said finally.

'What I want is irrelevant,' Mitchell replied as though disgusted. 'But it is clear to those who govern these factors that the fossil fuel era is at an end, and that every company that does not move on as swiftly as possible will be doomed to extinction. My superiors require a vehicle to ensure that their interests are aligned with those of the companies that control the supply of power to the people. Your company can be the part of that alliance, or it can be history. The decision is yours.'

'The price?' Seavers repeated.

'The controlling share, of course,' Mitchell replied. 'Seavers Incorporated will become the property of Majestic Twelve.'

'The controlling share?!' Seavers almost shouted. 'You want to control my company completely? They could fire me overnight as soon as the deal is done!'

'And you would be a very wealthy man for the rest of your life,' Mitchell pointed out, 'as you are now. Compare that with the consequences of not complying ... '

Mitchell turned away and strode from the aircraft before Seavers could reply, leaving the man standing alone and facing either complete ruin or the loss of a family business almost half a century in the making.

In the wake of Mitchell's departure Seavers looked at his watch and the date upon it, and made a decision. The Bilderberg meeting was due to start tomorrow and Seavers knew he had little time left to waste.

As Mitchell vanished, so Seaver's wife and children boarded the jet. Huck got out of his seat and forced a smile onto his face. His wife, Andrea, saw through him like glass as she looked over her shoulder out of the jet's entrance.

'Who was that?' she asked. 'What's wrong?'

'Nothing!' Huck boomed as he hugged his children. 'Everything's going to be great!'

***

VIII

Seavers Incorporated,

Kentucky

'I guess this is what you get for a lifetime in fossil fuels.'

Lopez looked up at the glossy, immaculate headquarters building of one of the most powerful energy companies in the country and removed her sunglasses to better absorb the affluence on display.

Chrome, glass and marble dominated the foyer of the building, which was built using purposefully unnatural angles, all sloping roofs and angular outcrops of marble and glass. Ethan had imagined that an oil company or similar based in Kentucky would have wanted to blend in somewhat with the folksy nature of the state rather than construct something as ugly as the building before him now and slap it in the middle of Lexington.

'I saw at least three limousines in the parking lot as we pulled in,' Lopez said as they walked toward the foyer entrance.

'We've seen this sort of thing before in New Mexico,' Ethan pointed out. 'Generally, the more money there is to be made, the more corrupt the people behind it will become.'

The foyer's glass doors opened automatically as they approached with a soft hiss, and Ethan walked inside with Lopez to be confronted with marble floors, more glass and a single reception desk. A young woman sitting behind the desk welcomed them with a broad smile that actually looked as though she meant it.

'Good morning, how can I help?'

Ethan affected an equivalent smile as he strode up to the desk.

'Good morning, we'd like to speak to Huck Seavers to determine whether he was responsible for the disappearance of three hundred people from the town of Clearwater, Missouri.'

The receptionist's studied smile slipped a little as clouds of confusion passed behind her eyes.

'Um, our CEO is not in today and I don't know anything about a town called Clearwater. Do you have an appointment?'

'No, we don't,' Lopez admitted. 'However, it's important that we speak to Mr Seavers. We understand that his company was involved in a mining application close to Clearwater and that the town was involved in a legal battle to try to prevent him from beginning operations. Every single person in that town has vanished, and we need to know why.'

'As I said, I don't know anything about a town called Clearwater, but I'll make contact with Mr Seavers and see if he is able to meet with you in the future.'

'Where is Mr Seavers?' Ethan asked.

'He boarded his private jet this morning,' the receptionist replied with some satisfaction. 'I believe that he is on his way to Holland, and from there to the Middle East. He won't be home for several days I'm afraid.'

'Thanks for your time,' Ethan said to the receptionist and promptly turned his back on her and strode for the exit.

'We not going to be able to get anything out of anybody who works here,' Lopez pointed out as they returned to the sunshine outside the building. 'The only thing we can really do is try to figure out a way of tracking down the people who lived in Clearwater. Three hundred people can't have just vanished into thin air.'

Ethan reached their vehicle, an unmarked SUV as unremarkable as any other in the state or even the country. He and Lopez climbed in to be met with Amber's ferocious glare.

'Was *he* in there?'

'No,' Lopez replied. 'He's out of the country on business.'

Amber folded her arms across her chest and fumed in silence as Doug Jarvis looked over the passenger seat into the back, having joined them from Washington DC.

'Europe?'

'Yeah,' Lopez said. 'Seavers is out of the country for some days. The receptionist made it pretty clear we wouldn't be getting any further than the foyer.'

'What have you got on the company's financials?' Ethan asked.

Jarvis was holding a thick file that he leafed through idly as he spoke.

'Seavers Incorporated is a very large company, but given that it's fully invested in mountaintop mining its accounts are actually rather simple. The business is divided into regions named alpha one, beta three, charlie five and so on, with individual sub companies founded for each region to simplify bookkeeping at a state level. I had a team at the DIA go over the accounts with a fine tooth comb going back ten years, and we found nothing unusual to suggest that there are any kind of financial indiscretions occurring at Seavers Incorporated. In fact, as far as major corporations go, it appears on the face of it to be clean as a whistle.'

'On the face of it?' Lopez asked.

Jarvis opened a particular section of the file which had been marked with colored tabs.

'The company's profits and dividends are drawn via a series of offshore accounts, much like most corporations who seek to avoid excessive taxation by using such havens to store company profits. Huck Seavers and his family's finances are operated out of these accounts, and our people did manage to find a few minor discrepancies that they haven't yet been able to solve.'

'What kind of discrepancies?'

'Seemingly random withdrawals of large sums into temporary accounts,' Jarvis replied. 'We're tracing where those sums went, but it's going to take a while. In short, Seavers Incorporated is making payments to accounts that no longer exist, shifting money around various countries and banks before it finally vanishes into thin air, rather like the population of Clearwater.'

'So, you think they're money laundering or something?' Lopez asked.

'Seavers Incorporated has been involved in numerous lawsuits over the past ten years,' Jarvis explained. 'Their mountaintop mining programs are claimed to be environmentally sound operations that do not affect the surrounding terrain and wilderness. However, multiple claims have been made of contaminated groundwater and inadequate clean–up operations over the years, mostly by townsfolk living within a few miles of Huck Seaver's operations. The vast majority of these claims are being quashed, Huck's lawyers far too powerful for ordinary townsfolk to take on and have any hope of winning. However, of the few that have been successful in gaining damages against Seavers incorporated, the pay outs involved do not match the payouts listed by Seavers Incorporated as having gone to claimants over the years. That means that the money is going somewhere else, and it's not a small amount. My guys estimate that Seavers Incorporated has paid something in excess of three hundred million dollars in the last decade alone, and we have no idea where that money has gone.'

Ethan leaned back in the seat as the SUV drove along the highway, heading back to the roadside motel where they had decided to hole up. The town of Clearwater had deliberately been made to look as though nobody had lived there for fifty years, and the extent of the changes had gone far beyond simply coating the town in a layer of grime. National census details had been altered and trees felled to block access to deter civilians from wandering aimlessly into the remains of the town. The digital details of hundreds of people had been completely removed from the national archives. The power required to do that in terms of legal access and sheer workforce was considerable, and seemed far beyond the reach of Seavers Incorporated and even the shadowy machinations of Majestic Twelve.

'There has to be some kind of government connection,' Ethan said. 'What if we're looking at this the wrong way around?'

'What you mean?' Lopez asked.

'What if the government or whoever is behind this did not make the people of Clearwater vanish? What if the people of Clearwater vanished voluntarily?'

'I doubt that three hundred people are going to simultaneously decide to up sticks and leave their entire lives behind,' Jarvis pointed out. 'What could possibly make them do something like that in such a hurry and … '

Jarvis's eyes widened as he understood where Ethan was coming from.

'Money,' Ethan said. 'You said that towns have disappeared before, in Africa and Siberia?'

'Yes, several years ago.'

'So what if the residents were *paid* to move?' Ethan suggested. 'What if what we've got here is in fact bribery? It would not be expensive to move an African tribe, as they have little money to start with. Presumably a town in Siberia would also be inherently poor, the task of paying sufficient money for them to disappear and start new lives elsewhere within the reach of a company like Seavers Incorporated.'

'But why?' Lopez asked. 'If Seavers Incorporated or indeed Majestic Twelve is behind this they've already recovered the device that Stanley Meyer supposedly created. They could simply have walked out of here, never to be seen again, and the whole thing would have been swept under the carpet.'

'That's my point,' Ethan said. 'It wouldn't have been swept under the carpet because the townsfolk were in on all this, and they would have approached the media. It's possible that the media could be silenced by the government, but not by a corporation like Seaver's. If what Stanley Meyer created was a world changing energy creation device … '

'It was,' Amber insisted sulkily.

' … then the risk would be too great if the townsfolk suddenly decided to make a big noise about what had happened. They needed to be silenced, completely, and presumably mass murder is not on the cards for government agencies. The only way they could reasonably do that is to offer them a sum of money sufficient that they would never *want* to talk about what happened.'

It was, in some respects, rather simple. A government like that of the United States, with its close ties to energy companies and the oil of the Middle East, would undoubtedly lose trillions of dollars in revenue for the loss of taxation and profit from fossil fuels should a device like Stanley Meyer's ever come to see the light of day. Even if they offered every family in the town of Clearwater ten million dollars, six hundred million dollars in total, still a tremendous sum of money and beyond even the coffers of Seavers Incorporated, it remained a paltry sum compared to the lost revenue that Stanley's Meyer's device represented. The US government could, and would, generate that sum of money in order to maintain profits over the coming years and decades.

'You said that Seavers Incorporated had somehow managed to lose three hundred million dollars,' Lopez said to Jarvis. 'That's about half of the arbitrary sum that Ethan just mentioned. What if Seavers is involved with the people that are behind this, maybe providing some of the cost of paying them off in order to maintain his mining rights in the area? It's a *quid pro quo*; Seavers Incorporated gets to continue making profit from fossil fuels dug from the mountains of Kentucky, while Majestic Twelve or the government or whoever else is behind this continues to keep any kind of novel energy device under wraps, thus keeping control of power generation countrywide.'

Jarvis was nodding slowly as Lopez spoke, assessing the information as the vehicle in which they drove descended off the highway and turned south for a small town just outside the city.

'It's not impossible,' he admitted. 'But in order to make people completely vanish, you would need something like the FBI's Witness Protection Scheme in order to give them new lives, new documents, legal papers and so on. It wouldn't be enough to simply forge them a new life – it would have to be a life that would stand up to scrutiny from local law enforcement, not to mention the fact that if these people have been paid off they suddenly possess large sums of money. The IRS would become suspicious of any such activity in the accounts of people who had been previously modest in their incomes, so that would also have to be addressed. I doubt that a small, albeit powerful cabal like Majestic Twelve would be able to organise all of this and make it happen.'

Ethan nodded.

'It's gotta be the FBI,' he said. 'They're the only ones with sufficient expertise to make people disappear completely. The question is, how do we get paperwork from the FBI concerning a program that's specifically designed to stop anybody from *getting* paperwork for it?'

'We don't,' Jarvis admitted. 'We'll have to do it the old way. People disappear when they want to, but most of them are terrible at it. They take up old hobbies, let slip their identities in conversation, although we have to remember that the people we're seeking have a good financial reason to stay quiet and they're not fleeing from anything. They have a lot of money to spend, and it's my guess that some will be more thrifty than others. We need to find out if there's anybody in the town of Clearwater that had an unusual hobby, or was perhaps poor in their judgement of how to spend money.'

'It's also worth a shot that many of the people involved would not have wanted to leave Missouri,' Lopez pointed out. 'They could be convinced to move town, but they may not have wanted to go too far. They may have families, other dependents, people who relied upon them and whom they would not want to be separated from. The FBI might be behind this, but these people aren't criminals or in fear of their lives from criminal gangs, so it would have been a hard push for the FBI to convince them to break full contact with their nearest and dearest. Silence is all that's required, on what happened at Clearwater.'

Amber Ryan looked up at her. 'Red McKenzie.'

'Who?'

'He's a mechanic, spends all his time fixing up old trucks for the loggers,' Amber explained. 'His house looked like a junkyard, old rusting chassis on the lawn and stuff like that. He was never happy unless his head was buried under a hood, a total petrol head. He won't change his ways much and he likely won't have gone very far.'

Ethan closed the file.

'It's the only way, if McKenzie's a weak link in the disappearances then we can maybe track him down. Why not try pulling a list of recent home purchases within fifty clicks of Clearwater and see if anything pops?'

***

IX

Winchester, Missouri

The quiet, leafy cul–de–sac that Ethan and Lopez drove into was a far cry from the cramped surroundings of Clearwater some fifty miles to the south. Large, modern homes with double garages overlooked perfectly manicured lawns, flawless asphalt roads and spotless sidewalks as Ethan pulled into the curb and switched off the engine.

'Looks like somebody's gone up in the world,' Lopez observed as she climbed out of the vehicle, the sun warm on her face and the sky flecked with a handful of white clouds.

Amber climbed out behind Lopez as Ethan glanced at a photograph of a man named Red McKenzie, or *Mac* for short. Mac had worked in the town of Clearwater for more than thirty years as an automobile repair man, carving a trade fixing the four–wheel drives of loggers moving in and out of the town. His property in Clearwater had been in a trailer park out back of the town and fairly close to the local bar, presumably so he could stagger his way home with greater ease at night.

Ethan looked up at the five bedroom house before him, complete with double garage and what looked like a brand–new Ford Ranger parked on the drive. The garage was open, as was the hood of the Ford Ranger, and he could hear somebody tinkering with tools as they walked up the drive.

Ethan glanced at Lopez, who understood what Ethan wanted without even so much as a gesture. Lopez walked up one side of the truck as Ethan walked up the other, Amber hanging back out of sight as they approached Mac.

It was possible that Mac was partially deaf, or more likely that he was so engrossed in tinkering beneath the hood of the Ford that he did not notice either Ethan or Lopez moving to stand either side of him. Despite the immaculate house and brand–new vehicle, Mac was dressed in an ancient pair of dungarees smeared with paint, grease and oil, and he was wearing a baseball cap of a similar vintage. His jaw was heavily forested with silvery stubble and there was a faint whiff of cigarettes and alcohol about the guy as Ethan rapped his knuckles on the Ford's hood.

Mac McKenzie jerked upright and a pair of hazy gray eyes fixed upon Ethan in surprise.

'Who the hell are you?' he croaked, one hand tightly gripping a wrench.

'Take it easy,' Ethan said as he raised his hands. 'We're just here to ask you some questions.'

Mac turned and saw Lopez standing behind him, and his frosty demeanour changed instantly.

'Well you can ask me any questions you like, honey,' he said as a toothy yellow grin spread across his features.

'That's just as well, because we've got a lot of questions to ask,' Lopez purred in reply. 'How's the new house working out?'

McKenzie peered back and forth between Ethan and Lopez, and he replied carefully.

'Me, I've lived here all my life. My Pa and my grandpa both lived just down the road, you can check the census if you like.'

Ethan grinned, McKenzie's response clearly a patter taught by whoever paid him off.

'Yeah, we know,' Ethan replied. 'The census will show exactly what the people that paid you to come here want it to show, and there will be no record of you or your family ever living in a town called Clearwater.'

McKenzie shrugged vaguely. 'Clearwater? Don't recall me ever hearing of a town called that.'

At that moment, Amber strode around from the rear of the Ford Ranger and pointed at McKenzie.

'The hell you don't, Mac!' she snapped furiously. 'What the hell are you doing here and how did you come by this house?!'

McKenzie's eyes flew wide as he looked at Amber, and then he struggled to drag a look of confusion across his face.

'I'm sorry Missy but I don't know what you're talking about. Who are you?'

Amber took a single pace forward and Ethan winced as he heard a sharp crack as the girl's knuckles collided with McKenzie's jaw and sent him sprawling across the wing of the Ford Ranger.

'You know damn well who I am and why I'm here!' Amber almost shouted. 'Where the hell are my folks?! Who paid you all this money to come and live out here!'

McKenzie's shock was replaced with an anger sufficient for Ethan to step forward in front of Amber and pin McKenzie's wrist down to prevent him from using the wrench.

'We know you were all paid off,' Ethan said.

'And we know that you're not going to talk and risk losing everything you've gained here,' Lopez added. 'But not everybody was as lucky as you, and we need to know what the hell happened in Clearwater.'

Ethan released McKenzie's wrist and the old man pulled himself off the Ranger's hood and glared at them.

'I got nothing to say to you folks. I don't know any Clearwater.'

Amber seemed to get control of her anger as she hissed at McKenzie.

'Paid you a lot of money, didn't they,' Amber said as she gestured to the house and the new truck. 'I expect you're looking forward to a nice future without the need to work. But my father has disappeared, and he was going to be worth a thousand times what you've been paid to keep your rotting mouth shut. You really think that Stan would have abandoned his friends, not brought them along with him? He shared that device with all of you, took away your energy bills, and this is how you repay him?'

McKenzie's face fell in shame but he clung to his fortune and future as tightly as he did the wrench in his hand.

'We didn't have no choice,' he uttered. 'It was accept the terms or walk with nothing. What would you expect us all to have done? Stanley took off, fled before the troops arrived. They sat me down, offered me more money than I could have earned in ten lifetimes to just up sticks somewhere else and say nothing to anybody about it.'

'Who?' Ethan asked. 'Who offered you money?'

McKenzie beckoned them in closer, looking about him as though suddenly nervous that they were being listened to.

'I don't know who they were and frankly I don't give a damn. They were good to their word and I've never seen them again since.'

'Tell us,' Lopez insisted. 'We not going to go to these people and tell them that Mac McKenzie ratted them out. We're already on their trail, you'll just be saving us some time and I have a feeling that they're not likely to take away what they've given you for fear of you shouting about it. Tell us what you know, and we'll be on our way.'

McKenzie peered at them certainly. 'Who are you folks?'

'Truthfully?' Ethan said. 'We're working for the Defense Intelligence Agency and we know what happened at Clearwater stinks. We know that the entire town was paid off to remain silent, and that the money offered was a powerful incentive to do so. We're not here to take it from you, just to find out what happened.'

'It's important, Mac,' Amber insisted. 'What my father did may now cost him his life, and if somebody doesn't help us then we can't help him. Just tell us what happened.'

McKenzie sighed and tossed his wrench down alongside the Ford as he rubbed his temples with his fingers, leaving greasy smears across his forehead.

'Old Stan called a meeting down in the town hall, one night during the week. The councillors were there too and a couple of the bosses of the local logging firms. Stan told them that he wanted to wire up the town's electricity supply to something he had designed. He said that if it didn't work out, then they would simply rewire to the National Grid and carry on as normal. But he said that if it did work, we'd never pay another energy bill as long as we lived.' McKenzie chuckled. 'That got everybody's attention. We figured we had nothing to lose, so we went ahead and let 'im do it.'

'What happened after that?' Lopez asked.

'Stan was as good as his word. The power supply went off while he wired up this device of his, and then suddenly the power was back on and that was that. Nothing changed, except the fact that our electricity bills stopped coming in, because all the bills read zero.'

'Didn't the local electricity companies come in and ask what was going on?' Ethan asked. 'Surely they must have had a stake in it all?'

'They showed up a couple of days later,' McKenzie said. 'We all just said the same thing, that we were on oil burners now and we didn't need an external electricity supply. That's what Stan told us to say, that we were to say nothing about the device he had installed. Those electricity company guys weren't impressed and they didn't like it, but using oil burners is quite common in these parts and there's really nothing they could do about it. We didn't hear anything from them after that.'

'Somebody must have noticed though,' Lopez pointed out. 'How long was it before the troops showed up?'

McKenzie leaned against the Ford and folded his arms as he frowned thoughtfully.

'About a week. Things were going great and everyone was really excited about getting energy for free. Many of the houses that had previously been on oil burners took advantage of Stan's device and were delighted at the savings they were making. Everybody was really amped

I guess, about what might happen in the future. Stan was adamant that we must keep quiet about it, that there'd be those who'd attempt to stop him from developing the device further, especially the oil and gas companies. But the town's council were keen to publicise what had happened, because they knew it would stop that local company from mining the mountaintops outside of Clearwater.' McKenzie looked at Ethan. 'Stan was against that, of course. He said we should wait, get things more sorted before we started advertising what had happened.'

'Did the council listen to him?' Ethan asked.

'Yeah, they listened,' McKenzie said. 'They knew how Seavers Incorporated had used dirty tactics in the past to gain mining rights in other towns in other states, so they knew they had to play their hand right. All of the councillors were on board and agreed to say nothing about the device.' McKenzie sighed again. 'That's the damnedest thing about it. Stanley insisted that when the time came, the device schematics, the plans for making these things were to be distributed by mail and by Internet across the globe as fast as possible. He had this crazy plan of printing thousands and thousands of copies of the blueprints and just mailing them to all corners of the country, so that people could build these things for themselves rather than buy them from Stan.'

Ethan looked at Lopez and she shook her head in amazement.

'I'll be damned, he really was planning to give it all away for nothing,' she said.

'Just like I told you,' Amber replied. 'My father wasn't going to make a fortune from this, he was going to give it away to humanity for the better of us all.'

McKenzie nodded, clearly ashamed at his own selling out in the face of Stanley Meyer's extraordinary altruism.

'Stan was apparently about to get ready to distribute his plans when suddenly he and his wife just took off as fast as they could in the middle of the night. Only reason I knew they'd gone was because I was on my way home from the local bar and saw their car leave, the trunk packed full of suitcases. I was pretty much drunk at the time, but in the morning I figured that they decided to get themselves out of sight before the storm broke just in case Stan was right and somebody was out to get them.'

'And you never saw them again?' Ethan pressed.

'Nope,' McKenzie replied. 'That was the last I ever saw of Stan and Mary, and the soldiers showed up less than two days later.'

'Tell us about them,' Amber insisted. 'Anything you can remember.'

'That is pretty much everything,' McKenzie admitted with a frown. 'It's not every day your town gets shut off by the military, and men in sharp suits offer you twenty million bucks to say nothin'.'

'Twenty million,' Ethan echoed. 'That was the price of silence for you?'

'For all of us,' McKenzie replied. 'It was a once only deal, take it or leave it. No taxes, paperwork all sorted. New name, new home, family included. They just wanted us to disappear and say nothing 'bout what happened, and they made it real clear that we should never, ever return to Clearwater or mention it ever again.'

'And what about Stan's device, the one that was powering the town?' Ethan asked.

'Whisked away as soon as we'd all agreed to the deal,' McKenzie replied. 'I was one of the last to leave, mostly because I hadn't tidied my trailer in years and it took me forever to find all the crap I wanted to take with me. The power went out just before I was finished, and I saw them taking away some sort of bright device that they had shielded with large tarpaulins and placed on the back of a truck. I'd have taken the damn thing to be a UFO or something if I hadn't known what Stan had been up to.'

'What about the men who offered you the deal?' Lopez asked. 'Did they identify the agency with which they were working, or give any clue as to who they were?'

'Nothing,' McKenzie said. 'They were straight–talking folk, no wasted words, and made clear that time was of the essence, if y'know what I mean. From what I saw of the troops outside the barricade around town, their uniforms carried no insignia and their vehicles were unmarked. I did some time in the army back in the day, and I've never seen soldiers moving without any insignia like that on US soil.'

'Paramilitary,' Ethan said, 'pretty much what we already knew.'

'Twenty million,' Amber murmured. 'There are not many families who would have turned down a sum of money like that. It's the kind of cash sufficient to last a lifetime if it's handled well.'

'Yeah, there were conditions,' McKenzie admitted. 'At least half a million committed to the purchasin' of a property, and a limit on how much we could spend each year. It was all in the contract, which we signed, some kind of nondisclosure agreement.'

'Clever,' Lopez observed. 'They were trying to minimise the chances of any of you being tracked down by overspending or drawing attention to yourselves.'

'That figures,' McKenzie admitted. 'They wanted everything to be done on the quiet, no big fuss, no big announcements. Just get out of Clearwater, never come back and never say anything about what happened.'

'You got any idea where everybody else went?' Amber asked. 'Old Jeff, Lauren Gardener, any of the logging contractors or hotel staff?'

'Nope,' McKenzie said. 'We were all questioned separately and it was intimated that we should not discuss with any of the other folk what we'd been promised or where we were headed. I don't think any of us were thinking of anything but the twenty million bucks that were waitin' for us outside of Clearwater. Which reminds me, you all should be goin' now, 'cause I ain't risking losing my fortune talking to you.'

Ethan figured that the old man had risked enough, and after thanking him he led Lopez and Amber back to their car.

'He's the smoking gun,' Amber said. 'If we can get him to go public, it'll blow the whole thing wide open.'

'Nobody will believe a word of it,' Ethan said, 'and I don't think that Mac there is going to sing for us and lose his new fortune. We need a different angle here.'

'Is there anybody your father might have confided in, a long–time friend perhaps?'

Amber nodded.

'Doctor Cecil Grant,' she replied. 'He works at the National Ignition Facility in California, was there with my dad for years.'

'We need to pay him a visit.'

Lopez glanced at Amber with interest. 'And what about your angle, Amber? There's twenty million bucks out there waiting for you and your own silence. Have you not thought about heading back to college and letting Majestic Twelve come striding into your life?'

Amber offered Lopez a curt smile. 'I have something called integrity. You ever heard of it?'

Amber opened the car door and got in, slamming it behind her.

'Glad I asked,' Lopez replied.

***

Dean Crawford

X

National Ignition Facility,

Livermore, California

'Are you sure this is the place to come?'

The flight from Missouri to California had been a long one but Ethan felt certain that the best place for Amber Ryan was as far away from Clearwater as possible, and travelling to California was not something that Majestic Twelve might predict, fake ID documents provided by Jarvis further veiling their path.

'Cecil Grant still works here,' Amber explained from the backseat, where she was lying down on a pillow to avoid even the slightest chance of detection by road cameras or other surveillance. 'I know that dad reached out to Cecil from time to time, that he trusted him.'

The National Ignition Facility was an enormous building, the entrance to which was emblazoned with a promising logo:

Bringing Star Power to Earth

Ethan could not help but be fascinated by the sight of it as he drove past the facility's main gates. Access to this most secure location was normally limited to employees and special invitees only, the NIF having been used as the set for the USS Enterprise's warp core in the movie *Star Trek: Into Darkness*, but Amber had been able to recover from her cell phone the number of Doctor Cecil Grant, an astrophysicist employed at the NIF and a former colleague of Stanley Meyer. Dr Grant had been more than willing to meet with Amber, but he considered the NIF building to be too dangerous and too well monitored to be a safe place to meet in light of what had happened at Clearwater. Instead, he had arranged a meeting at a local cafe where he felt more likely they could talk without being observed.

Ethan drove into the cafe lot and pulled up.

'Shades, baseball cap, collar up okay?' Ethan asked Amber.

'I feel like I'm in a lousy spy movie,' Amber replied, tucking her thick black hair under the cap.

'It's the easiest way to break up your outline without looking too ridiculous,' Lopez informed her as she climbed out of the car.

'Does the government really have that kind of ability to track people?' Amber asked as she too climbed out and slammed her door shut.

'Oh yeah,' Ethan replied. 'Trust us, they can follow you anywhere if they really want to, but to do that they've first got to pin you down. Facial recognition software is widely used now, but I'm hoping that the extent of the surveillance won't reach that far in your case. It's your father they're really after.'

Ethan led the way into the cafe, which was really more of a diner and at this hour was barely a quarter full, the air laden with the odours of coffee and fried breakfasts. Ethan stood to one side as Amber entered, letting her lead the way toward one of the tables in the back corner of the diner while Ethan and Lopez scanned the other people seated around them in search of any evidence of government agents or anything else that might make them feel uneasy. Ethan saw nothing to concern himself as he followed Amber toward where an elderly gentleman was sitting with a coffee and watching expectantly as Amber approached him.

Dr Cecil Grant stood up and embraced Amber with a warm smile, then looked her up and down as he rested his hands on her shoulders.

'I can't believe I once held you as a baby,' he said appraisingly as he looked over her shoulder at Ethan and Lopez.

'They're with me,' Amber said.

'Do they know what happened?'

'They're working on it,' Amber said as she sat down opposite Dr Grant and introduced Ethan and Lopez.

'Stanley Meyer is a stubborn *sonofabitch*,' Dr Grant said as Ethan sat down opposite him with Lopez. 'It doesn't surprise me that he's got himself up to his neck in trouble.'

'He done anything like this before?' Ethan asked.

'Has he pissed off the authorities more than once? Yes,' Dr Grant replied. 'Stanley is one of those guys for whom the phrase "thinking out of the box" was invented. He never liked to conform, and that often meant that sometimes his methods got him into hot water with his superiors at the NIF. They tolerated it, because that same out–of–the–box thinking helped him to make considerable strides in physics during his tenure, and to be honest the NIF wouldn't be what it is today without Stanley's contributions.'

'How much do you know about what he was working on in Clearwater?' Lopez asked.

Dr Grant humphed and shook his head as he replied. 'He started out building cars that ran on steam.'

'Seriously?' Lopez asked.

'It's a big deal,' Doctor Grant replied. 'There's even a Steam Automobile Club of America. Stanley did it as a hobby and built a vehicle that runs entirely on steam using a boiler system. He used a Ford 272 engine with a flat crank and a ninety–degree V design, which made a single–acting steam engine that's self–starting. Each cam was actuating two opposed poppet valves and used only one cylinder casting design. It was really very clever, and showed that a steam car could run fairly normally, like an ordinary combustion engine powered vehicle, on almost any fuel at all: vegetable oil, methanol, anything. He put the damned thing in an old Chevrolet and cruised around the country showing it to people at events.'

'He loved that old car,' Amber reflected with a smile. 'It cost him virtually nothing to run it for years, and the only exhaust it gave off was steam.'

'I'd have thought that it was impossible to run a car efficiently from steam,' Lopez said. 'Look how much coal those old steam trains used to use, all that smoke. Environmentalists would go insane.'

'If you're burning coal to get energy then yes, it would be,' Doctor Grant admitted. 'But Stanley wasn't, and anyway most attempts to produce pollution free engines are all to do with efficiency, and how the methods we use to produce electrical energy to heat our homes and the engines we use to drive our cars are hugely *inefficient*.'

'And dad found much better ways of doing it,' Amber enthused. 'He loved those Sterling Engines too.'

Doctor Grant nodded in agreement.

'What's a Sterling Engine?' Ethan asked.

'A fully enclosed combustion engine,' Grant explained, 'with a heat exchanger and two cylinders, which can be fuelled by almost anything with huge efficiency because it uses its own exhaust gas as part of the burning process. Stanley could get hugely excited about them because the average vehicle on the road, powered by the internal combustion engine, can produce a maximum efficiency of just fifteen per cent. That means that of all the power produced, eighty five per cent goes into overcoming friction within the engine or is lost as heat. A Sterling Engine, on the other hand, can produce energy with an efficiency of as much as sixty per cent.'

'So how come they're not powering cars the world over then?' Lopez asked.

'Size, slow start times and other minor issues, but Stanley was working on improving the smaller designs he'd come up with. Sterling Engines are found aboard most ships, for instance, because the vessels are big enough to house them.'

'So his work on these Sterling Engines led onto bigger things, I take it?' Ethan guessed.

'Stanley was obsessed with the idea that we were going about energy generation the wrong way,' he said simply. 'He's one of those guys that felt that nature did things in the opposite direction to what *we* do when it comes to generating power.'

'In what way?' Ethan asked.

'Well, when humans generate power we use explosive energy to do so. We heat water to power steam turbines, or burn coal in power stations to produce steam. We ignite fuel in car engines to drive them forward, which in principle is the same as letting little bombs off in the car's engine every fraction of a second. Explosive energy is how we power our world, but nature uses the complete *opposite* means to generate energy. If you doubt that then simply look at the power of a hurricane or tornado.'

'They are low–pressure systems, right?' Lopez asked.

'That's correct,' Dr Grant replied. 'Nature uses a low–pressure system to create motion energy. We see it in weather patterns all the time, in the maelstrom of a whirlpool in the oceans and even in the immense gravity generated by black holes which pulls galaxies in around them in exactly the same symmetrical whirlpool pattern. Stanley noted this repeatedly during his tenure at the NIF, and spent many hours telling anybody with a will to listen about how it was much more efficient to create low–pressure systems than it was to produce the high–pressure systems we normally use for energy generation. Of course, nobody bothered listening to him.'

'Why not?' Ethan asked. 'Surely he was onto something?'

'Of course he was, but that's not how the business of energy generation works,' Dr Grant said. 'Billions are invested every year in the search for more power, for cleaner power, for power that governments can control. If somebody suddenly turned around and created some kind of novel energy generation device that rendered all of those other expensive methods irrelevant, the existing energy industry would implode with the loss of countless jobs and livelihoods, not to mention those of the scientists involved in furthering currently accepted methods of generating energy.'

Amber nodded, clearly recalling similar things said to her by her father.

'Dad was convinced that any attempt to publicly patent or otherwise sell any kind of advanced energy generation technology that defied the accepted laws of physics would be met with accusations of fraud, possibly arrest by the authorities, and certainly refusal by the government patent office to consider the technology.'

'That's illegal, surely?' Lopez said.

'The US Government's Patent Office has a policy of refusing any applications for devices that contain claims of producing what is known as "perpetual motion",' Dr Grant explained. 'This broad brush approach extends to any devices which are claimed to produce free energy of any kind, which is really just a clever way of making sure that nobody can actually get a Patent for such a device should they actually manage to invent one. The policy is in place within all the world's countries – even if somebody invented such a device, they could never commercialize it.'

'So what you're saying is that if Stanley invented a free energy device, there's literally nowhere to go to actually get the thing into production?'

'At a very basic level, yes,' Dr Grant admitted. 'But Stanley did not invent a free energy device because there is no such thing as free energy. The conservation of energy, one of the governing laws of thermodynamics, prohibits energy gain in a closed system. It simply isn't possible to get more energy out of a device than you put in – if such a thing were possible, we would have dispensed with fossil fuels decades or even centuries ago.'

'And yet there is nuclear fusion,' Ethan murmured in reply.

'Nuclear fusion liberates the energy already contained within the atomic nucleus,' Dr Grant replied. 'That's not creating energy from nowhere, it's simply a conversion process and does not violate any of the known laws of physics.'

Ethan realised that Amber was watching Dr Grant intensely, and she nudged the old man with her elbow. Cecil looked at her for a moment and sighed as he went on.

'However, when radiation was first discovered it was also considered to be in violation of the laws of thermodynamics because those witnessing simply didn't understand what it was at the time. It was only with Einstein's discoveries and the publications of his famous papers that govern the laws of energy and matter that scientists finally understood what was taking place – the decay of radioactive materials from one element to another. Once understood, there were no violations of the rules of thermodynamics and the process was thus accepted by the scientific community.'

'So you're saying, in effect, that what Stanley Meyer discovered may actually be real?' Lopez pressed.

It was Amber, not Dr Grant, who replied.

'I think that my father uncovered the solution to something known as cold fusion.'

Dr Grant winced at the mere mention of the words, shaking his head.

'What's cold fusion?' Ethan asked.

'A debacle,' Dr Grant replied without hesitation.

'So everybody says,' Amber shot back, 'but if there was nothing in it then how come my parents are on the run and three hundred people have vanished from Clearwater?'

Doctor Grant scowled but said nothing.

'We need to know,' Lopez said to him. 'If there's something about this cold fusion that's behind why Stanley has fled then it could also lead us to him and help us protect him from whoever is behind all of this.'

Dr Grant sighed and spoke quietly.

'In 1989 one of the world's leading electro chemist's, Martin Fleischmann and his partner Stanley Pons, created a device that produced what was known at the time as anomalous or excess heat in sufficient quantities that they could only be explained in terms of nuclear processes. Their work was based on the idea that if you load enough hydrogen or deuterium atoms inside a metal lattice made from nickel or palladium, they become so tightly packed together that they begin to fuse: nuclear fusion. They also reported the detection of neutrons and tritium, by–products of nuclear reactions. What was remarkable about this experiment and the device was that it occurred on a table top and involved the electrolysis of heavy water on the surface of a palladium electrode. They called the process cold fusion, because it mimicked the processes going on within stars but without the millions of degrees of temperatures and intense pressures required to fuse atoms together.'

'What happened to this cold fusion, and why is it not powering my home and car right now?' Lopez asked.

'What makes science so successful is the process by which fresh claims in any discipline are tested, the process being known as peer review. If a scientist makes a great discovery, he then publishes the method of his experiments widely in journals and allows others to test it to see if they can find a flaw. Many scientists attempted to replicate cold fusion but were unable to do so. As the number of negative replications increased, suddenly the positive replications that had occurred were withdrawn and before long the entire cold fusion research community became embroiled in scandal. Cold fusion eventually gained a reputation as pathological science, and reviews by the United States Department of energy in 1989 and 2004 reached a conclusion that cold fusion was dead, although they did offer what they called a sympathetic view towards modest support for further experiments.'

'So cold fusion was a scam then, or a mistake?' Ethan said.

'Yes.'

Grant winced as Amber nudged him again. Dr Grant tilted his head this way and that as he spoke.

'Over the years certain things have happened that have caused some degree of doubt among scientists over the initial assessment of cold fusion by the Department of Energy and by the scientists employed by them to study the phenomena,' Grant admitted. 'You have to remember that both Fleischmann and Pons were expert scientists, leaders in their fields and not prone to coming up with spurious results or publishing papers when they were not certain of their conclusions. And yet both men were completely ostracised by the scientific community, their funding removed, their reputations tarnished and even smeared. Neither of the men ever recovered their prior scientific prowess.'

'You think that a smear campaign was orchestrated deliberately?' Lopez asked. 'In order to reduce the impact of what they discovered?'

'What nobody in the scientific community actually disputes is that they discovered *something*,' Dr Grant said. 'Yes, it's possible that their anomalous excess heat data was the result of some other phenomena rather than nuclear reactions, but nonetheless they discovered something. That something, the anomalous heat, was surprising and encouraging enough for them to go public with the discovery. You don't do that lightly in the scientific community, especially when what you found goes against the grain of all known physical processes. Although I'm not a supporter of cold fusion, I am a supporter of the fact that those two men must have been pretty damn sure of what they were seeing before they went wide with it. And there were also questions over the method used by the scientists who failed to replicate Fleischmann's and Pon's results.'

'Such as?' Ethan asked.

'There are two studies that are cited by Patent Offices worldwide for refusing all applications concerning cold fusion devices, and those studies were the ones commissioned by the Department of Energy's Energy Research Advisory Board. They were conducted by the Massachusetts Institute of Technology and Caltech, and were designed to determine federal responses to cold fusion claims and even to shape energy policy at the highest level of government. The problem is that a man named Dr Eugene Mallove wrote an article for the MIT press in which he claims that MIT actually did observe excess heat in their cells and then covered it up. Another scientist, Dr Maleeva, was so incensed at the complete disregard for proper scientific process that he resigned his position at MIT in protest. Yet another noted scientist, Dr Peter Hagelstein, noted that the MIT experiments could not have possibly seen enough excess heat because their loading was not high enough, the scientists concerned having not packed enough deuterium molecules inside their cathodes to reach the reaction range.'

'So they fudged the results on purpose,' Amber said, anger clear in her voice although she was staring at the table top. 'My father said that it was not the first time that such research had been quashed by the government's involvement in silencing creators of novel energy devices.'

'However, times are changing,' Dr Grant said. 'A symposium was held at MIT in 2014 regarding cold fusion, and the scientists involved explained that according to their experiments excess heat is never seen in cold fusion devices unless a ninety per cent deuterium–to–palladium loading ratio is created. The Caltech and MIT experiments never got above eighty per cent, which is why their experiments failed to produce excess heat. More recent tests involving more modern devices have, allegedly, produced the excess heat that's been missing from prior experiments, but of course the mainstream scientific community still denounces them and no papers are being published by respected journals because they are always refused on the basis that cold fusion is dead science.'

'Catch Twenty Two,' Amber said. 'You can't get funding to develop a device, and if you build one yourself nobody will test or review it in public journals. The science is buried.'

Ethan sat back as he thought about what Dr Grant had said.

'So at least some people in the scientific community still accept the possibility that cold fusion is real, and as a result scientists are going out on their own.'

'Precisely,' Dr Grant said. 'This is why Stanley resigned his position at the National Ignition Facility. He was determined to do something about all of this, his experience and knowledge in the field meant that he could do it on his own on a table top, just like Fleischmann and Pons claimed to have done. Although I can barely believe I'm saying it, it would appear that he achieved what he set out to do, and that the government were there waiting and ready to ensure that it never saw the light of day.' Dr Grant sighed. 'I don't think I need to elaborate on what our world would look like now had cold fusion found the traction that it needed to become a fully–fledged scientific theory. Oil crises, climate change, the rising price of gas and other fossil fuels, all would be a thing of the past because the cold fusion device that Fleischmann and Pons created works on nothing more than a low electrical supply and heavy water or deuterium, which is easy to produce and cheap too. Your entire house could be powered by a cold fusion device no larger than a shoebox, and there are plenty of people out there who don't want to ever see that happen.'

'But I thought the government was keen to do things like that, to get rid of fossil fuels forever,' Lopez said. 'Even if this were just about money or corporations, surely they're flogging a dead horse and everybody knows it?'

'It's not just about the money,' Dr Grant explained. 'It's true that the corporations want to continue earning money from the sale of fossil fuels, but there is far more to it than just cash. The government has a vested interest in ensuring that people do not have energy security.'

'That's crazy?' Ethan said. 'Energy security is widely known to be one of people's greatest concerns.'

'That's right,' Dr Grant said with a smile. 'And that's why the government doesn't want anybody else to have it. They must control the power because without power, the people are nothing. It's the control that is important, the knowledge or belief that the people cannot have their electricity without the government and power corporations to supply it. If you put a private power supply in every home in the United States, and there are enough farms to provide food and water for everybody, then ask yourself Ethan: *who needs a government?*'

Lopez shot Ethan a glance. 'More to the point, what would a government do if their authority was under such a threat?'

Ethan sat for a moment and then he asked Cecil Grant a straight–out question.

'If you were Stanley Meyer and you had built something like that, what would you do?'

Doctor Grant sighed.

'Truthfully? I'd do what Stanley told me he would do, and fly one of them out to Saudi Arabia to sell it to the highest bidder, then retire on my fortune.'

'My dad wouldn't do that,' Amber insisted.

'You sure about that?' Grant challenged. 'He even borrowed money off me to buy his tickets.'

'He's in Saudi Arabia?' Ethan asked in amazement, and was rewarded with a nod from Grant.

'If Stan really has invented a device that could render fossil fuels archaic, it would be utterly priceless.'

'And worth killing for,' Lopez added.

Ethan nodded in agreement as he pulled out his cell phone. 'We need to speak to Huck Seavers, he's the only direct link in all of this.'

***

XI

Bilderberg Hotel,

Oosterbeek, Holland

Aaron James Mitchell sat in the plush surroundings of a penthouse suite in the Bilderberg Hotel, looking out of the window at the sumptuous grounds as he tried to quell the sense of impending doom enshrouding him. The annual Bilderberg Conference, a three day event which was due to begin the following day, would mark a turning–point in the global obsession with fossil fuels. It was known, but only to those fortunate and powerful enough to be attending, that the future of humanity's fuel would be decided not by environmental or resource factors but by the whims and requirements of a small handful of the world's most powerful and wealthy men. The facts would be laid before the Steering Committee of Bilderberg and discussed at length by its members and invitees as a matter of global importance.

Even Aaron could admit to himself that the security of Bilderberg and the sheer influence of its regular attendees virtually premeditated the suspicion of those who regarded the political leaders of their respective countries with contempt. It was only in recent years that lists of the attendees at Bilderberg were even released to the public, and then only in places where those interested knew where to look. Combined with a permanent block on media reporting and the flood of security and secret services operations that surrounded the meetings, it was a marvel to Aaron that the whole world didn't know about Bilderberg. The methodology of the meetings certainly flew in the face of Aaron's own opinions on how to apply effective security, such as that surrounding Majestic Twelve. None the less, obscure and unknown the meetings remained, as did the events that took place within. However Aaron, and his close connection with those who both attended and even influenced the meetings themselves, had managed to gleen crumbs of information over the years about what went on within the shadowy corridors of Bilderberg.

At the top of the list of their priorities was economic policies based upon the trade in fossil fuels. Oil, in every form, in every country of the globe, was a concern that dominated most Bilderberg meetings at one point or another. Shell, Exxon, Oppenheimer, OPEC; all of the largest and most powerful petrochemical corporations were represented at Bilderberg, and all of them intensely interested in where oil was going to come from over the next ten, twenty or fifty years.

The great irony, Aaron reflected, was the fact that the vast majority of easily accessible oil in large quantities lay beneath the sands of the Middle East, and no Arab leaders were Bilderberg invitees. Thus, in the face of Arab distrust of the West, of the murderous and mindless hatred of Islamic fundamentalists, did the countries represented by Bilderberg have to discuss how their countries could do business with their unpredictable oil bearing foes in the Middle East. Many ordinary citizens considered the dominance of the fat–cat oil businesses and their continued manipulation of said oil–bearing nations to be the ultimate in oppression and self–serving greed, the pursuit of profit despite the suffering of the Muslim nations' ordinary people beneath the yoke of their splendour–loving monarchies and dictators. Yet, in fact, the general public had the whole image the wrong way around.

The nations of the West had long possessed the ability to drill oil in places far from the Middle East. Even Russia, now a tentative ally of the West, was possessed of oil reserves vast and plenty. Oil fields were being discovered on a regular basis at greater and greater depths and further afield, even in Antarctica, and only the development of efficient technology prevented the mining of these precious fields. This was without mention of the immense capacity of the science of the West to provide energy from a hundred different alternative sources which, although heavily screened from the public domain, would render the need for oil completely unnecessary. Even electro–magnetic research had shown considerable potential for energy generation, and that at the turn of the 20th Century at the hands of men like Nikola Tesla.

No. The West did not use the Middle East for oil, for oil was not a permanent nor current requirement of the West. It did so because, without this tenuous yet essential link between East and West, the ultimate goal of the Bilderbergs could not be achieved.

The New World Order.

The New World Order had been shaped in the late 1950's by the earliest Bilderberg meetings. It was not a self–serving plan for global domination, although it was placed largely in the hands of globalised mega–corporations. It was, in Aaron's opinion, one of the most noble and yet fraught with danger policies that he had ever heard of.

Global unity.

The dream; the Utopian jewel of a global society no longer torn by racial oppression nor religious intolerance. It was the spread of democratic rule, the triumph of trade over war. Already, the steady and inexorable spread of the European Union, absorbing countries beneath its protective umbrella, was the advancement of that dream. The N.A.T.O. alliance had been its birth, a vast cooperating super–army that had allowed the coalition forces to so completely overwhelm Iraq in the early 1990's. With the military force of the United States at its side, no single country outside the E.U. could hope to stand up to its advance. The New World Order was an advancing of the hope for unity, the bringing of democracy, by *choice*, to countries hitherto far beyond the reach of the West. But for that policy to be implemented, the populace of the countries involved must be under the control of their respective governments: most people operated in fear of the laws of their governments, but the greatest fear of all political establishments was the people rising up against them, too numerous to put down with words or war. The Arab Spring had been a stark reminder for many leaders that, when pushed too far, the people *could* coordinate themselves in their millions, and bring down entire governments and armies almost overnight.

The doorbell of Aaron's suite rang and he roused himself from his thoughts, walked to the hall and pressed a button on a small console set into the wall. A small screen there lit up and Aaron stared into the face of a Bilderberg invitee. He opened the door and the man walked in silently, waiting for Aaron to shut the door before he turned and spoke.

'What news?'

There was no preamble. The man was older than Aaron, his suit perfectly pressed, not a hair out of place. He would not of course be a member of MJ–12, for to reveal one's identity was a cardinal sin as far as the cabal was concerned, but clearly he was acting on their behalf. Aaron realized that he was probably sharing a hotel with the entire cabal, with no idea of who they were.

'The device has been recovered but Stanley Meyer is in the wind, as is his wife and daughter.'

'No matter,' the man said. 'As long as the device is in our hands Stanley Meyer will be unable to distribute it to other people or demonstrate it to potential buyers. He has nowhere that he can go, and as soon as possible will you ensure that a media campaign to further tarnish his reputation is instigated. The less trustworthy Stanley Meyer appears, the less likely it is that anybody will listen to his story.'

'Will that be enough?' Aaron asked.

The man shook his head.

'Not to change the world,' he replied. 'The revolution is coming and there is nothing that we can do to stop it, but we don't need to stop it – only to maintain control. Already, our major corporations are investing in technologies that will change the shape of our world in a matter of decades. Lockheed Martin has recently unveiled a nuclear–fusion generator that fits on the back of a truck and could power thousands of homes. Saudi Arabia is investing heavily in solar power and other renewable energy ventures – when the world's leading exporter of oil becomes interested in the very things that devalue oil, you know a change is coming.'

'This is a tide that not even Majestic Twelve can stop,' Aaron agreed softly. 'Sooner or later, somebody, somewhere is going to reveal this technology to a wide enough audience to create a shift in the balance of power. Is it not wiser to get ahead of that tide and obtain the rights to the technology before somebody does something stupid and gives it away for free?'

The man laughed, and it seemed as though the effort almost split his jaw.

'Do you really think that any sensible human being would be able to turn away the opportunity to earn a billion dollars overnight? Everybody has their price.'

'Stanley Meyer didn't,' Aaron pointed out.

'I said *sensible* human being,' the man replied. 'Stanley Meyer is an idiot. He could be relaxing on a beach on his own private island by now instead of hiding in the gutters of God knows where. He will be found, eventually, and when he is he will have nothing. I will make it my personal mission to ensure that he ends up destitute for the rest of his life without a dime to his name.'

Aaron nodded quietly as he pictured in his mind the old inventor shivering on a street corner in Detroit's south side, babbling about a conspiracy to deny the world free energy. The perfect foil, a man reduced to such a meagre state that nobody would believe him.

'I need to know what measures I may use to ensure that this stays under wraps,' Aaron said finally. 'If I locate Stanley Meyer, do you wish me to further make offers on your behalf, or should we simply dispose of the problem?'

The man stared out of the windows across the park outside for a long moment before he replied.

'Make offers if you can,' he said finally. 'We don't want to make more mess than we have to, agreed?'

'Agreed,' Aaron Mitchell replied, not without a flutter of mild relief as he stood. Murder was tough, especially when the target was a man who was clearly attempting to do the right thing with an altruism that would in other circumstances have earned him a Nobel Prize.

'Resources?'

'Continue to operate beneath the auspices of Seavers Incorporated, and allow them to supply any paramilitary or mercenary forces that you require. If law enforcement gets onto the case, the trail will lead to Huck Seavers rather than us. Ensure that you vanish as soon as the task at hand is complete.'

Aaron turned and walked for the door, opening it and exiting onto the corridor outside, his footfalls silent on a thickly carpeted floor. A man in a grey suit awaited him, an earpiece microphone and designer shades partially concealing his features. The hard line of his jaw and the short cut to his hair betrayed him as a former military man, the agent falling into step alongside Aaron as he walked.

'Get me everything on Stanley Meyer,' Aaron ordered without preamble, 'and his family. We have limited time and they must be found, is that clear?'

'Yes sir,' the agent replied and hurried away ahead of Aaron.

***

Dean Crawford

XII

King Khalid International Airport, Riyadh,

Saudi Arabia

'This is insane,' Amber uttered in a whisper. 'I feel like a criminal.'

The *Saudia* Boeing 747–400 from Los Angeles to Riyadh had landed thirty minutes before on the sun–baked runway some twenty miles north of Saudi Arabia's capital city. Ethan, Lopez and Amber were all travelling light with just hand luggage as they exited the airport's air conditioning and were immediately assaulted by the scorched air and brilliant flare of sunlight outside.

'Not as insane as your father,' Lopez replied as she lowered a pair of sunglasses over her eyes and looked at the unfamiliar surroundings. 'He invents a device that will render oil obsolete and promptly travels to the oil capital of the world. It's a wonder he wasn't shot the moment he stepped off the plane.'

'I think he's a genius,' Ethan said with a smile as he sought the private vehicle Jarvis had hired for them before they had left America with false passports, their passage smoothed with the DIA's help. 'If Majestic Twelve are seeking him out the last place they're going to look is Riyadh.'

'I think he's an idiot,' Amber informed him, once again. 'Dad hasn't been outside the United States in his life except for short trips to Europe to attend scientific conferences when he was younger. What the hell he's doing coming out here I have no idea.'

A wave of heat drenched Ethan in sweat as he stepped from the air–conditioned interior of the terminal. He squinted up into the hard and unforgiving blue sky as he stepped onto the flawless asphalt outside the main terminal. Few cars were visible, just a couple of dusty tan–colored sedans parked across the street.

A sleek, white sedan pulled up alongside them and a tinted window lowered to reveal a smartly dressed chauffeur who held up a placard with the name Warner upon it. Behind the sedan an equally immaculate white SUV slid in alongside the sidewalk and a man climbed out, his eyes concealed behind sunglasses, a microphone earpiece in place and a muscular torso bulging against his thin cotton shirt.

'Ethan Warner?' he asked in heavily accented English. 'Assim Khan. We will be your escort for the duration of your stay in the Kingdom.'

Ethan peered into the 4x4's interior as he shook Khan's hand, and saw there three other guards, all of them carrying weapons in discreet shoulder holsters.

'Who sent you?' Ethan asked.

'Courtesy of Huck Seavers,' Assim announced. 'He understands that you wish to meet with him here in the Kingdom.'

Ethan blinked. Somehow, for some reason, the receptionist way back in Kentucky must have gotten word to Seavers about their visit. He couldn't be sure, and perhaps Seaver's sudden interest in them was due to the legal battle for Clearwater's mining rights rather than any wrongdoing on the CEO's part, but he felt that they must be on the right lines of enquiry for Seavers to have followed their travels and been ready to assist them upon their arrival. Either he had something to hide, or he didn't.

'I didn't realize we needed an escort,' Lopez said to Assim.

'Then you have never travelled to Saudi Arabia before, ma'am,' Assim replied with an oily smile. 'You will need to wear these, due to the laws here.'

Khan handed both Lopez and Amber an *abaya*, a long and quite elegant dress that covered their bodies and arms. Although the Kingdom did not require women to wear the *hijab* demanded of more hard–line Muslim countries, it did enforce abaya's on both residents and visitors alike. Lopez and Amber both donned the dresses as Assim Khan spoke.

'Riyadh is less relaxed than Jeddah, which allows women to wear the abaya open rather than closed, but it is best not to draw attention to yourselves. Just being an American in this country is enough to make you a target.'

Ethan placed their luggage into the trunk of the sedan and then they climbed together into the rear seats and the chauffeur pulled away and increased the air conditioning inside the vehicle to cater for the new occupants. Behind, Ethan observed the 4x4 with Assim and his guards pull into escort position a few car lengths behind them.

'You said that your father intended to give away the device free,' Lopez said to Amber as the vehicle left the airport and joined the highway heading towards the distant city. 'Why would he come here to the one place where the ruling family would like to see such a device destroyed?'

'Who says that they would?' Ethan challenged. 'There are powerful people such as Majestic Twelve who do not want to see Stanley's device be commercialized, not to mention the US government itself. America is trying to get itself off and away from fossil fuels, which if they should achieve such a noble aim will leave the Saudi royal family in the lurch out here. Maybe Stanley is looking for new allies, people with a vested interest in what happens to the future of oil consumption around the world.'

'And what's he going to say to them?' Amber asked. 'Hello, here's a device that will render you destitute by the end of the year. Fancy getting involved?'

'He's clearly not intending to sell out,' Lopez admitted. 'But then it makes no sense why he would come here to Saudi Arabia. Even if the House of Saud believed that he could develop such a device, what could they offer him in return if he doesn't want money?'

'I don't think he's in it for money,' Ethan said. 'The only logical reason for him fleeing to Saudi Arabia is to blackmail the House of Saud.'

Amber looked to Ethan as though he had gone mad. 'You're kidding? He wouldn't do that. Even my father knows that the laws out here aren't like they are in America. I don't doubt that the Saudis would imprison him on a whim never to see the light of day again if they even thought he was capable of blackmailing them.'

'I'm not so sure,' Ethan said as he opened a file that he'd been given by Jarvis before they had departed Los Angeles. 'Saudi Arabia may be the oil capital of the world, but they know as well as anybody else that the writing is on the wall for fossil fuels and for their own future exports.'

'Already?' Lopez asked. 'I thought they'd have waited until every last drop was out of the ground?'

'Not according to this,' Ethan replied. 'The Saudis are getting in on the solar power game before the oil dries up. Due to the decreasing costs of utility–scale solar installations, solar power in Saudi Arabia has achieved grid parity and can produce electricity at costs comparable to conventional sources. In 2011, over fifty per cent of electricity was produced by burning oil. The Saudi agency in charge of developing the nation's renewable energy sector, *Ka–care*, announced in 2012 that the nation would install forty one gigawatts of solar capacity by 2032. It is projected to be composed of twenty five gigawatts of solar thermal and sixteen gigawatts of photovoltaics. A total of fifty four gigawatts of energy will be delivered by renewable means here by 2032.'

'So even the Saudis are preparing to get out of the oil game, and simply export their supplies to other countries?' Amber said.

'It would appear so, and that assertion is bolstered by the fact that as oil prices fell as demand reduced at the end of the first decade of the twenty first century, for the first time Saudi Arabia did not raise the price of oil to compensate. They knew that by doing so they could push other oil producing countries into debt by maintaining the low price, whereas Saudi Arabia could carry the losses for years, even decades, due to its reserves of both the oil itself and state–held capital.' Ethan glanced thoughtfully out of the window of the vehicle. 'They've got the whole world over a barrel, pardon the pun, and they're using it to bolster their own position as an energy supplier of oil or of future clean energy.'

'So what about my dad's device?' Amber asked. 'If the Kingdom has the market sewn up in their favour?'

'Why build solar plants that cost millions when you can have a cold fusion device churning away for little cost in every home?' Ethan surmised. 'The Saudi Royal family rules this Kingdom simply because they control the oil. Once that oil is gone, they'd be up and out of this country with their fortune overnight because the country has nothing else to export, not even any real tourism industry. This would become a desert as soon as the oil money dried up.'

Lopez shook her head. 'The Saudis won't stay here on the basis of national pride just because Stanley Meyer has given them a way out. The people will rise up against them quickly enough just like in the Arab Spring if they tried to … '

Lopez broke off and Ethan grinned.

'The people are what counts,' he said. 'The greatest fear of any government is being overthrown by their own people. The more the people are forced to rely upon their government, the less chance there is of that occurring. The Saudi people hate America because our government props–up a Royal Family who hoard the vast majority of revenue from the oil in their country and live in spectacular wealth while many of their people live in abject poverty. But if the people are suddenly presented with a means of shaking off their royal leaders and denying them their fortune, what do you think they'll do with it?'

Lopez nodded.

'There must be some kind of underground movement here, or maybe even environmentalists who Stanley could run to.'

'In an anti–American populace, they would gladly hide such an ally from prying eyes long enough for him to prove to them that he can build a device that will render the House of Saud penniless overnight,' Ethan said. 'He's not trying to start a revolution in America, but in the country that *supplies* America with oil.'

Amber held her head in her hands. 'He's playing with fire, literally. Dissident movement leaders in this country have been publicly beheaded in the past and the legal system is governed by Sharia Law. He's going to get himself killed out here!'

'We need to track him down and fast,' Ethan agreed. 'Majestic Twelve, if they're behind all of this, will have been able to track him too. It's only a matter of time before they figure out where he is.'

'And where we are,' Lopez reminded him. 'We're on their radar too after Argentina.'

'I don't think that they'll have anticipated us coming out here so soon after what happened in Clearwater,' Ethan replied, and on instinct he glanced over his shoulder out of the rear window of the sedan.

Behind them on the dark asphalt, beyond the escorting SUV, were several vehicles on the multi–lane highway heading south toward Riyadh. Two of them were the dusty sedans Ethan had seen earlier, following a respectable distance behind Assim Khan's escort.

'Well, somebody other than Seavers knows we're here,' he said.

**

Dean Crawford

XIII

Seavers Incorporated,

Saudi Arabia

'You stay in the car.'

Amber shot Ethan hurt look as he climbed out of the vehicle. 'No way. I want to look this guy in the eye and find out what's happened to my father.'

'If Seavers is behind any of this, the first thing he'll try to do is use you as leverage against Stanley,' Ethan insisted. 'Right now it's my guess that the guards he sent to escort us don't know of your significance, but if you give any indication you're somebody Seavers wants to get hold of we're going to find ourselves in a whole world of hurt. Stay here, let Nicola and I find out what's going on and we'll report back as soon as we're done.'

Amber smouldered with fury, still gripping the door handle.

'He's right,' Lopez soothed. 'We need to keep you out of sight, or what happened to your father may happen to you, too. We won't be long.'

Amber, her teeth gritted, released the door handle and folded her arms as she stared out of the tinted windows at the elaborate building nearby.

Ethan climbed out of the vehicle and watched as Assim and his three associates approached them. The two vehicles had passed through a security checkpoint, which itself was the only point of access past a twelve foot high razor wire fence that encircled the entire compound. Outside, a loose gathering of Saudi protesters were watching with dark eyes that smouldered with suppressed rage.

'Those guys always there?' Ethan asked Assim as the escort joined them.

'Most days,' Assim admitted. 'There is a strong anti–American feeling in this country. Most foreign compounds are heavily guarded, little patches of Americana in the desert that are often the target of attempted suicide bombers and other militant attacks. Trust me, it's not possible to be safe in Saudi Arabia as an American.'

'Reassuring,' Ethan said as they walked towards the building. 'Those two sedans followed us from the airport,' he added as he gestured to the two vehicles now parked beyond the protest line.

'We kept one eye on them,' Assim replied without concern. 'They cannot harm you here. What of your friend?' Assim asked as he looked back at to where Amber was sitting inside the vehicle and staring out of the tinted glass. 'Will she not be joining us?'

'Catherine is a journalist,' Lopez replied for Ethan, whipping up the first name that popped into her head. 'We have some delicate questions for Huck Seavers and the presence of a journalist may cause him to doubt whether his answers will be kept in confidence. We've asked Catherine to stay in the car for now.'

Assim nodded, apparently appreciative of the gesture.

'Mr Seavers has a lot of problems with journalists in the United States, so I've heard,' he said as they walked into the building's elaborate foyer. 'I don't suppose he'll be wanting any further issues with them out here, although the kingdom has very strict rules governing the work of journalists.'

'I wonder why,' Ethan murmured, his words heavily laden with satire.

Khan led them to an elevator on one side of the foyer, as one of his associates handed out identity badges to them. Ethan was surprised to see that his name and image was already on the badge.

'Just how long has Seavers known that we were coming here?' he asked.

'I have no idea,' Khan said with a shrug as the elevator climbed away from the foyer. 'We were given the badges this morning.'

Ethan glanced at Lopez but said nothing as the elevator carried them up to the third floor and opened out onto a plush corridor that led to a pair of wide, open mahogany doors. They walked into a conference room dominated by a long, slender glass table arrayed with glasses and vases filled with exotic desert flower species. Broad windows looked out across the scorched desert, tinted with a film that shielded them from some of the sun's brilliant glare. As Ethan walked toward the windows he could see the protesters far away beyond the brutal wire fences that glittered brightly in the sunlight, the crowd looking a little larger than it had before.

'Mr Warner?'

Ethan turned as a tall, broad–shouldered man in a sharp suit of dark grey charcoal and a crisp white shirt strode into the room behind them, his hands in his pockets and a broad smile on his face.

Huck Seavers looked good for his age, which Ethan recalled from the file as being forty five. Seavers had inherited the family fortune, rather than digging in the dirt for it for the better part of his life, and thus Ethan assumed he had lived in the lap of luxury all that time.

'Mr Seavers,' Ethan said as he shook the CEO's hand. Seavers' skin was soft, the hands of an office worker.

Ethan introduced Lopez, as Assim Khan and his three associates moved out of the conference room and closed the door quietly behind them.

'Please, sit down,' Seavers said as he strode to the head of the table.

Ethan took a seat, his back to the windows and Lopez sitting down opposite as Seavers stretched out in his chair, crossed his legs at the ankle and folded his hands in his lap.

'Now, you've come along way so what can I do for you folks?' Seavers asked.

Seavers exuded the folksy charm of a Kentucky oil man made–good, and it appeared to Ethan as though he had spent many years perfecting the image. Seavers clearly wanted himself to be seen as the ordinary man who had simply struck lucky, probably cultivating the natural image of his father. Whether Seavers thought his charade fooled anyone was anyone's guess, but Ethan wasn't interested in the image, more the man beneath it.

'We've come to discuss what happened in Clearwater,' Ethan said.

Seavers inclined his head in acquiescence, gestured with his open palm hands in what looked to Ethan a carefully choreographed display of honesty.

'One of our more successful campaigns,' Seavers said. 'It's likely we'll begin excavating there within a few months, once the final legal technicalities are in place.'

'You know that's not what we're talking about,' Lopez said.

'I don't know what you mean.'

'It's been a very thorough cover–up,' Ethan observed casually. 'Not just in the way that the town of Clearwater, Missouri has been given a makeover that makes it appear to have been abandoned for half a century, but in the sheer scale of the media cover–up. I'm incredibly impressed that a company as small as Seavers Incorporated has been able to eradicate not just any media references to the legal case brought against your company by the town Council of Clearwater, but also to silence the judges involved in the case, the lawyers, the supporters of the case in neighbouring towns, literally anybody with any knowledge of events in Clearwater. And that's not including the three hundred people who lived in the town who have suddenly just disappeared.'

Seavers frowned as he raised his hands and linked his fingers together to form a cradle upon which he rested his chin.

'Really, I don't know what you're talking about. The town of Clearwater has not been inhabited for at least forty years according to the census, and the surrounding terrain has been legally cleared for mountaintop mining operations. The paperwork's already on its way through.'

Ethan leaned casually back in his seat as he examined the tips of his fingernails.

'That's strange,' he said idly, 'because despite the apparent thoroughness of your work you missed a few of the town's inhabitants.'

Ethan figured that Huck Seavers had never really been a poker player. Although the CEO's expression remained unchanged, his eyes wobbled in their sockets as he began to realize the depth of Ethan's knowledge of what had happened.

'Missed a few inhabitants?' Seavers echoed, his voice less steady than before as he attempted to conceal his concern. 'Really, what are you two talking about? Nobody has lived in Clearwater for ... '

'The town of Clearwater was inhabited by three hundred people,' Lopez cut him off, a touch of irritation in tones. 'We know it and we're interested in what happened to them. Did it not cross your mind that living in a wilderness town would result in many of the people going camping, hunting, to have pursuits that may have taken them out of the town while you and your men were going about the business of making the rest of the inhabitants vanish?'

Huck Seavers sat for a long moment staring at Lopez, either thinking fast or unable to bring himself to speak. Ethan took full advantage of the silence.

'There are survivors,' he said softly. 'They were not present in the town when you made your alterations. It's time to stop pretending, Huck. We don't think that the people of Clearwater were murdered because we also know that they were paid quite substantial sums for them to simply disappear. There are a few more people who would like to disappear too, but understandably they're a bit cautious about coming forward because if a person like you is willing to make three hundred people disappear, you're probably willing to do just about anything to ensure you gain mining rights to that town. In fact, we suspect there may be more to it than just the mining rights, don't we Nicola?'

'Yes we do, Ethan,' Lopez picked up her cue smoothly. 'We're enormously interested in the device that apparently was loaded onto a truck and whisked away from Clearwater in the wake of its inhabitants disappearing. Tremendous energy emissions, so it turns out. The sort of thing that might represent an alternative form of energy and might render Seavers Incorporated worth, oh, I don't know, *nothing* for instance.'

Huck Seavers features gradually imploded as Ethan and Lopez assaulted him with their narrative, and he finally folded his hands together in a tight ball.

'What do you want?'

Ethan smiled a cold little smile. 'What do you mean, Huck? We have tremendous evidence to show that Seavers Incorporated is behind the vanishing of three hundred people, and is behind the concealing of a device that could provide our country, and perhaps the entire world, with free energy. I should imagine that the price for silence in such an explosive story would be far beyond even the means of your company. Unless of course, you *didn't* pay them off and what we're looking at here is a form of genocide?'

'Nobody has been murdered!' Seavers snapped and slammed a clenched fist down on the table with a sharp crack.

A long silence enveloped the conference room, broken finally by Lopez's voice, a degree softer now than before.

'To know that, of course you would have had to be involved,' she observed. 'Tell us what happened, Huck. Better to hear it from you than to see all of this evidence presented before major news networks across the planet, maybe even Congress and the Supreme Court.'

'It won't happen,' Seavers said with a tight smile, rage radiating from his eyes. 'You're dealing with people you really don't want to cross.'

'Yeah,' Ethan murmured. 'The problem is we've made a career out of doing that, so threats aren't going to change anything. Either you speak to us or by tomorrow morning every newspaper and news channel across the world will be reporting on how Seavers Incorporated is suspected of mass murder and possibly the greatest cover–up in the history of the United States.'

Seavers glanced at the scorching desert outside for a long beat before he spoke.

'Ten million,' he said. 'Each.'

Ethan felt a flush of excitement tingle down his spine as he realised the position he had suddenly put himself and Lopez in. Ten million dollars was a tremendous amount of money and more than he could ever hope to earn in an entire lifetime. Now, it was being presented to him on a plate in return for nothing more than remaining silent about what he knew. It crossed his mind he should have tried this years ago, considering the number of people of means they had encountered over the years.

'Twenty million each,' Lopez said from beside him.

Ethan looked at her sharply in surprise, only to see a stony face glaring at Huck Seavers, dark eyes smouldering like hot coals as she called the man's bluff. Ethan looked at Seavers and watched him fold like a deck of cards.

'Twenty it is,' he said simply. 'You will be required to sign nondisclosure agreements, to leave this country, to never approach Seavers Incorporated or any of its subsidiaries again. You will also be required to relinquish any evidence into my hands. Should you renege on this agreement you will lose everything that you have been given, every last dime. You will be left destitute, is that clear?'

'It's clear,' Lopez chirped.

Huck Seavers leaned forward on the glass table, the smile back on his face now as he returned to more stable ground. With tens of millions of dollars hanging in the balance, Seavers clearly felt that he had control of the situation.

'You will also be required to hand over any of the survivors you have referenced. Without them, there is no deal.'

'Ah,' Ethan murmured. 'That's a shame. You see, without them you could simply have us eliminated as soon as we leave this building. In fact, once we've handed over all of our evidence there's nothing to stop you from having us shot on the street.'

'I am not a murderer!' Huck Seavers almost shouted, and for a moment Ethan thought he was going to get out of his chair and swing for him.

Ethan was struck by sudden realization that despite his involvement, Huck Seavers may actually represent a half–decent human being stuck in an impossible situation. Ethan leaned on the table and watched Seavers closely as he spoke.

'You're not on your own in this,' he said. 'Your company does not have the ability to achieve what's been done at Clearwater on its own. We know damn well that you'd have needed the assistance of the FBI in order to make those people disappear into new lives. We know that Seavers Incorporated does not have sufficient influence, money or power to sway the media, to silence the news channels or to influence criminal courts in Virginia. Who are you working with, Huck?'

Ethan did not expect Seavers to reveal anything about those assisting him in his mission to destroy every last scrap of evidence of Stanley Meyer's device, but he did want to see the Kentucky man's reaction to his question. Seavers' eyes narrowed as conflict raged behind them, the desire to share his woes warring with his need to remain silent.

'You'd be surprised at the influence I'm able to generate,' Seavers replied. 'The buck stops here, Mr Warner, and so does your offer. You either take the twenty million now, or you leave this office with nothing.'

Ethan leaned back in his chair for a long moment, purposefully drawing the moment out. He had to admit, even to himself, that the temptation to take the offer right there and then was almost overwhelming. *Twenty million bucks*. He wouldn't have to work another day in his life. He could buy the boat he had always wanted, moor it outside a property on Lake Michigan that he had often dreamed of and while his days away in solitude and comfort, free of the constant financial worries that it seemed plagued every single person in the Western world.

Stay the course Ethan, people's lives are depending upon it.

Ethan made to get out of his chair and he realised that his legs were resisting him, as though every fibre of his being was screaming at him to take the offer and simply walk away from the Defense Intelligence Agency. The hell with them, they had never paid much anyway.

Ethan gripped the seat rests more tightly and pushed himself up onto his feet.

'You and I both know that's not true,' Ethan said, trying not to let his voice croak. 'There's somebody else behind this, somebody powerful, and believe me they'll drop you like a rock should news of this device get out.'

Ethan looked down expectantly Lopez and her dark eyes shot to his in desperation. He could see that she was struggling with the dilemma that she faced, just as he was, and it was almost out of embarrassment it seemed that she clambered to her feet and stood by his side.

'You're making a mistake,' Huck Seavers said, 'probably the biggest of your lives.'

Ethan shook his head.

'No Huck, you are,' he replied. 'We know what Stanley Meyer invented and we also know that he intended to give it away to the world. But even if he does, even if he hands it out to the world for free, you and

I both know that the spirit of humanity is far stronger than the greed of the powerful few. Stanley Meyer will be sent money from every corner of the world by people who have never met him, simply for saving them thousands of dollars a year on their energy bills. If every person in America only offered him a dollar he'd be on his way to his first half billion.' Ethan smiled as he warmed to his theme, that of a man who had invented a device that could save the planet and yet still put that planet ahead of his own financial security. 'Your twenty million bucks is nothing compared to what Stanley Meyer will soon be worth, so I'll be throwing my lot in with him thanks.'

Ethan turned his back on Huck and made for the door, discreetly reaching out for the corner of Lopez's jacket to tug her along with him. She almost stumbled as she was pulled towards the door, and Ethan could feel the exasperation radiating out from her like a force field as he opened the door.

Ethan barely had time to react as Amber Ryan blasted past them, evidently having listened to the entire conversation from the other side of the door.

'Bastard!' she screamed.

Ethan managed to catch hold of Amber's collar. She fought to break free as Huck approached them.

'I haven't done anything to your father!' he snapped.

Amber yanked herself free from Ethan's grip, took a single stride and swung a punch that connected with the coal man's jaw with a sharp crack that made even Lopez wince. Huck Seavers span to one side and crashed down onto the long table, one hand flying instinctively to his injured jaw.

'You're a murderer!' Amber screeched, loudly enough for her voice to carry through the open door and into the building beyond. 'You're paying people off and killing those who don't agree to a deal!'

Assim Khan and his men rushed into the room and grabbed hold of Amber before she could strike Seavers again. She writhed in their grip as they manhandled her away from the CEO, who regained his feet and rubbed his jaw.

'Show these people out of the building,' he growled, his skin reddening.

Assim and his men obeyed and turned, in time to see an attractive woman with long auburn hair hurry into the room and stare at Huck in amazement.

'What's going on here? Who are these people?'

Before Huck could reply, Amber spat in her direction.

'You should be ashamed of yourself, marrying a black–hearted murderer like him!'

Lopez took Amber's shoulder and directed her out of the door. 'Let's just get out of here, okay?'

As Lopez led Amber outside, Ethan cast Huck a last glance.

'You're playing a dangerous game Huck, and the only winners are the people you're answering to. They'll crush you, believe me.'

Huck did not reply as Ethan turned and left the room.

***

Dean Crawford

XIV

'I told you to stay in the car!'

Amber shrugged Ethan off as they walked through the foyer. 'Gee I'm sorry, *dad*.'

'Huck knows you're here,' Lopez warned her. 'He knows who you are.'

'We need to get out of here, fast,' Ethan agreed.

'What's he going to do?' Amber challenged them. 'Shoot me?'

'You're the one accusing him of murder,' Lopez shot back. 'Maybe you should have thought of that before you hit him?'

As they stepped out of the foyer, a chaotic melody of shouting drifted to them on the hot desert wind.

'What's going on?'

Ethan scanned the road and saw ranks of demonstrators waving placards and shouting in an Arabic dialect he could not understand. Many were chanting and punching the air as they marched, dark eyes above dark beards blazing with outrage, pink mouths agape as they vented their anger.

'Islamists,' Assim Khan suggested. They will be crushed, as they always are. Stay close to us.'

The phalanx of guards moved closer around Ethan, Lopez and Amber as they moved down the steps of the building toward the main street. Ethan noted that the guards were now walking with their hands on the butts of their side–arms, not drawing the weapons but ensuring that they could be used at a moment's notice.

Ethan saw Assim push a finger to his ear, listening intently to a series of instructions and then nod as he replied, but the noise of the protesters meant that Ethan could not tell what he was saying.

'This way,' Assim said finally.

Hordes of Saudis surged and swayed en masse before them, banners flying in the hot wind, deep voices soaring in a communion of protest, eyes bright and fierce. Ethan stopped just outside the main entrance of the compound and stared at the vast and imposing sea of faces before him.

Police armed with masks, riot shields and short, hard looking sticks loitered in loose formations around the fringes of the crowd, eyes flicking nervously across their renegade charges. Riot vehicles were idling nearby armed with water cannon, watching as the crowd chanted and pointed and accused, and already they had started to notice the foreigners amid the protective ring of Saudi guards as they approached the vehicles alongside the gates.

'Stay tight,' Ethan whispered harshly to Lopez. 'This could get rough.'

From the centre of the crowd rose a terrifying sight, one that sent a spasm of concern lurching through Ethan's bowels. A crude effigy of the American flag drenched with gasoline and oil was hoisted into the air and in an instant engulfed within a writhing coil of flame. A gust of bellowed cheers erupted from the crowd as the burning flag sent a billowing pall of smoke into the blue sky.

'They hate the House of Saud,' Assim rumbled darkly beside Ethan.

Ethan saw the two dusty tan sedans still nearby, their occupants nowhere to be seen, but now they were parked alongside the compound fence. He watched as the crowd surged against the security fences around the compound, and then a sharp crack split the air as a cloud of acrid grey smoke spiralled up from the hood of one of the sedans.

'Bomb!' he yelled.

Assim Khan's men reacted instantly and grabbed Amber Ryan as they formed a protective huddle around her and rushed toward the 4x4 nearby.

The sedan exploded with an ear–shattering roar, the trunk engulfed in an expanding fireball as the vehicle was lifted off its wheels and flipped over onto its back. A cloud of shrapnel from the blast sliced through the fences, and as a billowing cloud of smoke dissipated on the hot wind Ethan saw the fences lacerated and weakened by the blast.

In an instant, the crowd cheered and surged toward the damaged fences.

Assim gave Ethan a gentle shove toward the escort vehicle parked nearby, further down the road from the chaotic mass of humanity plunging into the fence.

'Go, get to your vehicle!'

Even as Ethan moved, a phalanx of armed soldiers broke away from the guard post at the main gates and rushed between their charges and the chanting crowd.

'This is going to get ugly!' Lopez shouted with clairvoyant certainty as the crowd surged against the fences. Ethan was half way to the car when the fence failed and crashed down onto the desert floor. A protester broke out from the crowd and rushed toward him, eyes filled with the fury or the desperation of the insane, one finger jabbing accusingly at him.

'American, American thieves!'

Before the man could impart any further gems of information the guards broke ranks and swarmed upon him, flicking open combat sticks from their belts to cut the Saudi down in a frenzied cloud of blows. The crowd turned to watch as their comrade was beaten to the ground.

'Belay there!' Ethan shouted above the chanting.

Lopez instantly recognized the seriousness of the situation and dashed toward their car as the deep and melodious chanting of the crowd underwent a sudden and grotesque mutation, a bellowed roar of indignation and rage. Retreating from the beaten man, the guards had drawn their firearms, holding them at port arms as they fell back. Confronting them was the advancing mob, a turbulent milieu from which flew a sudden and brutal cloud of rocks and bottles.

Ethan ducked as the projectiles showered down around him, and to his disbelief Assim's guards broke their defensive line and fled for the safety of their vehicle. Assim Khan grabbed hold of Amber, one forearm wrapping around her neck as he jammed a pistol against her side and hauled her away toward the 4x4.

'Wait!' Lopez yelled.

One of Assim's men aimed his pistol at Lopez, who froze in horror. Assim bundled the writhing Amber into the rear of the vehicle as strong hands hauled her inside, and then Assim jumped into the passenger seat in the front. The 4x4's doors slammed shut and Ethan watched the vehicle accelerate past them toward the main gate, Assim Khan watching him through the partially tinted windows with a sneer on his face. Behind the 4x4, their sedan also accelerated away from the impending crisis, its driver's eyes wide with fear.

'We've been set up!' Ethan yelled above the din of the crowd.

The 4x4 raced through the gates and disappeared around a far corner of the street in a cloud of dusty haze as Lopez backed away from the crowd toward Ethan.

Ethan looked up at the riot vehicles arrayed further down the street, and to his dismay he realised they were not moving forward to confront the growing mob. The soldiers atop the vehicles were holding the water cannons pointing at the ground, a clear sign that they were not yet prepared to take on the crowd.

'We're on our own!' Ethan yelled. 'Run, now!'

The burning American flag tumbled onto the dark asphalt amid the crowd as dozens of them swarmed upon it, stamping on it with cries of mindless hate. Lopez dashed across the street even as an enraged preacher lunged for Ethan with fury writ large across his features. Ethan saw a long, narrow blade clasped in his hand flash in the sunlight as the preacher tried to conceal it with his robes while at the same time lashing out towards Ethan with the weapon.

Ethan whirled and bought his right arm crashing down upon the preacher's wrist, blocking the weapon and pushing it to one side as he instinctively swung his left fist across the preacher's face. The preacher staggered backwards in shock and collapsed onto his back amid the crowd, his fury gone and replaced with an expression of shocked indignity. Ethan did not wait to see what the reaction of the crowd would be. He whirled and dashed in pursuit of Lopez as she sprinted away through the open gates and across the street and then vaulted over a low wall.

A shower of broken bottles and other debris crashed down around Ethan as he ran, pursued by the roar of the crowd as they launched themselves after him. He vaulted over the low wall and saw Lopez reach a battered truck parked in a lot that was caked in dust. Lopez lifted one boot and drove it into the passenger door window, shattering the glass.

'There's no time!' Ethan yelled as he joined her.

Lopez yanked open the door, used her boot once more to smash the plastic guard from the driving column.

'Get in!' she yelled as she yanked a handful of wires from the column and began re–wiring them together.

Ethan hurled himself across the hood as he heard dozens of heavy footfalls thundering across the parking lot behind him. He turned to see countless men flooding over the wall, some of them waving bats and other threatening objects in his direction as they screamed and yelled.

Ethan jumped into the passenger seat of the truck and slammed the door shut.

'Hurry up!'

'Thanks for the hot tip!' Lopez snapped back as she focused on the mass of wires.

Ethan leaned across her and grabbed her door, slamming it shut just as the crowd rushed upon the vehicle. The truck rocked violently as the angry mob slammed against it and a man's hands reached in for Lopez.

Ethan reached out and grabbed one of the man's arms and hauled him into the vehicle straight over Lopez's lap, instantly blocking the window and preventing further attackers from reaching inside. He saw others moving around the vehicle, tyre irons in their hands as they prepared to smash the windscreen out.

'Any time now would be good!'

An iron bar smashed into the screen and Ethan saw a spider's web of cracks blossom around the impact point as a Saudi with features ablaze with righteous fury smashed the bar across the glass again and again.

Lopez, reaching now over the back of the captive man's waist as she attempted to start the truck, finally found the correct wires and wound them together. The truck's engine spluttered into life and Ethan reached down and yanked off the handbrake as Lopez slammed the automatic drive into reverse. The truck lurched backwards to the sound of panicked yelps as the crowd attempted to get out of the way.

A deafening rattle of tire irons and cricket bats slammed down across the vehicle like hail on a tin roof as the angry crowd fought to get inside and stop the vehicle from moving. The man across Lopez's lap screamed as his legs were pulled violently by the bodies outside the truck, and Ethan immediately let him go. Lopez jerked her head back and her hands out the way as the man's body was ripped from the truck and she grabbed the wheel as she slammed one boot down on the throttle.

The tires squealed as the truck accelerated backwards and swung around, enraged Saudis hurling themselves clear as Ethan shoved the transmission into drive and Lopez once again accelerated. A hail of debris crashed down across the shattered windscreen from the Saudis in front of the vehicle as they threw what they held in their hands at the vehicle and then hurled themselves clear.

The truck blasted through the compound gates and swung hard left as Lopez aimed the vehicle away from the crowd. Ethan got himself a brief glimpse through the rear view window of streams of high pressure water blasting into the crowd and sending civilians reeling aside in the bright sunshine as the Saudi troops finally began moving in.

'That bastard Assim set us up,' Lopez snarled as she drove. 'Those guards made sure that we were a target before they took off.'

'We've got to assume Majestic Twelve are already on to us,' Ethan agreed. 'Huck Seavers must be in their pocket in one way or another, maybe over those mining rights.'

'Seavers isn't going to let us anywhere near him now,' Lopez pointed out. 'Our best bet is to get the hell out of Saudi Arabia before somebody torches our asses.'

Ethan looked over his shoulder and saw in the distance against the desert skyline a faint smear of dirty brown smoke against the perfect blue sky.

'They've got Amber.'

'Huck will offer her a deal!' Lopez snapped. 'Just like he did with us, except I hope that she has the brains to take it and run.'

'I think we both know that she won't do that.'

'Then she's as insane as her father and … '

Ethan saw the sedan at the same time as Lopez did, just as it smashed into the front fender of their truck and sent it spinning to one side. Ethan's head smacked into the window beside him with a deep thump and he saw Lopez's hair flying under the impact as the truck's tires screeched and it span across the road.

A second vehicle hit them from behind, impact cushions bursting into Ethan's face from the dashboard to absorb the blows as the engine cut out amid a cloud of dirty smoke that spilled across the windscreen as the truck hit the sidewalk and came to a halt.

Ethan fumbled for the door handle but he could not focus, his head swimming and his fingers numb. A twist of nausea poisoned his innards as he tried to get out of the truck. He reached out again for the handle but it was suddenly pulled from of his sight.

The door swung open and hands grabbed for Ethan. He pushed out and tried to swing a punch at the masked man looming before him, but his arm felt like rubber and he almost fell out of the car. The smell of burning oil stung his nostrils and he heard shouts in Arabic, sharp and staccato like gunfire as he was dragged out into the heat.

He squinted in the brilliant sunlight and just had time to see the dusty canvass sack that was rammed down onto his head as something hard clubbed across his face and everything went black.

***

XV

Office of the Director of National Intelligence,

Tyson's Corner, Washington DC

Lieutenant General Nellis strode down the fifth floor corridor to his office and hoped that the meeting he was due to attend would not end his career. A former Chair of the Military Intelligence Board and a much respected figure at the Pentagon, Nellis was one of the US military's most powerful figures. Yet today Nellis knew that he was heading for a serious grilling.

He walked into his office and closed the door as two men awaiting him stood from their seats. One was a former Navy SEAL by the name of Miller, who as a soldier was a man with whom Nellis could identify. The other was a tall man with a formidable physique, an African–American with slightly graying hair who despite his age looked capable of causing severe physical damage to anybody who stood in his way. The name Nellis had been given for him was Mister Mitchell, and that in itself was enough to send alarm bells ringing in Nellis's mind: a man supposedly a civilian sitting in on a classified meeting in the headquarters of the DIA.

'Gentlemen,' Nellis greeted them without preamble. 'What can I do for you?'

Miller and Mitchell sat down opposite Nellis as he eased himself into his chair. Miller spoke with a gravelly voice.

'We've been sent up here regarding a breach of security by one of your team.'

Nellis raised an eyebrow. 'Whom?'

'Douglas Jarvis,' Miller replied. 'Former United States Marine, works under your watch. Homeland sent us because they have no access to files.'

Nellis remained motionless for a moment. Miller was maintaining a formal bearing but he was clearly trying to project a reasonable persona.

Mitchell, on the other hand, simply watched Nellis with an unblinking gaze utterly devoid of any emotion he could recognize.

'Jarvis is responsible for the oversight of a classified research program for the agency,' Nellis replied. 'It's an autonomous program, so neither Homeland nor the Pentagon would have access to it.'

'Why is that?' Mitchell asked, speaking for the first time. His voice was both soft and yet threatening at the same time, his forged–in–granite confidence apparently divesting him of the need to project an attitude.

'Intelligence security,' Nellis replied. 'The program has assets on the ground and exposure of their activities could render them at risk.'

Miller's controlled expression slipped. Mitchell remained silent. Nellis became aware of the sound of people walking past beyond his office door as the silence stretched out for several seconds until Miller finally spoke.

'We have identified two individuals connected to this program.' He slid a pair of glossy images across the desk to Nellis. 'Do you recognize them?'

Nellis looked down and saw a black and white mug shot of Ethan Warner staring up at him. It was typical of the Pentagon that they would have provided a shot of Warner taken years ago in Cook County Jail, and not one from the much easier to acquire service record from the US Marine Corp's primary training base at Quantico, Virginia. Beside Warner's haggard features was a shot of Nicola Lopez, again taken via a surveillance team and not a more formal shot of her proudly wearing the blues of the Washington Police Department.

He looked up at Mitchell and Miller.

'They work for Jarvis,' he replied.

Mitchell folded his hands in his lap as he spoke.

'You are aware that these two agents were responsible for disrupting a sensitive operation in Argentina a few months ago?'

Nellis nodded. Ethan and Lopez, working with Jarvis, had deployed across the globe in search of something that even Nellis had difficulty in understanding: the remains of a species not of this Earth, a fossilized remnant of something that had died thousands of years ago and may have influenced human history and development. They had uncovered startling evidence of mankind's ancient record of extra–terrestrial involvement in early civilizations, all of which had swiftly been recovered and concealed by Majestic Twelve. What Nellis could not be sure of was whether Mitchell and Miller were working for MJ–12 or were, like him, trying to get to the bottom of it all.

'Jarvis's agents were deployed to South America in that timeframe,' he confirmed. 'However I am not at liberty to discuss the operation due to national security considerations.'

Mitchell smiled without warmth but remained silent.

'Your man Jarvis allowed both Ethan Warner and his partner, Nicola Lopez, access to highly classified material,' Miller pointed out.

'Their exposure to sensitive programs is more than justified by their success in utilizing the information obtained.'

'That would be true,' Mitchell added, 'were Warner and Lopez not civilian contractors.'

Nellis levelled Mitchell with a cold gaze.

'Warner and Lopez are only given cases that the rest of the intelligence community has already rejected as unworkable. Perhaps you should ask yourself why it is that the Pentagon has turned away from at least six major investigations that presented clear and present dangers to both American security and the lives of our citizens? And if I may, I'd like to point out that you are also a civilian, are you not?'

'This isn't about blame,' Miller intervened. 'We're being asked to ensure that the security of our most sensitive operations cannot be blown by two people over whom we have no control. This program represents a very weak link in a long chain of security measures. I can't go back to the Secretary of Defense and tell him, hey, everything's just fine, chill out. If any DIA programs were exposed to the public, all of our careers would be on the line.'

Nellis remained impassive.

'Over half of all DIA employees are civilians. Who sent you, exactly?' Neither Miller or Mitchell replied, which pretty much was an answer in itself. 'So, the spooks at the CIA have taken a fresh interest in what Doug's achieving down here?' He looked at Mitchell. 'Let me guess: Warner and Lopez have done what you guys couldn't so now you're looking to take over the operation.'

'This is about security,' Mitchell replied, 'nothing more.'

'Of course it is,' Nellis replied without losing the smile. 'So much so that you want me to breach my own agency's security protocols because you're *worried* about breaches of security protocol. Not going to happen.'

'We're on the same side,' Miller said, making a stab at keeping the mood cordial. 'We just need to keep everybody's borders tight, is all. If this program were such a big deal then maybe you could run it through the NRO and cut Warner and Lopez loose. That way it's all internal and we're not farming work out to people like that.'

Miller gestured to the images of Lopez and Warner.

'People like what?' Nellis rumbled.

'A convicted felon and a gumshoe,' Miller chuckled in response. 'We've got much better people available for this kind of work who won't set off alarm bells in DC.'

Nellis's fists balled of their own accord on his desk.

'If you'd bothered to look into the history of these two investigators instead of just sucking up the crap that the CIA has obviously fed you, you'd know that Ethan Warner is decorated former United States Marine, as is Doug Jarvis, and that Nicola Lopez is a former DC police detective. Neither of them are amateurs at anything.'

'They're both liabilities,' Mitchell snapped. 'Ethan Warner has a reputation for directly disobeying authority and Lopez is known to be a short fuse at the best of times. Yet they're both wandering around the country with access to all manner of classified material. Jarvis has in the past used assets of our Navy and Air Force to achieve his aims in support of these investigations, which have often led to extreme exposure events such as exploding civilian apartment buildings, violent incidents in allied countries such as Israel and repeated firearms violations in public areas throughout the country. Our business is both covert and classified.' Mitchell gestured at the photographs. 'They're a danger to national security, not an asset to it.'

Nellis leaned across the desk, his eyes glowering into Mitchell's.

'The Pentagon has acquired extraordinary technology as a direct result of Jarvis's investigations and I'll be damned if I'll let the CIA kick the door down now.'

Mitchell leaned forward. 'Where are Warner and Lopez, right now?'

'Busy, somewhere.'

Mitchell seemed about to make a move when a discreet buzzing sound broke the silence. Mitchell reached down and retrieved a cell phone from his pocket, answering it and listening for a few moments. Then he stood from his seat without another word and stalked out of the office. Nellis waited until the door had closed behind him before he looked at Miller. The soldier's expression said it all.

'Are you really in bed with the spooks?' Nellis asked.

'This isn't about the CIA,' Miller said quietly. 'It's far beyond that. That call means that wherever your two intrepid agents have gone, Mitchell now knows about it.'

Nellis looked at the soldier for a long moment, and then he reached out and grabbed a post–it note and a pen as he spoke.

'You know I want to help but all of our agencies have their respective boundaries. I can't just start exposing my own people to potential law suits should any of this become public knowledge. I have a loyalty to my agents just as much as the CIA, the Pentagon or anybody else.'

Nellis wrote a word on the note and turned it to face Miller, who looked down at it as he replied.

MJ–12?

'I'm just doing my job here,' Miller said as he read the note and looked back at Nellis. He nodded slowly. 'You understand, of course?'

'It's nothing personal,' Nellis replied.

'It never is,' Miller agreed. 'We've all got our place and we all have to fulfil our obligations, regardless of the cost. Sometimes, the powers that be are so influential that they can alter the course of history. That's not an enemy that you want to make.'

'Watch your back,' Nellis warned. 'Such people have a long history of self–preservation at the expense of their agents.'

'Don't worry, I've got myself covered,' Miller said with an easy smile as he stood. The smile slipped as he regarded the general for a moment. 'They'll get what they want in the end.'

'I know. Just going to try to hold them off for a while longer, is all.'

'Don't try too hard. There's too much at stake, for all three of us now that we're involved and for your man Jarvis,' Miller warned him. 'It's better for you all if you handle their investigations directly through this office and keep us in the loop.'

'Why's that?' Nellis asked.

'Because I'm only here due to Warner's military history,' Miller replied. 'Truth is, I've got very little control here over what CIA might try to do. I'm consulting, not controlling.'

'Mitchell's in charge?' Nellis asked in surprise.

Miller nodded.

'If Mitchell gets his claws into this alone, Ethan Warner and Nicola Lopez are likely to end up as targets themselves.'

***

XVI

Breathe.

Ethan sucked in a mouthful of dusty air that scratched the back of his throat and made him cough. The choked coughs reverberated through his chest like war drums, fear scraping the lining of his stomach like a convict's nails down the walls of a cell.

He could see nothing through the coarse sack that was bound with rough cord around his neck and filling his nostrils with musty, stale air. His arms were tied behind his back with rope that tore the skin on his wrists. He knelt with his head between his knees, kept breathing and tried to remain calm.

Fear scalded like acid through his veins, and the blackness messed with his sense of balance, further amplifying his asphyxia. He had been incarcerated by Saudi militants who would kill both him and Lopez without hesitation, and their captors had wasted no time in transporting them through Riyadh's dangerous streets to what he presumed was a safe house likely far from the reach of the authorities.

Breathe.

He was buzzing now on nervous energy, poisoned with paranoia, fear and hallucinations. The oppressive heat closed in around him and a brief burst of Arabic punctured the silence.

A door opened with a crash and rough hands grabbed him and hauled him to his feet. Ethan tried to stand but his legs would not respond and he sprawled awkwardly as the unseen hands dragged him across the rough, uneven ground.

'Get up!'

Broken, accented English. Ethan staggered upright and swayed as stars of light sparkled in the darkness before his eyes.

'This way!'

A hand shoved him and he stumbled blindly forwards, colliding with the walls of a corridor. Footfalls around him suggested two men, one in front of him and the other behind.

He was shoved into what sounded, from the echoes and timbre of the sounds from outside, like a larger room and a hand grabbed his shoulder, turned him around and shoved him down. Ethan thumped into a wooden chair. Before he could react he felt himself being tied to the chair.

Something wrenched at the hood over his face and a harsh white light burst into his eyes. He blinked away from it, squinting and struggling to focus on his surroundings.

A bare room, one shuttered window facing out across the city, bright sunlight outside and blue sky. Heat, close and oppressive, the stench of old tobacco heavy in the room.

'Welcome.'

Ethan squinted up and to his right to see a pair of dark eyes observing him. The man was young and fuelled with the arrogance of that youth, perhaps twenty–five years old, his hair thick and black, coarse stubble darkening his jaw.

'Who are you?' Ethan asked.

'What does it matter?'

Ethan managed to hold the man's gaze with a thin veneer of bravado.

'It matters to me, I'm the one tied to a chair.'

The man leaned close to him. 'You're an American. You deserve to be tied to a chair.'

'Where is the woman I was brought here with?'

The features creased into a smile poisoned with brutal delight. 'She is safe, in a manner of speaking.'

'I need to see her.'

The man whirled and ploughed his fist deep into Ethan's stomach. Ethan's eyes almost burst from their sockets as he bolted forward over the blow.

'Who sent you here?' his captor demanded.

Ethan sucked in a pained lungful of air, waves of nausea flushing through his guts.

'We're looking for somebody.'

The militant sighed and shook his head.

'You were inside the Seavers compound, talking with the American oil man.'

Ethan shook his head, slowly gaining control of his breathing.

'We came here looking for a man named Stanley Meyer. We think that Seavers may have abducted him.'

The militant looked across at his companion, whose face was almost completely concealed behind a thick beard.

'That would seem highly unlikely,' Ethan's interrogator leaned close to him, the smell of tobacco thick on his breath. 'Why would an American abduct an American? That's our job.'

Ethan looked at the man and performed a swift mental calculation. *Keep telling the truth. Don't get caught in a lie or they'll cut your throat and feed what's left to the carrion birds.*

'There's more to it than that,' he said. 'Stanley Meyer is who they're looking for too.'

A cruel smile creased the man's features. 'Yes, so I keep hearing.'

He raised a hand and clicked his fingers. Instantly the bearded militant grabbed something from inside one of the nearby crates. The man reached inside and produced a series of images, handing them to his companion.

The militant held the images out one by one to Ethan, shots taken from a parked car of armed police guards beating a Saudi protester, of the water cannons hosing them down in droves, and of Ethan and Lopez fleeing the scene in the stolen truck.

'You're a servant of the Great Satan, are you not?' he hissed. 'And now you're here, seeking to conspire with the oil men in their compounds.'

'Where is Lopez?' Ethan demanded.

'Your friend, the woman?' the militant asked. 'Where she ends up depends very much on what you do next.'

***

Dean Crawford

XVII

'Let Lopez go,' Ethan recalled, staring at the photographs. 'We've already lost track of Amber.'

'The younger woman who was with you,' the militant said. 'How tragic.'

'She's just a child,' Ethan said quickly, aware of the sweat soaking his skin. 'Are you going to just let her die at the hands of people like Huck Seavers?!'

The militant's features tightened as sheet lightning danced behind his dark eyes.

'Die?' he snarled with a wide grin of fury. 'She's been taken to Huck Seaver's personal home in a gated compound in the city, in a limousine, no less. She will be sipping fine wine as we sit out here in the baking desert searching for scraps to feed our children.'

'Her father is on the run,' Ethan snapped back. 'This is about things far bigger than you can possibly imagine!'

'Enlighten me.'

Ethan shook his head as he closed his eyes and spoke almost mechanically as he recounted what had happened and why they had travelled to Saudi Arabia. The militant listened for a long time, watching Ethan with his dark eyes and his arms folded until, finally, Ethan finished and the militant looked at Ethan for a long moment.

The man's jaw creased in a broad smile and he glanced at his companion.

'So, you are the victim of a conspiracy by corporate leaders of, what was it, MJ–12? And they are here to kill you, and your friends, all because this Stanley Meyer invented a device that makes oil useless?'

Ethan nodded, and the militant looked over his shoulder at his bearded companion and smiled broadly.

'I think he's been watching too much Hollywood films, no?'

The bearded militant smiled as Ethan's interrogator turned back to him and produced an elegantly carved blade that he examined as he spoke.

'Americans,' he uttered. 'Your presidents demand from the world honourable leadership, the dignity of your people, justice and liberty for all, and yet they then smile and shake hands with Saudi princes who take our country's money and spend it on luxury yachts and cars and private jets while we sweat in poverty. You rally against terrorism and yet supply Israel with arms with which to subjugate and torture Palestine. You decry injustice, yet prop up a corrupt House of Saud that is stealing our wealth from beneath our deserts and punishes, brutally, anybody who dares demand equality in this land.'

Ethan managed to drag his eyes away from the blade, looking instead at his captor.

'I don't make or agree with United States foreign policy.'

'I believe you,' the militant said. 'But it matters little. You see, my brother was a journalist who tried to expose the rotten core of our beloved House of Saud. When he was arrested, he was tried without jury in a court and sentenced to life imprisonment and one thousand lashes. I'm told he made it to about three hundred before his heart gave out. Where was your country's liberty and justice then? We sent images of his body to your news networks, but they wouldn't show the pictures of his remains on your western television networks because it might *offend*.' The militant suddenly grabbed Ethan's hair, yanked it back until it hurt and pressed the blade against his throat. Ethan felt the cold steel touch his skin, felt his pulse throbbing against the blade. 'Are you offended, right now?'

Ethan peered at the man and his voice sounded thin in his own ears.

'I was asked to search for Meyer by the Defense Intelligence Agency.'

'Why did they ask you?!' the militant shouted, spittle flying into Ethan's face. 'Why would you care?!'

'Why wouldn't I?!' Ethan snapped back. 'Show me a country where the leaders follow the will of their people! It never happens! Half of America would like to see Israel out of Palestine and who knows what else, just the same as you! We're people, not politicians, and killing me or any number of Americans won't change the ways of any member of Congress or the Senate because they don't damned well care! They're all making too much money to give a damn about you, me or anybody else! So go ahead, kill me, blow some more innocent people into oblivion, because the only damned thing that's for sure is that it'll never fix any of our countries problems, *idiot!*'

The militant held the blade still, transfixed by Ethan's outburst, and then he abruptly stood up straight and nodded to his companion. The bearded man left the room. Ethan watched as his captor opened a bottle of water and drank deeply from it, quenching his thirst until the bearded man returned with another captive, likewise hooded and bound.

'Release him,' the militant ordered.

The bearded man yanked off his captive's bonds and pulled the hood from his head. Ethan saw an elderly man blink dust from his eyes and struggle to focus on his surroundings. He looked at Ethan in surprise.

'Who is this?'

The militant looked at Ethan. 'Apparently, he's looking for you.'

Ethan stared at the thin and bespectacled figure, his features drawn and lightly touched with greying stubble.

'Stanley Meyer?'

'Who are you?' Meyer demanded. 'What do they mean you're looking for me?'

'I'm with the Defense Intelligence Agency,' Ethan said, flushed with relief that he was finally talking to another American. 'Amber is with us.'

'Amber?!' Stanley gasped in horror. 'She's here?! Where?!'

'Huck Seavers has her,' Ethan replied, and nodded toward their captors. 'You can thank these guys for that.'

Stanley glared at the militants. 'My daughter, is this true?'

The militant nodded. 'She escaped us.'

Ethan blinked in confusion as the militant moved behind him and began loosening the restraints from his wrists.

'Is what this man has claimed the truth?' the militant demanded of Ethan. 'What was his device called?'

'A fusion cage,' Ethan replied as he stood and looked at Stanley. 'We know what happened in Clearwater.'

Meyer staggered sideways and propped himself against the wall. 'My God, we had to flee, to leave Amber. We tried to find her but there was no time. I never thought that.., she would come so far.'

'She held out,' Ethan promised. 'She's okay. I don't know what Seavers will do, but I don't think that he has murder on his mind.'

'Huck Seavers is a coward, a slave to greenbacks,' Stanley snapped. 'But you're right, he's no murderer. But it's not him I'm worried about.'

'Majestic Twelve?'

'Who?' Stanley asked.

'Long story,' Ethan replied as he glanced at their captors and took a gamble that they might be willing to listen to Ethan now. 'You're abducting the wrong people. Stanley's work could cause the fall of the House of Saud, give you what you're fighting for.'

'That depends on what you think we're fighting for,' the militant growled. 'The only reason you're still alive is because you told exactly the same story as Stanley here. Either you are both equally insane, or you have something that I want.'

'I told you,' Stanley said wearily, 'I don't have a fusion cage, but I can *build* one for you. I just need the parts, and your promise that you'll build more of them and distribute them to the people for free.'

Ethan looked at the insurgent, who was frowning at Stanley. 'So you've said, but why would you do this?'

'Because we're not all oil–guzzling megalomaniacs,' Stanley replied wearily, Ethan guessing he may have been trying to convince his captors of this for some time. 'If you'd only let me build the damned thing, you could have had a dozen of them by now.'

The militant sighed and glanced at his companion as he left the room. 'Americans, you are all insane.'

'We figured you'd be abducted by insurgents eventually,' Ethan said to Meyer. 'Coming here was a bad idea.'

'It was all I could think of,' he replied. 'To come somewhere where even America would find it hard to track me down.'

Ethan turned as Lopez was led into the room by a Saudi woman dressed from head to foot in a *burqua*, only her dark eyes visible. Lopez's hair was in disarray where a hood had recently been removed. He saw the concern writ large across her face as she hurried to his side.

'Are you okay?' she asked.

Ethan nodded, felt warmth spread through his chest and down into his belly as he smiled at her.

'I'm fine,' he said, and then looked at Stanley Meyer. 'Who are these people?'

'This,' Stanley said, 'is the leadership of *Saudi Dawn*, a protest opposition group dedicated to exposing the corruption of the Saudi regime. They grabbed me two days ago.'

'If the Saudi authorities knew what you've achieved and they got hold of you, that would probably be the last anybody would see of Stanley Meyer.'

'I'm more than aware of that,' Meyer replied, somewhat affronted. 'But then I'm sure that Huck Seavers and all of the other bloodsucking corporate entities who would like to see my device eradicated from existence would also be unlikely to think that I would come here. It was a good idea, while it lasted.'

Ethan glanced at the Saudi Dawn militants. 'While you've been hiding out with these guys, Seavers has somehow managed to track you down. He abandoned us with the intention of us dying at the hands of enraged Saudi protesters, and it would have looked like nothing more than another tragic militant attack on Western journalists.'

'You were nearly torn to pieces,' the nearest militant said. 'I might have been one of them, were it not for Stanley's devotion to his cause. He kept saying that Seavers Incorporated was behind his woes, and so we checked them out. You showed up a day later.'

'Along with Amber,' Stanley said. 'Is it possible to get her back?'

'Our escort prioritized her safety at our request,' Ethan admitted. 'As soon as they got her clear, they took off. We inadvertently assured her capture.'

'You were acting in her best interests,' Stanley replied without the slightest hubris. 'Which is more than can be said for Huck Seavers.'

'We need to get her out of there,' Lopez said. 'There's no telling what Seavers will do to her.'

Stanley Meyer perched on the edge of a tired looking table and shook his head.

'He won't hurt her,' he replied without concern. 'At least I don't think that he will. Huck Seavers is the archetypical corporate monster, the embodiment of the American dream. He inherited his fortune and empire from his father and, to his credit, he has successfully grown the business over the years and gained huge respect for his abilities as a businessman.'

Ethan's blinked in surprise. 'You sound like you actually *like* the man.'

'Like? No. Have respect for, have sympathy for? Yes.'

'Sympathy?' Lopez echoed. 'He just abducted your daughter, a teenage girl who has travelled half way round the world to find you.'

Meyer smiled fondly as he stared into the distance, clearly thinking of Amber.

'Amber always was an adventurous soul, an outdoors woman and livewire. I'm constantly surprised that she wants to become a lawyer and not a soldier or a pilot or something. But you have to see this situation for what it really is. Huck Seavers is not a murderer, he's a businessman and he's way out of his depth. He'll offer Amber money, and keep offering it to her until she takes it, which I dearly hope that she does.'

'You want her to sell out?' Ethan asked.

'Of course I do,' Stanley said. 'This is my battle to fight, my decision. I'm an old man, Mister Warner. All the money in the world won't keep me alive for long enough to really enjoy it, but Amber could live a life of luxury for decades and still enjoy my device should I ever get it out into the public realm.'

'Damn it!' Lopez cursed. 'I knew we should have taken that offer!'

Meyer looked at her curiously.

'We both turned down twenty million bucks in favour of finding you and resolving all of this,' Ethan explained. 'It wasn't easy.'

The two militants stared at Ethan with sudden amazement and perhaps even a hint of respect.

'You turned down twenty million American dollars?' the militant asked.

'This asshole did,' Lopez uttered contemptuously as she jabbed a thumb in Ethan's direction.

Stanley watched Ethan silently for a moment with an admiring smile touching his old features, but then the gruff exterior fell back into place.

'Idiots, both of you,' he uttered. 'There's no good reason for you to have not sold out. You could have taken the money and run, that would have been the smart thing to do. No sense in getting heroic about it.'

'I think I'm going to faint,' Lopez mumbled.

'It's done now,' Ethan replied. 'Tell me what you're hoping to achieve out here.'

Meyer gestured to the militants watching them in silence.

'What it turns out, clearly, that I couldn't in Clearwater. These people live in the greatest oil producing nation on earth,' Stanley explained, 'and their Royal Family takes the lion's share of that wealth while they live in poverty. They are sick of the inequality, of the arbitrary use of Sharia Law to silence dissidents, of America's support for a Kingdom whose leaders are essentially corrupt and greedy. I was wrong to trust the people of Clearwater, because they did not truly appreciate what I was doing, and they sold out at the first opportunity.'

'Twenty million dollars,' Ethan replied, 'so we heard.'

'Hard to blame them,' Stanley admitted, 'but they could have had so much more. But these people here in Saudi Arabia and others like them, the poor and the weak and the abused, are those who would most *appreciate* what it is that I've managed to create. It will be these people and others like them who will spread the word of my device with glee, because they understand what it's like to have nothing. They know that passing on my device for free, so that nobody can profit financially from it, will benefit others like them across the world.'

Meyer smiled as he looked at the heavily armed militants.

'The meek truly shall inherit the Earth,' he said finally, 'for they outnumber the strong by billions. They will ensure that my Fusion Cage is distributed among the masses, for it is in their own interests to do so, and the act of kindness will also cause the collapse of the House of Saud.'

Stanley looked at Ethan, the smile still broad on his features.

'This is where the end begins, Mister Warner. The end of greed, the end of corruption, the end of energy wars and pollution: right under the noses of those who most want that all to continue. All I ask of you now is to help me protect my daughter. I will shoulder any further burden of risk alone.'

Ethan glanced at the militants, who had watched the exchange in silence.

'You guys really want to get back at your royal leaders?' he asked. 'If we can liberate Amber Ryan, then Stanley here will be able to give you the device that will render them powerless. Do you have any idea where Amber is, right now I mean?'

The lead militant nodded slowly.

'I know where she is,' he replied, 'and I know what will happen to her next.'

***

XVIII

Urayarah, 100km west of Damman,

Saudi Arabia

The desert was cold in the pale light of pre–dawn, the horizon a sharply defined line of blackness against a flawless deep blue. Ethan rode in silence alongside Lopez, following a line of militants making their way across the trackless wastes like shadowy demons traversing the barren plains of hell. Stars sparkled above them in the vault of the heavens, and the silence was broken only by the occasional snort from one of the splendid Arab horses as they climbed a dune at a gentle gradient.

As Ethan's mount crested the dune's ridge he could see in the distance a feint line crossing the endless expanses of the desert, a metalled road linking Riyadh and Damman, both cities beyond sight but marked by the glow of their lights against the horizon.

The plan was simple. Huck Seavers always travelled as part of an armed convoy, the cautious American always mindful of the risk of abduction for ransom. The militants would set up a staggered ambush, attacking the convoy from both in front and behind and pinning the vehicles in a cross fire. Amber would then be extracted and spirited away into the lonely deserts, far from the reach of Huck Seavers. Or so the militants figured, with the brash arrogance of those fighting with a god supposedly on their side.

Ethan had extensive experience of the ability of the US military to probe deep into even the most inhospitable of terrain using UAVs, Unmanned Aerial Vehicles, capable of deploying Hellfire missiles and staying aloft for days at a time. With Saudi Arabia such a close ally and themselves deploying US military aircraft and drones, the idea that anybody could simply vanish into the wilderness was fast becoming a thing of the past.

'You know we're going to have to high–tail it out of here, even if we do get hold of Amber?' he whispered to Lopez as they rode.

'I know,' she replied. 'We can't trust the natives as far as we can throw them. The question is, where? Can Jarvis deploy anything to get us out of the immediate area? Can we even get hold of him out here?'

Ethan rested one hand on his satchel, which contained a satellite phone Jarvis had supplied them with before they had left Chicago.

'Probably, but I don't doubt that the Saudis will detect the call. There won't be much time before they vector military assets onto our position, and we won't be able to get far before jets arrive.'

Lopez nodded and glanced at the militants. 'They've survived out here for long enough with the Saudi authorities breathing down their necks. Maybe they've got something up their sleeves that we don't know about?'

Ethan shrugged as they rode on toward the metalled road. It was true that despite having tremendous firepower behind them the combined might of the US Army, Navy, Air Force and Marines had effectively failed in Iraq and Afghanistan in quelling an enemy familiar with its terrain and fuelled by an unholy determination to repel the "infidels". Numbers and local knowledge had effectively trumped superior technology and firepower even on the modern battlefield, the ephemeral nature of militant groups hard to combat, tough to bring out into open battle. Where one force was struck down, three more emerged in their place. The brutality of the suicide bomber was impossible to predict, the cruelty of the Islamic militants so terrifying that few military folk could predict just what their limits were, knowing only that they would not stop, ever.

Saudi Dawn had planned an armed attack on a convoy belonging to an American company, and Ethan was acutely aware that he was effectively assisting them. It was only his knowledge of the corruption at the heart of Seavers Incorporated that compelled him to continue with the mission.

'I don't care,' he said finally to Lopez. 'We need to break off from these guys as soon as we can and get the hell out of Saudi Arabia.'

'Done and done,' Lopez agreed.

Ethan spurred his horse up alongside Stanley Meyer's. 'So, are you going to tell me that this is all worth it, that we're doing the right thing, that the world will be powered for free if this device of yours goes public?'

'I'm hoping so,' Stanley replied. 'Things aren't going exactly to plan though.'

'From what I've heard about cold fusion, they never have.'

'It's not cold fusion,' Stanley uttered angrily. 'It's Low Energy Nuclear Reactions.'

'If you say so.'

'Look,' Stanley persisted, 'cold fusion has become a byword for pseudoscience, but they clearly witnessed something or the scientists behind it would not have dared to go public. Those still researching the subject think that rather than nuclear fusion, what Fleischmann and Pons really observed was the conversion of one element into another, a transmutation that releases energy in the process: a low energy nuclear reaction.'

'You mean like alchemy, lead into gold? You can't be serious?'

'I'm serious,' Stanley said, 'and so is NASA. Both their Langley Research Center and the Jet Propulsion Laboratory are studying the conversion of stable elements like nickel, carbon, and hydrogen to produce stable products like copper or nitrogen, along with heat and electricity. They have already demonstrated the ability to produce excess amounts of energy, cleanly, without hazardous ionizing radiation and waste.'

'And that's the same process your fusion cages uses?' Ethan asked.

'Precisely the same, except I've added a fuel cell that massively increases the yeild,' Stanley explained. 'I've calculated that just one percent of the nickel mined each year around the world could produce the entire world's energy requirements at a quarter of the cost of coal, if my fusion cage was adopted globally.'

Ethan blinked, surprised at how plausible the whole thing sounded.

'Doesn't that mean you're in a race against NASA?' he asked.

'In a sense. They'll wish to commercialize the technology, whereas I wish to give it away. The science isn't even that radical. NASA researchers rely heavily on the Widom–Larsen Theory published in 2006, which speculates that low energy nuclear reactions already occur on Earth in lightning, and may be responsible for occasional fires in lithium–ion batteries, which highlights that even low–energy nuclear reactors can produce dangerous amounts of energy. I've heard of several explosions in laboratories researching this LENR technology, which is another danger.'

'What's that?'

'Like any energy source, they could easily be weaponized in the wrong hands,' Stanley replied.

*

The interior of the SUV was plush, black leather and dark wood panelling with chrome trim. Through the tinted windows the sunrise was visible breaking across the distant desert wastes, the whisper of the SUV's tires on the asphalt road distant as though Amber were in a dream, all sound muted and vague.

'As soon as we get you to Damman, you'll be safe. To be brutally honest few women are safe in this country, especially Americans.'

Amber turned from the panoramic view to look at Huck Seavers, who was sitting in the opposite seat with his hat in his lap and watching her with interest.

'You call this safe? Abduction?'

'Liberation,' Huck corrected her without taking offence. 'You were under attack from protesters, and I can't imagine what would have happened had they gotten hold of you.'

'They got hold of Ethan and Nicola,' Amber shot back. 'I don't suppose you're concerned about what happened to them?'

'They're adults and they're journalists, always poking their noses where they don't belong,' Huck snapped dismissively. 'I had my people track them down to a lousy two–bit bail bondsmen service operating out of Chicago, Illinois. They haven't been within a hundred miles of the Defense Intelligence Agency and they're fools for having brought you here. I won't be happy until you're back in America.'

'Like you care,' Amber muttered and turned back to looking at the sunrise.

'You've got me all wrong,' Huck insisted.

'Sure I have.'

'You think I'm the bad guy in all this, but for no reason.'

Amber rubbed her temples wearily with one hand and shook her head. 'No reason? The disappearance of three hundred people with whom I shared the town of Clearwater? The pursuit of my father, Stanley Meyer. Threats, violence, corruption and payoffs in order to keep people silent. Legal challenges quashed by lawyers too expensive for anybody else to fight, just so you can tear the tops off of mountains for profit.' Amber looked at Huck for a long moment and then looked away again.

Huck Seavers sat quietly for a moment before he replied.

'I have a family, you know?' he said finally. 'My wife and I have been married fifteen years and we have a son and a daughter, twelve and eight years old respectively. My parents died a decade ago and I have no siblings, so my family is everything to me. You say that I used expensive lawyers to quash legal challenges and you're right, I have. That's because often the challenges are from environmentalists who have absolutely no understanding of how important it is for people, for our country, to have power. Have I made villages disappear or murdered countless people? No, I challenge them in the courts, and I win. I win because our country can't face an ever–growing energy demand with nobody to fulfil it. I win because my business is a legitimate one and because I want to provide for my family in the future. This is a business, the business of supplying energy for the things you want in your own home; your lights, your television, your hot water and your heating. Without companies like Seavers Incorporated, you'll have none of that.'

Amber shot him look of pure disgust.

'At what cost? The poisoning of the atmosphere and the water table and of countless species, the destruction of habitat that can never be replaced, the warming of the oceans and the atmosphere that will change the face of our planet forever, all just to see your kids go to a more expensive school or own a more powerful car? You can't use the excuse anymore that there is no other option, that we can't power our world by other means. Even before my father devised his fusion cage he already understood, as I do, that we could power our entire world off the back of either solar or tidal power if the world's governments simply got their act together and committed to it. But they won't of course, because capitalism demands profit: if something can be done for profit but is too expensive to initiate, then it is ignored. You're not the solution Huck, you're the disease. My father is the cure, and because his solution didn't involve profit you're trying to shut him down. Don't you dare sit there and try to justify the things that you've done with a plea for sympathy and understanding, when more sympathy and understanding on your part might have turned this into the best thing that ever happened to our planet, the planet that your son and daughter will inherit.'

Huck remained silent for a moment.

'You're living in a dream world,' he uttered finally. 'You're right that there's enough energy falling on the planet every day from the sun to power our world for a year, but without anywhere to store that power it's useless to us. Likewise tidal power, which no country can afford to implement on the scales required to power *everything*. You people, you always seek a singular answer to complex questions when no such answers exist. The environmentalists cry that nuclear power is dirty and dangerous, when in fact it is clean and safe. Any kind of coal burning is considered heresy, even though clean coal is now available to us. Oil is the sworn enemy of any environmentalist seeking to ban motor vehicles, and yet only a tiny fraction of the oil that we buy goes into our vehicles –

the vast majority is used in manufacturing and lubricants. Aeroplanes are hated by the green movement, and yet now one of the most efficient forms of travel available to humanity. Left to you and your kind we would all be living in mud huts, our children suffering from hideous diseases long since cured by science, unable to read or write, but hey, at least we'd be able to hug a tree or two.'

'It's you who's living in the past,' Amber hissed as she shook with fury. 'What use are fossil fuels when they're going to run out? They're going to be gone, Huck, sooner than you probably think. We're using more and more every day and yet there is only a finite supply. It's like those idiots hunting tigers in Russia and India to grind up their bones for use in mythical medicines, the Japanese catching sharks just for their fins and whales just for their blubber. Once they're gone, they're all gone! They're so busy chasing profit that they don't realise that before they know it, the source of that profit will be gone entirely. And then where will they go? Your company makes its fortune from coal, but that coal will be totally gone eventually, Huck. What are you going to do then? Any smart businessman worth their salt would already be looking for somebody like my father to give them an advantage in the future to start the revolution now, but no. Far better for you to simply take the cash and run, and let your poor son have to sort it all out in twenty or thirty or fifty years time when Seavers Incorporated collapses into ruin at his feet.' Amber shot him a jubilant smile of distaste. 'Well played, Huck, well played.'

'Don't you think I've already thought of that?'

'Doesn't look like it to me.'

'It wouldn't, would it? Because to you, people like me are the enemy, our black hearts filled with oil and coal, determined to destroy the world. But we did not create this problem, it was created for us hundred years ago and now we labour beneath its consequences. I don't want to blow the tops off mountains to make a living. I didn't want to make the inhabitants of Clearwater disappear. This isn't about environmentalism, Amber, it's about control. It's about the fear of governments losing control over their people because the government becomes irrelevant, no longer needed for people to survive happily. The people I'm answering to don't want that to happen, ever.'

Amber stared at Huck for a long moment, never having considered for herself the possibility that Huck Seavers was merely one more pawn in a long chain that led to heights of government she had never really thought about before.

'Who are they?'

Huck shook his head. 'I can't tell you that because in truth I don't actually know, but they are incredibly powerful and believe me they have a firm grip on what's happening. If I'd discovered that your father had created his fusion cage before they did, I'd have offered to buy him out. I wouldn't have given the device away for free, I admit, because there's so much potential in it. But by Christ I would have bought it and I would have created a whole new industry, made billionaires of both myself and your father and changed the world at the same time. Don't you think I would rather have done that than sent people up a mountain to slice the top off it? Don't think I'd rather have done that than fight long and complex legal battles, regardless of how powerful my lawyers might be? Don't you think I'd rather be selling something that could fit into anybody's boiler cupboard, worldwide, than pissing about digging in the cold in Virginia?'

Amber felt her blood run cold and she sat in absolute silence as she stared at Huck for what felt like a very long time.

'You'd have gone with my father's device?' she uttered in disbelief.

'Of course I would!' Huck almost shouted in exasperation. 'But they had me over a barrel! If I hadn't complied they'd have got somebody else to do it and Huck Seavers would have been destitute by the end of the week! You think I have powerful lawyers? These people appear to be able to control entire governments – they would have crushed me like a worm and left me with nothing. Your war, it shouldn't be with me. It should be against this shadow government that seems to operate behind the scenes! Your father is running from the wrong people and straight into the arms of his enemies.'

Amber suddenly realised the depths to which some people had gone in order to keep her father's device safely out of the public eye. Huck Seavers, the perfect foil to the environmental movement, in fact a human shield for those with the power to save humanity or destroy it.

'We have to find my father as fast as we can,' Amber said, 'and I think that I can call my mom.'

'You can reach her?' Huck asked.

'I have my cell phone,' Amber said. 'I've carried it ever since I left Clearwater.'

'Finally,' Huck said with a heave of relief. 'The sooner we can get your family to safety, the sooner we can figure something out. I want in on this, Amber. Yes, I want to profit from it, but if this gets out it effectively neutralises the very people who are causing all of this – they won't hold power over me any longer and they won't be able to stop what's happening.'

Amber felt excitement rippling through her veins as she sat upright in her seat.

'Do you have any idea where my dad is?'

'I think so,' Huck replied. 'Let's try to call your mom first, and find out where she is so that we can warn her of … '

A sudden deafening blast shook the vehicle and a clatter of gunfire caused Amber to scream as she threw herself down on the back seat. Bullets crashed through the SUV's windscreen and it swerved violently off the asphalt road and plunged into the desert dunes.

***

XIX

Ethan saw the first grenade lobbed from the side of the asphalt road arc through the air, a black speck against the brilliant sunrise as the small convoy of vehicles approached. The militants had set up their ambush well, positioning themselves in a staggered line with the sun almost at their backs, the glare helping to conceal them from the view of the drivers.

Two more grenades bounced across the sun–scorched asphalt and Ethan threw his hands over his ears and ducked his head down behind a low dune just before the weapons detonated with a series of deafening blasts. He counted all three before he dared look up to see the four vehicles in the convoy swerving across the road, tires screeching as they slid to a halt and a clatter of machine–gun fire rattled out across the desert as the militants opened fire on the vehicles.

'Hold your fire!'

Ethan's cry was muted by the staccato gunshots as the militants swarmed up the sandy banks by the side of the road and dashed toward the vehicles, yelling threats in Arabic and broken English.

'Move, now!' Ethan yelled at Lopez.

They dashed together onto the road and headed directly for the SUV in the centre of the convoy even as Ethan saw flashes of gunfire coming from the cabs of the vehicles in front as Huck Seavers' escort began returning fire against the militants. Ethan reacted instinctively, dropping down onto the asphalt as he drew his pistol and aimed at the nearest escort guard, a man with a scar on his cheek who was now shielding himself behind an open door and firing through the shattered window at the militants.

Ethan could see from his position the SUV that almost certainly contained Huck Seavers and Amber, the vehicle having left the road and slammed into a sand dune. Clouds of wispy blue smoke slithered from beneath the hood where the radiator must have ruptured, while oil spilling from a damaged filter onto the hot engine smouldered with brown coils of smoke.

Ethan took a breath and held it for a brief second before pulling the trigger of the pistol. The shot crackled out and he saw the guard with a scar on his cheek hurled backwards as the round hit him in the shoulder. The guard slumped against the side of the vehicle with his legs out in front of him.

'Go now, I'll cover you!' Ethan yelled at Lopez.

Lopez responded instantly and sprinted for the SUV, a pistol in her hand as she reached out and yanked the vehicle's door open. Ethan advanced forwards in a low run, crouched in order to avoid any of the wildfire coming from the militants to his left, and he reached the SUV just as Lopez was hauling Amber's disorientated form out of the vehicle.

Amber pushed angrily away from Lopez, clearly unsteady on her feet from the impact and with a trickle of blood spilling from just above her left eye where she must have struck the back of a seat or perhaps the interior door.

'Go, now!' Ethan snapped.

Lopez dragged Amber with her across the asphalt as behind them Ethan heard horses galloping across the dunes toward the road, riders sweeping in to pick up survivors and flee with them into the desert wastes. Their Arabian horses looked born to traverse the deserts, with arched necks on a clean throatlatch and high tails.

Ethan leaned into the SUV with his pistol held before him, and at once saw Huck Seavers slumped in his seat. The businessman was unconscious, and Ethan reached out to his neck in search of a pulse. He found it immediately. Satisfied that the man was not dead, Ethan backed away and immediately ducked as a fist swung towards his face with lightning speed.

The blow cracked across the top of Ethan's skull, Ethan's defensive manoeuvre barely avoiding the blow as he felt somebody grab his wrist and twist hard, driving all of their weight behind it as they attempted to force the pistol out of his grip.

Ethan twisted in pain with the force of the grip, but he managed to keep his mind focused as he deliberately released his grip on his pistol and swung his left hand in to catch it. A knee drove up into his rib cage and Ethan gasped as pain ripped across his side and his right leg quivered and almost failed him. The pistol brushed past his fingers to clatter onto the asphalt, and his attacker's boot landed on top of it to prevent Ethan from grabbing it again.

Ethan felt his arm twisted over his back with a violent tug that almost tore it out of its socket and he flipped awkwardly over. Ethan slammed onto his back on the hard asphalt and looked up against the bright sky to see Seavers' senior bodyguard, Assim Khan, looking down at him over the barrel of a compact *Sig* pistol.

Assim aimed for Ethan's forehead, anger twisting his features with fury, blood trickling from his nose, and then he squeezed the trigger. The gunshot shattered the air around Ethan's head and he threw his hands uselessly to protect his skull even as Khan's body shuddered and his legs gave way beneath him as the bullet passed through his chest and out with a faint spray of scarlet blood that stained his crisp white shirt.

Ethan leaped up and twisted the pistol from Assim's grip, even as the guard slumped onto his back, his chest heaving as the dark scarlet stain spread across his shirt. Ethan looked up to see Lopez on the far side of the road, her pistol still aimed at Assim. Ethan looked down, shocked at how close he'd come to death, and saw Assim Khan staring up at him with a pained expression.

'You don't know what you're doing,' the guard gasped.

Ethan looked up and saw the militants withdrawing, firing still at the damaged vehicles to keep any of the remaining guards pinned down. Ethan dashed away across the road, jumping down into the safety of the dunes as the militants mounted their horses and one of them held the reins of an animal for Ethan.

'Come, now, before it's too late!'

Ethan vaulted into the saddle and checked over his shoulder to see Lopez already astride a horse, with Amber sitting in front of her and struggling to get out of the saddle.

'Amber!'

Stanley Meyer called out to his daughter, and she looked up in shock and stopped fighting against Lopez as together the horses turned again and galloped away across the desert. Ethan heard the staccato blasts of the AK–47s behind them fall silent as the militants fled across the open desert, and behind him he heard a few feeble cracks as the guards attempted to return fire on their attackers. But the shots were wild and distant, and pistols simply too inaccurate at such long–range, and within a few moments they were galloping alone through the desert sunrise.

'Dad?!' Amber gasped, shouting above the wind.

'They're with me!' Stanley called back.

They rode for almost twenty minutes, following ancient tracks that wound through the desert *wadis*, deep canyons carved by ancient, long–extinct rivers that sliced through the wilderness. Ethan could see that the militants were seeking an escape from the open dunes as they rode through ancient riverbeds long since desiccated by the Arabian sun, the high walls of the *wadis* shielding them from view of the drones and jets that would soon converge upon the shattered convoy far behind them.

The rising heat and the effort of galloping across open sand dunes had exhausted their mounts, but the militants had long learned to plan well ahead in the hostile environment and as they slowed the animals to a trot so Ethan saw ahead a small encampment concealed deep below the ragged walls of the *wadi*. There he saw wide buckets of water, the contents concealed by elaborate blankets laid across them by women completely concealed by their black *burqa*, only their dark eyes observing the militants as they dismounted from the horses and allowed the animals to drink. The *Rabicano* horses' lean flanks were sheened with sweat that glistened in the morning light.

Ethan climbed down from the saddle and guided his horse out of sight of the sky above and towards the water pales. The animal drank gratefully as he turned to see Stanley Meyer stagger across to his daughter and embrace her, Amber throwing her arms around her father's neck. To Ethan she looked far more attractive as she smiled broadly, compared to the sullen expression that she normally wore.

He turned and pulled from his satchel the satellite phone that Jarvis had given him, and within moments he was dialling.

'*Jarvis?*'

'We need an out,' Ethan replied hurriedly, not wanting to remain on the line for any longer than was absolutely necessary. 'We're near Riyadh, hostiles in pursuit, and need to leave the country fast.'

There was a moment's silence on the line before Jarvis replied.

'*Damman, and Al Qatif seaport. We have people there, they'll make contact. Your recognition call sign is Vanquish. Memorize this number and call it when you reach the city.*'

Jarvis recited a phone number and then the line went dead, and Ethan slipped the phone back into his bag as he heard one of the militants talking to Stanley Meyer.

'We must hurry. The Saudi military are not fools and they will soon guess where we have gone.'

Stanley released Amber and nodded as his daughter looked up at him.

'Why did you come here?' Amber asked.

'I was about to ask you the same question,' Stanley said in reply. 'There is much that I need to tell you.'

'I already know about the device, the fusion cage,' Amber said. 'We all do. But there is much that you need to know also.'

'We can share stories later,' Ethan said as he strode up to them. 'Right now, we need to get away from here.'

'No, we don't,' Amber insisted. 'We've got it all wrong. Huck Seavers wants in on this.'

'I'll bet he does,' Stanley uttered in disgust. 'Seavers would kill us all sooner than see the fusion cage come to light.'

'No,' Amber said desperately. 'He wants in. He's not the one behind this, his hands are tied. He said there's somebody else behind it, kept going on about some kind of shadow government.'

'I don't care what he said,' Stanley insisted. 'The man paid millions to have everybody go silent and abandon what I'd achieved. Clearwater sold out, Amber, the whole town. They didn't give a damn about what I'd done as soon as Seavers waved a few million bucks in their faces. He stole the device from me, Amber.'

'He says he doesn't have it,' Amber replied. 'He's just the company through which those people were paid off, but most of the money came from elsewhere. If we can prove that, then we can show that Seavers is not behind this and that somebody else is paying people off to remain silent.'

'Seavers is a liar,' Stanley almost shouted. 'He would say anything in order to turn you to his side. I will never sell–out to somebody like him.'

'Seavers might be lying about his motivation,' Ethan said, 'but this stuff about the shadow government? Did he ever mention something called Majestic Twelve?'

Amber shook her head. 'He never mentioned names of any kind, and he said he didn't know any of the members of the shadow government he insists is behind all of this. He said they could crush him like a worm if he didn't do as they said.'

'It's too late now,' Lopez pointed out. 'We just abducted you from that convoy, and these trigger–happy goons probably killed a few of Seavers' guards. That's murder in any country, and Sharia Law's not going to look favourably upon us. We need to leave before we find ourselves rotting in a Saudi jail for the next five hundred years.'

Ethan was about to reply when he heard a faint humming sound that drifted down the *wadi* from somewhere above them. He froze in motion and raised a hand to forestall any more conversation as he focused all of his senses on the sound, closed his eyes and tried to identify from where it was coming. The militants around him beat him to it.

'Predator drone, probably within a mile of us,' one of them identified the noise. 'It must have taken off from Damman and hasn't had time to get to enough height to be inaudible to us.'

Ethan opened his eyes and pointed at Stanley.

'We need to split up,' he said. 'The only way we can ensure the maximum number of us escape is to provide too many targets for them to follow once.'

'Agreed,' the lead militant said. 'But we can also fight back.'

Without prompting, two of the women guarding the water reached beneath their *burqas* and produced a pair of rocket–propelled grenade launchers, the long barrelled weapons easily concealed beneath their flowing robes.

The militants took the weapons and began jogging away down the *wadi* in an attempt to gain a visual on the circling drone before it climbed out of sight.

'What about us?' Stanley asked.

'We have further transport for you,' the militant leader said as he beckoned for them to follow him down the *wadi*.

Ethan followed them at a jog as they made their way through the winding confines of the canyon, the heat rising and the air scented with the musk of ancient desert sand. They reached a tight curve in the *wadi*, and there parked beneath the soaring cliffs were several motorbikes and two non–descript looking vehicles, sedans with peeling paint and ancient, almost flat tires devoid of grip.

'There will be more traffic on the roads by now,' the militant said. 'The police will set up roadblocks into and out of the city. My men and I will ride further out into the desert and meet you on the outskirts of Damman, where we will once again change vehicles in order to help conceal you as you enter the city. Make sure you leave the road before you reach the city, we will be waiting for you at An Nandah.'

The militant slid a grenade launcher from his shoulder and pressed it into Ethan's hands.

'May Allah walk with you. *Inshallah.*'

Ethan walked quickly across to the motorbikes, all three of which were fairly powerful and designed for off–road use. They were older machines, but fully functional and kept clean and likely well–maintained. He climbed aboard one, switched on the fuel valve and then brought his boot down on the kick starter. The engine roared into life immediately and he nodded with satisfaction as he looked at Amber.

'Time to leave. Get on.'

As if on cue, Ethan heard a clatter of gunfire and a sudden thumping sound that reverberated down the *wadi* as a helicopter thundered overhead.

'Saudi Arabia has arrived!' the militant yelled.

'Let's get out of here!' Stanley shouted as he looked at the lead militant. 'You have the plans now! Can you build it?'

'We can try,' the militant replied. 'Now go, all of you! Get to Damman as fast as you can!'

***

XX

Ethan twisted the motorbike's throttle and it swung around on the dusty floor of the *wadi* and accelerated downhill toward where once, long ago, a river had flowed out of the canyon onto a fertile flood plain. He saw Lopez following him with Stanley Meyer on her pillion seat as Amber yelled at Ethan above the wind, her arms wrapped around his waist.

'We're running the wrong way! Huck Seavers wants to help!'

'He can't be trusted!' Ethan shouted back. 'Hang on!'

They were gathering speed and the breeze was a welcome relief from the overwhelming heat. The deep *wadi* wound left and right ahead of them, but now the lofty walls of the chasm were coming down and he could see the *wadi* exit ahead, a brilliant flare of sunlight searing the horizon and blazing into his eyes.

Then, above the crunching of their tires on the dusty track, Ethan heard a new sound growing in intensity, and quickly he was able to distinguish the rhythmic *thump–thump–thump* of rotor blades beating the air as the helicopter returned.

He saw at the end of the *wadi* the two militants who had rushed away earlier, both armed with rocket–propelled grenade launchers. Before them, sweeping across the glowing sky, was the formidable shape of an AH–64 *Apache* gunship.

'Damn,' he uttered.

The Apache was a lethal weapons platform, the most feared of all attack helicopter gunships and sold to the Saudis by America. Ethan glanced over his shoulder and saw Lopez following close behind, and behind her the militants on horseback, galloping in pursuit and leaving swirling clouds of glowing dust in their wake.

Ethan twisted the throttle wide open and the little motorbike surged toward the *wadi* exit as the two gunmen took aim at the circling Apache. Even before they could open fire, the attack helicopter surged upward and sideways into the air, its rotors kicking up billowing clouds of desert sand as a series of brilliantly burning orbs sprayed in a fearsome pyrotechnic light show to fall toward the desert.

'Decoy flares!' Ethan yelled. 'They've seen the grenade launchers!'

Ethan craned his neck back as the Apache swung out of sight over the *wadi*, and then plunged back into view behind them.

'Hang on!' Ethan yelled as he twisted the bike's throttle wide open.

Ethan looked back again and saw the helicopter sweeping in, a black silhouette against the brilliant sky, and then suddenly something let out a cloud of smoke and screeched down toward the floor of the *wadi*.

'Incoming!'

Ethan hunched his shoulders and squinted as the motorbike shot from out of the *wadi's* confines and into the open desert as a Hellfire missile slammed into the *wadi's* depths and exploded with a deafening blast. The shockwave thumped into Amber's back and she slammed into Ethan as he fought to keep the bike upright, clouds of flame and debris blasting by them.

A wash of heat enveloped Ethan and he looked over his shoulder to see the *wadi* enveloped in an expanding fireball and a veil of thick black smoke. Lopez's motorcycle hung on grimly behind him, and he could see horses galloping out of the maelstrom and splitting up into different directions, the bodies of several militants and their mounts strewn across the desert.

'They're not taking any prisoners!' Amber yelled. 'We should have stayed with Huck Seavers!'

'Seavers probably called the Saudis in!' Ethan snapped back. 'Forget about him!'

Ethan's shirt was drenched with sweat, his hair and eyes thick with windblown sand, the motorcycle slipping and sliding as Ethan sought out the line of least resistance toward the main road.

A deafening crackle burst the air around Ethan as the Apache opened fire with its cannons on the fleeing horses and vehicles, a loud buzzing sound as the cannons whirled and bullets ripped across the dunes. He saw one animal go down in a tangle of limbs as one of the militants fired an RPG up at the helicopter. Ethan saw the grenade miss but burst into flame just alongside the Apache, the pilot yanking the craft clear of the lethal blast as he turned back toward the militants still concealed within the wadi's mouth.

'This is our chance to get clear!' he shouted to Lopez.

Ethan swerved toward the open desert, Amber hanging on grimly behind him as they fled. The motorbike weaved on the dunes and Ethan closed the throttle to give the bike a chance to steady itself as he looked ahead and saw a line of low hills. He yelled over his shoulder to Lopez.

'Head for those hills and stay sharp!'

Ethan looked over his shoulder toward the *wadi* rapidly receding behind them. The Apache was firing its cannons into the *wadi's* depths, while Ethan could see the last of the horses galloping out into the wastes in all directions, mere specks now trailing plumes of golden sand into the morning air.

He turned back to the controls, and then saw a plume of sand billowing up from the far side of a dune directly ahead of them. He felt his blood run cold in his veins as from behind the dune a second Apache rose up, its cockpit glass glinting in the sunlight searing the horizon behind it and its fearsome weapons array pointing directly at Ethan and Lopez's motorbikes.

'Enemy front!'

Ethan hauled the motorbike to one side as he changed direction, Lopez peeling away to his right just as the Apache's guns opened fire with a whirring crescendo like screaming demons as a hail of bullets churned the dunes around them. Ethan plunged over the crest of a dune and down into a valley of sand on the far side, out of sight of the Apache's crew.

'We can't get away from them!' Amber yelled. 'The bikes aren't fast enough!'

Ethan concentrated on guiding the bike down the gulley between the dunes, trying to head as much as possible toward the metalled road in order to give them a decent chance at putting some distance between themselves and the Apaches.

He heard the thumping of the gunship's blades nearby and then the whining sound of the cannons firing once more, and he knew that Lopez had come under attack. Fear for her coursed like ice lightning through his body as the motorbike crested a low dune and then descended down alongside the road once more.

Ethan squeezed the brakes and the motorbike shuddered to a halt on the sand as he turned to look over his shoulder.

'Can you ride?'

'Sure, but why ... ?'

'Take the bike,' Ethan said as he leaped out of the saddle and grabbed the grenade launcher from his shoulder. 'When I'm in position, ride, and let them see you.'

Amber blanched. 'They'll open fire!'

'I'll hit them first,' Ethan promised. 'If they're not taken down, get off the road again and get into the dunes, okay? Keep running, no matter what!'

Ethan didn't give Amber the chance to argue and instead dashed out across the main road to the far side, then began running hard to the east. He could hear the Apache nearby, the occasional *burr* of its machine guns as it tried to kill Lopez and Stanley. Ethan had no choice but to draw the Apache out. He kept running until he was a hundred yards further up the road, and then he hurled himself down beside the sandy edge of the road, driving himself down into the sand like a snake trying to bury itself, hurling handfuls of it over his back to conceal himself. Then, satisfied that he would remain out of sight until it was too late, he signalled to Amber to start riding.

Amber burst out onto the road into plain view of the Apache, which was circling back for another pass at wherever Lopez was pinned down. She rode the bike out into the centre of the road and gunned the throttle wide open, the bike accelerating wildly toward Ethan as Amber ducked down over the fuel tank, her black hair flying in the wind.

The Apache swung around almost immediately as its crew spotted the fleeing motorcycle, and as Ethan had hoped the pilot instinctively used the road itself to line up on the target, the helicopter moving directly overhead the road and descending as it tilted forward. Ethan pulled the RPG launcher into his shoulder, activated the sights and settled them on the gunship as it surged forward, the blades hammering the desert air as it rocketed in pursuit of Amber.

Ethan saw the two pilots in their tandem seating cockpit, and in the intense moment he saw the gunship's seeker assembly beneath the nose following the movements of the pilot's head as he sought to aim at Amber's motorcycle, saw the gunship's wicked cannons being brought to bear as the pilot gently pulled the nose up, tracking the centre line of the road. Ethan knew that the pilot would squeeze the trigger just before his gun sights tracked onto Amber's position, sweeping the road with high velocity, armour piercing shells that would shred the asphalt and anything else that got in their way.

Ethan kept his aim steady, the Apache bearing down upon him almost head–on and presenting a perfect target with minimal lateral motion and its swirling rotors and gearbox assembly in full view.

Ethan squeezed the trigger and the launcher shuddered amid a cloud of acrid gray smoke that stung his eyes as the projectile screeched like a banshee out of the barrel and rocketed toward the Apache.

The gunship pilot saw the launch the moment Ethan squeezed the trigger and Ethan saw the gunship pull up and to the left, but at such close range there was no time for even the finest pilot to avoid the weapon.

The grenade impacted the gunship just starboard of the rotor assembly with a brilliant explosion that Ethan glimpsed just before he ducked down to avoid the shrapnel blast that he was counting on to do most of the damage as it smashed into the helicopter's spinning rotors and they flew apart in a lethal cloud of blades and debris.

Ethan covered his head with his hands and pulled his legs up protectively as shrapnel hammered the asphalt road and the helicopter's engines shrieked with an ear piercing whine as the Apache banked away out of control and spun a complete revolution. Ethan squinted up through a cloud of billowing sand as the Apache's engines and rotors tore themselves apart in a frenzy of rending metal. The gunship plunged down into the desert with a crash amid a plume of sand and the engines split open and ignited their fuel.

The Apache exploded in a brilliant fireball that blossomed like a second sunrise against the desert before it was swallowed by black smoke and flames. Ethan dragged himself to his feet and back up onto the road as Lopez's motorcycle burst into view with Stanley clinging to her for dear life as they rode up to Ethan's side.

'We need to get the hell out of here before the other gunship comes back,' Lopez informed him breathlessly as she skidded to a halt.

'You're welcome,' Ethan replied as Amber rode up alongside him.

'Is this, like, normal for you two?!' Amber almost shouted in horror, appalled by the destruction around them.

'It is for *her/him*,' Ethan and Lopez replied in unison.

Ethan heard the sound of the other Apache helicopter further out over the desert, almost certainly trying to hunt down the fleeing horsemen.

'They'll be back,' Ethan said. 'Let's go, before the other helicopter or that drone gets a fix on us.'

Ethan clambered onto the motorbike once again as Amber shifted position back onto the pillion seat, and then he turned the bike around and twisted the throttle wide open.

Together, the two motorbikes accelerated away toward the distant deserts and the city of Damman.

***

XXI

Kingdom Palace, Riyadh

'This way, please.'

Assim Khan walked slowly, his shoes making no sound on the thick carpets. The interior of the palace was as hushed as the empty deserts and yet as cool as the breath of the clearest morning. His chest ached and twinged where the bullet had passed through it, and he knew that it was no more than luck and Allah's guidance that had spared his life: an inch to the left and he would have been dead. Now, heavily dressed in bandages beneath his shirt, Assim mastered the pain and observed his unfamiliar surroundings.

Assim knew little of the residence in which he walked, led by two young manservants immaculately dressed and groomed. The palace was sand colored on the outside and had been built at a cost of some three hundred million dollars, that much he did know, but the rest was rumour. It was said to contain over three hundred rooms and one and a half thousand tons of Italian marble, with gold plated faucets and oriental silk carpets. He had heard it even had its own cinema and no less than five kitchens, each specializing in different cultural cuisines.

Assim was led through the cavernous interior to a plush waiting room adorned with some of the carpets he had heard about, great canvasses adorning the walls depicting members of the House of Saud and historical battle victories, epic desert scenes filled with war horses and flashing cutlasses.

Assim did not have to wait long before a tall man approached him from a side room, dressed in a designer suit. As was befitting Muslim dress codes, he wore no tie around the collar of his silk shirt, and his hair was immaculately parted as though painted upon his scalp. Assim noted the scent of a cologne likely more expensive than some cars, and a thick gold ring on the man's finger encrusted with diamonds.

'Assim,' the man greeted him warmly. 'I have heard much about you. My name is Rasheed, and I will not take too much of your time.'

'It is my honor to be here,' Assim replied, shaking his host's firm, dry hand.

'I apologize for not being able to bring you before the prince himself, but matters beyond the Kingdom keep him long overdue.'

Yemen, Assim recalled briefly, another uprising.

'It is not a problem. What can I do for you, Rasheed?'

'You have been working for an American, Huck Seavers, on our behalf.'

'Yes, escort duties, some investigatory work.'

'We have some further tasks for you to complete but now you will work for us directly, if that is okay with you?'

Assim shook himself out of the spell that Rasheed and this immaculate palace had put him under. This was business, and despite being made to feel as though he should do anything these people asked, he was not about to be manipulated.

'That would depend on the terms,' he said in a reasonable tone.

'Of course,' Rasheed smiled. 'Perhaps your payment from Seavers Incorporated, multiplied by eight, would be satisfactory?'

Assim forced himself not to smile. 'That would be perfectly acceptable.'

Rasheed smiled that perfect smile and produced five black and white photographs which he handed to Assim.

'The payment will be made, in full, immediately. Please feel free to add any costs incurred to you between now and completion of the task. I take it you are familiar with the individuals in these images?'

Assim looked down at the pictures and he nodded. 'I am. What would you have me do?'

Rasheed smiled and his voice dropped lower.

'Find all of them and make them disappear. Permanently.'

Assim forced himself once again to nod, to not show any unwillingness to perform the actions required or to hesitate and cause doubt in his new employer.

'It will be done,' he said. 'Do we have any idea where they are heading at this time?'

'They were last seen fleeing for Damman and it is believed that they are Americans. We have solid evidence, intercepted from Mossad, that they and another American operative are at large in the Kingdom and are pursuing a man named Stanley Meyer.'

'I've heard of him,' Assim confirmed.

'Remove them all,' Rasheed said again. 'No questions asked.'

Assim nodded as he scanned the images. 'I have no questions. I will send word privately when the task is completed.'

'Your professionalism precedes you,' Rasheed said. 'Good luck, Assim.'

Rasheed shook his hand once more, then turned and walked casually away having just condemned three men and two women to death. Assim looked down at the images and allowed a grim smile to spread upon his features, the pain in his chest forgotten now.

Ethan Warner, Nicola Lopez, Stanley Meyer and Amber Ryan were all to die. He had only to learn the name of the dark, tall American photographed leaving a private jet in Riyadh, the tail code clear in the background. Whoever he was, Assim thought to himself as he walked toward the palace exits, he was not long for this world.

*

The sun was high in the sky when Aaron Mitchell stepped out of the air–conditioned interior of the sedan and out onto the scorched asphalt of the metalled road. The heat of the lonely desert cloaked Mitchell, and for once he was dressed simply in slacks and a loose shirt, his sunglasses reflecting the barren wastes as he observed the oily pall of smoke spiralling up into the hard blue sky.

The wreckage of the Apache gunship was shielded from the view of any passing traffic by a series of white canvass walls that rumbled in the wind, erected by soldiers who now stood guard, assault rifles at the ready as Aaron was waved through by a senior officer.

'The event has been presented as a militant action,' the officer reported brusquely, clearly displeased with the overt American presence at the scene of Saudi deaths, 'despite my own personal preferences.'

Aaron did not respond as he strode down the embankment and across the dusty plain to the canvass barriers and walked past them.

The Apache was a twisted, blackened mass of smouldering metal and glass that seemed to still be baking beneath the desert sun. Aaron could smell aviation fuel and the acrid stench of burned plastics and other chemicals staining the wind. He removed his sunglasses for a moment as he searched the deserts around them and saw more troops gathered near the entrance to a distant *wadi*.

Nearby, more troops guarded a hastily–erected field hospital around which worked a group of nurses. Aaron strode across to them, and as he reached the side of the hospital he saw a raggedly dressed man lying on a gurney beneath a sunshield, his legs stained with blood and an intravenous line in his arm.

Aaron paced closer to him, saw a wedge of bone protruding from a tear in his thigh, the broken leg the subject of the nurse's hurried ministrations. The man turned his head at Aaron's approach, dark eyes aflame with pain and eternal rage. As if sensing Satan close by, the man scowled and turned his head away.

'A moment,' Aaron said to the nurses.

His words were almost quiet in the desert wind, but they were deep enough to cause every one of the nurses to look at him and back away. The phalanx of armed guards accompanying Aaron ushered the nurses away, beyond the canvass shields as Aaron approached the gurney and looked down at the wounded militant.

'Where did they go?' he demanded, his Arabic broken and accented but easily understandable.

The militant looked up at Aaron, confusion in his eyes.

'My brothers and sisters of the resistance will already be in Paradise,' he seethed, 'a place of greater glory that you will never know.'

'If it's the place where terrorists and the murderers of innocent Americans go after they die, the only reason I'd travel there is to destroy it,' Aaron rumbled back. 'Last chance: where did they go, the Americans who were with you?'

The militants smiled through his pain, gritted white teeth bright against his dark skin, and he shook his head. Aaron regarded the man for a moment and then he reached down and with one hand wrenched the bone protruding from the militant's shattered thigh.

A wretched, keening scream echoed out across the desert above the rumbling wind and the militant writhed against his restraints as Aaron twisted and shoved the bone. Aaron heard the weeping of the horrified nurses nearby competing with the injured militant's agonised screams.

He released the damaged bone and the militant sagged onto the gurney, his chest heaving and sobs of pain spilling like poison from his mouth onto the hot air.

'There are many drugs here,' Aaron rumbled softly. 'I can keep you alive for many hours, and if you do not tell me what I need to know, I will have you buried alive in these deserts. It will take the animals a long time to kill you, the birds of prey to peck out your eyes, the rodents to scour the flesh from your face. Likewise, you could also be released without harm and nobody would know any the wiser.'

The militant stared up helplessly at Aaron through eyes swimming with torment, and he shook his head as beads of sweat spilled to dampen his hair.

'Never,' he rasped.

Aaron reached out for the ragged chunk of bone once more, when from behind him one of his men spoke.

'We have them,' he said. 'Communications channel intercept, they're heading for Al Qatif seaport.'

Aaron saw the grief twisting the militant's features as he realized that his courage and fortitude had all been for nothing. Aaron smiled down at him.

'Bury him in the desert, far from here,' he ordered his men.

'Murderer!' the militant spat at Aaron. 'This is what you truly are!'

'I'm doing you a favour,' Aaron replied as he turned to leave. 'What could you possibly be afraid of, when paradise is awaiting you?'

***

XXII

Darin Corniche Seaport, Al Qatif

The diplomatic vehicle slid to a halt alongside a vast jetty that extended out into the pristine waters, the sparkling azure ocean in sharp contrast to the flaring golden sands of Saudi Arabia.

Doug Jarvis had worked fast, Ethan's *vanquish* call sign accessing a DIA safe house used by overseas operatives to eavesdrop on Iranian communications and monitor the flow of Iranian–backed militia moving in and out of Iraq. Ethan and his companions had been spirited out of Damman's dangerous streets within an hour of their arrival by a tired looking, middle aged agent going by the name of Jones – easy to remember Ethan guessed, and the less real names used, the better.

'You're going to need to stay off the radar,' Jones reported as he handed Ethan a series of documents including passports, visas and some currency that had obviously been cobbled together with extreme rapidity. 'They're not gonna last long but they should get you through customs and out of the Kingdom, then far enough away before anybody raises the alarm.'

Ethan took the documents as Jones handed similar papers to Amber, Stanley and Lopez.

'The ship you're boarding is called *Huron* and is bound for India,' Jones added. 'Your next contact is aboard. The ship is also calling into Abu Dhabi to pick up cargo. Disembark in India and get the hell back to America while you still can.'

Ethan climbed out of the vehicle, closely followed by Lopez, Stanley and Amber. As soon as they closed their doors the vehicle moved off, swinging sharply around to accelerate away back down the dock. Ethan turned and observed a series of non–descript cargo vessels, none of them particularly large but all laden with the standard shipping containers seen on most major merchant vessels. He spotted across the stern of one particularly dirty–looking ship the name *Huron* and immediately began walking toward it.

'I need to talk to Doug again,' Ethan said to Lopez as they walked. 'Getting us here must have cost him dearly, given his non official status with the DIA.'

'It's the least he can do,' Lopez said. 'He's not the one dodging bullets again.'

'Amber seems to think that Huck Seavers might be willing to strike a deal with her father,' Ethan suggested.

'They're not compatible,' Lopez pointed out. 'Stanley is the philanthropist, Huck the capitalist businessman. Any alliance they tried to form would be broken within days as soon as the cost of development is measured up against the lack of profit that Stanley's aiming for.'

Ethan looked up at the *Huron*, the ship's hull stained and dirty, pockets of ugly brown rust around the anchor chain stays and railings.

'Looks like the DIA's budget has been severely cut,' Lopez observed dryly.

'If it gets us out of Saudi Arabia unobserved, it's good enough for me,' Ethan replied as he walked to the boarding ramp and began climbing toward the deck. 'Let's hope they're planning to set sail this morning.'

As Ethan reached the deck an angry looking man with skin as dark as obsidian and wearing a set of grey overalls confronted him.

'Warner?' he asked, as though it was an accusation. 'Captain Youssef Alem.'

'Pleasure to meet you too,' Ethan replied as he stepped aboard.

There was no handshake, no welcome from the captain as he gestured with a lazy jab of his thumb over his shoulder toward the bridge at the stern.

'Your quarters are back there, B deck, port side. I'd appreciate it if you all stay out of the way, we have work to do.'

Ethan glanced across the deck to see various deckhands engaged in their duties, checking braces on the shipping containers and preparing to winch in the enormous anchor chains and jetty ties keeping the ship in place.

Lopez, Amber and Stanley joined him on the deck and watched the captain suspiciously before another man appeared from the bridge and hurried forward. Dressed in overalls not dissimilar to the captain's, he extended his hand to Ethan.

'Mike Willis, DIA,' he announced himself with a smile, all bright eyed enthusiasm.

Ethan raised an eyebrow as he shook Willis's hand. 'You're posted here?'

'We have a small presence using trade vessels as a platform for discrete intelligence gathering. The ship's crew's appreciate the extra revenue in return for allowing us to come along for the ride.'

Ethan glanced at Captain Alem, who had returned to his work with his crew and showed very little interest at all in the new arrivals.

'Call me clairvoyant, but I sense a reluctance,' Ethan said.

'They fear retaliation by Iran should signals equipment be detected and the ship boarded, although they are careful to stay inside international waters as instructed. Of course, their fear is easily surmounted by cash. I'll show you to your quarters, such as they are.'

Ethan followed Willis along with Lopez and the others as they descended into the bowels of the ship, the vessel's hull now shuddering and reverberating as the engines were started and the ship moved away slowly from the dock.

'It's not exactly the Hilton, but it will do for tonight until we can get you out of Abu Dhabi in the morning.'

The interior of the ship smelled of grease and metal and looked as though it hadn't been swabbed down in at least fifty years. The cabins that Willis presented to them were little more than prison cells with open doors, thin mattresses and a tiny port hole along with a sink.

'The latrine is down the end of the hall and best used as little as possible,' Willis admitted.

'It'll do,' Ethan said as he tossed his satchel into one of the cabins. 'I don't plan on getting much sleeping done anyway.'

He intercepted a look of reluctance from Lopez and Amber as they ambled slowly into their respective cabins.

'Do you have a direct line to the DIA, to Jarvis? Something that doesn't use commercial satellites?'

'I don't have any names I'm afraid,' Willis admitted. 'I got a direct call from director Nellis himself and was ordered to set you up at short order. Is Jarvis your handler?'

'Something like that,' Ethan replied as he reached into his satchel and grabbed the satellite phone. 'I can't use this now because the Saudis will have identified it and will track its movements if I turn it on. I need to make a call.'

'Come this way,' Willis said in reply.

Ethan hurried in pursuit of Willis as he led him to the radio room of the ship, situated on the deck below the bridge. Little more than an old storage cupboard, a makeshift desk had been created using a piece of shelving bolted to the wall, and before it sat an uncomfortable looking wooden chair.

On the shelf was an old metal box that was bolted in place to the wall. Willis opened the box and retrieved from it a very modern looking radio set, glossy black and with a digital interface. He switched the device on and then reached around the back and attached a cable to a receptor concealed in the wall. Immediately, the radio display identified itself and became active, Ethan guessing that a direct satellite link had been established via a receiver mounted somewhere externally on the ship.

'Five layers of encryption,' Willis reported with satisfaction. 'A direct line to Virginia courtesy of the top brass. It's on a shortwave, modulating frequency that even the Saudis won't be able to monitor for more than a split second before it changes, and they've never been able to detect it before.'

'Variable receivers?' Ethan asked.

'Pretty much anything you want to tap into,' Willis said with a smile. 'I use it to talk to my wife from time to time. Nobody complains as long as you're discreet and don't take too long.'

Ethan sat down on the uncomfortable chair as Willis left the room, pulling the door behind him to give Ethan some privacy as he punched a number into the keypad attached to one side of the radio box. A whirring sound was issued from the headset he donned as he pulled the microphone down to his mouth and waited. The whirring sounds were replaced with a warble, and then the more familiar sound of a ring tone.

It took several rings before there was an answer.

'Doug Jarvis?'

'It's me,' Ethan replied simply.

Jarvis's tone immediately became somewhat more clandestine.

'Well you've done it again, Ethan. Apparently, the Saudis lost a helicopter yesterday morning in some kind of accident, possibly the action of militant groups in the desert west of Damman.'

'We heard a bang,' Ethan replied, conscious of not revealing any details even over such a secure line. 'I suspect it was a completely defensive action against a hostile force.'

'Anybody fleeing an event like that will be under extreme surveillance should they be observed,' Jarvis said. *'Any cover they may have obtained will be temporary at best. I'd say their best bet is to completely disappear as fast as possible until the dust settles.'*

'I'd agree,' Ethan said. 'They have acquired assets, most likely, those most prized by the enemy. Those assets need to be protected as a high priority.'

There was a long silence as Jarvis digested this new information and formulated his response.

'The assets should be bought back to home turf,' he said. *'They'll be safer there and it may be possible to arrange some kind of protection.'*

'Sounds like a plan,' Ethan said. 'Their journey will probably be complex and will involve more than one stop. It may not be possible to achieve under normal circumstances, so they may even need assistance of some kind.'

Despite the digital distortion down the line Ethan could detect the tension in Jarvis's voice.

'Things are not easy here. There are forces at work behind the scenes, attempting to sabotage our efforts. It's not certain how long I can maintain support, especially in light of recent events. I've been called to a major meeting with the brass, and I can only assume they're going to start yelling at me.'

'Support need only be in terms of concealment,' Ethan replied. 'Or even deception. Do what you can, and we'll be back as soon as possible. Can you get us out of Abu Dhabi?'

'Agent Willis will enact the protocol, but you won't have much time. He'll assign you a passage out of Abu Dhabi leaving tonight. It's the best I could do at such short notice.'

'Perfect,' Ethan said as a plan formed in his mind. 'I'll be in touch as soon as I can.'

The line went dead as Jarvis cut off the connection and Ethan leaned back in his seat, the old wood creaking beneath him as he considered what Jarvis said. The Defense Intelligence Agency was a very powerful organisation within the US government, but just as Ethan and Lopez had found on previous investigations for the DIA, even official ones, there were higher powers quite capable of infiltrating and disrupting operations even within the DIA. With Majestic Twelve likely representing the highest power of any organisation in the world, and with them being more than aware of Lopez in Ethan's presence in the Middle East, he could only assume that they might be able to eavesdrop on any conversation, no matter how secure.

If they were pressuring Jarvis and the DIA, then they could no longer be considered secure.

Ethan got out of his seat and hurried forward to the cabins once more, and found Stanley attempting to lay a threadbare blanket over a particularly ugly stain on his mattress.

'Stanley, is there anybody that can help us right now? Somebody you know in your industry perhaps, who you might be willing to reach out to?'

Meyer looked at Ethan for a long moment and perhaps for the first time he began to realise the depth of the trouble he was in. The old man had clearly been shaken by their encounter with the Apache gunships, and perhaps not as able as he thought he was to evade the authorities in order to bring his remarkable device to the masses.

'Perhaps,' he said after a moment's thought. 'There is a place in France, we might be able to find somebody there willing to help us.'

'France?' Ethan asked, somewhat surprised. 'What are they doing in France that could possibly help us?'

'Something quite similar to me, actually,' Stanley replied. 'They are trying to produce free energy for the world. But their method is somewhat different to mine, it's a bit bigger.'

'How much bigger?' Ethan asked.

Stanley shrugged.

'They're trying to build a sun here on earth, and capture its energy.'

***

XXIII

Pentagon, Washington DC

Doug Jarvis strode into a briefing room in the Pentagon four minutes late for a meeting, the importance of which had been flagged in his message from General Nellis as "*Stellar*". When he got into the room, he realised why.

Before him sat the Joint Chiefs of Staff, the United States miltary's highest ranking officers and the men responsible for the overall command of the Army, Navy, Air Force and intelligence community. Jarvis hesitated before the array of top brass before him, then closed the door behind him.

A single spare chair awaited him, which meant that he was the only individual invited to the meeting. Heading the table was DIA Director General Nellis, flanked by the Director of the National Security Agency, Morris Tyler, and FBI Director Gordon LeMay, a gaunt looking man with a hooked nose and cold eyes who reminded Jarvis somewhat of a bird of prey. The chiefs of staff sat alongside each other on each side of the table and at the far end was the forlorn empty chair, which Jarvis sat down in. It felt just a little bit like being positioned in front of a firing squad. Nellis's voice rumbled like an avalanche of boulders toward him.

'We have a problem,' he said. 'Have you been apprised of events in Saudi Arabia?'

Jarvis felt an itch developing at the back of his neck and fought the urge to scratch it as an image of Ethan Warner flickered unbidden before his eyes. 'No sir, I have not.'

'We have, from high level sources,' Gordon LeMay snapped. 'A Saudi attack gunship was lost this morning in an action against militant groups in the desert east of Riyadh.'

'A tragedy,' Jarvis said.

'The tragedy is that two DIA agents were identified among the militants,' Morris Tyler cut in, restraint written in pained lines across his features. 'Americans.'

'Do we know these Americans?' Jarvis asked.

'You know damned well who we're talking about,' LeMay snapped. 'Your two hound dogs are on the rampage again!'

LeMay tossed a grainy black and white image to Jarvis. Shot from what looked like the sensors of an attack chopper, maybe an *Apache*, it showed Ethan Warner and Nicola Lopez running across open desert in the company of armed militants, some of them carrying grenade launchers and assault rifles.

'Ethan Warner,' Morris Tyler said as though spitting something unpleasant from his mouth. 'This guy is responsible for more international incidents than I care to recall. The Israelis still want to talk to him about something he dug up in their desert a few years back. We have it on record that he blew up an entire apartment building in New Mexico and caused a major blast off the Florida coast some years ago.'

'That's not to mention the death of an entire paramilitary squad in Idaho,' LeMay added, 'the unsolved murder of a homicide captain in New York City who has since had his record marred by corruption charges, and a major international incident in Argentina earlier this year! This guy is a disaster for our departments and yet you're sponsoring him to do more work for us! Why the hell would you do this?!'

'In order to protect the same interests you have just described,' Jarvis replied. 'Without the intelligence provided, the cases upon which we were working could not have been solved. It was a necessary step for which I take full responsibility.'

Nellis's features creased into a tight smile. Jarvis could tell that Nellis was under pressure to show a united front with the Joint Chiefs of Staff, no matter what the general was agreeing to with Jarvis behind closed doors.

'A necessary step,' Nellis echoed, 'which you had no authority to make, then or now.'

'This isn't about authority,' Jarvis snapped, provoking a look of surprise on the general's craggy features. 'This is about getting the job done with the resources we have available at the time.'

Gordon LeMay glanced down the table at him.

'This agency can call upon all manner of elite forces, trained specialists. It doesn't require the services of Ethan Warner.'

'Yes it does,' Jarvis growled back. 'I'd rather employ Ethan than have your paramilitary units betray them again, as they did in Idaho. Or have you already forgotten about that, Gordon?'

LeMay's eyes flew wide in surprise. Jarvis didn't wait for the director's response.

'What's the problem here?' Jarvis asked the Joint Chiefs. 'I take it that this is about my department's hiring of Warner & Lopez Inc. to carry out investigations on the DIA's behalf?'

'The Department of Defense believes that it is a tactical folly to employ civilians in what should be an internally sourced investigative outfit,' Morris Tyler said.

'Then the department should look more carefully at its own charter,' Jarvis snapped back. 'All of the intelligence agencies out–source work, even clandestine operations. Every single one of Warner & Lopez's investigations at the DIA was previously rejected or denied resources by other agencies, including the CIA and FBI, before we picked them up.'

'Why put these things into the hands of civilians at all?' Tyler asked.

'Budgets,' Jarvis replied, 'resources, equipment, time. Warner and Lopez, they're just as reliable as any government agent.' Jarvis shot another dirty look at LeMay. 'Sometimes even more so.'

Admiral John Griffiths, chief of the Navy, leaned forward on the table.

'We were briefed this morning on the scope of your operations. I know that everybody in this room is aware of the full details of each of these investigations, so I'll make this simple. Since starting this department of yours, Ethan Warner and Nicola Lopez have overseen investigations into alien remains found in a seven–thousand year old tomb in Israel; into immortalised veterans of the Civil War living in seclusion in New Mexico and the arrest and death of the philanthropist Joaquin Abell who had used his fortune to build a device capable of seeing into the future. Then there was the CIA fiasco in Idaho surrounding the animals they had "modified" there, the hauntings in New York city and the search for alien artifacts in Peru's Andes mountains. You put all of this into the hands of a washed–out former Marine and a DC detective turned bounty–hunter?'

Jarvis maintained a stern expression.

'Yes sir, that's right. Ethan and Nicola have served their country with a courage and self–sacrifice that puts many of our supposedly elite operatives to shame. They're unpredictable and often vulnerable, but they've pulled through every single time and should be decorated, not denigrated. Who arranged this meeting, if I may ask?'

LeMay's tone darkened further.

'No, Mister Jarvis, you may not. This is about *your* people.'

Jarvis's eyes narrowed.

'That's utter crap and every man around this table knows it. I had a similar conversation with the JCOS years ago, when they tried to shut my unit down. Who called the meeting?'

Tyler Morris raised a hand, silencing LeMay's response.

'Gentlemen, let's stay the course here shall we?'

General Hank Butcher, Chief of the Army, shook his head.

'What's your problem here?' he asked Jarvis. 'What are you insinuating?'

'This is not about Ethan and Nicola,' Jarvis replied. 'This is about control. There is somebody behind the scenes pulling strings here because they don't like what we're digging in to.'

'That's rubbish,' Gordon LeMay snapped. 'You've been watching too many episodes of *24*.'

A chuckle went around the room.

'It's probably served me well,' Jarvis said. 'Who called this meeting? Was it any one of us in this room?'

LeMay squirmed. Jarvis could see him grinding his teeth in his jaw.

'It doesn't matter a damn.' LeMay replied. 'Right now the Saudis are screaming down our diplomatic channels for the blood of the two Americans in that image, and you're hiding them from view. Do you have any idea of the political damage that this could cause if it went public? American agents killing Saudi servicemen during the course of their duty?'

'It would be devastating,' Jarvis agreed. 'Which begs the question: *why* did they do it? I notice that they're running away from the camera in that image, as are the militants, so they were likely under attack from the two gunships. Why? Who ordered an attack on two American agents? Who knew they were there?'

'The Saudi's claim that they were rooting out militants during normal operations after an attack on a private contractor's convoy,' Nellis replied. 'They only saw the Americans when they recovered the data from the crashed helicopters.'

'Of course they would,' Jarvis grinned without warmth. 'But it makes no difference. Warner and Lopez will return fire if attacked, it's what they're trained to do. If the Saudi gunships were outclassed by a gumshoe and a retired cop, as you call them, that's their business.'

LeMay intervened, his voice quiet but forceful enough to cut through the tension.

'Doug, for now I think it's best if we draw this operation to a close until something can be worked out.'

Jarvis looked at Nellis and slowly shook his head.

'Again, on whose orders?' Jarvis shot back. 'Who's calling the shots here? The FBI? What jurisdiction would they have in Saudi Arabia?'

'Every man at this table is in basic agreement except you,' LeMay snapped.

'I don't suppose this has gone up as far as the White House?' Jarvis said, ignoring LeMay.

'It's not something we need to off–load onto the administration,' Tyler pointed out.

'Perish the thought,' Jarvis said. 'I wonder what would happen if I called a meeting there and told the President everything?'

'I don't think you'd get anywhere near the White House,' LeMay smiled. 'They'd turn you away as nothing more than a madman.'

'Unless I knew the president personally,' Jarvis murmured casually in reply. 'Or if Ethan Warner had once saved his life, when he was still a senator. You must recall the file of Isaiah Black, general?'

Nellis raised an eyebrow.

'We'd shut you down long before you got there,' LeMay uttered.

Jarvis stood up from his seat and looked at the men before him. 'You represent the most powerful nation on earth, but clearly none of you really understand why you're even here. What makes you think that I have any respect for your authority when you're being strong–armed and can't even admit it?'

The men around the table stared back at Jarvis in silence.

'Jarvis. Where are Warner and Lopez right now?' Nellis asked.

'Busy,' Jarvis said as he strode for the door.

'Busy *where*?' LeMay snapped.

Nellis looked at Jarvis. 'Doug, their whereabouts is not a big deal.'

'Pull them out, immediately,' Tyler added.

'They're dark, out of reach,' Jarvis lied as he opened the door. 'I'll pull them out when they make contact, or are we intending to put their lives at risk by going in there and searching for them in plain view of potential enemies of the state?'

Jarvis saw a tremor of unease flicker like a shadow behind Nellis's eyes.

'Where were they last headed?' LeMay demanded. 'Give us that much at least, and we'll ensure that they come to no harm and that there are no.., charges threatened, if you know what I mean?'

Jarvis sighed. He knew that he had to be seen to throw the joint chiefs a bone or he could possibly be arrested himself for treason, the threat thinly veiled. If any one of the brass in the room were on the payroll of Majestic Twelve, as he suspected, it could be even worse than that. A light of inspiration flickered into life in his mind as he opened the door to exit the room.

'They're headed for Abu Dhabi aboard a ship named Huron. That's all I'll say.'

Jarvis closed the door behind him and immediately reached for his cell phone as he hurried away.

***

XXIV

Port Zayed, Abu Dhabi

'Move, now!'

The convoy of four sleek white sedans supplied by the House of Saud cruised through the city streets even as the sun was glowing across the desert horizon, glinting off the tallest buildings of Abu Dhabi's immense glassy skyline. The city looked like a gigantic steel crown encrusted with diamonds and embedded against the vast deserts.

Aaron Mitchell's last command has just been received by the agents in the other vehicles, all of whom were now accelerating toward a ship moored in the port. Aaron could see the vessel's form against the peculiarly vivid desert dawn, a container vessel streaked with the filth of countless voyages across the open oceans. She was stacked with cargo brought from Europe that was being unloaded by large cranes onto the dock, and was due to depart that morning for India.

The cars swept into the docks, their security access cleared in advance from the highest levels of government. Aaron watched through the tinted windows as the form of the vessel hove into view, a hive of activity before its massive hull as dock workers hurried to complete their unloading and turn the ship around for departure.

Mitchell's sedan swung around and came to a halt behind the leading three vehicles, from which spilled armed agents who quickly contained the dock workers in confused rings, dark eyes wide with alarm as the agents corralled them near the loading cranes. Aaron waited until the area was secure and all of the captive workers had been forced to turn their backs before he opened the door of the sedan and stepped out.

The air smelled of salt, desert sand and metal as Aaron walked toward *Huron's* boarding ramp, which rose from the dock up into the ship's cavernous interior. He strode with purpose, four of his agents splitting off wordlessly from their comrades and escorting him toward the ship's entrance.

They were almost there when a man appeared in the entrance. Broad, imposing and dark skinned, he glared at the intruders with barely concealed contempt.

'Who the hell are you and what are you doing to my ... '

'Captain Youssef Alem,' Aaron rumbled as he came to stand within arm's reach of the ship's captain. 'Ten thousand dollars, right here and now, if you give up the Americans aboard this ship.'

Youssef stared at Aaron for a long moment, momentarily surprised by the offer. Moments later the veil of enforced confusion fell back down across his dark features.

'I don't know what you're talking about.'

'I will only make the offer one last time.'

Aaron remained impassive, his hands in the pockets of his dark coat despite the growing warmth radiating from the sunrise blazing across the eastern sky.

'Ten thousand dollars does not go far,' Youssef replied finally, a mercenary gleam in his eye. 'Not as far as the payment I already received.'

Aaron took one pace closer to the captain, his voice quiet and yet brittle as ice.

'Then you have earned enough for your compliance. Ten thousand more for the Americans. If you do not release them to me now, I will ensure that what remains of you will be found floating in this dock by sundown.'

Youssef's excitement at the prospect of more money flickered out like a dying flame as he glared at Aaron.

'You would not dare to ... '

Aaron was quick. Perhaps not as quick as he had once been in the jungles of Vietnam, but far too fast for the ship's captain to prevent the knuckles of Aaron's right hand from plunging into his throat in a blur of motion.

The impact collapsed Youssef's windpipe and his eyes bulged as he staggered back into the ship, one hand reaching for a Bowie knife thrust into the belt around his waist. Aaron lunged forward, one hand closing around Youssef's wrist as he dropped his weight forward behind his forehead and smashed if across the captain's face.

Youssef's nasal bridge collapsed as blood spilled across his face and he twisted away, his legs failing beneath him as his eyes rolled briefly up into their sockets. As the captain collapsed toward the deck, Aaron twisted the man's wrist up and around as he grabbed his hand and folded it over.

Youssef hit the deck and sprawled face down as Aaron folded the captain's arm over at an awkward angle. Youssef regained consciousness and opened his mouth, sucking in air and screaming as his arm neared breaking point.

'The offer has changed,' Aaron whispered softly as his men moved into the ship, their side arms drawn. 'Your life, in return for the Americans.'

Youssef gagged in agony as he tried to speak above the pain wracking his body.

'Deck B, port aft quarter!'

Aaron did not need to order his men into motion. With extraordinary fluidity and speed born of Special Forces training they deployed into the ship's gloomy interior. Aaron looked down at Youssef for a long moment, and then with his free hand he drew the Bowie knife from Youssef's belt. The blade was long and stained with age, had perhaps sailed the oceans with Youssef his entire life.

'Who paid you?'

Youssef squirmed and writhed on the ship's grimy deck.

'I don't know, it was all done by telephone and Internet. They paid into my ship's account and that was it.'

'Who arranged the American's presence here?'

Youssef continued to squirm and Aaron lowered the blade to his neck.

'The American agent,' Youssef finally spluttered. 'Willis! His name is Willis!'

Aaron heard shouting coming from somewhere further inside the ship. He yanked Youssef's arm upwards, forcing the captain to clamber painfully up onto his knees and then to his feet. With the blade pressed firmly against Youssef's flank and his arm twisted up against his spine, Aaron forced him to walk through the ship's ugly corridors of unpainted metal toward the uproar.

The odours of damp, salt and neglected machinery grew as they descended toward the sounds of distress. Aaron walked Youssef out into a cargo area deep inside the ship, just above the open holds. Fresh air wafted across them as Aaron saw his men standing in a ring, their weapons pointed down at a man lying face down on the deck, his hands over his head.

The agents separated to let Aaron through. He shoved Youssef inside the ring of agents and looked up briefly to the massive hatch open in the decks above them, a crane suspended above the ship's cavernous interior and the blue sky flawless beyond it. A massive shipping container was dangling from the crane's hooks, suspended ready to be transferred to the dock alongside the ship.

'We caught him fleeing here,' one of Aaron's agents said. 'Looks like he was going to climb up to the deck from this cargo bay.'

Aaron looked down to see the man lying before him, peering up with fearful eyes.

'Agent Willis,' Aaron said. 'Where are Ethan Warner, Nicola Lopez and Stanley Meyer?'

Willis's brow creased in confusion. 'Who?'

Aaron looked up at the crane above them and then he gestured to Willis. His men grabbed the terrified agent and hauled him to his feet. Aaron stepped across and in one fluid motion he swung a giant bunched fist into Willis's belly. The agent's face bulged and he doubled over as his legs gave way beneath him, the agents dragging him to one side as Aaron turned his attention to Youssef where he lay on the deck.

The captain scrambled backwards and away, but Aaron stomped one heavy boot across the captain's ankle with a furious effort. A sharp, brittle crack echoed across the storage hold and Youssef screamed once again, the cry bouncing off the walls and escaping out into the brightening sky above.

Before Youssef could suck in enough air for another sob of pain, Aaron stamped down on the other ankle and it snapped with an equally sickening crackle of fractured bone. Youssef gagged, his face sheened with sweat as he slumped, weeping, onto the deck.

Aaron turned and left the crippled captain where he lay and walked toward Agent Willis, held in the firm grip of Aaron's men and with a pistol jammed against his ribs. The smaller man cowered and blubbed without further provocation.

'I'll tell you where they are,' he cried. 'I'll tell you!'

Aaron turned away from Willis and strode across to a control panel affixed to one wall of the hold. Usually manned by the crane's operator but currently abandoned, Aaron surveyed the controls only for a moment before he spoke.

'Where did they go?'

Aaron activated the controls and the crane above them hummed into life, the massive shipping container shifting position slightly in the light breeze.

'They jumped ship,' Willis mumbled. 'They didn't trust me to keep them safe ashore.'

Aaron grinned without warmth as he pressed a button and the massive shipping container above them began descending to the sound of whining hydraulic winches. Youssef yelped in fright as he looked up from where he lay crippled in the centre of the hold and saw the huge container descending toward him.

'What the hell are you doing?!' Willis cried out in horror.

Aaron watched as Youssef began trying to pull himself out from beneath the container, dragging his ruined legs behind him and crying out in pain as he did so, his yellowing teeth gritted against his dark skin.

'Don't do it!' Willis gasped in grief, his voice trembling.

'Please!' Youssef wailed in agony as the descending container's shadow consumed him, the base of the weighty container now just four feet from the deck.

Aaron did not look at Willis as he spoke.

'Who was Ethan Warner's direct contact at the Defense Intelligence Agency?'

Willis's features collapsed in defeat and he shouted his response.

'Jarvis! It was some guy called Jarvis!'

Aaron flipped a switch on the control panel and the container hissed to a halt, swinging just a couple of feet above the deck as Youssef appeared, tears glistening on his face as he crawled toward the edge of the container. Aaron looked at Willis.

'Where did they go?'

'The airport,' Willis blubbed. 'They got a jet to some place in France, I have the tail code. Take it, just take it!'

Aaron nodded slowly in satisfaction. He glanced at Youssef and then hit a button on the control panel. The crane's hooks released and the container dropped the last two feet and slammed down onto the deck with a deafening crash, Youssef vanishing beneath it. Willis cried out and turned away from the grisly scene.

Aaron stepped down from the control panel and moved slowly to tower over Willis, the agent coughing and spitting the acrid taste from his mouth as Aaron spoke.

'If I should hear that you have spoken to anybody in Washington, ever, about anything you have seen here, I will return and another tragic accident will occur. Do you understand?'

Willis, barely able to stand, nodded, his face pale and his eyes glazed with tears.

'The flight number, now,' Aaron demanded.

Willis blubbed a tail–code, weeping openly.

Aaron turned and Willis sank to his knees as Aaron and his guards left the storage hold.

As he left the docks in the white sedan, Aaron did not see the dark skinned man watching him quietly from the deep shadows thrown by the rising sun across the quay.

Assim Khan watched Mitchell's convoy depart from the dock, noted the registration plate of Mitchell's vehicle, and then flicked away the cigarette he was smoking into the nearby black water as he strode to a motorcycle and climbed aboard.

***

XXV

ITER,

Cadarache, France

'Wow.'

Lopez's voice sounded small as they climbed out of the car they had leased for cash, in Euros, from a small dealership in Roquemaure alongside the Le Rhone river that wound its way through the picturesque valleys of southern France.

The flight out of Abu Dhabi that Ethan had booked had resulted in them abandoning Agent Willis in the city, an act for which Ethan felt some degree of shame. However, Stanley and Amber were his priorities and he felt certain that Majestic Twelve would have located them before *Huron* had gotten far from the docks. Jarvis had texted him and warned of a possible breach, confirming Ethan's suspicions and urging him to make alternative plans. A commercial flight out of the city using the cash and fake documents Jones had provided a better option, and they had landed in France tired but beyond the reach of the Saudi authorities, for now at least.

'It's a temporary victory,' Lopez had warned him. 'The Saudis have strong ties with our own administration. They could easily demand our arrest and extradition to face charges.'

'One thing at a time,' Ethan had replied with more confidence than he had felt. 'Let's just get back to America first – we'll be better able to operate on home ground.'

A vast facility was arrayed before them containing many huge buildings, many of which were still under construction. Ethan could see heavy trucks moving to and fro, cranes operating and countless workmen labouring beneath the warm sunshine.

Stanley Meyer looked up at the vast construction site with his hands on his hips and a scowl on his features.

'Biggest waste of the world's money I've ever seen,' he muttered.

'What is this place?' Lopez asked.

'ITER is Latin for '*the way*',' Amber explained, apparently well enough versed in her father's work to know about the site. 'It's an international research and engineering project to build the world's first nuclear fusion reactor.'

'The project is funded and run by seven member entities,' Stanley said as they began walking toward the massive site. 'The European Union, India, Japan, People's Republic of China, Russia, South Korea and the United States. All of them have agreed to waste enormous sums of money building what is really just a giant plasma accelerator using a tokamak chamber.'

'A torus to contain the plasma in magnetic fields,' Ethan recalled from a previous investigation for the DIA, deep beneath the waves of the Florida coast.

'Indeed,' Stanley said, raising a surprised eyebrow at Ethan. 'The reactor uses deuterium fuel, which is easily extracted from seawater, and tritium which is generated once the fusion reactions begin, thus creating a runaway reaction which is effectively self–sustaining. It's being designed to produce five hundred megawatts of output power while only needing fifty megawatts of ingoing power to operate.'

'Free energy,' Lopez remarked. 'How come that's possible?'

'It's the same process going on inside our sun,' Stanley explained as he glanced up at the bright orb in the hard blue sky. 'The sun's gravity is so immense that it attempts to crush itself under its own weight. This compresses the nuclei of hydrogen that mostly make up the sun so much that they fuse together, a process known as nuclear fusion. Immense volumes of energy are emitted during this process, in line with $E=mc2$, and are emitted from the sun as the heat and the light that we feel on our faces right now.'

'Isn't that what all nuclear power stations do?' Lopez asked.

'No,' Stanley said. 'They use nuclear fission, the opposite process: once again, mankind chooses to use the opposite method to nature for producing energy. They *split* the atom, releasing vast amounts of energy but also radiation with it. A fission reactor can melt down in a runaway chain reaction should it overheat, as witnessed at Chernobyl in 1986. A fusion reactor, however, will simply cease to operate if the temperatures or pressures fall below the required level. Fusion also produces very little waste product – it's the perfect energy supply for mankind if it can be harnessed.'

'Then why are you so against it?' Ethan pressed.

'I'm not against it, I'm against the methods employed to achieve it,' Stanley insisted. 'All of this, some sixteen billion dollars of investment, all to produce what is in effect nothing more than a proof of concept. This reactor won't be able to power the world even if it works perfectly and confounds the critics who say it's a waste of time. Our National Ignition Facility in California has already proved the concept on a smaller scale and initiated nuclear fusion reactions, and the aerospace giant Lockheed Martin has announced plans for a fusion reactor small enough to fit on the back of a truck that may be commercialized within a decade, long before this monstrosity even gets fully completed.'

Stanley huffed and puffed his way to a low ridge of dirt alongside the edge of the compound where the reactor was to be built and surveyed it through the high fences that surrounded the enormous site.

'I have witnessed energetic reactions emitting excess heat phenomena in an apparatus made from things you could buy in a local hardware store,' he said gloomily. 'It's all about efficiency, not a free lunch. Our governments are building this not because they need it, but because they want to show the people how much they need their governments and leaders to achieve such things. If only the people knew that they don't, that if they simply made an effort to research these things themselves they could take their own futures into their own hands and shake off these ridiculous gestures of power.'

The reply to Stanley Meyer's oratory came from one side of where they stood.

'The cynic as ever, Stanley.'

Ethan turned to see an elderly man watching them from the foot of the ridge, his hands in the pockets of his jacket and a kindly smile on his face.

'Hans!'

Stanley hurried down the ridge with remarkable agility for one so old and the two men embraced briefly.

'This is Hans Furgen,' Stanley introduced his friend, 'the best electrochemist I ever knew and somebody who knows more about nuclear reactions than everybody else in the world combined.'

Furgen appeared to almost blush as he shook Ethan's hand.

'That's something of an exaggeration,' he murmured in reply.

'Blah blah,' Stanley said, more animated than Ethan had ever seen him. 'You're the top dog, Hans, it's why these damned fools picked you to run this project.'

'You're ITER's project leader?' Lopez asked.

'I'm in charge of developing the tokamak chamber,' Hans replied. 'It's a crucial part of the assembly and one so large has not been built before. Stanley's right that excess heat phenomena have already been achieved at the NIF in California, but only on a very short time scale and at lower energies than we plan to achieve. This facility is to prove that it can be done at a commercial scale, and thus will hopefully pave the way to a future devoid of fossil fuels and the dangers of fission meltdowns and radioactive waste.'

'That's a big responsibility,' Ethan noted with considerable admiration for Han's role. 'And if somebody else were to come along and do the same thing on a desktop with some beakers and electrodes they bought at Walmart, how would that go down at ITER?'

Hans sighed and his shoulders slumped as he glanced at Stanley.

'I wondered why you had come all the way out here,' he said to his fellow scientist. 'I thought that you'd given up on that pipe dream a long time ago.'

Stanley offered his friend a tight smile. 'That's the thing–I didn't, and it paid off.'

Hans shook his head. 'That's what you said the last time, and the time before that, and the time before that. You do realise the entire Department of Energy has been studying cold fusion for years and they've come to the same conclusion as I did: it doesn't damned well work.'

'They fudged it all,' Stanley argued in desperation. 'It worked, Hans. I powered an entire town for weeks with it and everybody had all the power they needed for nothing more than the water I was siphoning out of the stream that ran through the middle of Clearwater.'

Hans peered at Stanley for a long moment and then looked at Ethan.

'It's true,' Ethan said, 'as far as we can make out. Their only mistake was to disconnect from the National Grid and draw attention to what they had achieved. A few days later, the entire town was paid off to disappear and remain silent about what had happened. Stanley here fled, along with his wife, and Amber witnessed the whole thing.'

Hans looked at Amber in surprise, and she nodded.

'They made the town look as though nobody had lived there for decades,' she said. 'They're covering it up, Hans. They don't want this out because they know what it will mean for projects like this, for the amount of control that governments have over their people.'

Hans looked across at the massive construction site to his right and then back at Stanley once more.

'Why are you here, Stanley?'

'We need your help,' Ethan replied for Stanley. 'There's no way that this is going to get out without somebody on the inside. Every scientist, every builder, everybody working on this project would be likely opposed to anything like Stanley's device getting out. The fusion cage is the greatest threat to all energy producing corporations in the world, not to mention every oil–producing nation and countries like Russia with vast gas reserves. Every single ounce of those fossil fuels will be worth nothing, less than bare rock, if Stanley's fusion cage goes public.'

Lopez stepped forward. 'We want you to help make that happen,' she said.

Hans took an involuntary pace back from them and his pale skin turned even whiter than his eyes as they wobbled in their sockets.

'You don't know what you're doing,' he uttered in disbelief. 'Even if Stanley had managed to do what you say he has done, it would require months or even years of testing to validate, to ensure that there was no mistake. Such a delay could call into question this entire project and many others like it. The public would jump upon the chance to have free energy, and there would be a massive outcry and political pressure to stop investing in major projects that are so essential to our survival. If Stanley turned out to be wrong, or even just mistaken, or if the reactions could not be sustained for long enough, or if the devices are found to blow up due to the heat and pressure over time, and proved themselves unsafe and incapable of commercialisation, then ITER would have lost years of research data, perhaps even the chance to develop a new form of energy before oil, coal and gas run out or a runaway reaction occurs in our atmosphere and environment. It's just too damned risky.'

'No risk without gain,' Ethan observed quietly.

'That statement that makes no attempt to measure the sheer magnitude of the consequences of failure,' Hans shot back. 'Many Western countries are already facing blackouts during periods of high demand due to the fact that we simply cannot maintain an energy supply across such a vast population addicted to electrical devices and in need of heat and light. ITER is not some immense monstrosity designed to keep the populace under the thumb of their politicians: it's a potential lifesaver for the entire planet and it operates on the basis of physics that is well understood. Nuclear fusion does work, whereas Stanley's supposed fusion cage is based on a science that has long ago since been invalidated by peer review.'

'There was no peer review!' Stanley almost shouted. 'There was a whitewash!'

'There always is, when a scientist begins to *believe* instead of needing to know,' Hans replied quietly. 'You say that it's a conspiracy against you, but the whole cold fusion science debacle has continued ever since the Fleischmann and Pons experiments of the 1980s. They give it a different name now, low–energy nuclear reaction research or something, but it's the same thing.'

'Doesn't that validate what Stanley's saying?' Lopez argued. 'That's it's real science after all, worth investigating?'

'No, it reveals only that we're desperate as a society for an alternative to fossil fuels! It's not about the environment, some noble crusade by governments to clean up our planet no matter how they might choose to dress it up. It's *business*. Governments make money from fuel, and they'll be powerless if the lights go out worldwide. Fossil fuels are running out, and they're terrified of the consequences of that happening.'

'Everybody is,' Stanley replied, 'all the more reason to help me.'

'All the more reason to ignore you and work here at ITER!' Hans retorted. 'This is the future Stanley, real science, a chance at real change! Independent laboratories continue to research cold fusion and attempt to replicate the results because it's just too valuable to ignore if there's any truth in it. There's not a government in the world that wouldn't want to get its hands on a free energy device such as the one you're describing, one that could be assembled on a desktop, to power the world, but they wouldn't hide it. Hell, they be the first to package and then sell it, to slap a label on the box and ship it out to billions of people. You're living in the past, Stanley, in a dream world of conspiracies that simply don't exist. If your device was so amazing, why the hell did you waste your time powering some backwater in Missouri? Why not build a couple of hundred of the damned things and ship them out to friends across the country and get the ball rolling? Why didn't you send one to me to test out for you?'

'I didn't have time,' Stanley lamented. 'We shouldn't have disconnected from the National Grid, I know that now. I fully intended to build more of them, to create a wave of the devices that would not be stopped by any government, but they were on to me before I was able to do so.'

'Isn't that always the way?' Hans lamented. 'Somebody supposedly invents something amazing, and then they do something stupid and it mysteriously disappears into thin air.'

'The big corporations are intent on shutting me down!' Stanley yelled. 'They'd be insane not to!'

'That's crap!' Hans snapped back. 'They're as interested as anybody in developing alternatives. The electric car maker Tesla in America is about to commercialize batteries that store solar energy as back–ups for consumers during blackouts. They're rechargeable lithium–ion units, designed to be paired up with solar panel energy supplies. General Electric and LG Cherm in South Korea are also now in on the emerging energy–storage market. Even the environmentalist groups have started singing the praises of these companies for what they're doing. The whole thing is a move away from fossil fuels and away from government controlled energy supplies. You really think that would be happening if there was some shadowy corporation hell–bent on keeping us slaved to their whims?'

'Battery storage isn't quite the same as free energy,' Stanley snapped. 'You're talking about products that will take years to filter into use, that require major investments! I'm talking about a device that people can install for themselves, overnight, and never need buy a battery again!'

'Pah!' Hans scoffed. 'You're living in a dreamworld.'

'They've shot at us,' Amber defended her father. 'We've been chased across the Middle East by people who want this to remain silent. There *is* a conspiracy, not perhaps by the government but certainly by people who don't want to see their livelihoods and their earnings threatened by something like the fusion cage.'

'Help us,' Stanley begged his friend. 'This could be the beginning of a revolution that will make your ITER facility look like a farce. What we have to do is be stronger than those who seek to protect their money rather than our planet, and give it away, to everybody, for nothing.'

Hans stared at Stanley in disbelief for a long moment. 'You're going to give it away?'

'To everybody,' Stanley acknowledged. 'To every man, woman and child on the planet, to every single person who needs it the most, and deny the profits to anybody who puts greed before altruism. This is the future, Hans. Be a part of it, go public and support me.'

Hans stared at them for a long moment and then he shook his head.

'I have a family,' he uttered. 'I have a career, a life, a future. Do you really think I'm going to jeopardise that for your pipedream? My career would be over the moment I announced any such thing. I may as well go out there and say that climate change is a fallacy, that we never landed on the moon and that the Earth is actually flat after all.'

Stanley's hands clapped against his forehead in exasperation.

'You're walking away from the future of mankind,' he gasped. 'You've lost your humanity.'

Hance backed away further from the group and shook his head as he turned to leave.

'No, Stanley. You've lost your mind. Now get out of here, before I'm forced to call security and have you removed from the premises.'

Hans turned his back on them and hurried away as though afraid to be seen anywhere near them.

Lopez turned to Ethan. 'We need to get out of here and back to America. If he fears for his career as much as he appears to, he may be the first person to pick up the phone to somebody we don't want to meet.'

Ethan nodded and looked at Stanley.

'Is there anywhere we can go? Do you know of anybody who might be willing to let us hold out for a while and figure out a new play?'

Stanley nodded slowly, his shoulders sagging in despair as he watched his friend walking hurriedly away. 'There's only one person I can think of who might listen to us, but it's a long shot.'

'Where are they?' Lopez asked.

'Virginia.'

***

XXVI

DIAC Building,

Washington DC

Doug Jarvis drove back into the parking lot at the DIAC just over an hour after he'd left the Pentagon, his mind still buzzing with paranoia and fear over what had transpired since he had left the center of the United States military command structure.

A source in Dubai had informed him that at dawn, local time, a small unit of unidentified agents had stormed the maritime vessel Huron at its dock in Abu Dhabi. In the wake of their presence, the ship's captain had become the victim of a tragic accident, crushed beyond recognition beneath a seventeen ton shipping container. The local DIA agent, a man named Willis with whom Jarvis had spoken only the previous day, had been relieved of his post after suffering what was believed to be a nervous breakdown and was already being repatriated to the US for debrief and counselling. All that Jarvis had been able to glean was that whatever had happened, Willis had witnessed it first–hand and wasn't talking to anybody about it.

Jarvis parked his car and hurried into the building, then took an elevator up to the fourth floor, hoping against hope that his team had managed to provide Ethan and Nicola with an exit out of Abu Dhabi. He walked into his office and was met with a toothy grin.

'We did it,' Hellerman said.

Hellerman was a short, slightly built man with a thick beard and a youthful expression. Barely out of his teens, he had served the DIA for six years and been on Jarvis's team under General Mitchell before transferring to the DIAC.

Jarvis felt a wave of relief flush through his body. 'Tell me, everything.'

'Your guy Warner knows how to smell a rat, just like you,' Hellerman said with what sounded almost like a fatherly pride. 'He must have booked a commercial flight out of Abu Dhabi before leaving Damman. They were airborne even before the raid on Huron.'

'Where did they go?' Jarvis asked.

'Charles De Gaulle airport in Paris, France,' Hellerman replied. 'I managed to track their fake documents but the trail goes cold there. My only guess as to why they're in France is to do with Stanley Meyer. France is home to ITER, a nuclear fusion project – he may have allies there.'

'Makes sense,' Jarvis agreed. 'There's no other reason to go there unless Ethan wanted to be off that plane in case MJ–12 tracked him just like you have.'

'It's only a matter of time,' Hellerman pointed out. 'There are only so many flights out of Abu Dhabi each day, and those documents they were supplied with will only hold up so long. Once they're identified as having travelled to Paris, MJ–12 will be able to pick up the trail right there and then, and they'll likely be able to draw in assets on the ground that we cannot.' 'Can we get anybody to them from here?' Jarvis asked.

'You mean like friends of mine who live in Lyon?' Hellerman replied with a grin. 'Who I called, and who might have been able to find them and pass word from us?'

Jarvis's jaw dropped open. 'You've found them?'

'They're on a private jet out of Lyon–Saint–Exupery airport,' Hellerman chortled in delight. 'The flight plan's filed and they'll land in Virginia about three o'clock local time.'

'Was the flight chartered?'

'Private,' Hellerman reported proudly, 'using a payment chain that will take the feds days to follow up. If they're looking for a digital trail, they won't find it. All they can do is figure that Ethan and his companions will arrive in the USA on a flight from somewhere in France, and that's a lot of flights to check through.'

'Don't think that they won't do it,' Jarvis cautioned. 'They'll put agents at all civilian fields on the east coast within range of that aircraft. We need to be there to spirit them away from any FBI intercept. What about Huck Seavers?'

'Heading back from Saudi Arabia,' Hellerman replied. 'His crew filed a flight plan direct to Cincinnati. They'll land somewhere behind our privately hired jet.'

'What about the Saudis?'

The technician's jubilant expression faltered slightly.

'We've been monitoring the channels and it's not looking good. The story of a militant attack on Saudi helicopters appears to have been accepted at face value by the media, but behind the scenes the Saudis are screaming for blood. All they care about is that their Apache was downed by a couple of American fugitives and they're piling pressure on the administration to hand over those responsible.'

Jarvis winced. The events in the Kingdom had played directly into the Bureau's hands, giving them every reason they needed to hunt Ethan down.

'We need to figure out a way for them to disappear once they land in Virginia,' Jarvis said.

'Not much we can do for them,' Hellerman said. 'The jet's flight plan is for Charlottesville. I guess we could change it at the last minute, but that might in itself raise a flag if the feds are watching incoming air traffic from Europe.'

Jarvis's mind began racing. 'Where's the nearest air–intercept unit based?'

'Langley Field,' Hellerman replied. 'F22 Raptors.'

Jarvis thought long and hard. 'They won't shoot them down if they identify the jet, but they might be able to escort it forcefully to Langley Field and search the plane. Charlottesville is a customs airport – as soon as they land they'll be picked up.'

Hellerman said nothing as Jarvis thought long and hard about what he knew. His reveal to the Joint Chiefs of Staff of Ethan's plans to escape Saudi Arabia had resulted in a storming of that very same vessel within a few hours. That the leak could only have come from the JCOS meeting was obvious, and that it resulted in the raid by unknown agents suggested assets of MJ–12. Jarvis could only assume that FBI Director LeMay was behind the leak, but he could be wrong.

Intelligence was a game of chance, and only those willing to bet the farm made big gains. He knew that he would be for the chop as soon as LeMay figured out what Jarvis had in mind, but Jarvis reminded himself that he wasn't the one leaking intelligence to private organisations presumably in return for professional or financial favours.

'I've got an idea,' Jarvis said finally and pulled out his cell phone. 'I need you to remain here and if Ethan calls, you give him whatever support he needs, okay?'

'Where are you going?' Hellerman asked.

Jarvis did not answer as he left the office.

*

Charlottesville, Virginia

'Our target is a Caucasian male, late thirties, six feet tall and in the company of a Latino woman, another Caucasian male and a teenage girl. The target is considered dangerous and should not be approached without the presence of back–up.'

Special Agent in Charge Valery Jenkins was a formidable woman, almost six feet tall and with dark hair tied in a severe bun behind her head, streaked with fine lines of silver that only seemed to make her look more stern. Special Agent Hannah Ford watched as Jenkins gave her brief in an abandoned lot to the south of the airport, the entire operation one of the swiftest Hannah had ever witnessed.

Photographs of the fugitives were handed out to each of the twelve agents present, all of them wearing their distinctive FBI jackets and bullet–proof vests. Hannah looked down at the image of Ethan Warner and his accomplices and briefly scanned the biographies attached to them.

'Who's the kid?' somebody asked.

'Amber Ryan, seventeen,' Jenkins replied. 'According to reports, she has been abducted by Warner and Lopez.'

Hannah frowned. The brief said that Ryan had vanished from somewhere in Missouri but now the fugitives, having fled to the Middle East, were apparently on their way back to the USA.

'What's the evidence that this is an abduction case?' she asked.

Jenkins directed a cold glare in her direction.

'What, you mean apart from two adults scurrying around the world with a missing teenager?'

A ripple of chuckles floated across the gathered agents and Hannah felt color rising in her cheeks. She swallowed her embarrassment down, hoping that her voice wasn't trembling. 'They abduct her, flee to Saudi Arabia, then they come back again? Doesn't make sense if they want to remain undetected – they were already clear and away. And how did we catch this case when nobody has reported the girl missing?'

Jenkins smiled without warmth.

'If you pay attention to catching them instead of asking questions that nobody can answer yet, then I'll guess we'll find out.' Jenkins looked at the rest of the team. 'We don't know what these folks are up to, but orders are they're fugitives from the law and it's our task to apprehend them and bring them to justice. We have agents at fifteen civilian fields

174

on the east coast, that's how important this case is, and Charlottesville is considered their most likely point of entry. Focus on finding them, understood?'

A chorus of *yes ma'am* followed and then the FBI team split into groups and headed for their vehicles.

'Good call.'

The voice of Hannah's partner, Mickey Vaughn, served to calm Hannah's beating heart as they climbed into the pool car they'd been assigned. Mickey was a stocky, blond junior agent not long out of Quantico and assigned to Hannah. Hannah was a ten year veteran of the bureau and had already been disciplined twice for aggression in the field and an unlawful discharge of her weapon that had brought some disrepute to her field office and the wrath of Valery Jenkins.

'The White Witch didn't seem to think so.'

Vaughn's eyes widened. 'Your mic's on!'

Hannah panicked and looked down, then slapped Mickey across the shoulder as she saw him chuckling to himself.

'She's been gunning for me ever since we iced Sylvester Ruslo down in Auburn Hills.'

'He was a damned child molester, he got what he deserved,' Mickey said as they drove out of the lot, following the rest of the team.

'Civil rights didn't agree,' Hannah uttered in disgust. 'Jenkins has had it in for me ever since.'

'Jenkins is an asshole,' Mickey pointed out. 'She missed out on Langley because of her divorce and now she sees herself being stuck down here as some kind of punishment. She's venting on you – don't give her the satisfaction.'

Hannah sighed and saw her reflection in the mirror, auburn hair flowing in the wind from the open window, pale skin across a slightly too–wide jaw and freckles populating her cheeks. Vivid blue eyes stared back at her, angry and afraid all at once.

'When's the jet due to land?'

Hannah looked at her notes. 'Fifteen minutes. You read this guy's rap sheet?'

'A few arrests from years back, former Marine Corps right?'

'Iraq and Afghanistan,' Hannah confirmed. 'Supposedly has done some work for the government recently, runs a bail bondsmen business out of River Forest, Chicago with this Lopez woman. She's an ex–DC cop. Nothing fits an abduction case.'

'Sometimes even the good guys go bad,' Mickey pointed out. 'Don't start personalizing them. Jenkins was right, we need to get them into custody and then we can figure this all out.'

The cars swept into Charlottesville–Albermarle airport as Jenkin's voice warbled over the intercom.

'I want agents in the terminal and at all airport exits. Be ready to apprehend the suspects at all costs. As soon as the aircraft comes to a rest at the terminal, we move in.'

Hannah did not respond to the call as she surveyed the airport. A large terminal faced out onto a long runway orientated 03–21, with aircraft landing on the 21 runway according to the orange windsock she could see gusting in the light breeze far out across the field.

'Take us to the southern–most point you can find,' she instructed Mickey. 'I want to keep an eye on that plane from the moment it touches down.'

'Roger that,' Mickey replied as he turned into an airport parking lot.

Hannah reached down and checked her service firearm one more time before they deployed from the vehicle.

*

Ethan looked out of the jet's windows as it turned onto final approach to land, the aircraft wallowing and rocking on the wind currents as it extended undercarriage and flaps.

'You think there's anybody waiting for us?' Lopez asked.

Ethan nodded slowly, trying to get a better view ahead as he pressed his face to the window.

'It's what I'd do,' he replied. 'There can't be many trans–Atlantic flights coming into this field from France. We can't just walk off the jet and through the terminal or customs will spot us – we'll have to figure something out.'

The rolling hills below basked in the sunshine as the jet flew gracefully over fields and forests and then Ethan spotted the airfield perimeter and the parking lots filled with assorted vehicles flashing as their windows caught the sunlight.

'What's the plan then?' Stanley asked. 'We can't just jump out.'

Ethan thought for a moment, and then pushed away from the window as he finished surveying the rest of the airport. He looked at the jet's interior, the exit hatches and the general shape of the aircraft, and he sighed and shrugged.

'We can't do anything,' he said finally. 'We'd better get ready.'

*

Hannah Ford watched as the impressive, sleek white jet landed on the runway and rocketed past them. She heard the engines whine into reverse thrust and the aircraft braked as it rolled toward the end of the runway, almost a mile away. Hannah shielded her eyes against the bright sunlight and squinted as the aircraft slowed to a stop at the end of the runway, heat haze rippling and obscuring the jet as it turned slowly and began taxiing toward the parking area in front of the main terminal.

'That's them,' Mickey confirmed. 'The tail code matches the FBI alert notice.'

Valery Jenkin's voice blared over the radio. 'All units, go now!'

Mickey accelerated their car and Hannah watched as half a dozen vehicles all emerged from within parking lots or from behind hangars and converged on the jet as it reached the main terminal and rolled to a halt. The engines were still whining as Hannah jumped out of her vehicle and ran toward the aircraft, the engines mercifully shutting down as she reached the entrance hatch just as a female attendant lowered it and then stared at Hannah in shock.

'Freeze, FBI!'

The attendant threw her hands in the air in surprise and backed up into the aircraft as Hannah advanced up the steps and inside. Mickey followed her, and together they turned and looked down the jet's plush interior.

Two men, one woman and one young girl stared back at them in horror.

Hannah lowered her pistol as she looked at their faces and in an instant she knew.

'It's not them,' Mickey said.

Ten more agents piled into the aircraft, followed by Valery Jenkins, who stared at the unfamiliar faces sitting in the aircraft's leather seats.

'What the hell is going on here?!' asked the older of the two men as he got out of his seat. 'This is a *private* aircraft!'

Hannah pushed past Mickey and the other agents and approached the cockpit. There, two pilots, one male and one female, stared in surprise at her.

'Is there a problem?' the captain asked in amazement.

Hannah slid her pistol into its holster. 'Yeah, there's a problem.'

*

'It's not going to take them long to figure out what happened to us.'

Ethan sat in an SUV, a fresh cell phone in his hand as Lopez drove.

'It's enough of a diversion to give you time to get out of sight,' Jarvis replied. *'I dropped the leak to the FBI but it won't take long for LeMay to figure that out. Once they solve what happened to you, I won't be unable to offer any further assistance. One DIA leak could be ignored, but not two.'*

'I know.'

The SUV pulled out of Yeager International Airport in West Virginia as Lopez aimed south, Stanley Meyer and Amber Ryan in the rear seats behind them. The airport was shared with the Charleston Air National Guard's 130th Airlift Wing, a connection that had enabled Jarvis to arrange the false lead and then divert their aircraft to West Virginia.

'The feds are all over this,' Jarvis informed him. *'MJ–12 have players within the bureau, so they'll know by now they've been duped. Whatever you're thinking of doing next, do it fast. They know you're on US soil and they'll be using every resource at their disposal to track you down. I have a reliable contact here at the DIAC named Hellerman. You can call this number if you need to move long distance, but that's it for me. Go dark as of now, and good luck.'*

'Understood.'

The line went silent and Ethan switched the cell off, ensuring that it could not be tracked until he next was forced to use it. Now, they were all in Stanley's hands as he searched for his mysterious contact in Virginia.

***

XXVII

Nathalie, Virginia

'This isn't going to work.'

The sun was already low in the sky, bleeding molten metal across the horizon behind Virginia's rolling hills. The clatter of a freight train passing somewhere far to the south faded into the distance, only the sound of birds in the trees accompanying them as they walked along a dirt track half a mile to the north of the main road.

'We can't take the car up here,' Ethan replied to Amber as they walked. 'And it's only a matter of time before Majestic Twelve track our movements.'

'We have to stay off the grid,' Stanley agreed. 'Any time spent in major conurbations could result in our arrest, or more likely our being shot on sight.'

'This isn't our first rodeo, Amber,' Lopez added as they walked. 'Ethan and I once remained off the grid for six months, completely undetected even by the CIA who were hunting us at the time.'

Amber shot Lopez a concerned glance. 'You never mentioned that! What did the CIA want with you two?'

'It's a long story,' Ethan said by way of an explanation. 'Let's just say we're used to staying out of the way of government agencies. What I want to know is why here? We're not that far from Washington DC as the crow flies.'

'Keep your friends close,' Stanley smiled in the fading light as they walked. 'There's a community out here somewhere and we need to find them. They may be able to help us.'

Ethan looked to his left, where amid the dense trees he could see a few distant lights where the tiny town of Nathalie was nestled in the forests.

'Doesn't look like a very large town,' he pointed out as they walked. 'You really think that somebody there that can help us?'

'There is nobody in Nathalie who can help,' Stanley said. 'The kind of people we need don't live in houses.'

'What the hell are you talking about?' Amber asked.

'The only allies left that we can trust are those who don't trust the government themselves, who have already chosen to live off the grid and away from electrical supplies and the constant surveillance that goes with it.'

Lopez cast a concerned glance at Ethan. 'I don't like where he's going with this.'

'Nonetheless, I think I know what he's got in mind,' Ethan replied as he looked at Stanley. 'Preppers?'

'Preppers,' Stanley confirmed as they walked, the dusty track becoming ever more vague as it wound its way into the darkening wilderness. 'Some of them have become quite sophisticated over the years and are able to support themselves on private ranches without any outside intervention. In all fairness to them, our government does not restrict such activity and has not in any way attempted to interfere with the communities that have been formed, however they also don't advertise or advocate other people to do so. I think that Washington is more than aware that any completely self–sustaining community outside of their control represents a dangerous threat to the balance of power across the country.'

Lopez frowned. 'That doesn't really make any sense. The Amish have been living in that way for centuries and won't allow any electrical goods into their communities. It hasn't resulted in the rest of the entire American population building barns and buying horses has it?'

'No,' Stanley agreed. 'But that's only because the vast majority of people like their creature comforts and don't have any desire to live with Civil War era technology. But give them the ability to have all of their electrical devices fully functional, and yet still be without dependence on the government and you've got a whole different ballgame. No administration wants to see that happen on their watch, they're just too afraid of the consequences of relinquishing too much control to the populace, no matter what you hear the Republicans yelling in Congress.'

The track finally vanished at the edge of a long abandoned field that was overrun with tall, swaying grasses glowing in the low sunlight.

'End of the line,' Amber said as she observed the field.

'Only if you don't know what you're looking for,' Ethan replied as he surveyed the terrain ahead.

'Since when did you become the great white hunter?' Amber asked.

Ethan did not reply as he looked through the various copses of trees and saw what he was looking for probably half a mile in the distance.

'It's that way,' he pointed.

Lopez frowned as she looked at the distant valleys and hills. 'What, our doom in the wilderness?'

'The prepper community,' Stanley said as he followed Ethan across the overgrown field.

Ethan smiled as Lopez rolled her eyes and followed them, and decided to put her out of her misery.

'Any decent size community requires crops if they're completely self–sufficient,' Ethan said. 'These fields are all long overgrown and abandoned, but those near that hillside look like they've been tended recently and possibly ploughed. It's a good bet that the community's somewhere over there, possibly concealed within the trees.'

'Top marks, Mr Warner,' Stanley said. 'Hopefully we'll be able to stay with them for long enough to come up with an alternative plan of action. Right now, I feel as though I have half the country's armed forces chasing after me.'

'Frankly, you probably do,' Lopez said unhelpfully. 'But hey, we'll be safe out here living in mud huts with a bunch of tree–huggers.'

'Would you rather be in DC?' Stanley demanded.

'I'd rather be in a hotel in some out of the way place, with a beer and some potato chips,' Lopez replied. 'I don't get why we have to be all Cody Lundin about this.'

Ethan ignored Lopez's grumbling as he led the way through a dense copse of trees that separated the abandoned fields from the ploughed ones he'd seen from the track. The trees virtually blotted out the darkening sky above, already speckled with a thousand tiny stars that flickered like beacons as he walked carefully in the darkness.

'I can't see a damned thing,' Amber muttered miserably, then cursed as her foot smacked into a gnarled tree root.

Ethan was about to answer when he froze mid–stride on the track, the hairs on his neck tingling as he stared into the darkness.

'What is it?' Lopez asked, whispering as she almost clairvoyantly sensed the sudden tension in Ethan.

Ethan saw her raise her chin slightly as she detected the same threat as he had done. The odour on the air was faint, just enough to stand out from the pristine scent of the forest itself, as the breeze carried a waft of tobacco and old fabric past them.

Ethan knew that the source of the odour could not be more than a few yards away to have carried so easily on the almost still air, and even before he could say anything he saw a figure step out onto the track before them, a shadow against the shadows, and heard the sound of a shotgun being cocked, pump action.

'Don't move.'

The voice was threatening, and Ethan realized that they had technically trespassed on private land.

'We already stopped,' Ethan managed to quip, hoping to defuse any confrontation quickly. 'We were looking for somebody.'

'Who?'

Ethan could not make out the individual's appearance in the gloom, but he was smart enough to be standing well out of reach of Ethan or any of his companions, and Ethan had the sense that he might be willing to open fire if he felt truly threatened.

Lopez's voice cut through the silence.

'Somebody who can help us,' she said.

Smart move, make us sound like we're defenceless and on the run, which in fact they actually were, Ethan realized. It was Stanley who stepped forward, his hands in the air.

'I'm looking for Jesse McVey,' he said. 'Is he still living out here?'

The figure turned slightly to look at Stanley and Ethan heard the man dig around in his jacket for a moment.

'Who's askin'?'

'Stanley Meyer, I'm here to see if Jesse might be willing to … '

A brilliant light blazed into their eyes and Ethan squinted and turned his head away in an attempt to protect his night vision, but already all he could see was a blurry orb of light seared onto his retina.

'Jesus, will you cut it out?!' Lopez snapped. 'We're unarmed, okay?!'

Ethan squinted past the bright light as the man stared at Stanley for a long beat and then lowered the flashlight.

'*The* Stanley Meyer?' he asked in apparent amazement. 'The steam car builder?!'

Stanley nodded, rubbing his eyes.

'I've moved on a bit from cars now,' he replied.

Ethan saw the shotgun turned aside and made safe as the man strode forward, a broad grin on his features, his hair a brilliant red that sparkled in the flashlight's glow, a thin beard adorning his jaw.

'I'll be damned,' he gasped. 'It is you.'

'You've got a fan club?' Lopez asked Stanley.

'You bet your last damned dollar he has,' the man replied, extending one hand and shaking Stanley's so vigorously Ethan thought he might yank it from its socket. 'This guy virtually revolutionized car travel, until the government stepped in and banned his inventions.'

'They didn't ban them, exactly,' Stanley said. 'They claimed the boilers in the cars were unsafe.'

'Unsafe my ass!' the man boomed. 'I've been driving a Lincoln with one of your boilers in it for the last ten years! It's never gone wrong, not once!'

'Who are you?' Amber asked, bemused.

'My name is Jesse McVey,' he replied in delight. 'And you are all welcome here. Follow me, it's this way.'

Jesse turned, and without checking that they were actually following him he set off into the now blackened forests.

*

DIAC Building, Washington DC

'Douglas Jarvis?'

The FBI agents arrived even before Jarvis had the chance to book out of the building and head for the parking lot. As he approached the security pen that protected the main building from the foyer beyond, guards at their posts alongside each check–point and scanner, so they flooded into the building and locked eyes with him immediately.

Jarvis considered retreating into the building once more, but he knew that it would be a pointless exercise. General Nellis would then have to become involved in allowing the FBI agents access to the building, further exposing his involvement in what Jarvis had been doing, just the kind of embarrassment he would be keen to avoid.

Jarvis had never been one for falling on his sword, but now there was nowhere left to run.

'It's okay Mike,' he said to the nearest security guard, who was looking at Jarvis in confusion. 'I'm coming through.'

'Is everything all right Mister Jarvis?' the guard asked as Jarvis eased his way through the checkpoint and removed his identity badge.

'Everything's fine,' Jarvis replied, and leaned close to Mike. 'Inform General Nellis that the FBI are here and they've taken me into custody. They're peeved at my breaking one of their cases, Nellis already knows about it.'

The guard nodded as Jarvis walked through the check point and moved to confront the FBI agents amassed before him. Jarvis counted at least ten men, all of them wearing stern expressions.

'My reputation must have become somewhat exaggerated,' he greeted them. 'Ten men, all to apprehend me? Do pass on my regards to Director LeMay.'

'Douglas Jarvis,' said the lead agent as he stepped up with a pair of handcuffs, 'you're under arrest for suspected treason. Anything you say may be taken in evidence and used against you at any trial or court martial you may be subjected to.'

Jarvis said nothing as he allowed the agent to cuff his hands behind his back.

***

XXVIII

Ethan followed the light of Jesse's flashlight through the dense forest, a thin strip of blue–white that illuminated the forest floor before them. Ethan walked alongside Lopez, Amber and Stanley behind them, with a handful of Jesse's faithful followers bringing up the rear guard. The quiet folk had materialized like phantoms from the darkness of the forest upon a commanding whistle from Jesse.

Without them, Ethan realized that he would have been utterly lost out here. They were so deep in the woods that there were no city lights visible, the glow from them on the clouds above shielded from view by the hills rising all around, themselves only visible because they blocked the light from the stars spanning the heavens. The only evidence of civilization out here was the occasional blinking lights of an aircraft as it passed high overhead, the sound of their engines barely audible.

'You remember Idaho?' he asked Lopez.

'I'm trying not to.'

He and Lopez had spent many nights camping out in the mountain wilderness of Idaho on another investigation for the DIA some years before, and then a few nights more fleeing something not quite human out in the deep woods. Now, he too found it difficult to think about anything else as he followed the faint light ahead of him.

To his surprise, Jesse finally stopped in a pitch black spot deep in the forest and turned, his features ghoulishly lit by the glow of his flashlight as he spoke softly in the darkness.

'We're here.'

Ethan blinked, keeping his eyes off the flashlight beam as he looked about and saw nothing but ranks of dense trees, low grassy mounds and thick foliage all around them.

'It could use some work,' he observed dryly.

'On the contrary,' Jesse replied cheerfully, 'it's complete in every way.'

Jesse let out a low whistle that echoed into the darkness. A long silence followed, and Ethan wondered whether the hippy had completely lost his mind as they stood in the darkness and waited.

Then, to Ethan's amazement, a glowing rectangle of light appeared to his right in the front of one of the mounds and a woman stepped out. Then another, and then more rectangles of light appeared as people began emerging from the earthy mounds dotted around the site.

'Welcome to Earthville,' Jesse announced grandly as he spread his arms to encompass the entire camp.

The glow from the interiors illuminated perhaps twenty low mounds, each of them covered in grass and completely hidden, at least at night, from observation. Ethan was startled to see heat emanating from within the mounds as Jesse led them to a slightly larger one in the centre and reached down in the grass. Ethan heard Jesse pull hard on what sounded like a metal handle, and the grass and earth opened before him to reveal another well–lit interior as Jesse stepped inside.

'Come on, quickly, we don't want to let the heat out.'

Ethan followed Jesse inside and the hippy hauled the door shut behind them and let them get a look at the interior.

The mound was merely the top of a home deeply excavated into the earth beneath the forest. Open plan in nature, and with an entirely wooden construction, the home resembled a large apartment that had no windows. Polished wooden floors, plush sofas, even a television and modern oven were installed, along with lighting that gave off an interesting glow, more like sunlight than the unnatural flare of a halogen bulb.

'Welcome to my home,' Jesse said. 'Please, make yourselves comfortable. Drink, anyone?'

Jesse strolled across to a fridge–freezer and opened it to reveal plentiful stocks of food and drink.

'What is this place?' Lopez uttered in amazement, a genuine smile on her face.

'My home,' Jesse repeated. 'I built it nearly ten years ago, although it wasn't quite as plush back then. But I've added refinements as I've gone along and now all of the homes here look more or less similar. They take a lot of man–hours to construct, but once done they're for life.'

Jesse poured fresh orange juice from cartons into glasses and shared them around.

'You still need the supermarket then,' Amber observed with interest.

Jesse laughed. 'No matter how much I achieve, always people seek to pick holes in it. Yes, I still use a supermarket – why wouldn't I when good food is so plentiful in them? And I still have a job in the hardware store in town, although I mountain bike to and from work. It's only if society collapsed that I'd have to fall back on hunting and gathering to subsist.'

'Where's the power coming from?' Stanley asked as he glanced at the lights.

'Oil generators,' Jesse replied, 'or gas–powered spares in emergencies. They're used just for the normal appliances, although we like to cook outdoors using barbeques as much as possible in the community and we grow what food we can ourselves. Because these homes are built mostly underground they have natural insulation, on the top as well as to either side. We have heaters but we rarely need them either in winter or summer because the homes maintain a natural temperature of about sixty degrees Fahrenheit. I'm hoping to install solar panels too somewhere nearby and channel the supply to these homes, but that's a big step and quite expensive. We're working on the logistics right now.'

Jesse sat down on a sofa as he sipped orange juice.

'So you're off the grid completely?' Ethan asked, starting to develop a grudging respect for the strange man before him.

'For ten years now,' Jesse confirmed. 'You'd be amazed how much money that saves. I was lucky, my father owned this land so I inherited it from him when he passed away and could do what I liked with it. I'd always dreamed of trying something like this and when I achieved it and people, friends and such like saw what I was doing, they wanted to join in too. In all there are nine homes here, all of them built by our hands, all of them independent of energy supplies but for the essentials that we all like. We also have hot water storage tanks installed, use old car tires cut up for extra wall insulation and such like to improve our living conditions. The heating is piped under the floors for maximum efficiency when we need it.'

'What about light?' Lopez asked. 'Isn't it always dark down here?'

'Not at all,' Jesse said and gestured to the corners of the walls where they met the ceiling. 'There are strips of transparent plastic on the surface above the home that allow sunlight into shafts along the edges of the walls. A mirror deflects that sunlight into the home, providing natural light during daylight hours. It's not as bright as a full window, but because we're in a forest it's further diluted, but it does the job as long as we clean the upper panels daily. We also use natural light LEDs for night time, which have a more natural glow. That's the blue light you see reflected off the walls.'

'And you can do everything else down here without any trouble at all?' Amber asked.

'Everything,' Jesse confirmed. 'We have composting toilets, rainwater collection devices, pretty much all that you need to survive. The one thing that we've made the most effort to preserve when we all came out here is human contact. You might be surprised to learn that there are many communities like this all across the United States, and all across Europe for that matter. Disconnecting from the grid and living a simpler life, but one which does not deprive people of the creature comforts of modern society, is a surprisingly popular pastime. But for most a pastime is exactly what it is, people moving into and out of such communes as their own requirements dictate. New jobs take them away too but most of all it's just a need for human contact because for some reason most off–grid communities are built way out in the middle of nowhere – you know, like Washington state nowhere, far from urban centres. I built our commune here because I wanted to stay reasonably close to major towns. Frankly, I like being able to go and rent a DVD or buy a pint of milk whenever I want to, rather than having to trek fifty miles just to find a loaf of bread.'

'You said you had a job,' Stanley said. 'How come the government hasn't penalised you for avoiding taxes?'

'Because I pay them,' Jesse replied. 'I don't earn much from my job and it could hardly be called a career move, but what I do more than covers the cost of my food, travel and holidays should I want to take them. We actually live pretty normal lives here and we don't need to earn a fortune in order to do so. I don't have to pay rent, I don't have a mortgage and thanks to Stanley here, my car costs almost nothing to run because it uses water for fuel. One of the guys living here is actually a lawyer in St Louis and pulls down a pretty respectable salary, which he uses to travel on his holidays rather than paying a mortgage on some enormous house that he doesn't even need.'

Ethan looked about them and realised that were it not for the knowledge they were sitting ten feet underground, he wouldn't really have known any different. The interior of the house looked pretty much as any home would except for the unusually open plan nature and slightly smaller size.

'And you're not worried about something coming through here and destroying everything?' Lopez asked.

'I suppose,' Jesse answered, 'but there's not much to go wrong really. Forest fires are easily the greatest threat because of the damage they obviously cause, and if one of the big trees decided to come down it could cause a great deal of damage to any one of the homes, although it's unlikely it would be unrepairable as they're constructed from wood anyway. For me the greatest problem is the local state council deciding that such properties are illegal, which isn't unheard of. They don't like people having such complete independence. It seems that being a part of the grid, and I don't mean just the National Grid but our interconnected digital society, means that they can keep an eye on everybody. Out here, short of my taxes, they don't really know what I'm up to.'

'Exactly as I've been saying,' Stanley confirmed. 'These things aren't always about money. If Jesse here became successful enough from what he did, and others began emulating him as swiftly as possible, you could start a wave that would see thousands if not millions of families breaking away from the structure of normal society and becoming fully independent but for their food and emergency fuel supplies.'

'That's right,' Jesse agreed. 'The main opposition to communes like this is health and safety, especially for children who may not have been able to make the decision for themselves to come here, but it's usually a veil for more base motives such as collectible taxes, profits for fuel companies and such like. They all earn their revenue from people's dependence on the energy grid – take that away in big enough numbers and they'll start to fight for their right to charge us for the right to be warm. To me, it's like bottled water – nobody needs it because we have water coming out of our taps, or in our case here out of the sky, but still millions of people will go and buy bottled water just because they can. It's insane, but it happens every day.'

Jesse looked at them all for a moment and then set his glass down. 'I digress, as I often do. You said that you were looking for me. Why?'

Stanley leaned forward in his seat. 'How would you like to be able to get rid of your generators and yet still have more power than you will ever need for free?'

Jesse raised an eyebrow.

'You'd be amazed how many people come by here saying things like that,' he replied. 'I did my physics at high school, and I know that such things require either large wind turbines or major solar arrays to generate enough energy. Regrettably, the amount of land I own is not large enough to install either.'

'You won't need any more space than a boiler cupboard,' Stanley said. 'If you can get me the required components, I'll build the damned thing right here. All you have to promise to do is build another one just like it and pass it on to another community like yours, with the promise that they will do the same.'

Jesse stared at Stanley for a long moment, apparently stunned into silence. Something about Stanley's confidence and enthusiasm for his work compelled people to believe, so much so that even Ethan found himself hoping that he would be able to see the completed device in action soon.

'Why would you do that, and how would you do it?'

It took Stanley no more than about ten minutes to give a brief explanation of what he intended to do. As the old inventor described what had happened, how he had achieved what he had and of how the government was attempting to prevent it from becoming commercialized, so Jesse leaned further forward in his seat until he looked as though he were about to fall forwards out of it.

'How long?' he asked finally, 'to build one of these fusion cages?'

'Once I've got the pieces, about three days plus a few extra days of testing to make sure it's stable and performing as it should,' Stanley replied. 'A week, and you'll never have to worry about energy ever again.'

Jesse stared at Ethan, his features alive with excitement and hope.

'Do it,' he said, 'and if it works, I'll build enough of the damned things with you to power half of the country.'

Stanley reached out for Jesse and the younger man shook his hand firmly.

'Let's change the world, for the better,' Stanley said.

Ethan felt a surge of hope flicker into life like a pale flame within him as he realized that he might be witnessing a meeting that would herald the beginning of a new dawn for humanity, felt those high hopes thumping in his chest alongside his heart.

Lopez snapped him from his reverie.

'You hear that?'

Ethan blinked and realized that the thumping in his chest was not his heartbeat but a building crescendo of helicopter blades battering the night air outside.

Jesse leaped out of his seat even as a voice from outside cried out for help. His eyes raged as he glared at Ethan.

'Who have you brought here?! What is this?'

'They're onto us,' Lopez said urgently. 'How could they have found us out here?'

'Damn it, it doesn't matter,' Ethan snapped. 'Nicola, grab the shotgun. We're leaving!'

***

XXIX

'Move, now!'

Ethan bolted for the door of the home as the sound of helicopter blades thundered overhead. He hurled open the door and stepped out into the forest to see the trees billowing in the downdraft from half a dozen Sikorsky UH–60 *Black Hawk* helicopters that were hovering above the trees, one of them sufficiently close to the open door for the glow from the home's interior to faintly illuminate its cockpit and nose.

'Get out of the house!' Ethan yelled.

Lopez rushed out with Stanley and Amber close behind as Jesse sprinted out and shouted at Ethan.

'Why did you bring them here?!' he demanded, the wind from the rotor's downwash blustering through the commune. 'What have you done?!'

'We didn't bring them!' Ethan shouted back. 'You have to run, now!'

'I'm not leaving my home!'

Jesse dashed into the centre of the commune, spread his arms wide and shouted up at the helicopters.

'This is my home! You have no right to be here!'

The side doors of the helicopters suddenly slid open and Ethan saw rappel lines spill out in the faint light from the other homes as residents opened their doors as they sought to see what was going on outside.

'Get out of here!' Ethan shouted at them. 'Run!'

Jesse shouted out to his people. 'Stay where you are! You have nothing to fear! We have done nothing wrong!'

Lopez dashed to Ethan's side, Stanley alongside her with Amber. 'We need to go, now!'

Ethan nodded and gestured to the north.

'Get deeper into the forest, it's the only chance we have.'

Ethan ran toward Jesse as Lopez, Stanley and Amber fled.

'Get out of there!' he yelled at Jesse.

The commune leader shook his head, his arms still spread wide as he stared up at the helicopters, smiling now.

'They're our soldiers,' he shouted back. 'We have nothing to fear from them!'

Ethan slid to a halt behind a large cedar tree as he shouted back even as soldiers appeared on the rappel lines and began descending toward the forest floor.

'They're not our soldiers, Jesse!' he shouted. 'Run, now!'

Jesse looked at Ethan in confusion and then the first gunshots rang out.

Ethan saw Jesse take two rounds, a classic double–tap shot that zipped through his plexus and upper right chest. Jesse twitched once and then twice before his legs gave way beneath him and he slumped onto the forest floor amid a whirlwind of dislodged leaves and foliage.

Ethan looked up and saw brief flares of light as M–16 rifles opened up on the commune in a blaze of staccato flashes. Even before Jesse had hit the forest floor screams went up from the houses around him as the inhabitants dashed out and began fleeing into the darkened forests.

Ethan saw dozens of troops descending down the rappel lines toward the forest floor, firing indiscriminately into the darkened woods. He turned and ran across the compound, dashing left and right to spoil the aim of the soldiers, who would be concentrating on rappelling and getting onto solid ground before taking more careful aim at their targets.

Half a dozen deafening blasts and bright flares of light illuminated the forest around him as the attacking troops dropped *flash–bangs* to blind and disorientate their targets. Ethan could hear the screams of the commune's families as they sought to escape the assault, and he felt his desperate need to escape warring with his need to defend people who had no means of defending themselves. A cold dread enveloped him as he realized just how far Majestic Twelve were willing to go in order to capture and kill Stanley Meyer. The assassination of innocent civilians, however abhorrent to anybody else, was no obstacle to their goal.

Ethan threw himself into the cover of the forest, behind a broad trunked tree as he looked back into the compound. The helicopters were arrayed in a ring around it, the troops descending into the forest and then moving in toward the centre to prevent anybody from escaping. He sought to find Lopez, but he could see nothing in the darkness and he knew that he would not be able to locate her easily.

He looked up and saw a single Black Hawk helicopter blocking his path, hovering above the trees and with its rappel lines now empty. He knew that the soldiers would be equipped with the latest technology: night–vision goggles, infrared sensors and other gadgetry that would allow them to track their targets in complete darkness. For all he knew Ethan was probably already in clear view to the advancing soldiers, and even if he were not those from a different angle would be able to warn their comrades of his presence crouched alongside the trunk of the huge tree.

Ethan remained in position and ducked his head down to protect his vision against any more of the flash–bangs that might be tossed in his direction as he attempted to orientate himself to the camp. He recalled Jesse describing the diesel generators that were used by the camp to provide energy during particularly cold winter months, and he hunted around the forest floor for any sign of the power lines that must run to the houses. Most likely they would be buried, but there might be some kind of evidence of their passage. In the faint light of the compound he searched the forest, remaining perfectly still as he sought a likely route, the most sensible place for Jesse and his people to have built the generators.

Ethan spotted a narrow path between the trees that appeared unnaturally straight, as though the foliage had been cleared at some point and had not yet fully regrown. He peered into the darkness and saw a glint of reflected light, the kind of reflection that could only come from metal.

A noise to Ethan's left alerted him to the presence of the advancing soldiers and he turned just in time to see a flare of gunfire. A salvo of bullets smashed into the tree next to him and sprayed chips of bark and wood into his face as he fell away from the impacts and rolled across the forest floor. Ethan leaped to his feet and dashed across the path, sprinting down toward the metal object he had seen reflected in the firelight.

More gunshots pursued him immediately, his doom prevented only by his rapid motion and the dense trees around him that made a perfect shot almost impossible due to the nature of the night–vision goggles. Ethan knew from his own use of them in Afghanistan that they presented a flat image in only two dimensions that made it incredibly difficult to judge depth perception, meaning that any soldier using a rifle with them had to account for this change in perception, something very difficult to do against a moving target amid multiple obstacles.

Keep moving.

Ethan slid down into the foliage as he spotted ahead of him a rectangular metal wire cage, within which were two diesel generators that were currently switched off. The cage had a door which was sealed with a padlock. Ethan yanked at the lock but it was far too secure for him to break through. Instead, Ethan spotted the fuel lines that fed diesel from the tanks into the generator, which was then converted into electrical power and directed toward the homes.

Ethan pulled out a small knife from his satchel and managed to push the blade far enough through the wire fence to puncture one of the fuel lines. He levered the knife back and forth until the blade sliced through and the diesel fuel began to spill onto the forest floor beneath the tanks. Ethan tucked down behind the tanks and then began to retreat as fast as he could away from them. A second Black Hawk helicopter was to his left, still hovering and gusting hot air through the forest along with the smell of aviation fuel. Gunshots rang out as the soldiers closed in on the homes, completely encircling the compound.

Ethan reached into his pocket and pulled out a zippo lighter, one that he carried with him throughout the Gulf War. Ethan had never smoked, but in theatre one of the quickest ways to gain friends among the Iraqis was to offer cigarettes and to light them, breaking down social barriers with the people they were trying to protect as they sought information on whatever bad guys they may have been after at the time.

Ethan placed one hand on the ground and felt the tinder–dry leaves and twigs coating the forest floor beneath his touch. He gathered together a small pile of them, the gusting wind from the helicopter blades at his back as he crouched down over the kindling, shoved the zippo lighter deep into it and flicked the flint.

The makeshift kindling ignited immediately with a pale flame that quickly grew in intensity. Ethan leapt up as soon as the flames had taken hold and dashed to his right as another pair of gun shots cracked out and zipped through the space where he had been crouched moments before.

Ethan hurled himself behind another tree and then peeked around to see the flames from the small fire growing rapidly in the turbulent downdraught of the helicopter's blades as it blustered through the trees. The flames were already three feet high and spreading quickly to both the left and the right as they began marching toward the diesel generators. Ethan knew damned well that diesel was not flammable, but it did have a flashpoint and was combustible above a certain temperature. The flames were already crackling through the undergrowth and growing like some fearsome beast fed by the very power of the helicopter sent to kill them. The heat from the flames would also disguise his infrared signature and that of the fleeing civilians, rendering the soldier's night vision goggles and infra–red sensors useless at the same time.

Ethan heard further shouts of alarm, this time male voices, deeper than the shrieks of panic and terror from the inhabitants of the commune.

More gunshots crackled out, but this time they were not directed at Ethan and he heard returning fire from his left. Jesse's shotgun.

Lopez.

Ethan moved without conscious thought, his back now covered by the advancing wall of flames that would be driving the troops away from him and forcing them to circle around in order to reach the centre of the compound. With the flames in his rear Ethan hurried forward and caught a glimpse or two of Lopez firing, the shotgun's report differing from the distinctive rattle of the M–16s.

The forest was glowing now in the light of the ferociously growing fire, and Ethan suddenly saw the helicopters pull up and away from the forest as they sought to avoid fanning the flames any further, the pilots recognizing the danger to the troops on the ground. Ethan crouched lower and checked over his shoulder. The fire was now raging, driven this way and that by the turbulent downdraught from the helicopters, a twisting inferno that would be almost impossible to stop.

'Get down, hands on your head!'

Ethan froze, staring ahead, and in the light of the fire he saw troops advancing toward him, their weapons trained on a figure huddling on its knees with hands in the air.

As Ethan watched, he recognized from his silhouette the shape of Stanley Meyer as the troops surrounded him, and then they were placing manacles around his wrists and dragging him away from the commune. Ethan searched for any sign of Lopez, suddenly fearful that she had been shot and killed and that the troops had advanced to find Meyer alone in the forest.

The soldiers dragged the old man away, hurrying in retreat from the growing flames behind Ethan, and then suddenly Ethan sensed motion behind him and he whirled to see four heavily armed troops looming behind him, two of them holding Lopez and Amber in savage grips.

'On your feet!' one of them growled, his black fatigues smouldering where burning foliage had become lodged in the folds.

Ethan got to his feet, his hands in the air as he confronted the soldiers.

'Move!' one of them snapped as he rammed the barrel of an M–16 under Lopez's jaw, 'or I'll ventilate her skull right here and now!'

Ethan was about to turn when he saw a brief flare of light burst like a new–born star amid the flames behind the soldiers, and he ducked down as suddenly all noise and light vanished as a terrific blast ignited in the forest.

Ethan felt the shockwave from the blast hit him as the diesel generators exploded, the fearsome flames snarling through the forest igniting the fuel within them as the temperature reached its flashpoint.

Even as he ducked down he saw the blast hit the soldiers from behind, lifting them from their feet and hurling them to one side. He saw both Lopez and Amber still in the grasp of the soldiers and partially shielded from the impact of the blast as an immense fireball ripped through the trees and billowed up into the sky.

Ethan managed to get his hands over his ears to protect them from the raw fury of the detonation, but even so as he scrambled to his feet his head was dizzy and his legs felt weak as he struggled across to the nearest of the fallen soldiers before they were able to bring their weapons to bear upon him once more.

He saw the soldier look up at him and try to lift his M–16. Ethan brought one boot crashing down on the weapon to pin it against the forest floor as he lifted the other boot and smashed it down across the soldier's face. The soldier's head snapped to one side as he was plunged into unconsciousness, and Ethan grabbed the M–16 from his hands and turned it on the other fallen soldiers.

Cold fury gripped Ethan's heart as he took aim and fired three controlled shots, each round puncturing the soldier's skulls. These were not servants of the US government, these were mercenaries, killers for hire, probably former Special Forces and the kind of people who clearly had no problem killing civilians for their pay.

Lopez hauled herself to her feet and without prompting stumbled over to Amber and tried to help her up. Ethan turned and saw the entire forest filled with churning flames, felt the heat washing across him from the inferno as it grew. Somewhere beyond the darkened forest he could hear the helicopters waiting, holding clear of the blast zone as they prepared to land in the nearest clearing to allow the soldiers to regroup and climb aboard.

'We need to move, fast!' Ethan said as Amber struggled to her feet.

'Where's my father?' Amber asked, clearly shaken by the blast and the speed and ferocity of the attack.

'He's gone, Amber,' Ethan replied. 'They got him. There's nothing we can do, except get out of here before they come for us too.'

Ethan did not wait for a response, knowing that they didn't have time to debate the situation, stranded in the middle of nowhere and with a hostile force within a short distance of where they stood. Clutching the M–16 rifle, Ethan turned and led the way through the darkened forest in the hopes that the raging inferno behind them would conceal their presence for long enough to make good their escape.

***

XXX

Angel Springs Hotel, Virginia

Stanley Meyer sat in silence as he watched the dawn break across distant hills, the sky above a wonderful eggshell blue and a light mist hovering in the air across the nearby forests. It looked so much like the hills near Clearwater.

So much had changed, in so little time, that he felt as though he were in some kind of dream, that he would wake up eventually in his own bed with his wife beside him, Amber asleep in her room, and their lives back to normal. He realized, with some melancholy, that he almost wished it were true and that he had never gotten himself into this mess.

The hotel in which he had been forced to spend the night was far more luxurious than anything he had ever believed possible. From the cold, hard, dark confines of a military helicopter he had been transferred into a luxury limousine and from there to the hotel. The bathroom had marble floors and a voice activated pad on the wall allowed him to open the curtains, turn on the lights, alter the air conditioning and do pretty much anything he wanted without ever having to lift a finger. On one wall was mounted a television larger than the dining table in his home, the screen concave to prevent any reflections from marring the perfect image it produced.

Stanley knew that there were soldiers outside his door, dressed in smart suits and with their weapons concealed. His door was locked from the outside and the entire top floor of the hotel booked out to conceal him from observation. Stanley reckoned that the proprietors of the hotel probably assumed that a rock star was staying incognito upstairs, or perhaps a movie idol or something, not a retired scientist considered a lunatic by most of his peers.

Stanley had no idea whether Amber, Lopez and Ethan were still alive, but he did know that Jesse had been shot during their attempted escape. He had heard more gunfire afterward, and in the carnage that ensued he felt certain that there had been no survivors in Jesse's commune. The sight of people being shot and killed had affected him deeply, and sleep had not come to him despite the huge size and great comfort of the king–size bed that dominated his room. People were dying, dying because of what he had achieved and because of what so many other people wanted to see destroyed.

A great pall of depression settled on Stanley's shoulders as he watched the sunrise through the broad windows, all of which had been secured and locked shut and were made from a form of glass that could not be broken. Had he not already been informed in great depth of the security of his room, he might have been tempted to hurl himself through them and off the fifth floor balcony to his death below. He had chosen a course of action that he knew had been dangerous, but he had believed the danger to be only to himself. Never once had he considered the possibility that the brutality of those who were pursuing him would extend to innocent civilians, to people who had never heard of Stanley Meyer or Seavers Incorporated or free energy devices. His grief intensified as he reflected upon the nature of the people who had died, people who had been seeking a way to live peacefully outside of the National Grid, the kind of people that Stanley Meyer had hoped to champion with the fusion cage. Now, the first people to encounter him and his device, or the promise of it, were dead, their children with them.

Tears welled into his eyes, but the rage he had once felt for the machine that seemed determined to thwart him at all costs would not come. He knew that he had pushed too far, too soon, that he had challenged the powers that be and found their nature to be far more horrific than anything he could have imagined. Finally, after all this time, he realised something that he had not before considered: that perhaps many scientists refused to become involved in the free energy game not because they felt that it would not work, but because they feared the consequences of even attempting to do so. More than one inventor had died under mysterious circumstances after proclaiming to have discovered some form or other of extreme efficiency or free energy.

Stanley turned wearily to the television and switched it on. The screen glowed into life in an instant, an image of a news anchor from a local state television station appearing larger–than–life and clearer too, almost unrealistically high definition as though he were looking through a window to where the newsreader sat dictating her newsfeed directly to him. He had already watched the reports a dozen times, but once again found himself unable to tear his view from them.

' ... *reports are coming in once again from the fire service fighting the blaze near Nathalie, a fire which appears to have been started deliberately. Casualties are reported in the dozens, along with the destruction of a small commune belonging to one Jesse McVey, an employee of a private firm in Lynchburg who owned the compound and had built an off-grid community there over the last ten years ... '*

An image of Jesse appeared on the screen, all youth and vigour and bright smiles, photographed in front of the home he had built in the woods many years previously. Stanley's tears welled again as the news reporter continued.

' ... it is believed that an explosion of a gas canister or possibly a diesel generator started the blaze, which then consume the entire community. On–site explosive experts are already warning of the dangers of using such generators in wilderness conditions, citing dry conditions and the danger of natural sparks as well as the threat of arson. The blast at the site was heard as far away as Harrisburg, and although firefighters now have the forest fire under control they are maintaining a perimeter around the site to prevent contamination in order for forensics experts to search the scene. The local police department say they are now treating the event as a multiple homicide and are seeking witnesses. All victims found at the scene are confirmed to have died from asphyxiation or burning during the fire.'

The image on the screen switched to a series of mug–shots, each showing a face that Stanley recognized.

'Police are asking local residents to be on the look–out for these individuals, who were seen in the area at the time and are believed able to help police with their enquiries. All of them are wanted for questioning in connection with the events of last night and prior police investigations in several states. If you see them, do not attempt to approach them but instead call nine–one–one immediately.'

The faces of Ethan Warner, Nicola Lopez, Amber Ryan and Stanley Meyer stared out of the screen at him, all of the shots carefully picked to show them at their most glum: Warner's was clearly a police mug–shot taken years before, Lopez's a grainy image from CCTV somewhere, Amber's gothic visage staring sullenly from a school photo, and Stanley's taken from an identity badge he'd worn for years at the National Ignition Facility in California.

Stanley slumped into his seat as he switched the television off, and he sat for a long time watching the sunrise over the peaceful rolling valleys until he heard a key turning in the lock of his door. Stanley did not turn to look as he heard somebody walk into the room, the door closing behind them as they moved. A long silence followed before he heard a voice speak to him.

'Stanley,' it said softly, 'It's Huck.'

Stanley could not bring himself to turn his head, to look upon the man who had murdered so many people already. He simply continued stare out of the window.

Huck Seavers pulled up a chair from nearby and sat to Stanley's right, just in view out of the corner of his eye. Seavers linked his fingers together as he rested his elbows on his knees and looked at Stanley from beneath his Stetson.

'I know how you must feel right now,' he said softly. 'I would feel the same too, if all of this had happened to me. Believe me when I say that this is not what I wanted, that I would never have done this to you or to those people.'

Stanley did not move, stared out of the windows of the hotel room as he thought of Amber, of his wife and all that they had been forced to endure since this whole thing had begun. For the first time ever Stanley hated what he had become, hated what he had fought for and endured and forced upon others. He hated the thought of his fusion cage, hated the naivety with which he had believed that somehow, human compassion and cooperation would overcome greed and herald a new dawn of humanity, of a people free from crippling energy bills, pollution, climate change and the machinations of corporations hell–bent on profits, fuelled by greed, fearing nothing.

'There are forces at work here, Stanley,' Huck went on, 'forces that I would not have believed existed six months ago. They control everything, everything we think that is democratic. They scheme and conspire, and all of it in order to build and consolidate power over every human being, over every living thing, on this planet.'

Stanley remained silent.

'I have tried to resist them, tried to limit the danger that they have put people in, including me, Stanley, but there's just no stopping them. I talked to your daughter, Amber, and tried to make her understand but she wouldn't believe me. Then, they tracked you out of Saudi Arabia and to France, sent their own people in to talk to a guy who works there, Hans somebody or other.'

Stanley's chin lifted slightly, and with a chilling premonition he realized how Huck's people had found them despite their being located so deep in Virginia.

'They threatened him,' Huck said, 'with things that I don't even want to think about. I have children too, a wife, a family and a future. They've made it clear that if I don't do what they want I'll lose them all. They made the same threat at Cadarache in France, and then they told me that you were coming back to America. I had to stop you, Stanley, had to intervene in Clearwater, to silence the townsfolk. I didn't have a choice but to do what they wanted. If I hadn't done what needed to be done, they would have killed my wife and my children and taken away everything that I … '

'Shut up.'

The words spilled from Stanley's mouth like poison. He heard his own rage, mixed with regret and frustration and hopelessness.

'Where is Amber?' he demanded.

'She wasn't found,' Huck said, quick to inform Stanley that her body had not been recovered. 'I think that she escaped because only the inhabitants of the commune have been identified from their … '

Seavers broke off, apparently stunned by what had happened at Nathalie. Stanley sucked in air that filled his lungs but somehow failed to replenish him.

'I'll take the money,' Stanley said.

Huck Seavers looked up at him. 'What?'

Stanley did not look at the man, keeping his eyes focused on the distant hills.

'Enough people have died,' he uttered, barely able to conceive of the terrible course of action he had put into motion. 'I don't want anybody else's deaths on my hands for this, for the device that I built. I don't want it any more. I don't want any part of it anymore.'

Huck remained still, his eyes searching Stanley's face for some sign of deception.

'I don't know if they can be trusted,' he said finally. 'I don't know if they'll honour a promise to leave us be, or if they'll make any of this simply *go away*.'

For the first time Stanley began to realize that Seavers himself might actually be what Amber had suggested he was: a pawn, like Stanley, in a dangerous game much bigger than either of them.

'You got yourself in with them,' he growled, showing no sign of sympathy. 'It's on your hands, all of this. You killed those people, all of them.'

Huck's head hung low.

'I needed help to defeat the legal actions piling up against my company,' Huck said. 'They had leverage, power, they said they could make the cases go away and they did. But you have to believe me, Stanley – I had no idea that they would do anything like *this*. None at all. I don't even know who they are. I tried to find out at Bilderberg, and that's when they made the threats against my family.' Huck looked up again at Stanley. 'Is your wife okay?'

Stanley felt no warmth in Huck Seaver's concern. 'A bit late, Seavers, to be worrying about her.'

Seavers bit his lip. 'Someone once told me that it's never too late to try to put things right.'

Stanley scowled and finally looked Seavers in the eye.

'It's too late for black–hearted cowards like you,' he snapped. 'I'll take the money. One hundred million, all of it sent to accounts I've set up.'

Huck's eyes narrowed. 'You've already set up accounts?'

'I did it the moment I realized the fusion cage worked,' Stanley snapped. 'I'm not an idiot. I wanted to give the device away, but if it couldn't be done then I wanted to ensure that my family profited from what I'd achieved. It's called putting others first, Seavers. You should try it one day.'

'My family come first,' Huck replied coldly.

'No negotiations, no discussions,' Stanley said, ignoring Huck's last. 'In return, I'll cease all work on the fusion cage and I will sign anything to show that I will never again distribute any paperwork, prototypes or other reference material pertaining to the device. If Amber and my wife are harmed in any way, ever, I swear I'll release everything regardless of what happens to me, understood?'

Huck Seavers nodded slowly.

'I'll pass that along. I hope that it will bring these unfortunate events to a close, that we will never have to deal with anything like this again and … '

'It will never stop,' Stanley cut him off. 'It will never end, because somebody else will discover what I did. Others will know, will come to understand, and one way or another they'll bring your damned corporations to their knees. I just hope I'm alive to see it, so I can drink champagne and piss on the ashes of your company, Seavers.'

Huck sat for a moment longer, and then he got up and walked away from Stanley and let him watch the sunrise once more in peace.

***

XXXI

Richmond International Airport, Virginia

Aaron Mitchell strode off the corporate jet and into the sweltering mid–day heat of a Virginian summer, the sound of aircraft taking off behind him on the distant runway interspersed with a ripple of birdsong in nearby trees as he walked toward a sleek, glossy black limousine parked nearby.

The airport handled flights to Paris in Europe as part of its scheduled service, but Aaron as ever was able to call upon the near–limitless financial power of his employers to travel in corporate luxury. Flying under a local airline's call sign to further conceal his movements, he had landed only minutes before and was forcing himself to ignore the weariness aching through his bones as he opened the limousine's door and climbed inside.

The interior of the vehicle was as plush as that of the jet, and he looked into the eyes of Huck Seavers and was surprised to see relief and delight sparkling in the younger man's eyes.

'What news?' he demanded.

'Meyer folded,' Huck reported with glee. 'His price is one hundred million, no questions asked. He's even set up the accounts. We pay, he vanishes and it's over.'

Aaron looked down at a piece of paper that Huck handed him, containing account codes for numerous overseas banks.

'It's never over,' he said as he took the paper.

'That's what Stanley said,' Huck admitted. 'He thinks that somebody else will achieve what he has and carry the torch for him. Whatever.'

'What guarantees did he demand?'

'That his family be left alone,' Huck said. 'Anything happens to them, he blows it all wide open.'

'He could do that anyway.'

'Yes he could,' Huck agreed, eager to maintain the advantage he had created, 'but then if that's what you think then you would have simply killed him anyway, so why even attempt to make an offer through me? It wouldn't make any sense.'

'There are many, many things that you do not understand.'

Huck ground his teeth in his skull, suddenly nervous.

'I did what you asked,' he said. 'I got him to sell out. He's going to hand everything over to us and has promised never to speak of his device ever again, or promote it or anybody else's work. He's given up – that's what you people wanted.'

Aaron stared down at the accounts for a long moment.

'The money will be transferred to Seavers Incorporated by this afternoon, after which you may pass it on to these accounts.'

Huck's features fell.

'That's not what we agreed! You didn't say anything about me laundering money for you! If this ever did go public they'd trace the payments right back to me!'

'You are displeased?'

Aaron's voice rumbled like boulders tumbling down a cliff as he turned in his seat toward Huck, his eyes dark and foreboding. 'Perhaps you think that you're being treated unfairly?'

Huck's eyes wobbled in their sockets as he retreated in his seat.

'You're stacking the odds in your favour and putting me at risk,' Huck blustered. 'I can't face any more public investigations or legal threats!'

'Then you had best be sure that this deal you have struck with Meyer does not fall through,' Mitchell warned as he leaned closer. 'The consequences to Seavers Incorporated might be.., fatal.'

Huck swallowed thickly, his voice broken and an octave higher as he replied.

'Go to hell,' he spat with a feeble veneer of bravado. 'I've done what you asked, we're finished.'

Aaron watched Huck Seavers for a long moment, and then he twitched his shoulders as though he were about to strike. Seavers flinched in fright and recoiled further in his seat. Aaron watched him for a moment longer before he opened the limousine's door and climbed out once again.

He turned away from the vehicle and walked across the apron, heard the limo pull away as he pulled a cell phone from his pocket and dialled a secure number. After a series of prolonged digital buzzing sounds as various security protocols were activated, the line rang and was picked up almost immediately.

'Report?'

'Meyer is controlled,' Mitchell said. 'One hundred million must be wired into these accounts, stand by.'

There was a moment's pause, and then: *'Go.'*

Aaron relayed the account numbers and then waited patiently as they were diligently recorded.

'What of Meyer? What are the guarantees?'

'The man's word and not much else. That said, he's been pushed to the edge and he knows that any further provocation will be met with merciless retribution. Meyer has found his price and I believe that he can be contained without further need for bloodshed.'

'The assault in Nathalie was a mess,' came the retort. *'We barely had time to cover our presence and it's only good fortune that the Pentagon swallowed the story of a terrorist group hiding out in the woods.'*

'The media disinformation I initiated has taken the heat from us,' Aaron reassured the voice on the line. 'Right now, we have both removed Meyer from play and also ensured that General Nellis's lapdogs are neutralized. They'll be running from law enforcement for weeks and unable to interfere further in our operations. What of the DIA?'

'Nellis is under investigation as we speak and Jarvis is under arrest, but if we push too hard then we risk exposing ourselves and defeating the object. The General has the ear of the president and can still kick up a fuss that we might struggle to contain.'

Aaron stopped for a moment as he considered the delicate nature of what Majestic Twelve was attempting to achieve. General Nellis was far too high a figure to consider silencing permanently. Any threat against his life would draw far too much attention to the inner workings of the DIA and perhaps to their interest in MJ–12. The publicity such an event could generate was to the detriment of the cabal and absolutely must be avoided. However …

'He needs to receive a message,' Aaron replied finally, 'a clear message that any further digging into our affairs could be detrimental to more than just his career.'

'Agreed. But how do we send that message? Any threat to his family is as good as a threat to the man himself and would only entrench him further.'

'The threat must be close to home, but not personal enough to provoke aggression,' Aaron replied softly. 'I believe we have the perfect target.'

'Whom?'

'Jarvis.'

*

J. Edgar Hoover Building,

Washington DC

Jarvis heard the guards coming as he sat in a featureless cell, the mattress thin and uncomfortable. Half a lifetime served in the US Marine Corps had served him well and taught him the virtues of 'hurry up and wait', but none the less he was relieved that something was now happening.

The cell door opened and two armed guards stood back either side of it and beckoned him forward. Handcuffs were presented to him and Jarvis allowed himself to be restrained without complaint. The time for defiance would come later, not now when he was sealed deep in the heart of the FBI's Headquarters on Pennsylvania Avenue – resistance here would be both futile and likely to see him incarcerated beyond the view of the public or legal aid forever. That was how the intelligence community liked to deal with such things: in house. Jarvis knew that his greatest threat now was to simply disappear forever, much like the inhabitants of Clearwater, Missouri, but without the benefit of ten million bucks.

Nobody could hear you scream in a maximum security prison.

The guards led Jarvis through the small cell block to the elevators, where they then took a ride up through the building to the top floor, direct. No stopping on other floors, no access to witnesses or contact with people outside of his predicament. Jarvis was in the system now as an enemy combatant, in effect, and was being treated as such.

The top floor was deserted as he was led out of the elevator, something which would have been ordered a few minutes before his arrival. The guards guided him toward the Director's office, and Jarvis braced himself to find out what would happen to him and who had taken

General Nellis's place at the DIA. Replacement, in his experience, was what always happened to those who dug too deep. He had lost count of the number of well–intentioned senior officers in prime condition who had retired due to 'family matters', or 'ill health' or with an 'unblemished record'. Such men and women were staunch patriots and rarely retired until they were unable to walk or talk straight, unless they were pushed from behind the scenes.

The office door was opened by one of the guards and Jarvis was propelled inside. The door closed behind him and to Jarvis's surprise General Nellis awaited him, his hands folded before him. Nellis looked up at Jarvis, his features emotionless.

'I take it that I'm not about to be released with a presidential pardon and the Medal of Honor,' Jarvis said, his hands still cuffed.

No humour appeared on the general's face as he replied.

'They've got us over a barrel,' he replied simply. 'We're out of moves.'

'We're never out of moves.'

Nellis dragged a hand across his face and with the other pushed a photograph on his desk toward Jarvis, rotating it with his fingers. Jarvis looked down and saw a picture of a bright red Ford Ranger, its hood crushed as it lay on its roof in the middle of a highway, surrounded by fire–retardant foam and emergency service crews.

'This vehicle crashed on a Virginia Interstate yesterday evening,' Nellis said. 'The occupant was killed outright, pronounced dead at the hospital. Braking trails on the road suggest a hit and run according to local police, but there were no witnesses and nobody's come forward with information.'

Jarvis raised a questioning eyebrow, although he already suspected a connection with the case in which Warner and Lopez were embroiled.

'The occupant was Red McKenzie, one of the former inhabitants of Clearwater, Missouri, whom your people located and spoke to a few days ago.'

Jarvis closed his eyes.

'Could be a coincidence,' he suggested, hearing his own words and despising them. 'McKenzie was a drinker, he could have lost control.'

'The only thing that he lost control of was his life,' Nellis shot back as Jarvis opened his eyes again. 'The autopsy was completed out this morning. No alcohol in his system, no drugs. He died from blunt force trauma due to the impact from the oncoming vehicle, which flipped his truck over three times and partially crushed it. That requires a big damned impact, and yet there's no evidence of any debris from the other vehicle but some small fragments of glass and plastic. What does that tell you, Doug?'

Military truck, maybe a four tonne transporter or similar, Jarvis thought but didn't say.

'McKenzie broke the terms of his agreement,' Nellis went on, 'and Majestic Twelve sent both him and the other three hundred people from Clearwater a real clear message: stay silent by choice, or you'll be silenced permanently. This crash appeared on media networks in states across the east, Doug. An automobile wreck, one of countless dozens that occur in every state every day, and it's now national news? How does that happen without somebody pulling some heavy strings to put the word out? Every former Clearwater citizen would have seen or heard about it and will know damned well what it means.'

Jarvis thought briefly of the general's family.

'They won't target you,' he said finally. 'You're too high profile, too much of a risk.'

'Glad you think so,' Nellis shot back. 'Personally, I don't fancy taking any chances with the lives of my daughters. Would you?'

Jarvis avoided the challenge. 'What happens now?'

'Nothing happens now,' Nellis replied. 'We can't operate with these people breathing down our necks! They know we're onto them and they're applying pressure, letting us know that if we don't back down then things are going to get nasty – Red McKenzie nasty.'

'You're quitting?' Jarvis asked. 'You're the one who instigated this whole thing! You called me out here in the middle of the night to start this program up.'

'I didn't know what I was getting myself into,' Nellis countered. 'I've been dragged up here and informed, in no uncertain terms, that any further intervention by the DIA in these matters will result in direct action against my office, *against me*. I thought that this was about inter–agency corruption. I wasn't prepared for what I've found out since. These people are dangerous, Doug. They don't obey the law but are able to manipulate those same laws to hide behind them, to get whatever they want, even if that means strong–arming the administration itself. We're powerless against this kind of activity.'

Jarvis stared down at Nellis for a long moment.

'If we're powerless against such people, then why the hell are we even here? What's the point of having an intelligence service dedicated to wiping out the enemies of the United States if we're going to quit at the first sign of danger?'

'Because the enemy *is* the United States!' Nellis snapped. 'It's not our government we're fighting, it's the big businesses! They've acquired so much power, so much influence that our administration is no longer the governing force in our country. Eisenhower was right: we should have believed him when he warned of the growing power of the military–industrial factions that were cosying up to the president at the time. Their power exceeds that of the White House now in all but name: our president has become a cypher, the public face of something that even he does not understand and cannot influence. If the White House cannot control the machinations of global industry, what the hell can we do?'

Jarvis tried to maintain a confident expression.

'Bring it to the attention of the people who really own the power in our country: the people themselves.'

Nellis scoffed and waved Jarvis aside with a wince.

'Like hell,' he uttered. 'The media can be controlled by this Majestic Twelve, we've already seen that. Look at what Fox News does, pushing the opinions and upholding the preferences of its CEO instead of providing unbiased reporting. Majestic Twelve are powerful enough to make Fox look like a madman shouting in the street. We can't oppose that, we'd be crushed overnight. I take it that you haven't seen the latest reports coming out of Virginia?'

'I've been in a cell.'

Nellis used a remote to switch on a wall–mounted screen nearby and instantly Jarvis was treated to a report, recorded he guessed, showing Ethan, Nicola, Amber Ryan and Stanley Meyer as wanted fugitives.

'Local news, at the moment,' Nellis reported. 'I'm guessing that if Stanley Meyer doesn't fold to the demands of MJ–12, this will go nationwide by tomorrow and your people will spend the rest of their lives on the run.'

Nellis switched off the television and tossed the remote down onto his desk.

'I've been told that you're free to go,' he informed Jarvis.

'By whom?' Jarvis asked. 'And how come they're just going to let me go?'

'Damned good luck?!' Nellis suggested. 'You've directly assisted fugitives using agency resources, and not for the first time, to evade arrest in both Saudi Arabia and Virginia by the FBI. Any sudden moves,

Doug, and they'll bury you in a federal prison for the rest of your days. I'm sensing that this is our first, last and only warning. I'm shutting the program down and I suggest that you enjoy the rest of your retirement in peace, Doug, otherwise it's going to be a lot shorter than you planned.'

***

XXXII

Blackstone, Virginia

'You see anything?'

Ethan crouched low behind the wheel of the decrepit 1970's Dodge Fire truck that they had found abandoned on an old cotton farm. Ethan had managed to liberate a battery from a vehicle on the street and get the old truck running, and using it they had snuck into town and lay low as the sun rose.

'Nothing that screams FBI,' Ethan replied to Lopez in a whisper as she sat low in the driver's seat and watched a run–down motel nearby. 'If they're actively looking for us then motels are the way to go. We can't get in there without attracting attention to ourselves – you've seen the news reports.'

A pre–dawn drive through a nearby small town had taken them past a television repair shop, and there in the window behind the grated metal shutters had been a screen showing a local station. They had waited only minutes to see their faces emblazoned across the television. Straight afterward they had seen the report on the crashed Ford Ranger and an image of Red McKenzie had appeared, deceased, the victim of a late–night hit and run out on the Interstate.

'They've got us completely covered,' Lopez hissed. 'That was a local station, right? We haven't seen anything to suggest they're broadcasting that stuff nationwide.'

'Haven't seen anything to suggest they didn't either,' Amber pointed out from the back seat. 'I guess this is what Stanley was afraid of – total loss of control.'

'We've been in this situation before,' Ethan assured her as he watched the motel. 'Lopez and I were dark for almost six months and we never got caught.'

Amber smiled without warmth. 'That's lovely and I'm very happy for you both, but I'd very much like my life back if it's all the same to you. Living out of dirty motels and wearing disguises for five decades wasn't part of my game plan, y'know?'

'Me either,' Lopez agreed. 'I'm not going on the run because of those assholes. They murdered Red and now they're after us. I say we start fighting back.'

Ethan sighed as he kept his gaze fixed across the street.

'It's not about going on the run and hiding forever,' he said. 'We just need to lie low until this blows over and then we can start building ourselves back up again. Jarvis will come through for us, we need to give him more time.'

'Jarvis is out of the picture,' Lopez insisted. 'If the FBI are after us, they're sure to have figured out who's been assisting us. Jarvis said they were breathing down his neck, didn't he? We're fugitives now, so the first thing they'll do is shut him down.'

Ethan saw a vehicle pull up alongside the motel, a non–descript silver sedan with government plates and tinted windows.

'Here we go,' he said softly.

They watched as two FBI Agents got out of the vehicle and walked toward the old motel and into the reception.

'This isn't going to work,' Amber said from the backseat. 'Just because we're not there now doesn't mean they won't come back later, and who's to say there isn't a reward out for us?'

The two agents emerged from the motel and climbed back into their sedan. Moments later, they pulled away and vanished around a corner on the street.

'Okay, here we go,' Ethan said. 'Remember, stay in the truck while I go inside. The TV stations are using a mugshot that makes me look bad, but that's also different to the way I look now. Hopefully that will be enough to fool whoever's on the desk inside.'

'Or get us arrested,' Lopez muttered, but she said nothing more as Ethan eased the truck across the street and into the motel's lot.

Ethan killed the engine and climbed out. The sunlight was bright and the air clear and crisp as he put on a pair of sunglasses and pulled a baseball cap down over his thick brown hair. He took a deep breath and then strode across to the reception door and walked inside.

The interior smelled of old wax and polish, a pall of stale cigarette smoke wafting toward him from behind a security grill in the wall. Behind the grill sat a fat, ugly man with sweat–sheened skin, a small electric fan humming nearby and pointed up at the man's face. He looked up at Ethan with eyes devoid of any enthusiasm for life that Ethan could detect.

'Got a room?' Ethan asked, sensing that engaging this guy in conversation would be a pointless exercise.

'We're a motel, what do you think?'

The voice was rough from decades of smoking, brazen while behind the security grill. Ethan's gaze snapped to meet the hotelier's and anger flared inside him.

'Be nice, or I'll drag your fat ass out of that office and kick it all the way down the street.'

'You want a room or not?'

'Ground floor, my mother's a little weak legged after her operation and needs a rest from the journey.'

The lie came easily, as did the aggression. The fugitives on the TV would be expected to lay low and not draw attention to themselves by threatening people. Likewise, the story about his mother was dropped casually and would hopefully derail the fat man's interest in anything Ethan had to share.

'Do you take credit cards?' Ethan asked brusquely.

'Cash only.'

Ethan tutted irritably despite only having cash on him. The more deception he could throw at the dim–witted hotelier, the greater his chances of remaining unrecognized.

'How much?'

'Fifty bucks a day,' the man replied. 'Each.'

'A hundred fifty bucks for this flea–ridden dump?'

'You don't like it, go to Richmond,' the hotelier shrugged.

Ethan peeled off the money from his meagre funds and handed the notes over. Moments later, the hotelier slid a key under the security grill. Ethan saw his chance and grabbed the fat man's wrist, twisted it sideways and pinned his hand against the outside of the grill to a shriek of pain as he leaned in close.

The hotelier squealed in panic as his wrist was twisted and bent back at a sharp angle. Ethan offered him a cold grin.

'I ever see you outside of your little cage here, I'll shove this hand up your fat ass, understood?'

The hotelier nodded frantically, grunting as fresh sweat spilled from his forehead and his lank black hair hung in greasy fronds before his eyes. Ethan grabbed the key with one hand and gave the hotelier's wrist a last painful wrench before he released it and turned his back, walking for the door.

'That's assault,' the hotelier uttered weakly from behind Ethan as he opened the reception door.

'It's a friendly warning,' Ethan replied without looking back as he stepped out into the sunshine and strode back to the truck.

He opened the passenger door and leaned in to Amber's side to look at her. He took a fresh handkerchief from his pocket and handed it to her.

'What the hell am I supposed to do with this?' she asked.

'Wear it on your head. You're seventy five and have just had a hip operation,' Ethan replied. 'Stay between Nicola and I and act like it.'

Amber dutifully wrapped the kerchief over her head in the manner of a bonnet and hobbled out of the truck's rear seat as Lopez moved to her side and helped shield Amber from view of the hotel's reception. They held her between them and slowly crossed the parking lot toward a line of apartments with aged, sun–weathered doors and grubby windows.

'This is ridiculous,' Amber hissed. 'If anybody gets a look at me we'll be sold out before we even realize what's happened.'

'Keep moving,' Ethan whispered. 'One thing at a time, okay? Let's just get out of sight first.'

Ethan unlocked the apartment door and Lopez helped Amber inside as Ethan followed and then closed the door behind them.

'That's it,' Amber snapped as she tore the handkerchief from her head and tossed it onto the grubby sheets of a small bed, grabbing for her cell phone. 'I'm calling for help.'

'You can't,' Ethan snapped back. 'We need to sit this out and wait.'

'For what?!' Amber wailed. 'Divine intervention?!'

Ethan shook his head wearily as Lopez took up the mantle.

'We can't move, not until we've got a game plan. Stanley's gone, and if he's got any sense he'll sell out. It's all he can do now to prevent us from … '

'He already has,' Ethan said.

He had switched on a small, aged television propped on a wall mount in one corner of the room, so old in fact that it wasn't even a flat–screen but an old cathode ray tube with a thick layer of dust gracing its surface. Despite its age, however, the picture was more than clear enough as a news report appeared showing an image of Stanley Meyer.

'Turn it up!' Amber cried.

Ethan looked about for a remote, but it was Lopez who reached up and turned the volume knob on the television itself. The sound came in abruptly from the ancient speakers at the television's rear.

'Police this morning confirmed that they had eliminated four suspects from their enquiries into last night's forest fire after one of the four, renowned scientist Stanley Meyer, was able to confirm that all four suspects were in fact in Kentucky at the time of the blast. Police have announced that they are still searching for witnesses to the fire, and are urging anybody with information to come forward as soon as possible...'

Ethan could see that Stanley Meyer appeared unharmed and was walking between a police station and a pair of smart, black SUV's parked in a lot nearby. A lawyer was by his side and doing the talking for him, but it was clear that he was being released without charge and that the media were being used to spread the news to all concerned.

'He's sold out,' Lopez agreed. 'Only way he'd be walking like that on live television.'

Amber stared open–mouthed at the screen, for once lost for words as Ethan shifted his attention to the two vehicles parked in the lot on the screen.

'Government?' Lopez hazarded. 'Can't see the plates.'

'No,' Ethan shook his head. 'They wouldn't get themselves on film too close to Stanley. My guess, it's Huck Seavers.'

Amber managed to regain her voice as she shoved one hand in her pocket and retrieved her cell phone.

'I'm calling my mother, right now!' she snapped.

'No!' Ethan shot back. 'We can't be sure this is all over.'

'The hell it isn't!' Amber replied, the cell phone already in her hand and the screen aglow. 'My father's alive and he's free!'

'It might be a ploy to draw us out,' Lopez explained to her.

'They don't need us anymore!' Amber replied. 'They wouldn't bother with all of this. You said it yourself, they're using the media to get messages across to us. They've killed Red McKenzie and now my father's folded to their demands. They probably threatened our entire family with extinction for all I know. I understand what you're saying and I appreciate what you've done for me, but I don't answer to either of you. I need to call my mother and that's what I'm going to do, okay?'

Ethan looked at Lopez, who shrugged.

'Do it from across the street or something,' Ethan said. 'If this is a set–up of some kind, at least they won't be able to bag us all at once.'

Amber strode for the reception door and without another word she opened it and stomped outside, slamming the door behind her. Ethan felt something resembling relief as the room fell silent.

'Tenacious,' Lopez observed.

'Yeah, and I have to put up with both of you.'

'Oh come on, I'm not that bad!'

Ethan cast Lopez a weary glance. 'You're my boss, on paper at least. You ever meet a boss you could get on with?'

Lopez was about to answer when the door to the room burst open and Amber dashed inside.

'They're here!' she yelped.

Ethan dashed to the window and peered out to see two expensive looking vehicles pull into the lot and screech to a halt directly in front of the apartment.

'There a way out back?' Ethan asked Lopez, cursing himself for not checking already.

'Nothing,' Lopez called back from the bathroom. 'No way out!'

Ethan pulled Amber out of the way of the door as he heard heavy footsteps mount the sidewalk outside.

'Get behind me,' he ordered her. 'How long did you have that cell turned on for?'

Amber sulked and said nothing.

'How long, Amber?'

'I texted her, a couple hours ago,' Amber mumbled.

'Jesus,' Ethan uttered as he rubbed his temples. 'This is why I don't have kids.'

A long silence ensued as Lopez returned and stood alongside Ethan. Images of flash–bangs being tossed through the windows or a shotgun being used to blast open the door flashed through his mind. The silence drew out along with Ethan's thumping heart beats, and then there was a soft knock at the door.

Ethan hesitated for a moment, glanced at Lopez, and then reached out and opened the door.

***

218

XXXIII

Ethan sat in silence between Lopez and Amber, all three of them staring back at a pair of men in smart uniforms, clearly trained bodyguards of some kind, who sat facing them in the rear of the people carrier. The men remained impassive, making no attempt at conversation and hiding behind their sunglasses as the vehicle whispered along the highway.

Ethan had opened the door to the grubby motel room at the knock, and had been surprised to see the two men standing there, supported by a further two behind them. He had been able to tell from the cut of their suits that they were carrying, most likely pistols in shoulder holsters and perhaps assorted close–combat weapons in other, discreet sleeve pouches and such like.

Outnumbered and unarmed after ditching the M16 Ethan had taken from the soldiers near Nathalie , he and Lopez had known right away that there was little point in putting up a fight. If they defeated the first two men, the two behind them would be on hand to cut them both down with a single shot each, and the interior of the motel room offered no escape or cover. In the end the decision had been easy: Stanley Meyer had sold out, and so to an extent the visit by the armed men could simply be the end of the road or the promise of an escape.

Nothing to lose, Lopez had said, and maybe everything to gain.

Somehow, Ethan felt a certain degree of relief as he glanced out of the window and saw the city of Richmond passing by in the distance, tower blocks of metal and glass glinting in the dawn sunlight. There was also a hint of excitement that he was struggling to keep at bay from clouding his judgement. Meyer had sold out, and now it was possible that Majestic Twelve may be willing to buy his and Lopez's silence too.

Warner & Lopez Inc had no direct affiliation or loyalty to the Defense Intelligence Agency, and selling out did not mean that they would lose the business the agency provided. Hell, if any payout was generous enough they wouldn't need the damned business at all. Ten million bucks was a hell of a retirement fund, and would last Ethan the rest of his days and far beyond as long as he was careful and …

'Stop thinking about it.'

Ethan glanced at Lopez, who was watching him with her dark eyes.

'Kinda hard, don't you think?' he replied.

'Stop thinking about what?' Amber asked.

'The trouble we'll be in at the DIA,' Ethan lied smoothly. 'We've failed, in effect, and this is the first time. We didn't keep Stanley safe and we didn't recover all of the material surrounding his fusion cage. Presumably that is now in the hands of Huck Seavers, or whoever he's been answering to.'

'You did what you could,' Amber replied. 'I don't see how dad selling out will cause you any problems. It's the last thing that I expected him to do.'

Ethan nodded as he reflected on Stanley Meyer's stoic refusal to sell his device to anybody, to even *consider* doing so. Stanley's goal was a lofty one, to simply give away his device to the world for free and bask in the glow of an act of altruism that would be remembered for generations, perhaps forever. Ethan could see how the threats of violence against so many people and the death of Red McKenzie might have swayed him from his true purpose in life, but it seemed odd to Ethan that Stanley, prepared for the worst that the oil companies could throw at him, would have folded so completely and suddenly.

'I don't think anybody who knows Stanley expected him to do this,' Lopez agreed. 'Can't say I'm disappointed though.'

'I am,' Amber scowled, her arms folded across her chest. 'He could have been so much more than this, *was* so much more than this. People like Huck Seavers don't give a damn about the people, they're too interested in the size of their bank balance. I hope that my father has sold out to them and then uses the money to build ten thousand fusion cages and distributes them around the world. That would teach those damned corporate fat cats a lesson about money and their greed and … '

Amber's words drifted off in Ethan's mind as he sat absolutely still in his seat and stared vacantly straight ahead. A single sentence revolved around in his head over and over as the vehicle whispered along the asphalt.

' *… uses the money to build ten thousand fusion cages and distributes them around the world … '*

Stanley, if he had indeed sold out, would undoubtedly be under strict orders not to develop his device any more. The consequences of doing so would likely be literally fatal, so there was no way that the old man could get the word out about what he had achieved unless he intended to make the money disappear somewhere and then shout about his invention as loudly as he could before MJ–12 put a bullet in his skull.

No. Ethan scratched that off of his list. The media would be blacked out from any such broadcasts, MJ–12's reach seemingly long enough to prevent Stanley from achieving his aims through the media. None the less, Ethan could not square the old man's new course of action with the character that he knew. It didn't make sense, because Stanley already seemed aware that powerful corporations might attempt to take his life once he tried to go public: he seemed prepared for such an eventuality, willing to risk his life to …

'Oh no.'

Ethan stared into the middle distance as a sudden flurry of thoughts and realizations flashed through his mind in rapid succession.

'What?' Lopez asked.

Ethan leaned forward and stared into one of their escort's sunglasses. 'Can you tell us where we're going?'

The guard remained stone faced and silent. Ethan tried again.

'This isn't about us,' he said. 'Stanley Meyer may have duped everybody. I need to know where we're going because I think that he may have placed himself in great danger.'

'What do you mean?' Amber asked, leaning forward.

Ethan looked at her.

'I don't think that Stanley is behind all of this,' Ethan said. 'I think that he's deliberately made himself a *patsy*.'

'Patsy for who?' Lopez asked. 'What the hell's going on?'

Ethan looked at their escort again. 'Please, you need to call ahead and let them know about what's going on, or Stanley Meyer might not be alive when we find him. I know you're not FBI, or working for Majestic Twelve or Seavers Incorporated. Where are we going?'

The guard lifted his chin and then turned to his right and nodded at his accomplice, who pulled a cell phone from his pocket and began to dial. The guard looked back at Ethan and spoke in a monotone voice.

'Richmond International, for Las Vegas,' he said.

'We need to delay that, turn around and find Stanley before he gets himself killed.'

'Will you tell me what the hell's going on?!' Amber insisted.

Ethan leaned back in his seat as Amber's words of days before drifted through his mind. *I was adopted. Stanley and Mary couldn't have children, so they adopted me at the age of two. Mary was an electrochemist and they met as undergraduates at university. I think that because they couldn't have children they made their careers their priority, and then later in life decided to adopt me.*

Mary was an electrochemist.

'It's all a deception. We've all been chasing the wrong person.'

*

Huck Seavers strode down the plush corridor toward the hotel's penthouse suite and felt as though he were floating on an invisible ocean of joy, his footfalls making no sound on the deep carpets as he reached the door of the suite, which was guarded by two of his most trusted men. One of them unlocked the door and pushed it open for him to pass through.

Seavers had spent much of his life in such luxurious surroundings, the best that life could offer so familiar to him that he never really considered the fact that there were hundreds of other, less exuberant rooms on the floors below. He strode casually into the suite and saw Stanley Meyer sitting on a vast leather couch, a sparkling glass of chilled wine in one hand and a smile on his face as wide as the San Francisco bridge as he looked up at Seavers. The old man reached for a remote and switched off the vast plasma screen television dominating one wall.

'You're looking a tad more cheerful than this morning,' Seavers observed with a smile, buoyed up by his own relief that the whole sorry episode was over.

'Things have improved immensely,' Stanley replied and took a sip of his drink. 'To be honest, I wish I'd done this sooner.'

'So do I!' Seavers gasped, flopping down onto a deep armchair nearby and tossing his Stetson onto a glass table between them. 'I take it that the money has reached your accounts?'

'Half an hour ago,' Stanley acknowledged. 'I must say I admire that you have kept your word, Huck. The payment was immediate and in full, no questions asked.'

'An agreement was made and it was honored,' Huck replied. 'Do you have the documents regarding the fusion cage?'

Huck knew that as soon as Stanley had been paid, and with full access to the Internet and phones supplied, he had begun the process of gathering all of his research materials together into one place so that Huck, and by extension MJ–12, could take control of them, completely removing all trace of the fusion cage from the public domain. A motorcycle courier had delivered a package to the suite only minutes ago, the door guards informing Huck immediately, and he had hurried up in order to take possession of them.

The door to the suite opened, and Aaron Mitchell strode in. Stanley looked up at the towering agent, and his jovial expression withered away. Huck caught the change in mood and spoke quickly to smooth over it.

'You know, if only this had been done sooner when the offers were first made, then none of that bloodshed would have occurred,' Huck said as he watched Stanley rifle through a folder of papers. 'You would never have had to go on the run, your family would have remained safe and Red McKenzie would still be alive and well. Hiring those gumshoes to help you was a mistake.'

To Huck's surprise, Stanley chuckled and nodded.

'Well, it was a necessary evil although I didn't actually hire anybody myself. They found me in Saudi Arabia and were with my daughter when they arrived. In truth, I have no idea who hired them or even who they truly work for.'

Huck looked up at Mitchell, who glowered silently as he spoke.

'The Defense Intelligence Agency. They've been prying into things they have no business interfering with for some time now, under the guise of one program or another.'

Stanley closed the folder he was holding and walked across to Aaron, his features beaming with delight once more and his arms clutching the folder to his chest.

'And who do *you* work for?' he asked the towering agent.

'You don't need to know. Hand over the material and I will disappear.'

Stanley smiled almost pityingly at Aaron.

'You people, you wear the flag of our country and claim to act in the defence of what you call national security, but really you're just as corrupt as the people you work for. Majestic Twelve, isn't it?'

Huck's eyes almost burst from their sockets. 'How do you know about them?!'

'I made it my business,' Stanley snapped back as his happiness vanished in the blink of an eye and an incomparable fury grotesquely twisted his features. 'I did my homework for months and I found out all about that dirty little nest of vipers, feeding off the poverty of millions for their own greed.'

'The files,' Aaron growled.

'You want them?' Stanley asked. 'You want *these*?'

The old man looked down at the files he was holding, and then he tossed them onto the thick carpet at Aaron's feet and turned his back on the agent and strolled away with his hands in his pockets.

'Take them,' he said finally. 'Enjoy every last detail because it won't do you any good.'

Huck, a sliver of panic now slithering through his guts, watched as Aaron Mitchell swallowed his pride with a visible effort and picked up the thick folder. He opened it and leafed through the contents and then looked at Huck and nodded.

'Good enough, for now,' he said as he looked at Stanley. 'Any further mention of this device, or anything in connection with it, by you or any of your family, will result in your funds being taken from you and your own life coming to an abrupt end, is that clear?'

Stanley kept his back to Aaron as he replied.

'I will never speak of my device again,' he said softly. 'Now why don't you be a good little puppy dog and disappear back to your masters? Maybe they'll throw you a bone and pat your head for being such a good boy.'

Huck stared in disbelief at Stanley, astonished that he would so deliberately try to rile Mitchell, a clearly dangerous man. Mitchell glared at Stanley but said nothing as he turned his back and began striding toward the suite door.

Huck Seavers got to his feet and shook off Stanley's sudden aggression. He was probably pissed for having sold out to MJ–12, putting money before his own crazed mission to donate the most valuable energy generation device in the history of the planet to billions of people that he would never meet. The activists, they always took things too far and …

The door to the suite burst open as one of the guards, a phone clasped to his ear, cried out.

'It's gone public!'

Aaron Mitchell froze in mid–stride as Huck felt a ball of ice form around his heart as though it had stopped beating. Mitchell glared at the agent.

'What do you mean?'

'The fusion cage!' the agent almost shouted. 'It's going viral on Internet sites everywhere!'

Mitchell dropped the files in his grasp and immediately pulled a cell phone from his pocket and speed–dialled a number. He spoke clearly and quickly.

'Freeze all assets belonging to Stanley Meyer and initiate a lock–down on all broadcasts both digital and otherwise. Seal the system, now!'

As Huck watched, Stanley continued to look out of the window in silence, a gentle smile on his face.

***

Dean Crawford

XXXIV

Aaron Mitchell closed the door behind the agent with a stern order. 'Nobody is to come in.'

The door closed, Mitchell still holding the cell phone to his ear as he listened, and then finally he shut it off and slipped it back into his pocket.

'What's happened?' Huck asked in desperation. 'What's he done?'

Aaron glared at the inventor for a long moment before he replied.

'The money in the accounts he gave us has disappeared,' Aaron replied, his voice low and filled with a menace so appalling that Huck took an involuntary step back from the agent. 'One hundred million dollars has been spread across accounts in dozens of countries in an attempt to conceal its whereabouts. We'll find it, of course, but for now it is no longer accessible to us.'

Huck shot Stanley a glance. 'What have you done?!'

Stanley, his hands folded behind his back, finally turned away from the panoramic view and faced Mitchell, the smile still touching his face.

'You didn't really believe that I'd sell out to any of you black–hearted criminals, did you?'

Huck felt the world shift beneath his feet as though he were losing his balance as the world collapsed beneath him, which in many ways it had.

'You promised,' he gasped in a weak voice, barely able to speak. 'That you wouldn't share anything, that you would honour the deal.'

'And I have,' Stanley smiled, his gaze fixed upon Aaron Mitchell. 'I have shared nothing, nor have I stolen any of the money. I have completely honored my end of our deal.'

Aaron Mitchell moved closer to Stanley.

'Who?' he demanded. 'Where?'

Stanley's smile grew wider as he looked up at the towering agent and he shook his head.

'I think that you and I both know that no matter what happens to me, no matter what you evil cretins dream up, I'll never tell you anything and that's because I don't actually know. This whole thing was out of my hands long before you even started looking for me.'

To Huck's horror, Stanley's smile broadened and he began to laugh as he spoke.

'All this time, you and your greedy little cohorts have been chasing me around the world looking to silence me, but it gives me an immeasureable pleasure to tell you now that the whole thing has been a charade.'

Huck's legs finally gave way and he slumped back down onto the armchair, his lungs aching and his breath wheezing as though somebody had stuffed a sock down his throat. Aaron Mitchell loomed over Stanley, his giant fists clenched.

'Who, and where?'

'You've spent millions, perhaps billions of dollars now,' Stanley continued in delight, 'and all of it for nothing. Greed is blind, they say, and you're sure greedy!'

Huck tried to stand, to speak, but he could not. Tears welled in his eyes as he heard Stanley's delighted cackles echoing around the suite.

'I knew that you'd come after me, especially when Clearwater disconnected from the grid. It was only a matter of time, really, before somebody figured out that the town was getting its energy for free without a solar panel or a wind turbine in sight. News like that travels fast when there's money involved, so I decided to ensure that when the time came, you'd come for me first. I couldn't distribute the fusion cage without funds, which of course no company would provide as an investment without patents in place, so I needed a really big cash injection to get things moving.'

Aaron's voice rumbled back at Stanley.

'You didn't invent the fusion cage,' he said finally.

Stanley chuckled in delight and shrugged. 'Nope, sorry! I just plugged it in!'

Huck Seavers almost gagged as he saw an image of Seavers Incorporated stocks plunging, of the entire company folding before his eyes and legal cases piling up by the second as his support from MJ–12 vanished. He knew without a doubt that they would hang him out to dry, that his company would be bought out for a fraction of its value and that his life, his family's life, would never be the same again. They would lose everything: the house, the boat, the holidays, the cars, the security, the happiness ...

Stanley Meyer's voice chortled at Aaron Mitchell.

'You're finished,' he said. 'There's nothing on earth that you can do to stop it now! Mine was not the only fusion cage built!'

Aaron Mitchell stepped forward and one thick fist ploughed down into Stanley Meyer's plexus like a freight train through an eggshell.

Stanley's cries of delight mutated grotesquely into a wretch of agony as he folded over at the waist and plunged to his knees. A thin stream of bile spilled from his mouth to stain the carpet as he clutched his belly with both arms.

Mitchell grabbed the old man's collar with both hands and lifted him bodily off the ground, one thick hand gripping Meyer's throat as the other pinned him against a wall.

'Who, and where?'

Meyer's face was twisted in pain, his eyes streaming and blurred as he struggled both to breathe and to fight the pain from the blow that must have wrenched his innards apart. Huck could hear his sobs as Mitchell spoke again.

'Believe me, what happens to you will be nothing compared to what I will do to your family when I find them. Your daughter, your wife, everybody. I will personally exterminate them one by one unless you tell me, right now, what I need to know. Who, and when?'

Stanley, his knees struggling to pull up to his stomach in sympathy with his pain, shook his head and cried out.

'Never! I'll die sooner than tell you a damned thing!'

Mitchell held the old man in place for a moment longer, and then nodded. 'So be it.'

Mitchell hauled Stanley across the suite, the old man's legs dragging across the carpet. Mitchell used a key card to unlock the balcony doors, Stanley kicking and struggling as he was pulled out onto the balcony, five stories above the gardens below. Huck dragged himself off the sofa and staggered across the suite, one eye drawn to a large ornate vase as he heard Mitchell's voice from outside.

'Last chance, Meyer. Start talking or you'll end up as nothing more than a damp spot on that lawn.'

Stanley gabbled an agonized insult, and through the white blinds Huck saw Aaron Mitchell jerk one knee violently upward. The bony joint slammed into Stanley's groin and the old man let out a stifled, pinched groan of agony as he folded up against the railings, weeping and quivering as Mitchell pinned him in place.

'Your daughter will go first,' Mitchell growled. 'Painfully, slowly, while your wife watches. I'll take months over it, Meyer, years. Nobody will ever see them again and even if they did they wouldn't recognize what's left.'

Meyer twitched, his voice sawing and rasping in his throat as Huck reached the balcony and saw Mitchell drag the old man over the railings, his old head and shoulders dangling over the precipitous drop as Mitchell growled at him.

'Your suicide from this suite will be the first news report they hear,' he rumbled, 'just to let them know that we're coming for them, that they'll never be able to escape us. One call, Stanley, one call and your family will become the most wanted people on Earth. Tell me: who, and where?!'

Stanley Meyer sucked in a final, rattling breath.

'Go to hell!' he rasped.

Mitchell scowled and made to lift Meyer over the railing as the old man screamed in fear.

Huck lunged and swung with all of his might, and the ornate vase smashed across Mitchell's temple with a deep crack that sounded as though somebody had dropped a metal ball on wet mud. Mitchell's body flailed sideways as his eyes rolled up into their sockets and the huge man thumped down onto the balcony as Meyer cried out.

Huck Seavers whirled as the old man tilted over the edge and he lunged for Meyers. Huck threw himself half over the balcony railing and grabbed at Meyer's wrists, catching them even as they flailed. The old man hung onto Seaver's grip and looked up at him in amazement.

'Give me your hand!' Seavers groaned, barely able to maintain his grip.

Meyer stared at him through eyes smeared with tears of pain. 'Why?' he gasped.

Seavers knew what Meyer meant.

'Because without you I'm nothing now!' he said in a strained voice, fighting to keep a hold of Meyer. 'I can't survive now with or without your fusion cage, my business will collapse! You're my family's only hope!'

Stanley Meyer watched Huck for a long moment, suddenly it seemed unafraid any more.

'Las Vegas,' he said softly, still fighting back tears. 'My wife's in Vegas, and headed for the Crescent Dunes solar plant. Help her.'

'Grip my wrists!' Huck shouted. 'I can't pull you up like this!'

To Huck's horror Stanley did not grip back as his legs swung out over the abyss, his rheumy old eyes now calm.

'No! Don't you dare do it Stanley!'

Stanley smiled, his voice devoid of anger.

'Be the man you'd want your family to remember you as, not the man you need to be in the now.'

Huck stared at Stanley in amazement and then the old man's hand loosened and slipped through his and he plunged away from the balcony. Huck stared in horror for a moment and then averted his eyes before Stanley hit the patio far below. He heard a distant, sickening thump, and bile formed in his throat as he glanced at Mitchell. The agent was lying on his back, blood streaming from the deep wound in his head onto the balcony.

Huck staggered into the suite and struggled to think straight. He managed to set the vase back down on the glass table and then to fumble for his cell phone in his pocket. His fingers felt numb as he dialled a number, and then heard it connect on the first ring and his wife's voice.

'Honey, where are you?'

'Oh God, Angela, you're safe!'

'What do you mean?'

'Get the kids, Angela, get them and get in your car and run, okay?!'

'Huck, what's going on?!'

'Just do it! Run, Angela, as far as you can! Everything's gone, Angela. There's nothing that I can do now to stop it. Please just do as I say and run!'

'Okay!' Angela replied, Huck hearing the tears and the fear in her voice. *'Where are you?'*

Huck struggled to speak.

'I have some things that I need to do and I can't be there with you right now. Please, just keep running okay? You know how to access the accounts?'

'Yes, but ... '

'No buts! Empty them, all of them, and run! I'm so sorry honey, I love you and the girls!'

'I love you too, but you need to come with us and ... '

Huck shut the phone off, his own eyes blurred now with tears as he turned to shut the balcony door and buy himself some time. He locked it with Mitchell's key card and then hurried to a mirror in the bathroom and splashed water on his face from the faucet as he forced himself to think straight.

'Get out of here,' he whispered to himself.

Huck straightened his suit and walked back into the suite, grabbed his Stetson and set it onto his head. He took a deep breath and strode to the suite door, opened it and walked out into the corridor. Mitchell's two guards looked at him as he closed the door behind him.

'He's dealing with Meyer,' Huck informed them, 'and does not wish to be disturbed.'

The two guards nodded, and resumed their positions as Huck walked past them, his heart beating fast inside his chest as he reached the elevators, already thinking about his next move. He couldn't use his car, or his jet, and only had a few hundred bucks on him.

Huck made it down to the reception hall and walked from the hotel. He barely noticed the dark–skinned Saudi sitting watching the reception hall from the nearby cafÃ©. Huck was far too preoccupied with his dilemma. Somehow, he had to get to Vegas and find Mary Meyer before Majestic Twelve wiped her from the face of the planet.

***

XXXV

'Time of death?'

'Ten fifteen this morning,' the police officer said. 'We called you guys in as soon as we identified him. Looks like a suicide, but given what this guy's been through we figured it the smart play.

'You did good,' Hannah Ford replied.

The patio beneath the balcony was partially concealed by a canvass forensics tent that flared brightly in the sunshine as Hannah looked up at the fifth floor room. Mickey stood beside her.

'The guy's found innocent of any crime, then he commits suicide?' Mickey asked her.

'Doesn't add up,' she replied. 'Let's go take a look, shall we?'

Hannah led Mickey up to the fifth floor, where the entrance to the penthouse suite was being guarded by two police officers. They walked in to see the suite undisturbed, the balcony doors open and fine white nets billowing in the morning breeze.

'No sign of a struggle,' Mickey said, 'but forensics found evidence of vomit on the carpet over there by the wall.'

Hannah Ford glanced at the wine bottle on the nearby table, a half–empty glass alongside it, and the hastily applied marker tape surrounding a damp stain on the carpet nearby.

'Gets drunk?' Mickey hazarded, 'takes a fall outside?'

'Doesn't explain the blood trail,' Hannah said as they followed a faint trail of blood drops and walked outside onto the balcony to look down at the stain by their feet.

'Forensics have taken samples, so whoever this blood belonged to should show up if they're in the system. I'm guessing it's Meyer's though. Maybe he took a fall out here and then went over the edge?'

Hannah frowned and shook her head.

'On half a glass of wine?' she asked. 'If he fell out here, why are there blood drops inside the suite? And why haven't we found his wife and daughter yet? None of this makes any sense. The entire top floor to this hotel was rented out by Seavers Incorporated, a Kentucky mining firm, right?'

'According to the hotelier, yeah.'

'So where's the company's CEO? He's registered as having stayed at the hotel, but was seen leaving this morning. He hasn't booked out though. Stanley Meyer stayed in this room, so we're told, but has no connection to Huck Seavers that we know of. Stanley's cleared of any involvement in that commune fire and is no longer wanted by the Bureau, despite his case being classed as a high–priority, and now he's topped himself? What the hell is going on out here?'

'I don't know,' Mickey shrugged. 'Jenkins says we need to hand any evidence found at this scene over to her, something to do with orders from Langley.'

Hannah looked about her in confusion.

'Something else doesn't make sense about this,' she said. 'Meyer was supposedly on board that jet that we intercepted at Charlottesville, right. But he's not aboard, and neither are Warner, Lopez or Amber Ryan. We then hear they're all alive and well in Kentucky, but I didn't see any evidence to support that, did you?'

'Report came in from on high,' Mickey shrugged. 'I guess they didn't need to prove it.'

Hannah's mind raced as she looked down at the pool of blood at her feet. 'Somebody else was here. And who knew that Warner and his accomplices were both safe in Kentucky and not involved in the fire near Nathalie? One moment they're highly dangerous international fugitives, the next we're closing the case despite multiple civilian deaths?'

Mickey watched her for a moment before he replied.

'There's nothing connecting the deaths in Nathalie to Stanley Meyer or his accomplices,' he pointed out.

'There was yesterday, right up until Stanley here suddenly reappeared in the company of lawyers and Huck Seavers. This stinks, Mickey, and Jenkins wants it zipped up as soon as possible.'

'I don't like the way you're thinking.'

'I don't like the way the bureau's acting,' Hannah shot back.

She looked down at the blood, and on an impulse she knelt down and pulled an evidence kit from her pocket.

'What are you doing?' Mickey asked. 'Samples have already been taken.'

'I know,' she said. 'So I'm taking one for myself.'

*

Ethan did not know how the men with whom they travelled had gained access so quickly to police radios and other law enforcement agencies, although he had an idea, but they were supremely well equipped and within minutes of making a call their vehicle was travelling rapidly toward a massive hotel.

He could see through the windows that the hotel was located amid sumptuous grounds, forested hills and broad lawns that spread as far as the eye could see in the bright sunshine. The image would have been picture perfect were it not for the flashing hazard lights of multiple police cars, a pair of ambulances nearby.

Amber Ryan leaned forward in her seat as her face crumpled in grief.

'No,' she gasped.

Ethan remained silent as the vehicle pulled up alongside the police cordon and Amber yanked open the door and virtually threw herself out into the sunlight. Ethan followed, Lopez behind him as Amber ran to the nearest police officer, who was guarding a cordon preventing any vehicles from getting closer to the hotel.

'What's happened?!' she asked, the tension in her voice palpable.

'I'm afraid I can't discuss the details of the incident with you ma'am, would you kindly step back from … '

'Stanley Meyer,' Amber cut across the officer. 'Is he … '

Amber could not complete the sentence as the officer frowned. 'Are you family, ma'am?'

'He's her father,' Lopez informed the officer gently. 'We've been searching for him.'

The officer's eyebrows raised as he suddenly recognized Lopez and then Ethan, probably from a BOLO likely issued to local law enforcement, and his hand moved momentarily for his sidearm before he then recalled that the BOLO had been withdrawn recently.

'Can you tell us what happened?' Ethan asked.

The police officer gestured over his shoulder to the hotel, where Ethan could see a white tent pitched in front of the building, police maintaining a cordon to prevent the residents from seeing what was happening.

'Suspected suicide,' the police officer said. 'Victim has been identified as … ' The officer hesitated. 'I'm sorry ma'am, Stanley Meyer.'

Amber let out a wail of grief and threw her hands over her face as she turned away. Lopez moved to her side, arms wrapping around her as Ethan stepped closer to the officer.

'Do you have any details? I'm here with the Defense Intelligence Agency.'

'What's the DIA got to do with this?'

'It's a long story, believe me.'

'I can't divulge any information without the say–so of my superiors and with all due respect sir, you've recently been a suspect in a homicide case yourself.'

'I know,' Ethan said. 'The whole thing's a major set up and Stanley Meyer was its chief victim. All I need to know is whether this was a suicide or not.'

The officer chewed the inside of his cheek for a moment before replying.

'The officers called to the scene reported that staff witnessed many suits travelling to and from the fifth floor,' he said.

Ethan looked at the hotel, and up at the fifth floor balcony where a female detective was examining something.

'No evidence of anybody else in the suite at the time?' Ethan asked.

'Not that I'm aware of, but the feds like to keep their cards close to their chests. Makes them feel more important … '

'Feds?' Lopez asked as Amber was gently led away by her escorts.

'Yeah,' the officer shrugged. 'Can't imagine what they're doing here, and now you're with the DIA asking questions. Is this one of those big cover–ups or something?'

Ethan watched the detective on the hotel balcony as she produced an evidence bag from her jacket and began collecting something from the balcony floor.

'Does this place have security cameras in place?'

'That's the thing,' the officer replied. 'They've been wiped.'

'Right this morning before the suits left the building?'

'How did you know that?'

'Seen this sort of thing before,' Ethan explained. 'I think that there was somebody else involved. Chances are he's an African–American, over six feet tall and well built, mid–fifties. If any of the staff recall seeing a man of that appearance visit the hotel this morning, you might want to pass it on to the detectives – or take a little of the glory for yourself?'

The officer virtually beamed at Ethan.

'I'll check it out. Anything else?'

'Yeah, as a matter of fact. Do you think that you could get me a direct line to the DIA from here? I don't have my phone anymore and we need to place an urgent call.'

'Stand by,' the officer agreed, 'I'll get on it.'

As the officer walked away Ethan turned to see Amber now sitting on a low wall nearby, the two escorts watching over her and consoling her as Lopez approached Ethan.

'Are you going to tell me what this is all about?'

'Stanley did not invent the fusion cage,' Ethan replied. 'He deliberately drew attention to himself by fleeing, and of course given his history everybody assumed that he was the inventor. We've all spent this time chasing the wrong person around the globe.'

'Then who invented it?'

Ethan smiled, impressed by the ingenuity of it all.

'The only other person who disappeared but was not paid off,' he replied. 'Stanley's wife, Mary.'

Lopez stared into space for a moment and then her eyes lit up. 'Stanley said that she was a biochemist.'

'Exactly,' Ethan said. 'By the time she retired, Fleischmann and Pons had already had their cold fusion scandal. She would have been working at the time and would have had access to the data they produced in order to replicate the success, or alleged success, of their experiments. What if she saw something in the experiments that the others did not?'

'Maybe she decided not to report her findings,' Lopez echoed his thoughts, extrapolating what might have gone through Mary Meyer's head. 'Maybe she saw through the MIT fudging of the test results and realised that there was a conspiracy behind attempts to suppress the technology. If she is anywhere near as determined as her husband was, she might have decided to forge ahead alone.'

'And then planned to give the device away, for free,' Ethan finished the story. 'They've been in this together from the start. Mary did not flee because she was afraid of persecution, Mary was the target that should have been. Now she knows what's happened to Stanley, my guess is that she'll do everything she can to expose the technology and spread word of it before Majestic Twelve are able to pin her down.'

'We need to find her,' Lopez said urgently. 'We can use Amber's cell phone and … '

Ethan was about to agree with Lopez when suddenly he heard a car door slamming. Ethan whirled in time to see their escorts leaving in the people carrier, the vehicle cruising away from the hotel.

'Where the hell are they going?' Lopez snapped.

'Damn it, Amber's taking off on her own,' Ethan said. 'The only person who could have found us so accurately and sent heavies has to be somebody that Amber spoke to.'

Lopez closed her eyes. 'Amber's damned phone. She contacted her mother.'

'Mary's got a fortune to play with if Stanley did what I think he did, and sold out before sending the money to Mary. She'd have hired professional bodyguards to grab Amber – we just got carried along for the ride. Now, Amber's going to join her mother.'

Lopez watched as the vehicle disappeared down the drive and then she grabbed Ethan's arm.

'Majestic Twelve would do anything now to stop Mary from broadcasting anything about the fusion cage. They'll send that agent we ran into in Argentina, the tall guy, Mitchell?'

Ethan nodded. 'He'll stop at nothing. The moment Amber makes her move he'll cut her down without hesitation. Majestic Twelve are protecting him from prosecution, including this.'

Ethan gestured to the hotel behind them.

'You think that Mitchell did this?' Lopez asked.

'I think that he realised what Stanley had done, what Mary has done,' Ethan replied. 'Stanley didn't want to die, and had family relying upon him. Yes, he would fight tooth and nail, but throwing himself over a balcony would serve no purpose. He must have been pushed.'

As Ethan finished speaking the police officer hurried back down to the cordon. He had a cell phone in one hand and excited looking on his face.

'Looks like you were right,' he said conspiratorially as he handed Ethan the cell phone. 'The detective on site is not certain, but she thinks there's a second person involved. There are traces of blood on the balcony, and drag marks in the carpet that she thinks may have been caused by somebody dragging a body and throwing it over the balcony. So that means there's a homicide here. I passed on your description of the perpetrator to the team.'

'Thanks, I appreciate it,' Ethan said as he took the cell phone and dialled a number. 'The FBI can talk to our senior officer at the DIA, Doug Jarvis. I'm calling him right now.'

The line rang repeatedly for several long seconds, and then finally picked up.

'*Hellerman.*'

'Who?'

'*Warner, is that you?*'

'Where's Jarvis?'

'*Long story, man. Listen, get yourself under cover as fast as possible. There's a whole crap storm brewing here and yours and Lopez's names are all over it!*'

'What's happened?'

'*Jarvis has been forcibly retired and you're both being hunted again by the FBI for the murders of a bunch of tree–huggers in Virginia and some guy in a hotel.*'

Ethan felt his blood run cold as he looked at the hotel.

'Okay,' Ethan said, keeping his voice calm in front of the police officer. 'We need a ride out of here as fast as possible. We're at that hotel.'

'*You're what?!*' Hellerman replied. '*Get out of there now! Where do you need to go?*'

'Las Vegas,' Ethan replied. 'Mary Meyer is the one behind all of this, she invented the device and now she's about to release it to the public across just about any channel she can find. Majestic Twelve will do anything they can to stop her. They've already murdered Stanley Meyer, and I believe the agent we encountered in Argentina was behind it. Mitchell.'

'*There's a plan in place,*' Hellerman replied. '*Get to Shepherd Field Air National Guard Base in Martinsburg, West Virgnia, as fast as you can. Transport will await. Use the clearance code Have Gray at the gates, it'll get you through, now get out of there!*'

Even as Ethan shut off the phone, he saw FBI agents emerging from the hotel and looking around, and saw one of them point in his direction. A woman, with long auburn hair and a fresh face, reached for a radio at her belt.

'Time to leave,' Lopez said.

The police officer's radio crackled and he reached for it as a stern–sounding female voice shouted at him. Ethan lunged forward and un–holstered the officer's service pistol, yanked it free as he tucked one boot in behind the officer's ankle and shoved him onto the grass. He turned the pistol over in his hands as he and Lopez whirled and dashed across the lawns.

'Wait!'

Ethan plunged into the woods lining the hotel drive and followed Lopez through the thickets until they burst out onto the drive as a smart looking Lexus appeared ahead, driven by an elderly couple. Ethan stood in the middle of the road as he aimed the pistol at the car. The driver panicked and stopped, his eyes wide as he threw his hands up beside his head.

Ethan rushed forward and opened the driver's door.

'You're in no danger,' he said in a perfectly reasonable voice. 'We're working with the Defense Intelligence Agency. Get in back, and we'll give you back your car in a short while.'

The old man nodded frantically as on the other side Lopez helped the elderly wife out of her seat and installed her in the back.

Ethan jumped into the driver's seat and turned the Lexus around as they fled the scene, the sound of sirens somewhere behind them. Ethan turned hard right out of the hotel's drive and then took the first left he encountered, putting distance and direction to good use to avoid any pursuit.

'They won't take long to figure out what happened to us,' Lopez pointed out.

'This'll dupe them for a while,' Ethan replied. 'Mitchell has a head start on us, and he'll fly on a private jet no doubt with diplomatic immunity of some kind. The only advantage we have is that we know which vehicle Amber is travelling in and where it's headed. We've got to get to them before Mitchell or this is all over.'

***

XXXVI

Nellis Air Force Base, Nevada

The massive C–5A Galaxy of the 167th Airlift Wing out of Shepherd Field Air National Guard Base in Virginia had landed at Nellis Air Force Base in Nevada just before sunset, the sprawling military airfield within sight of Las Vegas's glittering galaxy of lights already shimmering in the fading light of dusk as Ethan watched the sun setting behind the sandy colored mountains of the Sierra Nevada range.

Despite General Nellis's lofty rank, the airfield was not named after him, but Ethan felt as though the senior officer deserved such an accolade for taking the chances that he had, along with Jarvis's mysterious assistant, Hellerman. Ethan walked with Lopez off the C–5A along with the crew, both of them wearing uniforms that made them appear as nothing more remarkable than loadmasters or engineers.

'This way.'

An Air Force sergeant guided them toward a dark blue personnel truck destined to carry the crew across the airfield to the crew rooms. There, Ethan and Lopez would split off from the main group and leave the base on their desperate mission to locate Mary Meyer and Amber.

'Why do you think that she's in Vegas?' Lopez asked quietly as they rode in the truck with the tanker's crew. 'Can't be the bright lights or the gambling, even with the money she must have taken from Majestic Twelve.'

'Not with the money she's got now,' Ethan agreed. 'I don't know what she's up to, but my guess is that she's going to try to do something with the fusion cage and it involves Vegas. Think about it, both she and Stanley hated capitalism, and what better icon to money than Sin City?'

'Good place to pick,' Lopez observed as she looked out of one of the windows to the west, where the glow of the city was easily visible against the darkening mountains. 'This place is lit up like Christmas every night of the year.'

On the journey down from Virginia, which had taken four hours in the C–5A as it travelled to take part in Nellis Air Force Base's annual international *'Red Flag'* combat exercise, Ethan had taken the opportunity to try to figure out why Mary would have chosen to conceal herself in such a brazenly excessive location.

A haven of pomp and glitz, Las Vegas was globally infamous for its excesses. The state of Nevada consumed more than twenty eight million megawatt–hours of power annually, that power drawn from the US national grid, which was supplied by more than six thousand power stations. However, Vegas's City Center complex of hotels and casinos was so large that it had developed its own 'off grid' electricity power plant.

'The whole central complex of one of the most illuminated cities on Earth is also completely off the US national grid,' Ethan said to Lopez as he read from the screen of his cell phone a file sent to him by Hellerman at the DIA. 'It has its own power station along with power supplied from the Hoover Dam complex. Most of Nevada's energy comes from out of state and has few fossil fuel resources but substantial potential for geothermal, solar, and some wind power development. According to this, Nevada's economy is not energy–intensive and consumption is well below the national average despite heavy use of air conditioning.'

'So Nevada's not as bad as people think?'

'Depends on how you look at it. Two thirds of the state's net electricity generation comes from natural gas fired plants but the state's consumption exceeds in–state generation, the excess being supplied by high–voltage lines from Arizona and the Pacific Northwest.'

'So it's worse than people think too?'

'Nevada takes fully one quarter of the energy created by the Hoover Dam,' Ethan said. 'Plus its two grids supply Vegas and the northern part of the state respectively, with a solar plant at a place called Crescent Dunes powering the strip in support. Only California takes more energy from the Hoover Dam. If there was ever a place where Mary might be able to make some kind of dramatic demonstration of what the fusion cage can do, it would be here.'

Lopez frowned.

'You think that she's going to do something dramatic? Cut the power off and then start things up again?'

'It's what I'd do in her position. There's no hiding now. She's taken the money from Majestic Twelve and run with it, and they'll be hot on her tail. Internet releases about what's happened and even print publications won't be enough to save her. The only way she can save herself is to do something so spectacular that everybody on the planet will hear her name and see her face. Majestic Twelve will be rendered powerless to touch her–if she reveals the scale of the conspiracy her family has been hiding from and then she's killed … '

'Too many questions,' Lopez agreed. 'It'll be enough to turn world attention on to the Bilderberg conference and, by extension, Majestic Twelve.'

'They've got to stop her or they'll lose control of the energy industry,' Ethan said as the truck slowed alongside the crew buildings on one side of the huge airbase. 'Mitchell will be here by now and looking for Mary in the city.'

The truck came to a halt and the tanker crew disembarked as the sergeant led Ethan and Lopez through a side building. The flight bags they carried, ostensibly filled with flying regalia, instead contained their civilian clothes.

'You can change in there,' the sergeant said, clearly uncomfortable with the covert nature of what was transpiring. 'A vehicle is awaiting you outside, silver, here's the key.'

The sergeant handed Ethan a key. 'You're already cleared to leave the base but once off site you're on your own, understood?'

'Understood,' Ethan replied.

With that, the sergeant turned on his heel and marched away as quickly as he could as Ethan and Lopez quickly changed out of their flight suits and back into civilian clothes. Ethan led the way outside to a large parking lot and hit the 'unlock' button on the key fob the sergeant had handed him. To his right, parked among a myriad of cars, a silver sedan's lights blinked and a short beep from the alarm rang out.

'Where do we start?' Lopez asked as they walked toward the car. 'Mary could be anywhere in the city and the FBI won't be far behind us.'

'She must have some kind of target in mind, something that she can both attack and then save at the last moment, that will be visual enough and obvious enough that the whole damned world will have to sit up and take notice.'

Lopez climbed into the sedan and opened a tablet computer she found in the glove compartment. She tapped in a few commands as Ethan started the engine and switched on the air conditioning to cool the vehicle's sweltering interior.

'According to this, the main supply of power to the Las Vegas area is delivered by the Edward Clark Generating Station in Whitney, east Las Vegas. It's a major station, over a thousand megawatts of power.'

Ethan nodded. 'That sounds like a good place to start. Mary and Amber must be together by now and she'll know that her husband is dead and that she's running out of time. Whatever she's got planned, it's going to happen tonight.'

*

'There can be no further mistakes.'

Aaron Mitchell sat inside the limousine that had ferried him from the airport and into Las Vegas. The car cruised in silence, the tinted windows veiling Mitchell from the view of the countless tourists and residents flowing along the sidewalks and reflecting some of the glare from the myriad lights of equally countless casinos and hotels.

The voice he had heard was that of the same man he had met in Holland, his distinct tone and accent audible even over the digital scrambling that protected their conversation from even the most adept of hackers.

'There can be little time remaining,' Mitchell replied. 'Mary Meyer knows by now that her husband is dead. She may not suspect us of involvement, but given Stanley's deception it is my opinion that this was all pre–planned directly because of their mutual suspicion of government involvement in the cover–up of the cold fusion debacle of the 1980s.'

'Then our cause is under direct threat,' the voice said.

'We have contained the Internet leaks,' Aaron assured him, 'and all other media outlets that Mary Meyer approached have been silenced on this matter. I can only assume that she now intends to do something direct in an attempt to draw attention to herself, and Stanley said that his fusion cage was not the only one in existence. We must assume that Mary Meyer, the actual inventor of the device, possesses another of its kind and may be building more of them as we speak.'

'I do not need to impress upon you how vital it is that any fusion cages in her possession be retrieved and their security maintained indefinitely. The consequences of their appearance in the public realm would be catastrophic, would see trillions wiped off the market share of every major fuel and oil company across the globe. The economic ramifications, not to mention the political fall–out and the collapse of financial markets globally would be unmatched by any prior economic event in history. Find Mary Meyer, find the fusion cage, and destroy them.'

The line went dead and Aaron Mitchell leaned back in his seat and closed his eyes. His head still throbbed from where Huck Seavers had hit him with the vase, and despite pain–killers and the attentions of a skilled make–up artist to conceal the wound, Mitchell was for the first time in a long time at a disadvantage. His main concern was locating Mary Meyer or Amber Ryan, either of whom would give him the required leverage to bring the entire charade down and prevent a catastrophe that would end his career and ruin the reputations of many other men vastly more powerful than he. However, his second major concern was Ethan Warner and Nicola Lopez.

Mitchell felt certain that Warner would already be in the city. The men he had dispatched to Virginia had reported that both Warner and Lopez had escaped local police and the FBI once again, this time commandeering an elderly couple's vehicle and covering forty miles to the outskirts of Richmond before vanishing once again. Mitchell suspected General Nellis's involvement but could not prove it and didn't have the time right now anyway. Likewise he wondered whether Jarvis had somehow been able to slip Warner a warning of some kind before he had been forcibly ejected from the Defense Intelligence Agency's headquarters, hopefully for the last time.

Both Warner and Lopez had developed a nasty habit of appearing at the most vital moments and throwing spanners in the works of Mitchell's missions, and he was growing tired of hearing their names. Freelancers, and bail–bondsmen at that, were harder both to control and to predict than paid employees of the government or armed forces.

Defense Intelligence Agency operative Douglas Jarvis had played a clever hand, keeping his own agents at arms–length and off the radar of the government, but that hand was now–defunct. Mitchell looked out of the windows at the glowing lights of the Las Vegas strip and cleared his mind of thought as he focused in on Mary Meyer and her single–minded mission to devastate the entire United States economy in a single, crushing blow. If Mitchell were in her shoes, where would he go and what would he do to complete his task before he was found and silenced?

Aaron's eyes focused on the bright shimmering lights of the strip, and in an instant he knew that Mary intended to somehow subvert the power supply to the strip itself, and to do that she would need access to at least one of the main power stations serving the Las Vegas area.

A moment's work brought up a series of power stations connected to the Nevada grid, and Mitchell knew that he would not have time to search them all in order to root out a single individual. More to the point, it would not be possible for Mary to hijack such vast industrialised sites in order to plug–in a fusion cage. In addition, how would Mary publicise the event? Nobody would know, and she had just one night in which to complete her task on her own...

Aaron thought of the commune that Stanley Meyer had hidden in, and in an instant he realized what Mary would most likely have done.

He reached for his cell phone, speed dialled a number and waited for the line to hook up.

'What is it?'

'I need every single resource we have in Nevada within the hour,' Aaron snarled. 'She's not here on her own, she's bought an army with her.'

***

XXXVII

'We don't have any record of those individuals passing through the airbase at this time ma'am.'

Special Agent Hannah Ford leaned against the security gates at Nellis Air Force Base and flashed her most winning smile at the soldier manning the gate house, let him catch a glimpse of her cleavage.

'We know that a C–5A Galaxy aircraft departed Shepherd Field Air National Guard Base four hours ago and landed here,' she said. 'We also know that two fugitives with support from at least one government department of the intelligence services made it aboard that aircraft. All I want to know is where they went after that, or in what vehicle they were travelling.'

The soldier remained impassive.

'I don't know what to tell you ma'am,' he replied. 'I have no record of them passing through this airbase, and no amount of eyelash fluttering is gonna change that.'

Hannah's winning smile evaporated and she pushed off the gate. 'You know that hiding fugitives is a federal offence?'

The soldier shrugged. 'Yes ma'am, but knowing nothing about it isn't. You have a nice day.'

Hannah turned and stormed away from the gates of the airbase back to the pool car where Mickey was waiting for her. She yanked open the door and slumped into the passenger seat.

'Never heard of them?' Mickey hazarded.

Hannah scowled but said nothing as she covered her face with her hands, took a deep breath and then pushed her hair up and away from her face.

'Warner and Lopez get out of that car somewhere near Richmond, and then we lose track of them. All we do have is the license plate of the vehicle they were seen arriving in, which was hired and later found abandoned outside a civilian airfield, and the occupants seen entering that field. The only aircraft that left that field in that time frame is a C–5A for Nellis, from where they've disappeared. Damn it, none of this makes any sense. Warner and Lopez arrived at the hotel in a vehicle! Why the hell did they steal another one?'

Mickey shook his head.

'We're chasing our tails here, Hannah. In my time at Quantico we were trained to track killers, to monitor suspected terrorists, to assist local law enforcement. Nothing I'm seeing here bears any reference to that. As far as I can make out, we're chasing a bunch of lunatics across the country and have no idea, for sure, if they're even criminals.'

'Defense Intelligence Agency,' Hannah said. 'That's what officer Morton said they'd claimed to be working for, right?'

'They claimed to be working for, being the operative statement. Hannah, these people are likely con artists, frauds. Nothing they've said can be taken at face value.'

Hannah leafed through a folder that contained everything they had on the current case, and found herself once again looking at an image of Mary Meyer.

'Why is nobody looking for this woman?' Amber asked. 'Her husband is now dead and she's been missing for just as long, as has their daughter, Amber, who also showed up at the hotel with Warner and Lopez in tow.'

'I don't know,' Mickey replied wearily. 'They could be in Europe by now. This is a waste of time, Hannah. You're just chasing this because you think that any success you have will piss Jenkins off.'

'That's not true.'

'Why are we here then?'

Hannah looked at Mickey for a moment, and then shrugged. 'Because it might piss Jenkins off a little, obviously.'

Mickey sighed at the sight of the tiny smile touching Hannah's freckled face. 'I don't know why I follow you into things like this.'

'Because you know it stinks,' Hannah replied, 'just like I do. They're all here, and they're up to something. Whatever it is, I can't just let it go – there's also a homicide to think about, remember?'

'Again, according to Ethan Warner, who then takes off before we can question him about how he knew there was a second person on the scene.'

'The DNA profile will take a while to figure out, but we know the blood wasn't Stanley Meyer's. Warner was right, so why would he then take off, and why the hell is he being held up as a suspect in the case? He wasn't there, can't have been.'

'And yet he knew somebody else was present at the scene,' Mickey pointed out. 'So he must be connected to the murder somehow.'

Hannah rubbed her temples wearily, her back still aching from the commercial flight that they had taken in order to pursue her wild hunch that they had all been missing something important that would tie all of the disparate threads together. Warner. Lopez. The Meyers, and the unknown killer she felt sure was …

Her cell phone buzzed in her pocket and she answered instantly.

'Tell me you've got something.'

'I've got something.'

The excitement in Special Agent Emma Granger's voice made Hannah sit up straight in her seat and switch the phone onto conference as Mickey glanced across at her.

'Tell me.'

'There's a common theme in the travels of Stanley Meyer and this Ethan Warner guy,' Emma reported. *'I've been reviewing CCTV footage from any locations that we can be certain they have travelled through within reasonable time–frames, and then cross–referencing those with …'*

'Stop pulling my chain, Granger, what have you got?' Hannah snapped impatiently.

'A Saudi security specialist,' Emma replied, *'by the name of Assim Khan. I'm sending a picture over to you right now.'*

Hannah looked down and saw an image of a Middle–Eastern looking man, his hair graying slightly at the temples and a broad jaw beneath dark eyes.

'What's his story?' Mickey asked.

'Former Saudi Special Forces,' Emma replied. *'He joined a Saudi firm that specializes in security but is suspected by the CIA of being a front for assassins for hire. Assim here has been implicated in a number of hits over the years but nothing's stuck.'*

'What's his connection to Stanley Meyer?' Hannah asked.

'Assim was hired by Seavers Incorporated to provide security during a visit to Saudi Arabia by none other than Ethan Warner and Nicola Lopez. I managed to find out that the Saudi's suffered a major military setback in the desert while Warner and Lopez were in the Kingdom but off the radar, lost an Apache gunship to militants and apparently are now trying to extradite Warner and Lopez back to stand trial.'

'They shot down an Apache gunship?' Hannah asked in amazement. 'What the hell for?'

'Who knows with these two,' Emma replied. *'Their names are all over files attached to the Defense Intelligence Agency, but they're so redacted that I can't make head nor tail out of them. At one point or another, the CIA has had an interest in the pair of them, and so has the National Reconnaissance Office.'*

'Who the hell are these guys?' Mickey uttered in amazement.

'Assim,' Hannah pressed. 'Why is he so important?'

'Because he's here,' Emma replied, *'in America, or more precisely, he landed an hour ago in Las Vegas. More than that, I've got images of him showing up in Virginia at the hotel. Assim Khan may be our guy, and get this, since he showed up in the country, Huck Seavers and his family have vanished.'*

Hannah and Mickey exchanged a glance.

'If Assim's the killer, then he's probably targeting either Warner and Lopez or the Meyers,' Mickey said.

'Or Huck Seavers and his family, or even all of them,' Hannah agreed. 'Do we have a fix on Assim Khan yet?'

'He hired a vehicle from a rental place down on the south side,' Emma informed Hannah and passed on the registration. *'Do you want me to alert the local field office and get you some support. Jenkins is still in the office and I'm sure she'd clear you to...'*

'Keep Jenkins out of the loop,' Hannah snapped. 'Contact the Las Vegas office and inform them of everything you just told me but keep local law enforcement out of it for now other than a BOLO for the rental vehicle. Any of them locates him, they're to pass it on to the field office. I don't want forty squad cars with screaming sirens letting this guy know we're onto him.'

There was a long pause on the line. *'Jenkins will be pissed at you cutting her out.'*

That smile appeared again on Hannah's face as she replied.

'Let her get as pissed as she likes, this one's slipped through her fingers because she was all for shutting it down. Send my number to the Special Agent in charge down here and I'll liase directly with them. Let's see if we can't close this guy down before he kills any more Americans.'

Hannah shut off the phone and turned to her partner. 'Any time, Mickey, you're welcome.'

'Damn, how the hell do you manage stuff like this?' Mickey uttered as he pulled out of the air base's gates.

'I got a nose for trouble,' Hannah replied gleefully as she looked at the image of Assim Khan on her phone. 'Let's hope this guy does too, and we'll let him lead us right to everybody else.'

***

Dean Crawford

XXXVIII

The Las Vegas crowds were dense, rivers of humanity flowing between endless sparkling lights flashing in the darkness. The city was like that, built in the centre of a desert plain and glowing like a galaxy of stars amid the blackness of space. Noise, heat, light, vehicles rushing to and fro, laughter, and beneath the glossy veneer a grimy underbelly of crime and suffering.

Vagrants rifled through bins overflowing with the casually discarded detritus of a humanity that possessed far more than it needed. Young dudes in shades and hoodies surreptitiously exchanged wads of cash for small packages. Hookers lingered on the corners of the darker streets, not all of them women, some of them neither fully woman nor man.

Society at both its best and its worst, a modern day Sodom intoxicated by the heady elixir of unrestrained capitalism.

Mary Meyer walked through this gloating apocalypse of excess as though striding through a valley of death. She saw nothing around her that made her admire what humanity had achieved, a life where nobody cared, where nothing really mattered but the next drink, the next hit, the next woman or man for hire in some dingy low–rent motel. She glanced up at the towering casinos and hotels, magnificent in their glamor and yet rotten to the core with greed and the criminal foundations upon which they had been built. Her beloved, brave Stanley had hated this city with all of his considerable passion, and now those who had built it had consumed him and spat him out, dead and derided and forgotten. Tears blurred her eyes, the flashing lights smeared into a kaleidoscope of color that sickened her with its unnatural haze.

She forged ahead, pulled her baseball cap low over her eyes. She was hot and uncomfortable, and not just due to the heat of the Nevada night or the disgusting display of profanity all around her. The padding she had placed under the sleeves of her shirt and trousers bulked her out, changing her appearance to conceal her from easy identification. Hair dye and clothes that she would not normally be seen dead in that emulated those of the tourists oggling at the city around them completed the illusion.

Mary knew that the government possessed the ability to identify faces from the merest glimpse on a CCTV camera, so she kept her head down and hoped that the dazzling casino lights would help camouflage her appearance further and fool the cameras. In her hand she held a cell phone, purchased for cash in a store downtown as soon as she had arrived. Upon the phone she had installed an *app*, which she had created herself, and distributed to a small network of people whom she had confided in from the moment she had fled Clearwater.

To have abandoned Amber in the wilderness had been the most heart–breaking thing that Mary Meyer had ever had to do in her life, and that pain only cemented in her mind the importance of what she was now endeavouring to do. Had Amber been caught, she would have been used as leverage against Mary and Stanley. But far out in the woods, she was safe enough and Mary had hoped, prayed even to a god that she did not believe in, that she would realize what had happened and find her way to safety, somewhere else.

Amber was a fighter, a spirited girl whom Mary had raised from just three months old. Her mother, a drunken drug abuser out of Bedford, had abandoned the baby girl on the doorstep of All Saint's Church in the town. Mary and Stanley had searched for just such a baby, one given no good start in life, and had been successful in adopting Amber. They had given her a life that otherwise would have been denied, for her mother had died of a drug overdose four years later in a shack in Villamont. Amber had never asked about her and Mary, with relief, had never made an attempt to speak of the dead woman.

The phone in her hand buzzed and she looked down at it.

The app revealed her location in the city, as tracked by local cell phone towers, and also displayed the location of some fifty accomplices moving through the city in various locations.

It had not been hard to recruit people to her cause. With one hundred million dollars available to her and a willingness to approach just the right kind of people for the job, she had assembled a small force of like–minded individuals who had followed her work on Low Energy Nuclear Reactions for years, and it had only cost her a couple of million dollars to do so – half the payments already in place, the other half when the task was complete. Now, her faithful minions were scurrying this way and that across the city, all of them with a small but essential task.

And now Amber was with her, and ready to play her part, a more crucial one now than Mary would ever have dared to hope for. But in the wake of Stanley's death, Amber had been clear: she wanted in.

Mary had spent a few weeks identifying the critical power–supply lines streaming into Las Vegas from the surrounding power stations that fed the city's enormous appetite for electrical power. Gorging itself like some gigantic, hideous monster, Las Vegas glowed with its greed for power, consuming more energy in one day than some towns did in an entire year. Each of those power cables represented a high–voltage intravenous line that kept the city alive and also prevented its inhabitants from suffering the heat of Nevada's mid–day sun, while also providing the power for water pressure to prevent them from dying of thirst, and energy for sewage works and treatment plants that spared them the ignoble fate of drowning in their own waste.

All of it required power, and Mary Meyer now held that power in her hand. On the screen as she glanced at it, amid all the tiny green dots that represented her work force, was a single blue dot that remained steady and still, far to the bottom right of the display.

The Fusion Cage.

Mary's plan was deceptively simple. At the required time, the minions she now employed would each detonate an explosive charge that would sever the high voltage lines coming into the city. In a single, bold stroke she would cut Las Vegas off from its energy supply, starving the beast within seconds. The lights of Las Vegas would go off, along with all computer networks, phones, Internet, air conditioning, water supply, sewage treatment, everything, gone, in an instant.

In the same instant, at a location only she herself knew, she would deactivate the only available source of power that could save Las Vegas's poisonous strip from economic collapse. Then, and only then, would she reveal her hand.

She knew that the casinos would bend to her will. Devoid of power and reliant upon generators that only possessed enough fuel for a few hours' of work, they would be facing ruin as the gamblers flocked away in their droves. Without power the casinos were nothing, gigantic monoliths to greed and cash that held no sway over their countless victims. But Mary could change all of that, and not only return the power to them but also provide it entirely for free, saving them millions of dollars in energy bills.

Mary had long ago accepted that to change the world, you first had to grab the people with the money by the balls.

Right now, unbeknown to the most powerful people in Las Vegas, Mary Meyer had her fingers curled tightly around their most prized possessions and was about to start squeezing.

*

'She could be anywhere.'

Ethan drove slowly onto Las Vegas strip and saw the galaxy of lights stretching away before him, a highway of color amid the immense blackness of the Nevada desert.

Lopez was right. Vegas was the perfect place for Mary Meyer to hide herself, to vanish amid the roiling crowds of tourists, card–sharks, drifters and addicts that made up so many of the city's countless inhabitants. Whatever she had in mind, and Ethan felt certain that she did indeed have a plan, it was likely going to involve switching the lights off across one of the most famously excessive cities on the planet.

'She'll blow the power stations,' Lopez guessed. 'It's the only thing that makes sense.'

Ethan shook his head.

'But that's just what bothers me, it doesn't make sense. Everything that Stanley set out to achieve involved helping the ordinary people of the world, not plunging them into darkness. Mary must share the same passion, and blowing up power stations won't achieve anything in the long run, unless ... '

Ethan imagined the sight of Las Vegas in absolute darkness. Of course, the casinos and hotels would be able to run off generators for a while, a standard back–up system to prevent the immense loss of revenue from black–outs that afflicted all cities from time to time. But the *control* of that power, that ability to switch it on at will and not have to worry about revenue, was a different matter. The power companies could not do that because they would lose revenue themselves, be held to account, profits and shareholder confidence vanishing overnight. But Mary, if she did indeed have a second fusion cage, could hold the entire city to ransom and ...

'She's not going to blow up the power stations,' Ethan said. 'That's not her plan.'

'How do you know?' Lopez challenged. 'Her husband was just murdered by the people she wants to stop. Revenge is a powerful motivator, believe me.'

'She wants revenge all right,' Ethan agreed, 'but this has always been about hitting the corporations where it hurts the most – their pockets. She doesn't want to destroy the city's infrastructure, she'll need it herself to distribute power from any fusion cage she might possess. She wants to shut down the power and then come to the rescue, to show the world that her husband was right, that Stanley Meyer was trying to save the planet and was murdered for his troubles.'

Lopez's dark eyes flew wide.

'The solar array!' she said suddenly. 'Crescent Dunes, wasn't it?'

'It's the city's back–up power source,' Ethan confirmed. 'Much of the power it produces is to light the Vegas Strip.'

'But that's solar power,' Lopez frowned. 'Why would she go there?'

'That's what she wants, the exposure, the visibility. The solar plant is iconic. If she's figured out a way to demonstrate the fusion cage in action that nobody can deny, she'll be untouchable–any attempt on her life will result in social unrest on a global scale.'

Ethan grabbed the wheel of the car and swerved off the main strip as he sought a fresh route out of the city.

'It's past midnight,' Lopez said as she glanced at her watch. 'Whatever she's going to do, it's going to be soon.'

Ethan's cell phone rang as he drove and Lopez picked it up.

'Ethan's phone.'

'I have a track for you,' came the response, and although she had never met Hellerman, Lopez could guess from the digital hiss of distortion on the line that matched the one she had heard whenever she spoke to Jarvis that she was speaking to his faithful assistant.

'Go ahead.'

'It's heading north on the I95 toward Tonopah, range twenty eight miles. The signal matches Amber's cell phone.'

'That's toward the Crescent Dunes project,' Lopez confirmed. 'Amber must already know what Mary is about to do. But it could be a decoy, something to throw us off.'

'We've got no choice but to follow her,' Ethan said, raising his voice enough so that Hellerman could hear it. 'There are no other leads right now and we can't search the Vegas Strip, it would take weeks and we only have hours. We've got to take the chance that Amber's letting us know where she's going.'

Lopez switched the cell to speakerphone as Hellerman replied.

'I can offer you no further assistance. The KH–12 Keyhole satellite I tasked for this is already moving on toward other regions and is out of range and Jarvis is out of the loop completely. Even General Nellis isn't playing ball any longer. Majestic Twelve, whoever they are, must have got to him somehow. In addition, according to transmissions intercepted recently, the FBI are on your tail again with agents deployed into Vegas and a BOLO out with local law enforcement. You're on your own now, I'm afraid. Good luck, Hellerman out.'

The line went dead and Lopez looked at Ethan.

'On our own again. Color me surprised.'

Ethan smiled grimly as he accelerated out of the Vegas Strip onto the I95.

***

XXXIX

Tonopah, Nevada

'Bullseye, Spirit Twelve, inbound to Initial Point, request vectors.'

The cockpit of the B2 *Spirit* Stealth bomber was shrouded in darkness, the instruments glowing a faint green through the pilot's visor as he glanced briefly out of the cockpit windscreen at the immense night surrounding them. Major Pete Grady heard the voice of a fighter controller in his earpiece as he concentrated on his instruments, climbing through banks of broken stratus cloud that glowed a faint blue in the starlight as he climbed toward his assigned altitude.

'Spirit Twelve, angels three two zero, maintain climb, no traffic.'

'Three two zero, wilco, Spirit Twelve.'

Beside him, the co–pilot was scrutinizing the displays, programming data into the aircraft's surveillance system. Both of them knew of the immense importance of this mission, which had been recorded as a routine training flight out of Whiteman Air Force Base, Missouri. It was rare for B2s to deploy operationally into theatre, and even rarer for that theatre to be the continental United States, but this was an extraordinary mission born of an extraordinary detection just days ago over Missouri.

Pete Grady had been able to analyse the data from the Spirit's surveillance sensors before that data had been whisked away by the Defense Intelligence Agency, and although he would not have admitted it to another soul, not even his wife, what he had seen there had fairly scared the crap out of him. An energy burst of significant proportions, deep in the Missouri wilderness, that should have been worldwide news by now. At the time his first assumption had been an asteroid impact or another energetic cosmic event, but the emergence in the data of nuclear by–products including a small neutron burst in the wake of the event suggested a nuclear accident. That was quickly ruled out, as there were no nuclear sites nearby and besides, there was no *smoking gun*: no crater, no fires, no nothing.

Whatever he and his co–pilot had detected that evening on their way back from a training flight, it had vanished completely. Now, with sensors adapted at no small cost to specifically locate that energy burst again, they were now airborne high over the Nevada desert having deployed to Groom Lake airbase, better known as *Area 51*, that very day. Pete Grady's rank was not senior enough to ask too many questions, but it was obvious that the whatever–it–was they had detected was believed to still be present, and clearly the powers that be felt it was in Nevada.

Area 51. Bright lights. High energy.

Nobody was saying UFO, but he knew damned well everybody had been thinking it.

Prior to their departure, they had been briefed on the presence of an unspecified weapon smuggled into the United States by insurgents from the Middle East. Powerful, dangerous, high technology that must be found at any cost. Lives, perhaps millions of lives, depended upon it. The orders came from the very, very top: *locate and destroy*.

The desert below him glowed with the light from Las Vegas, a sparkling jewel of color encrusted into the darkness. Grady looked down at it, knowing that up here at forty thousand feet he was utterly invisible to the people below, that *he* was the UFO sneaking around in the upper atmosphere. The gigantic, wedge–shaped B2 looked like an enormous, angular black bat haunting the troposphere.

'Sensors are set,' his co–pilot, Scott Reed, reported. 'We're ready.'

Grady checked the instruments one last time, made sure that he was ready for what could be a long night, and then nodded.

'Activate,' he ordered. 'Let's see what's out there.'

Reed switched the Spirit's passive sensors on and then set them to "Active", and moments later the radar displays began displaying images from the apparently empty desert below them.

'Good morning, America,' Reed said.

The darkness was alive with tiny specks of light and heat detected by the immensely powerful sensors. Vehicles on roads, campers far out in the desert, asphalt roads still glowing with residual heat from the previous day's sunshine like arteries flowing in an X–ray. But amid the countless specks of heat a single spot of bright blue–white shone like a new born star almost right in the centre of the main display on the cockpit before Grady.

'What's that?'

Reed studied the display, isolating the glow.

'It's the solar tower at Crescent Dunes,' he reported. 'Must still be much hotter than the surrounding area. Don't they have melted salts or something, heated by the solar arrays?'

Grady watched the display. He knew that solar towers glowed throughout the night and were extremely bright objects when compared with the rapidly cooling deserts that so often surrounded them, but there was something about this one ...

'Can you isolate and grab a spectrographic display?' he asked. 'If anyone was trying to hide a weapon down there, that hot spot would be the perfect place to do it.'

Reed began altering the filters on the optical sensors until he was able to display a spectrographic read–out on Grady's screen. The image had switched to one that portrayed the elements contained within the heat source far below them: all light had a signature that could be split and studied to determine what chemical components were contained within. Grady stared down at the read out and frowned.

'Hydrogen, oxygen, palladium, lithium,' Reed reported, 'nothing unusual at all.'

Grady's mind tried to determine what he was seeing. There was almost certainly water down there, which one might expect from the steam boiling off the turbines at the plant. As far as he could recall, most solar plants used the heated salts to boil water to turn steam–turbines, so some airborne exhaust would be expected. But palladium and lithium? He had heard of lithium salts but palladium was often used in catalytic converters and fuel cells, where hydrogen and oxygen were combined to produce heat, electricity and water.

'It's a solar tower,' Reed said. 'That's the kind of technology we'd expect to find in an installation like that, right? Green stuff, no pollutants?'

Grady nodded, still thinking. Their orders were to search and destroy, but he was also aware that the Crescent Dunes solar array was quite a famous installation. Built using government money and costing billions of dollars, dropping a few thousand pounds of high–explosive ordnance on such an installation would create political devastation in so many ways that Grady could not begin to calculate the consequences of such an action. The fall–out would be incalculable, and if covered by a story of an explosion or similar could render the solar industry redundant and perhaps even bring down the administration that funded the projects.

The perfect place, then, to hide a weapon from aerial bombardment.

'Search for another solar tower and use the spectrograph again,' Grady ordered. 'I want to compare the data and see if what we've got here isn't being used to hide something.'

'I've already got one in the data set,' Reed replied. 'Ivanpah, down in the Mojave desert. We flew overhead on the way to Groom Lake yesterday.'

Reed got to work immediately, pulling out the relevant data sets and comparing them to the crescent dunes signal from far below. Reed studied them for a moment and then looked at his pilot.

'No palladium,' he said. 'According to our data file the Ivanpah site uses much the same tower technology as Crescent Dunes, but no salts – it heats water directly.'

Grady looked at the displays and the sensors for a moment longer.

'Call it in,' he said finally. 'We can't bomb the damned tower, but somebody needs to get down there and check it out real fast.'

As Reed called their findings in to Groom Lake on a secure channel, Grady wondered just what the hell these terrorists had down there, and what on earth they were doing putting it up on top of a three hundred foot solar tower.

*

'All units, stand by.'

Special Agent Hannah Ford gripped her vehicle's radio switch tighter than was necessary as she watched her rear view mirror. Bright lights illuminated the huge pipes, conduits and towers that made up Las Vegas's Edward Clark Generating Station, the sky beyond deep black.

The vehicles were concealed behind a slip road onto the I65, looking north east over wire fences at transformers and power cables strung from metal towers that hummed in the warm night air.

'Why would Assim come here?' Mickey asked.

'His vehicle turned up here an hour ago,' Hannah replied. 'All we can do is try to figure out what his game plan is and hope we can intercept him.'

'We've got movement.'

Agent Vaughn nodded discreetly to Hannah's left, and she slowly turned her head to see several figures skulking along the fences outside the plant, hugging the shadows, crouched low and carrying bags.

'This is it,' she whispered once more into her microphone. 'Be ready to move on my mark.'

Ten agents from the Las Vegas Field Office were positioned around the plant, each in vehicles parked discreetly in side alleys and nearby roads, concealed by shadows. As Hannah watched the half–dozen figures skirting the edge of the power plant, she saw them stop and produce a large pair of bolt–croppers. Within moments, they were through the fence and inside the plant.

'They're going for it,' Mickey said urgently.

'Units one through three, take the front entrance,' Hannah ordered. 'The rest of you, with me! They'll go for the towers. Go now!'

Hannah shoved her door open and dashed out across the street to where the figures had sliced open the fences and slipped inside. The ground was dusty and hard, baked for decades by the fearsome desert sun as Hannah ran hard in pursuit of the figures she could see ahead of her, their shadows cast long by the powerful lighting of the station. She could hear Agent Vaughn right behind her, sprinting to keep up.

'They're going to drop the towers,' he gasped, 'the ones leading into Vegas.'

Hannah ran harder, saw the figures huddle around the base of the first tower they reached and begin unpacking their bags. Visions of high explosives shattering the legs of the towers and bringing Las Vegas to its knees raced through Hannah's mind as she ran and drew her pistol from its holster beneath her left arm.

'FBI! Freeze!'

The figures looked up at her, faces concealed by bandanas, but to her amazement they continued unpacking their bags and hurrying to secure something to the legs of the tower. Hannah heard the hum of the power lines as she dashed beneath them, saw other agents converging on her position through the plant.

'On your knees, hands where I can see them!'

Hannah skidded to a halt before the terrorists, her pistol held in both hands and pointed at them. Mickey Vaughn dashed to her side, covering her with his own weapon as from their right more agents rushed in, all armed.

The terrorists looked at the agents and as one they stood up and raised their hands.

Hannah checked that she was covered and then she strode forward to the nearest of the terrorists and yanked the bandana from his face. To her amazement, instead of Assim Khan' rugged features a young girl stared back at her, fresh faced like she was just out of college.

'Hello,' the girl said.

As Hannah watched, one by one every single one of the terrorists removed their bandanas to reveal young, college–aged faces. Hannah had never seen a more innocent looking bunch of kids, pinned down as they were now before a dozen armed federal agents.

'What's in the bag?' Hannah demanded, fearful of some kind of suicidal cult.

The girl's smile broadened.

'Nothing but banners protesting against our abuse of the planet's limited resources,' she replied softly. 'You can check the bags if you want.'

Hannah's mind whirled as she tried to figure out just what the hell was going on.

'Banners?'

'Banners,' the girl repeated. 'I was told to give you a message.' Hannah stared at the girl, speechless, as she went on. 'Wrong place, wrong people, wrong time.'

Hannah stared at the bags, at the supposed terrorists before them, and a creeping fear swelled inside her.

'Oh no,' was all that she could utter.

'What the hell's going on?' Vaughn demanded.

'This doesn't make any sense,' Hannah gasped, then whirled and shouted at the FBI team.

'Arrest them all and get us out of here! Assim's target is not in Las Vegas!'

Hannah stormed back the way she had come, Vaughn at her side.

'What do we do now?'

'How the hell am I supposed to know?!' Hannah snarled back.

Vaughn slowed, and Hannah forced herself to take a breath and stop walking. She closed her eyes for a moment and turned to face him. 'I'm sorry, I don't know what to do next, okay?'

Vaughn sighed but he offered her a faint smile. 'It's not an easy case.'

They both turned as they heard boots approaching, and saw Valery Jenkins striding toward them, flanked by two senior agents from the Las Vegas field office.

'Ford!'

Hannah felt her shoulders sink as she turned to face Jenkins. 'I can explain.'

'You can explain all you want! You're off the case, and suspended until further notice, is that clear?!'

Vaughn stepped forward. 'This was a legitimate lead. Hannah had good intel that could have led us to … '

'To what?!' Jenkins demanded. 'A different career?! You disobeyed a direct order, subverted the chain of command and caused a major operation out here for nothing, all in one evening! You're both done, understood? Now get out of here before I have you arrested!'

Hannah turned and walked away, her strides feeling stiff and unnatural as she set off for the vehicles they had left at the roadside. She heard Vaughn following her, pursued by Valery Jenkin's outraged voice.

'If I have my way, you'll never work an FBI case again. This was a farce, Ford. Nobody's ever going to destroy a power station like this one, and you're a fool for believing they'd even try to … '

Hannah saw the blast before she heard it, a blossoming ball of flame to her left as something detonated beneath the southern towers. The shockwave hit her a moment later, a solid wall of air moving at high speed that hurled her off her feet and sent her tumbling across the dusty earth.

The explosion lit up the power station as the failed tower toppled, power lines falling with it in a shower of bright sparks as though a billion stars were falling all at once from the night sky. Hannah covered her head with her hands as the tower crashed down to the sound of wrending metal and a snarl of wild electricity that ran like bright snakes up and down the severed wires and across the tower's superstructure.

Hannah, her ears ringing from the blast, pulled her head up to see the tower on its side and flames licking around the remains of its metal legs, high–voltage power cables draped across it and spitting sparks crackling with energy.

She staggered to her feet as Vaughn joined her.

'What the hell?' he uttered.

Hannah struggled to think straight, but she could see Jenkins and her entourage clambering to their feet nearby, and then Vaughn's cell phone buzzed in his pocket. He answered it, and then looked sharply at Hannah.

'Half of the Vegas Strip has lost its power supply,' he reported.

'Damn it,' Hannah cursed and kicked the dust. 'What the hell is going on here? We're one step behind all the time!' She ran her hands through her hair. 'I just don't know what to do here.'

Vaughn grinned as he listened to the voice on the other end of the line.

'Well, I do. Local law enforcement just received a call that a hire vehicle that matches the one hired by Assim Khan has been spotted by a traffic camera headed north on the I95, for Tonopah.'

Hannah whirled to face Vaughn. 'What the hell's up there?'

'I don't know,' Vaughn admitted, 'but it's our only remaining lead and Assim Khan clearly doesn't care what's happening in Vegas.'

Hannah glanced at the power station one last time, at Jenkin's bedraggled appearance, and then made her decision. 'Let's go.'

**

XL

Crescent Dunes, Nevada

The sun.

Mary Meyer had always loved the sight of the sun rising on a clear dawn, ever since her parents had taken her early morning fishing out on the lakes of her Missouri childhood home. Few things were more peaceful than a wilderness sunrise, all the more surprising considering how lethal was the sun's heat, how fatal exposure to its radiation could be for humans.

The solar plant was deserted, only a small number of employees based on site to monitor the tower and its boilers. Situated far enough out into the desert for Mary to have driven to its gates unnoticed, her headlamps extinguished to further conceal her approach, Mary had driven her car off the road and approached the site from across the dusty desert, aiming for a series of narrow trails that intersected the gigantic field of mirrors arrayed in a disc around the immense tower at the plant's centre.

The Crescent Dunes Solar Energy Project was a one hundred ten megawatt solar plant surrounded by seventeen and a half thousand heliostat mirrors. The immense array of mirrors collected and focused sunlight onto a five hundred forty foot tower, atop which was a huge chamber which contained flowing molten salts. Those salts, superheated by the sunlight, flowed to a storage tank where the energy was used to produce steam which then powered turbines to produce electricity. A marvel of human engineering, all of which would be rendered useless by Mary Meyer this very morning.

The horizon to her left beyond the mountains was aglow with the promise of another of those perfect dawns and this one she hoped would be more memorable than any of the others she cherished so dearly. It was just such a shame that she would have to do things this way, instead of the way that Stanley would have wanted – via the people themselves, rising up together as one and showing the governments and the corporations that they were nothing without the people themselves.

Instead she held a pistol firmly in her grip, pointed at a young, bearded technician cowering behind his computer panel.

'This won't take long,' she said. 'Do as I say and I absolutely promise that neither you or your colleagues will be harmed, okay?'

The man cowering before her glanced to his right, where half a dozen engineers lay with their wrists bound to their ankles, their backs arched as they lay facing the walls of the office that Mary had stormed barely ten minutes before.

'Okay.'

The man's voice was thin and reedy. Mary recognized him as an academic, not the kind of man used to being in physically stressful situations, which was precisely why she had chosen him. He would bend to her will for fear of his life and would not be prone to heroic defiance. If he knew what she intended, what she and her family had been through, he might well have helped her but Mary was already well–used to the response of scientists to her work, their dismissals and their ostracising of anybody who dared to think out of their comfortable little boxes.

The bearded man, who went by the name of Alan, had followed her very precise instructions after tying up his colleagues, and re–programmed the mirrors across the array. Now, there would be no power getting to Las Vegas, which was stricken by the power outage blackening the strip so beloved of the casinos and corporations.

'Get up,' she said softly.

Alan did not move, his eyes wide behind his thin–rimmed spectacles.

'I said get up, now!!'

Mary fired the pistol into the nearest wall and Alan shrieked in terror as he struggled up onto legs weak with fear.

'Out the door, move!'

Alan hurried away with Mary following, the gun never straying far from his back as they walked outside into the cool night air, the tremendous array of silent mirrors pointed straight upward into the blackness. Mary gestured toward the car she had travelled in, and she walked around to the passenger's side and ordered Alan into the driver's seat.

'Drive to the tower,' she commanded.

'Why?'

'Because if you don't I'll have to shoot you and pick another of your colleagues to do so, understood?'

Something in Mary's tone and expression convinced Alan that she was serious and he obeyed without further question. The car traversed the distance from the control station to the tower in less than a minute, its tires crunching along the track between the huge mirrors, each the size of an eighteen–wheeler truck, and Alan pulled up alongside the tower's main entrance.

Mary could see huge buildings, the size of aircraft hangars, and massive pipes and conduits of polished aluminium shining in the dawn light. Further back, on the far side of the tower, the two huge water tanks loomed.

'Get out.'

Mary kept her gun trained on Alan as she walked to the car's trunk and gestured to him. 'Open it.'

Whether Alan thought that he was going to be placed in the trunk or not, she couldn't be sure, but his legs almost gave way beneath him and he struggled to open and lift the trunk. Mary looked down and inside the trunk she saw the object for which governments had killed, for which businessmen had killed, for which so much had been lost and so many denied so much for so long. The answer to mankind's dreams.

'What's that?'

Alan's fear had vanished to be replaced with something that almost sounded like disappointment. A metallic box, no larger than a suitcase, was caged in aluminium tubes and attached to what looked like an oxygen cylinder. The whole device fitted easily into the trunk of the sedan.

'Lift it out.'

Alan reached in, somewhat emboldened by the fact that whatever it was, it wasn't a bomb. He hefted it out of the trunk and set it down on the ground before looking up at Mary.

'Now what?'

'Now, you carry it up there for me,' Mary replied.

She gestured with a nod of her head up to the top of the tower. Alan swallowed thickly and his fear returned.

'I don't like heights.'

'Do you like being shot?'

*

The horizon was awash with a pink glow as Huck Seavers drove off the main road and into the large open lot that served Crescent Dunes. He could see the main service building ahead of him, immaculate and white amid smaller out buildings and parked lorries.

His eyes ached from the long drive, his head fuzzy with weariness and worry for his wife and children as he pulled into a parking slot and killed the engine, wondering just what the hell he was going to do next. A local radio station had reported explosions at a major power station outside Las Vegas, half of the strip going dark, the presence of FBI agents at the scene and chaos as engineers struggled to restore the power.

The desert was silent as he got out of the car and began walking across the lot, and for a moment he felt as though he were in one of those post–apocalyptic movies, a last survivor of some global pandemic wandering a lonely planet. The stillness of the air and the silence did little to comfort him as he strode across toward the service building and peered into a window.

The interior was dark, the reception area devoid of personnel, to be expected at this early hour he supposed. He glanced left and right and then he saw it. A single door, the locks bust off, perhaps using a crowbar or similar. The door was ajar, a blackness inside that Huck did not want to confront. He spared a thought for his family, for Stanley Meyer, and then he took a breath and walked across to the door and swung it open.

Silence and darkness greeted him, but at the end of the hall he could see an open doorway from which spilled light. Emboldened, Huck walked down the corridor, trying to keep his footfalls as silent as possible as he approached the open door. Beyond, he could see flashing lights that looked like some kind of control room and then he heard the low, muffled moaning.

Huck stopped, listening intently and acutely aware that he was stranded half–way down the corridor with nowhere to hide. He watched and waited, listening to the low moaning and once again reminded of those horrible zombie movies, but then he pushed forward to the doorway and peered inside.

He saw the men tied up on the floor and immediately he hurried across to one of them and leaned down. The man was gagged, his wrists tied behind his back and bound to his ankles. Huck reached down and pulled off the gag.

'Call the police!' the man coughed as he gasped for air. 'She's insane and she's got a hostage!'

'Who? What did she look like?'

'Who the hell cares?! Call the police!'

Huck looked up at the control panels. Mary must have come through here and picked up a hostage for some reason, perhaps protection against Majestic Twelve should they manage to locate her in time, although it seemed MJ–12 cared little for collateral damage. She must have travelled to the tower, but he could not fathom what she intended to do.

'She reprogrammed the panels,' the scientist said in dismay. 'They're deactivated. You need to call the police and inform them of what's happened before … '

Huck replaced the man's gag to a groan of protest as he stood up. The moment the police were called, Majestic Twelve would send people and Mary would be killed, if they weren't on their way already. Huck knew that his best bet was to reach out to her himself, to do something, anything, to join forces with her and bring the fusion cage to the world.

Huck ran out of the service building, turned and sprinted into the massive mirror array as he headed toward the tower. Maybe, just maybe, he could get Mary out of here before it was too late.

*

She recognized the arrogant stride as soon as she saw it.

Huck Seavers walked from his car to the service building, and emerged a few minutes later at a run, headed toward the tower. He looked strange in the low light, disembodied, seen through a tunnel of darkness as a shadowy figure flashing past one solar mirror stand after another as he ran the five hundred metres from the service building to the tower's base.

Amber Ryan lay prone in a low depression alongside a heliostat, her position perfectly masked by the mirror itself. The rifle in her grasp was perfect for the job and it felt natural in her grasp, the telescopic optics perfectly aligned after she had "zeroed" them to her eyesight further out in the desert. The winds were light, the bullet drop at two hundred fifty yards already calibrated on the scope and range–finder.

Amber could hit a small bird at this range, even in a breeze.

Cover me, Mary had begged. *Just until this is over, so that they can't do to us what they did to Stanley.*

Mary had been in tears, shivering, shaking and her eyes both wide with fear and yet hard with determination. *For Stanley.*

The crosshairs tracked Huck as he moved but at a sprint and at such range and with the solar array supports forming a forest before her, Amber knew that a wild shot would be unlikely to finds its target and would only serve to alert Huck Seavers to Amber's presence. Besides, that was not what Mary wanted. Her instructions had been clear: she wanted no innocent people involved and Amber was just to be a back–up. If somebody tried to kill Mary, then she should act accordingly before fleeing the scene.

Huck was on his way to prevent Mary from revealing something amazing and wonderful to the world.

Huck had killed Stanley Meyer.

Amber kept him in her sights as he entered the tower, and prepared to pick him up again when he emerged at the top.

***

XLI

'Put it there.'

Alan set the fusion cage down on the floor alongside a set of steel doors, access panels that opened out onto a walkway that encircled the tower just below the salt chamber at the top.

The tower's base possessed only a narrow entrance, used to bring in the vast lengths of steel pipe used to transport the salts up and down the tower. The heat inside was intense, Mary's shirt soaked through and Alan's hair matted flat against his head, his beard glistening with sweat and his face sheened.

Mary could feel the even more intense heat generated by the chamber above them permeating the air and the walls as she positioned the fusion cage beneath the chamber and looked up to the ceiling. When the solar array was active, it directed the light from the mirrors to the heating chamber where they now stood and at the salt tower above them, heating those salts to more than a thousand degrees centigrade.

Alan stepped back from the fusion cage, staring at it as though confused.

'What is it?' he asked.

'You wouldn't understand.'

'It's not a bomb, there's no timer.'

'Be quiet.'

Mary turned to the steel doors. From her pocket she pulled a small set of folding bolt croppers and handed them to Alan.

'Break the lock,' she ordered.

'I don't know if I can,' Alan whimpered, the fear returning once more as he looked at the padlock holding the door latch in place.

'Try,' Mary replied, and jabbed the barrel of her pistol against his ribs.

Alan winced and turned, trying to fit the croppers around the padlock's thick steel bar.

'The latch,' Mary uttered as she rolled her eyes. 'It'll be easier to cut the latch.'

Alan shifted the croppers to the thinner metal of the latch and dug his shoulders in as he heaved the croppers closed around it. The pincers bit into the metal, and from her vantage point behind him Mary could see them cut through the latch a bit at a time.

Alan heaved and huffed as he fought his way through the unyielding metal, but eventually the croppers sliced through the last of the latch with a sharp click.

'Good, now open the doors.'

'We're three hundred feet above the desert!' Alan gasped. 'It's dangerous to … '

'Now!'

Mary's enraged yell was amplified by the confines of the chamber, and Alan visibly jumped in fright as he looked again at the gun in her hand and then turned and wrenched open a series of deadbolts keeping the doors in place. As the last of them was freed he reached for the handles and pulled the massive doors open.

A blaze of sunlight burst into the chamber as the doors opened to reveal the desert in all of its glory, a vast panorama of sandy terrain tiger–striped with black shadows as the sun began to rise on the far horizon. Mary was taken aback by the sheer spectacle of the huge heliostat array before her as a gust of fresh desert air billowed into the chamber.

Alan whimpered again and his knees buckled as he staggered back from the doors.

'Please, no more,' he begged.

'Sorry, Alan, but you're my insurance,' she replied. 'Out you go.'

Alan's eyes widened in terror and he shook his head. 'No, I won't go.'

Mary aimed at him, the pistol pointed between Alan's eyes. 'Now.'

Alan stared up at her, his eyes glazed with tears, but then to her surprise he shook his head.

'No. You'll have to just shoot me, I'm not going out there!'

*

Amber's eyes widened as she saw a pair of tiny looking doors open high up on the tower and Mary appeared, a gun held to the head of a man slumped on his knees before her.

'What the hell, Mary?'

Her mother had never before shown even the slightest hint of aggression or violence in all of the years Amber had known her. A pacifist, philanthropist and devotee of nature, Mary Meyer had never even owned a gun as far as Amber could recall. Now, she was threatening the life of a man who looked suspiciously like he worked in the facility and was likely as innocent as Amber.

I don't want any bystanders to get hurt, Mary had said. Amber's finger rested on the trigger of the rifle but she began to waver uncertainly as she watched the exchange high above her. The man was crawling away from Mary, one hand held uselessly up to shield himself from the gun as he inched his way toward the ledge outside the heat chamber, three hundred feet above the desert floor.

'Don't do it, Mary,' Amber whispered.

Mary shouted something at the cowering man, the wind now whipping at his hair as he backed out onto the ledge, and then she fired the gun over his head. The shot flashed brightly from the pistol's muzzle and a few seconds later Amber heard the faint report on the wind.

Without conscious thought Amber switched her aim from the cowering man to Mary Meyer.

'Don't do it mom,' she whispered again.

*

'Move!'

Alan crawled backwards, fully outside of the chamber now on the wide ledge that surrounded the heat chamber. He was barely three feet from the edge, and as he got his first good look down so he shook his head again, anger finally breaking through on his features.

'To hell with you, I'm not going any further!'

Mary aimed over his head and fired a single shot. The pistol jerked in her hand and the report rang in her ears, an unfamiliar burning smell assaulting her. Alan shook his head again, crying openly.

'No, I'm not going further!'

Mary lowered the pistol and aimed at Alan's head, steeled herself. Emotions churned through her mind as she thought about what Stanley had endured, at what had been done to him, and as she looked at the man cowering before her she realized that she had become what Stanley's enemies had become: inhumane.

'Mary, no!'

The shout from behind her sent a shockwave of alarm through her entire body and she whirled and aimed at the man who had appeared in the chamber behind her. Surprise gave way to fury as she saw Huck Seavers standing before her, his chest heaving as though he had been running.

'You!' she hissed.

'It wasn't what you think it was!' Huck said quickly. 'They had me over a barrel just like Stanley!'

Mary took a pace toward Huck, the pistol aimed squarely at his chest.

'You, the multi–millionaire coal man, comparing yourself to my late husband?! How dare you even speak his name?!'

'I didn't murder him, Mary!' Huck shouted, the wind picking up around the tower as the sunrise began to warm the deserts below. 'He let go!'

'What the hell are you talking about?'

'I had a hold of him!' Huck shouted. 'He was being attacked by a man, the same man who convinced me to go into business with Majestic Twelve! I helped Stanley because I realized, too late, that we would all be dead if somebody didn't make a stand!'

Mary shook her head. 'You were at the scene! You killed my husband!'

'I tried to save him!' Huck protested, his hands in the air beside his head. 'It's why I came here! My own family are being threatened now, just like yours! I've had to hide them away! I'm not your enemy, Majestic Twelve is!'

'What happened to Stanley?!'

'He let go!' Huck insisted. 'Said that he didn't want to give anything away about what you two had planned! He knew they'd get to him in the end! He told me you'd be here at Crescent Dunes, that's all!'

Mary wavered, tears staining her eyes as she tried to figure out who was lying in what felt to her to be a world of liars. She kept the pistol aimed at Huck.

'You're not interested in my husband, or me! All you want is your profits!'

'Yes!' Huck shouted back. 'And those profits are here!' He pointed at the fusion cage in the centre of the chamber. 'That's it, right? The fusion cage that everybody's chasing after? I don't want to destroy it, Mary, not any more. I understand what Stanley was trying to do! I want to help. I can manufacture it for you, produce ten thousand of them and ship them for free! It's the only way to stop Majestic Twelve from covering all of this up! Help me to help you, and let that man go! He's innocent!'

Mary stared at Huck for a long moment and then she realized that he was telling the truth, saw the same light of compassion in his eyes that she had so often seen in Stanley's. Huck Seavers, incredibly, had seen the light. Huck saw the change in her expression and he lowered his hands and took a pace toward her.

Mary lowered the pistol and turned to Alan, who was still lying in terror on the ledge.

The shot cracked past Mary, a snap on the wind like a bird's wing, and she turned to see Huck Seavers quiver. The coal man's chest shuddered and Mary saw a faint spray of crimson blood puff out on the gusty air from his back as the color drained from his face.

Huck Seavers looked down and saw a red stain spreading on his chest.

Mary dropped her pistol and dashed to Seaver's side as his legs gave way beneath him and he slumped onto the chamber floor, his eyes wide and his mouth gaping for air.

'No!'

Mary felt terror ripple through her belly as she held Huck in her arms and screamed at Alan.

'Go, get help!'

Alan, unsteady on his feet and pale now from the sight of so much blood, staggered past them and ran for the exit. He got as far as the stairwell and then Mary heard a deep thump. She looked up and saw Alan collapse, his eyes rolled up into their sockets.

Moments later a dark skinned, Middle Eastern looking man ascended the steps to the tower, a pistol in one hand as he walked out into the chamber and saw Mary.

***

Dean Crawford

XLII

'This is it!'

Ethan drove onto the parking lot and raced past the rows of vehicles there as he aimed directly for the nearest track that led toward the tower.

'Enemy front!'

Lopez's shout alerted Ethan and he swerved as several agents emerged from a parked SUV and aimed their pistols at them. A crackle of gunfire rattled out and Ethan hunched down in his seat alongside Lopez as bullets smashed through the windows and sprinkled glass chips across them.

The gunfire swept past them and the car lurched to one side as a round punctured a tire. Ethan heaved on the wheel to keep the vehicle straight as he came up again and saw a dark, tall figure leap out of the way of his vehicle. Ethan got a brief glimpse of the man's face, his dark skin and angry eyes, the salt and pepper hair cropped close to his scalp.

'That was Mitchell!' Lopez gasped as they raced by.

'Majestic Twelve are already here,' Ethan said. 'We don't have much time.'

The engine of their car coughed and spluttered as a cloud of gray steam billowed from beneath the hood. The vehicle slowed and Ethan instinctively slipped the car into neutral and let it coast toward the tower.

'There's somebody up there,' he said as he leaned forward and peered up at the dizzying heights.

The car rolled to a halt a hundred yards from the tower and Ethan climbed out to see Aaron Mitchell close behind them.

'Go,' Ethan said to Lopez as he backed up. 'Get to Mary and cover her until we can find a way out of here.'

'We're in the desert, Ethan,' Lopez said cautiously as Mitchell advanced, his guards in their vehicle close behind him.

'Get inside the tower and keep moving,' Ethan insisted. 'I'll hold them off as long as I can.'

Lopez glanced behind them at the soaring tower. 'Is this because you don't like heights?'

'Will you get on with it?!' Ethan snapped.

Lopez turned and dashed through the tower entrance, and Ethan slammed the doors shut and searched for something to seal them with. Huge overhead pipes hissed and hummed with energy, but he could find nothing suitable to protect Lopez inside the tower with. He grabbed a handful of sand from the ground and turned to face Aaron Mitchell.

Ethan stood in silence in front of the tower entrance as Mitchell approached, his dark coat billowing in the rising desert wind, his skin dark and his eyes concealed behind glossy black sunglasses, one hand casually tucked into the pocket of his coat. He looked every inch the avenging angel of death as he moved to stand within a couple of yards of the entrance and then raised a hand behind him. The SUV containing his men slowed and pulled up a hundred yards away, covering the escape route.

Mitchell turned back to Ethan and regarded him silently for a moment.

'Mister Warner. Once again you have placed yourself in a position of great jeopardy.'

'Bad luck and trouble seems to be my forte.'

'Stand aside, and I will let you live.'

No preamble, no threat, just a statement of fact. Ethan tensed. He saw no weapon on Mitchell, no sign of any intention to attack, and yet Mitchell was clearly under no doubts of his ability to crush Ethan. Mitchell probably had forty pounds on Ethan and a good three inches in height, likely a longer reach and, given the man's formidable size and confidence, a Special Forces background that Ethan lacked.

'No can do,' Ethan replied.

Mitchell's shoulders sagged slightly. 'So be it.'

Aaron was fast, incredibly so. The hand in the pocket of his jacket was not there at all, only the sleeve tucked in place, his arm instead behind his back with a pistol in his grip. It flashed around to aim at Ethan, who instantly tossed the handful of sand he held in his left palm and dropped into a forward roll.

Mitchell's shot cracked out, his rising arm countered by Ethan's rapid drop as the bullet zipped over Ethan's head and smacked into the tower with a metallic clang. Ethan threw his shoulder down as he rolled through and struck out with his right boot.

The hefty size ten slammed into Aaron's groin even as the sand stuck in his eyes, and Aaron groaned and folded over the blow. Ethan scrambled to his feet and reached up to slap one hand across Aaron's wrist to push the gun away and prevent him from taking a second shot while with the other he swung a bunched fist. The blow struck Aaron across the cheek with a crack but the agent was already making the only play that he could.

Aaron rushed in and let his entire body weight plummet into Ethan. Ethan hurtled backwards and down, turned his head aside in the direction of the gun just before Aaron's muscular chest crashed down onto his face, but even blinded and winded Aaron was quick enough to stretch the pistol out beyond Ethan's reach, pinning him in place with his weight.

Ethan heaved against the agent's huge body but he knew already that he would not be able to dislodge him. Aaron widened his legs to keep Ethan from toppling him off to either side, giving him the chance to recover from the devastating blow Ethan had delivered. Ethan forced one leg between Aaron's and jerked it up, driving his knee upward in an attempt to deliver more blows to the bigger man's groin, but despite groans of pain Aaron remained in place and folded his arms around Ethan's head as he pressed his chest down.

Ethan struggled against Mitchell's immense weight and strength but he quickly felt the bigger man regaining himself. Mitchell's wrist turned as he tried to aim the pistol at Ethan's head, only Ethan's grip on his wrist preventing him from fully bringing the weapon to bear. Pain bolted through Ethan's hand as he tried to keep the pistol at bay, his breathing laboured and his head pinned against the dusty desert.

Ethan reached down with his free hand and fumbled in his pocket and a moment later he found what he was looking for. Ethan flicked the Zippo lighter into life and held it against Aaron's coat, and moments later the stench of smoke and the heat of flames billowed from between them.

Aaron let out a roar of pain and hurled himself up and away from Ethan, his coat in flames as he tried to throw it off and aim at Ethan at the same time. Ethan shot to his feet, one hand still on Aaron's wrist and blocking the pistol, and he hopped off his right boot and onto his left as he then slammed his right knee up into Aarons' flank.

Aaron's ribs crackled beneath the impact and Ethan saw the agent double over in sympathy with the pain. Ethan turned in the opposite direction, twisting the pistol over in his grip and tearing it from Aaron's grasp. Aaron cried out in pain as he dropped to one knee, and Ethan grabbed the pistol and stepped back, aiming at Aaron.

'Hands behind your back, face down on the floor and I'll let *you* live,' Ethan gasped, short of breath.

Aaron did not look up, until a sudden gunshot echoed from within the tower and a scream followed. Ethan whirled without hesitation and dashed into the tower, Lopez on his mind as he tore up the steps.

*

Amber blinked and her heart raced in her chest as she saw Mary collapse beside Huck Seavers' body, and with some terrible certainty Amber knew that she had made a mistake. Through the telescopic sights she could see Mary trying to stem the flow of blood from Huck's wounds, his body no longer visible where it had collapsed, only Mary's grief stricken face.

Amber saw the man Mary had only moments before been threatening leap to his feet and flee the scene, disappearing out of sight. Then, slowly, Mary got to her feet and Amber saw her lips moving as she spoke to somebody out of sight, deeper inside the tower.

Amber's heart thumped in her chest as she thought of Seavers bleeding out in the tower. What if she had shot the wrong man? She recalled Seavers talking to her in the car in Saudi Arabia, of how she had believed him back then. What if she had been wrong about him killing Stanley Meyer? What if he had in fact been trying to help Mary?'

But she had turned her back on him, and he had moved toward her. He could have pushed her off the edge of the tower, tried to take her gun, anything.

Amber struggled to control her wildly swinging emotions as she watched Mary talking, saw her backing away toward the edge of the platform. Amber tried to still her beating heart as she took aim, seeking whoever was threatening Mary now.

Somewhere, far behind her across the desert, she heard the faint sound of police sirens echoing across the vast wastes.

***

XLIII

'You are a very brave lady. I did not think that you would do my work for me.'

Assim Khan looked appraisingly at Mary Meyer, and the body of Huck Seavers lying before her. Mary Meyer slowly got to her feet and glanced at the pistol she had dropped.

'Don't even think about it,' Assim Khan snapped as he kicked the weapon out over the edge of the chamber and into oblivion.

Mary swallowed thickly and began to move around Huck Seaver's body, hoping against hope that Amber was still watching. Having been sickened by the shot that had hit Huck, now she found herself begging to hear another like it.

'Who are you?'

'It doesn't matter, really,' Assim murmured. 'All that matters is that this thing here is removed from play.'

Assim gestured to the fusion cage with the pistol.

'Saudi Arabia,' Mary guessed on an impulse. 'They sent you, didn't they?'

Assim smiled but shrugged.

'I'd have come here for Lithuania, if the money had been right.'

Mary's heart turned cold as stone. 'Money. You know one day you'll die, and you can't take that money with you.'

'True,' Assim smiled without warmth. 'but it makes a life better to have it than be without it. Pick up the cage.'

'Pick it up yourself.'

Assim shrugged and aimed at Mary. 'Whatever.'

The shot was deafeningly loud in the confines of the heat chamber and Mary almost fainted as her hands shot to her chest and sought the blood that she felt sure must be pouring from her.

Instead she saw Assim slump down onto one knee, shock on his features as he turned to aim down the stairwell behind him. From nowhere a dark haired Latino woman burst into view, one heeled boot smashing into the pistol to send it spinning from Assim's hand out across the chamber. The pistol skittered past Mary and flew out over the edge of the tower.

Lopez slammed into Assim and sent him sprawling across the floor as she shouted at Mary.

'Run, now!'

Mary, stunned and uncertain, turned instead for the fusion cage and lunged for the control switches on its side.

*

Aaron Mitchell got out of his vehicle at the control centre even as he heard the sirens approaching from the far distance. He could see the flashing lights of a stream of law enforcement vehicles rushing toward Crescent Dunes, and he knew that behind them would be helicopters and probably the media too.

He had little time, and despite the pain in his ribs he knew that he had to complete his mission.

'Be ready to leave,' he ordered his driver, and then turned for the control centre.

The control centre was empty but for the bodies of five engineers lying on the ground, firmly bound and gagged. Aaron looked at them only for a moment to ensure they could not interfere with him, and then he turned to the control panel itself.

The array was controlled entirely by computers which handled the rotation and angle of each of the thousands of heliostats arrayed around the central heating tower. A cursory examination of the control panel confirmed that Mary Meyer had shut the entire array down, the mirrors pointing not at the tower but at the sky. On reflection, at last he understood what Mary had been trying to do: the power from the fusion cage would light Las Vegas, but the mirrors would remain deactivated in front of the television crews that would inevitably arrive behind the law enforcement. The tower would be ablaze with heat, even with no solar energy directed toward it, and that would pose too many questions for Majestic Twelve to possibly cover up.

In one simple move Mary would have proved the validity of her fusion cage and secured her place in history. Now, pained and injured, Aaron was filled with a fury that he had not felt since his youth amid the steaming forests of Vietnam, fighting hand to hand in the tunnels beneath the jungle against a much feared and hated enemy.

Aaron surveyed the controls one last time, and as an image of Ethan Warner flickered darkly through his mind he re–activated the solar array and re–set the controls to their default settings. The panel lit up before him as the control system re–booted itself and almost immediately he heard the sound of a siren going off somewhere in the distance, from the tower itself, as the heliostat mirrors suddenly hummed into life and their motors began turning the mirrors toward the tower.

Two birds, one stone.

In minutes, the heating chamber of the tower would be bombarded by the sun's rays reflected by nearly two thousand gigantic mirrors, and every memory of the fusion cage, Mary Meyer, Ethan Warner and Nicola Lopez would be quite literally vaporized from the face of the earth.

Aaron turned and limped from the control centre to his waiting car. He glanced up the road and saw the distant police motorcade still a couple of miles away. Without hesitation he climbed into the vehicle, which drove out of the compound and away to the north.

*

Lopez ducked down as Assim Khan leaped to his feet, blood spilling from his chest and hate radiating from his features as he swung for Lopez. His fist brushed through her hair as she drove a straight right into the wound in his chest.

Pain wracked the assassin's features and he cried out as he stumbled backward, struggling to stay focused on Lopez as she lunged forward with another roundhouse left. Assim blocked her blow with one solid forearm, a dull but terrible pain shuddering along the length of the bone. Lopez cried out as she was suddenly driven backward.

Lopez jerked left and raised her right arm, catching Assim's arm under her own. She closed her arm over his and yanked her left knee up into the assassin's ribcage. Assim grunted and Lopez felt brittle bones somewhere in the man's chest crunch against her knee cap.

Assim rallied, a fist flashing into Lopez's vision and smacking across her cheek. She reeled away, and before she could regain her balance the assassin slammed one foot into the inside of her left knee. The leg buckled with a lance of bright pain that bolted up her thigh as Lopez crashed down onto the unforgiving floor.

The assassin swivelled expertly on one foot, one leg smashing down on top of Lopez to pin her in place as in Assim's hand appeared a wicked blade that flashed toward her. Lopez brought one leg up against Assim's chest and caught the assassin in freefall with the blade a hair's breadth from her throat. Dull pain throbbed though her skull as she struggled against the weight and insane strength of her assailant as the tip of the blade touched her throat.

'You have fought bravely,' he said in a sombre tone, 'but now I must protect myself. And for that, you have to die.'

Assim leaned his weight into the blade.

And then a gunshot smacked the hot air.

The bullet slammed upward through Assim's hip, shattering bone and ploughing through his internal organs before bursting from his shoulder in a fine mist of bright blood. Lopez smashed the blade clear of her throat as Assim shuddered from the blast and rolled onto his side.

Ethan burst into the heating chamber and stared at Lopez. 'Are you okay?!'

'About time!' Lopez gasped.

Assim Khan groaned as Lopez looked at him. 'Christ, won't this asshole *ever* die?'

Ethan glanced at Mary, who was standing over the fusion cage, and then he saw something outside of the chamber. A brilliant, blinding flare of light that began to grow as though a star had suddenly burst into life out on the desert plains.

'The mirrors are working!' he yelled.

Ethan grabbed Lopez and propelled her toward the stairwell as he dashed to Mary's side. 'Move, now!'

'No! I must start it up!'

'It's too late!' Ethan insisted. 'We're about to be fried! Come on!'

Mary tried to activate the device and she hit a switch that lit up with a green glow before Ethan yanked her away from the fusion cage and they ran for the stairwell.

A terrible, fearsome heat seared the air as Ethan followed Mary and pushed her down ahead of him. They dashed down the stairs together, the heat in the chamber swelling with a remorseless power that seemed to burn the air around Ethan. He felt his eyes dry out, his skin seared and then he dashed through a series of heavy doors and saw Lopez slam them shut behind him.

*

Assim Khan staggered to his feet and grasped for the stairwell. The metal touched his hand and he saw his skin slough off in a bloody mess. He turned, delirious with pain and blood loss, barely able to see in the searing heat as a brilliant halo of light burned into his retina with the strength of a thousand suns.

To one side, he saw Huck Seaver's body consumed by flames, thick smoke billowing from the corpse as it burned.

To the other, he saw the fusion cage burst into life.

Assim screamed as a fearsome heat ignited his clothes and then his skin, as he felt his flesh and his bone seared by thousands of degrees of pure energy. With the last remaining synapses functioning in his body he dashed for the open air of the ledge outside, but he barely made two steps before his body was charred into an unrecognisable black mess of bone and tissue that burst into a flaming pyre and collapsed, smouldering ashes billowing out over the tower's ledge and into the desert sky.

*

Ethan staggered out into the open air beneath the huge tower, just in time to hear the sound of dozens of shotguns, rifles and pistols being cocked.

He looked up to see a dozen or so police cars, their lights flickering with brilliant colors before them and countless officers glaring at him down the barrels of their weapons.

Ethan dropped the pistol he still held in one hand and slowly raised his hands, Mary beside him doing the same as he watched Lopez standing with her hands in the air, her dark hair billowing in the hot desert wind.

'On your knees, hands behind your heads!'

The voice bellowed at them from a loud hailer and Ethan obeyed, placing his hands atop his head as he knelt down on the hard desert soil and watched as two FBI agents advanced toward them, pistols pointing at Ethan and Mary.

'My daughter,' Mary cried out. 'Is she okay?'

The two agents said nothing. One of them was a young guy, late twenties Ethan guessed, who covered his partner as she advanced. The partner was a little older, with long auburn hair and a determined expression, all cold blue eyes and no smiles.

'Ethan Warner,' she said as she looked at him. 'I've been wanting to talk to you for quite a while, but you keep avoiding me?'

Ethan managed a shrug and a grin.

'I won't avoid you anymore, let's be friends. What's your name?'

Special Agent Hannah Ford offered Ethan a tight grin devoid of warmth as she produced a set of hand cuffs.

'My name is: you're under arrest, asshole.'

'That from your mother's side?'

Ethan winced as Hannah Ford slammed the cuffs brutally hard around his wrists.

***

XLIV

FBI Field Office, Las Vegas

'I've been waiting for this moment.'

Special Agent Hannah Ford sat opposite Ethan Warner in the interview room, smiling as she glanced at the hand cuffs around Warner's wrists, manacling him to the table.

'So have I,' Ethan replied. 'I don't feel we got off to the best start in Virginia.'

'Running away does that,' Hannah pointed out.

'It wasn't like we were on a date.'

'Thankfully.'

'You'd have been disappointed if I'd run away?' Ethan asked with interest.

'Mister Warner, you've been embroiled in an international conspiracy that has resulted in several deaths.'

'I killed nobody,' Ethan replied. 'I did however see Huck Seavers before what happened in the tower. You know … '

'The incineration,' Hannah confirmed. 'We didn't recover much.'

'And Stanley Meyer was almost certainly murdered by a man named Aaron Mitchell, who escaped the scene at Crescent Dunes. Nicola Lopez, Mary Meyer and I were witnesses alone to everything that happened.'

Hannah looked down at her notes.

'The District Attorney won't see it like that. You left Saudi Arabia without a passport or papers, entered the United States illegally and then proceeded to injure several people, acquire a firearm for which you were not licensed and commit a homicide for which the FBI have been hunting you.' Hannah grinned. 'And that's the way I'll be presenting it.'

'You ever considered the fact that you might be missing the larger picture here? Aaron Mitchell is behind all of this. He's working for a cabal known as Majestic Twelve. They are dangerous, this isn't a game.'

'And this supposed fusion cage,' Hannah replied as she glanced down at her notes. 'Which cannot be found.'

'The solar array at Crescent Dunes produced energy for a brief few moments before those solar panels lined up on the tower,' Ethan replied. 'I take it that Vegas got its power back before the solar plant was producing electricity?'

'I checked that out for you,' Hannah replied. 'Turns out the salts atop the tower retain their heat for up to twelve hours after the sun's gone down, providing power even when they're not being directly heated. As soon as the engineers corrected what Mary Meyer had done, the plant operated as normal. As for this Majestic Twelve – I think you've been watching far too many episodes of *The Blacklist*, Mister Warner.'

'Check it out on the Internet for yourself,' Ethan muttered. 'Documents pertaining to MJ–12 have been available for decades. This isn't some kind of new conspiracy. Bilderberg is the same, it even has its own website.'

'So does Santa Claus I expect,' Hannah replied, 'but I'm not about to go to Lapland to arrest him for illegally crossing borders now, am I?'

'Check the pistol you took from me,' Ethan insisted. 'It will have my prints on it, but it will also have those of Aaron Mitchell.'

'The other assassin?' Hannah asked airily. 'Lots of assassins in your story, Ethan, and yet you expect me to believe that you have killed nobody. According to your testimony you and your partner, Nicola Lopez, work for the Defense Intelligence Agency and are merely the innocent victims of a multi–national cat and mouse game of corporate espionage.' She sighed, tilted her head to one side. 'How adorable. And you're also *James Bond* in your spare time?'

'Bilderberg is real, it all stems from there.'

Hannah's grin didn't slip as she stood.

'It appears to be nothing more than one of many international political conventions.'

'Talk to the DIA,' Ethan said. 'They'll confirm who we work for.'

'I already did,' Hannah replied as she slapped her files down on the table. 'Nobody at the agency has ever heard of you.'

Ethan felt his blood run cold.

'Seriously?'

'Seriously,' Hannah uttered. 'We have historical documents of your involvement with the DIA but nothing suggesting current support from that agency. I'm not surprised, of course. You're a fantasist, Warner, living some kind of bizarre dream. I'd have thought it just the act of some loser who couldn't face real life if it were not for the fact that people have died for being a part of your little charade here.'

'There is no charade,' Ethan snapped. 'We've been burned. Assim Khan is dead and with Mitchell gone, there's nobody to corroborate our story if the DIA have decided to drop us.'

'There is no DIA involvement,' Hannah snapped. 'You're going away for a very long time, Mister Warner. I've made it my personal mission to see you pay for your crimes, that's if the Saudis don't manage to extradite you.' She leaned on the table, looked into his eyes. 'What would you prefer? A ten year stretch here on US soil, or the end of your life in some Saudi hell hole instead?'

'I'd prefer to be freed, actually,' Ethan replied.

Hannah stood up. 'Not before hell freezes over.'

'I can wait.'

The cell door opened and two FBI agents walked in.

'Take him away,' Hannah ordered.

'You're not going to believe this,' Mickey Vaughn said, casting an uncertain glance at Ethan.

'Believe *what*?!' Hannah snapped.

'Orders from Langley, we've got to cut him loose.'

'He's our suspect!' Hannah shouted. 'We've got evidence, witnesses and … '

'Presidential pardon,' said Vaughn in reply. 'For all of them.'

Hannah's jaw worked for a few moments but no sound came forth.

'Presidential pardon?' she finally managed to echo. 'Who the hell has the authority for this? The president doesn't even know about what's … '

'That's classified, Defense Intelligence Agency and well above your pay grade,' Ethan cut in, enjoying himself immensely as relief coursed through his veins. 'But I'll happily chat to you about all of this over that drink.'

Hannah glared at Ethan with such ferocity that he thought for a moment she might burst into flames like Assim Khan had done. Then she whirled and stormed away, leaving the two agents to free Ethan and lead him out of the room.

Ethan saw two more agents appear ahead, Nicola Lopez wedged between them and looking equally bemused. They said nothing to each other as they were led to a parking lot outside the FBI building. A black SUV was waiting, and as they climbed aboard Doug Jarvis was waiting for them.

'I thought you'd been forcibly retired?' Ethan asked as he climbed aboard.

'I have,' Jarvis admitted. 'But I wanted to come down here and pick you both up. You tell them anything?' he asked as soon as they were on the move.

'Everything,' Lopez replied. 'I figured any chance to get this out in the open was a good one.'

'Did they buy the story?'

'Nope,' Ethan said. 'Special Agent Hannah Ford thinks it's all bunkum and wants our asses in a federal prison as fast as she can manage it.'

The SUVs drifted down the I95, headed south.

'Good,' Jarvis said.

'Good that she wants our asses in prison?' Lopez asked mildly.

'Good that she doesn't believe it,' Jarvis corrected. 'The world's not ready for this yet.'

'How are the DIA going to cover all of this up?' Lopez asked in disgust as she rolled her eyes.

Jarvis glanced out of the windows as he replied.

'Both of you have been pardoned by the president himself, despite FBI Director LeMay's protests, your saving of Isaiah Black's life all those years ago finally paying off. Huck Seavers was killed by a Saudi assassin by the name of Assim Khan, who also murdered Stanley Meyer. Huck Seaver's wife has inherited the family business, which has secured its mining rights in Missouri due to the population of a town named Clearwater voluntarily moving on after a generous re–housing initiative funded by Seavers Incorporated. I've heard that the old town has already been levelled by Seavers Incorporated's explosive tests before the mining begins.'

'Christ,' Lopez muttered as she shook her head. 'Your boys sure do move fast.'

'What about the FBI?' Ethan asked. 'Hellerman said that they were onto our case, sounded like they wouldn't let go.'

'Director LeMay backed off as soon as he heard that Mary Meyer was in FBI custody,' Jarvis replied. 'With the fusion cage no longer in danger of reaching the public sphere, his work is complete. But he got his message across real well. He's all in with Majestic Twelve.'

'Amber?' Ethan asked. 'Mary?'

'They have been apprised of the situation and now understand that the introduction of a device like the fusion cage cannot be carried out overnight. The socio–economic shockwave would create just as many problems as it would solve. The technology is coming, that is without doubt, and one day the fusion cage will be as ubiquitous as cell phones and fast food – just not today. It's my hope that with the fusion cage gone and Mary Meyer effectively controlled, Majestic Twelve will pursue her no longer, the risk of exposure now presented by taking her out too great.'

Ethan rubbed his eyes with his fingers as he spoke.

'Stanley Meyer died to give that thing away. You really believe that the corporations and governments involved in this will let that happen? They'll annex the technology and make money from it, just like always.'

'Perhaps,' Jarvis replied, 'but neither you nor I can control that. It would take the population of our entire country to stand up as one and say together that they won't stand for it. If the people of America were able to do that, to down tools as one and demand action, they could have anything they want, just as could the population of any country on this planet. But none of them ever do and as long as that continues, governments and corporations will continue to hold all of the cards.'

'Business as usual,' Lopez uttered. 'Same for you too, I see. I thought you'd been arrested.'

'A temporary set–back due to risking my neck getting you two out of trouble, again. '

'My condolences,' Lopez shot back. 'How does it feel to be working for governments and corporations that place profits above lives?'

'I don't choose the way our country works, Nicola, but I do try to do something about improving that country in whatever way I can,' Jarvis defended himself. 'However, unless the people themselves choose to act together and do something about it, nothing will change. The United States of America has become a business just like any other, and I can't change all of that on my own any more than you or Stanley Meyer could.'

'I take it that General Nellis has withdrawn his support for our work?' Ethan said wearily.

Jarvis folded his hands and leaned back in his seat.

'Far from it,' he replied. 'The administration has asked him to offer you more work through the DIA, with their promise of support. If, of course, you wish to undertake it?'

Ethan and Lopez exchanged a glance and both of them looked at Jarvis.

'Yesno. '

*

FBI Field Office, Richmond

Virginia

Hannah Ford sat at her desk and stared at her computer monitor in silence. For the first time in over ten years she had found doubt within herself, doubt over the motives and methods of an organisation, a country and a government she had come to love.

Hannah was no stranger to international espionage and the tragedies that it could cause, for in her years within the FBI she had seen enough reports and files detailing politically motivated murders, organised assassinations, genocides, terrorist activities and the like. Intelligence was a dirty game, played by those who must constantly war with what is within and humane, and what is required of them in order to protect the humanity which they served.

But the pictures of the slaughtered civilians in the commune in Virginia were a step too far. Somebody was responsible. *Ethan Warner* was responsible, or so she had thought.

Hannah clicked on her computer screen, entered her access code and accessed once again the file that had been waiting for her upon her return to the office. It contained the bloodwork for the specimen she had discreetly obtained from the hotel balcony, near where Stanley Meyer had died.

To her amazement, the DNA profile of the blood had found a match in the system that the FBI had claimed had not been found via their own official sample obtained by forensics at the site.

Data spilled down the screen and Hannah read as rapidly as she could, absorbing information like a sponge as she read page after page.

An image of a dark skinned Afro–American, born August 12th, 1959 – *Aaron James Mitchell. Mother; Florence Mitchell, nee Spencer, an American by birth, Detroit. Father; Jackson. J. Mitchell, former soldier, service record; Pacific Theatre, Iwo Jima, decorated veteran. Devout Catholics, both now deceased. No other siblings. Aaron Mitchell, service with United States Marines, Vietnam, decorated twice, two tours of active duty, two further tours as instructor ...*

Hannah had originally felt a deep sense of relief flood her nervous system upon reading the file. She had immediately believed she was reading the operational file of an all American boy and veteran.

Wife; Mary Allen Mitchell. Daughter; Ellen Amy Mitchell, born 1972, Oakland, California ...

Hannah scrolled down, and once again the warmth of relief within her turned to cold slime as she continued to read.

... died, 1978. Interred Oakland, California.

Aaron James Mitchell; Diagnosed with acute anxiety and depression, revised as Post Traumatic Stress Disorder. Original PTSD from combat service enflamed via suppressed grief after loss of family. Two years medical hospital, San Diego. Released 1981. Registered CIA 1983.

Hannah scrolled down rapidly toward the physician's report near the bottom of the file.

Physically impressive. Doctor's note: Aaron J Mitchell is without a doubt the most powerful and dangerous man I have ever attempted to treat.

Then she scrolled to the bottom of the page.

Died, 1998, Berlin, Germany.

Ethan Warner's words echoed in her mind as she stared at the face on the screen before her. *Aaron Mitchell is behind all of this. He's working for a cabal known as Majestic Twelve. They are dangerous, this isn't a game.*

Hannah stared into the middle–distance for a moment longer, and then she started making notes that began with three lines.

Majestic Twelve.

Aaron J Mitchell.

Ethan Warner.

***

Also by Dean Crawford:

The Warner & Lopez Series
The Nemesis Origin
The Fusion Cage

The Ethan Warner Series
Covenant
Immortal
Apocalypse
The Chimera Secret
The Eternity Project

Atlantia Series
Survivor
Retaliator
Aggressor
Endeavour
Defiance

Independent novels
Eden
Holo Sapiens
Soul Seekers
Stone Cold

Want to receive notification of new releases? Just sign up to Dean Crawford's newsletter via: www.deancrawfordbooks.com

ABOUT THE AUTHOR

Dean Crawford is the author of the internationally published series of thrillers featuring *Ethan Warner*, a former United States Marine now employed by a government agency tasked with investigating unusual scientific phenomena. The novels have been *Sunday Times* paperback best-sellers and have gained the interest of major Hollywood production studios. He is also the enthusiastic author of many independently published Science Fiction novels.

www.deancrawfordbooks.com

Printed in Great Britain
by Amazon

54606458R00180